THE ECUADORIAN DECEPTION

By

BEAR MILLS

©2013 Bear Mills

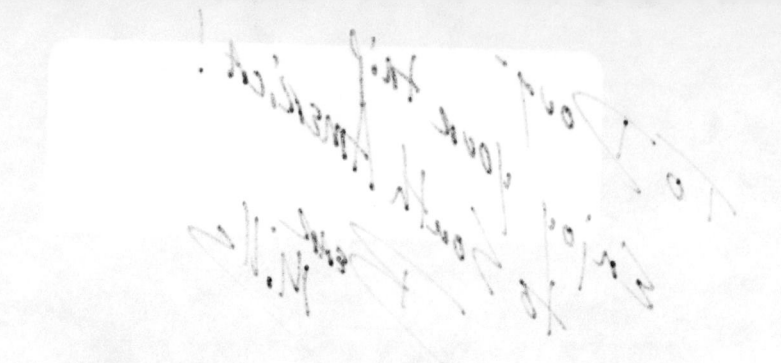

This book is a work of fiction. All names, characters, and incidents are the product of the author's imagination or are used fictitiously. Any resemblance to actual events or persons, living or dead, is purely coincidental.

Copyright Bear Mills, 2013

All rights reserved. No part of this publication may be reproduced, stored in a retrieval system, or transmitted in any form or by any means, electronic, mechanical, photocopying, recording, or otherwise, without the prior written permission of the author.

For information and inquiries, contact CLM Talent Management at 1-432-553-2368 or CLMmanagement@gmail.com.

ISBN: 1490325263

ISBN 13: 9781490325262

Library of Congress Control Number: 2013910305
CreateSpace Independent Publishing Platform
North Charleston, South Carolina

To Caryl, my traveling companion through the journey of life. Thanks also to Cody, Sarah J., Sarah A., and Sid for your technical assistance. I am indebted to the people of Ecuador for their great hospitality during the research on this book. Finally, thanks to Dolores Gay, who introduced us to Guayaquil and Cuenca. "Usted es muy amable."

PART ONE

CHAPTER 1

Sunday, 5 January
8:04 a.m.

"Are you sure this is safe? I'm really worried about you." Carol d'Hout peered deeply into her husband George's gray, clear eyes, seeking any hint of hesitation or second thought.

"I'm a consultant. A man is paying me to consult." George continued to pack, not looking up to meet his wife's imploring gaze.

"You're a consultant in the United States. This man, whoever he is, wants you to fly off to somewhere I don't even know how to pronounce. Besides, you barely speak Spanish. How are you even going to talk to people?"

"'This *man*, as you call him, learned about me from the Internet. You know that. It's no different than a job in Denver or Philadelphia. The name of the city is Guayaquil. I think in Spanish it's pronounced why-I-kill."

"And that's supposed to make me feel better about all this?"

George smiled mischievously. "I admit my Spanish is pretty poor. Come on, two years of high school Spanish; what do you expect? That was a long time ago. But surely if the guy wants to hire me, he knows it will be to work in English." George inspected his shaving kit once more before zipping it shut inside his suitcase. He had probably overpacked for just two weeks in the Ecuadorian port city, but he lived by his grandfather's motto: better to have it and not need it than to need it and not have it.

"Don't forget the biggest lure," George said, standing the suitcase up and placing his carry-on duffel bag atop it. "He's paying me fifty thousand dollars for two weeks work. Where am I going to make that in the United States?"

"Lures are for catching fish." Carol adjusted the tie on her pink bathrobe. "And any city with *kill* in the name is just plain spooky. What if he meant pesos instead of dollars? You'll end up making next to nothing." Her hair was still a jumble as she headed into their walk-in closet to dress in jeans and a hoodie before driving George to the airport. "What if this is all some scam?"

Carol pulled her hoodie over her head and looked out of the closet to see her husband's approving gaze. Twenty-five years of marriage hadn't diminished his appreciation for her considerable charms, for which she was extremely grateful.

"I can't promise it isn't," George said, rolling the suitcase toward the garage, where he would place it in the rear of their Honda Pilot. "But the guy bought me a round-trip airline ticket and sent a five-thousand-dollar retainer. I ought to at least go down there and check it out. Besides, any guy in his right mind would make his money quick and then get right back to the best looking babe in Texas."

"Lord, please keep him safe," Carol muttered as she stooped to pull on her running shoes. She and George stayed in shape by being active joggers, even competing in a few marathons over the years. While Carol was the faster of the two, George had a capacity for endurance few other men in their early fifties could match.

Carol adjusted the formfitting hoodie and made her way to the garage. George jabbed the wall control for the electric door opener. The garage door rattled open to a Sunday morning curtain of rain and fog. "Houston," George said. "Your basic traffic-and-moisture buffet. Nice."

Driving George to Intercontinental Airport, Carol tried not to continue the role of the anxiety-ridden wife. However, every question and inquiry came out that way. "How will we stay in contact if your cell phone doesn't have a signal? Did I mention you had a phone call this morning from a man named Edward Davies? He called while you were in the shower. Did you write down the name of the hotel you're staying at and leave it at the house? How do you know this Roberto Ordóñez is legit? Do you have everything you need for work? Have you told all your clients you won't be available for a few days?"

As Carol steered through the fog and rain, George found it hard to concentrate on the machine-gun spray of questions and comments. His mind was already boarding the Copa Airlines jet for Panama and then on to Guayaquil. He'd downloaded a myriad of books, movies, and podcasts on his MacBook Air to entertain him on the flight. However, a dull throbbing, like a looming headache, was coming over the horizon and heading his direction. It was the same sensation he got each time his conscience told him he should have been more careful to listen to his wife's advice.

His best hope for relief rested in the variety of entertainment he'd downloaded. Nothing ruined a perfectly rainy and gray day quite like an incessant "I told you so" planted firmly in the innermost regions of the brain.

He kissed Carol good-bye at the departure terminal and watched her drive off into the increasing downpour. Turning, George made his way to the Copa check-in desk. The agent looked at his passport. "d'Hout—is that Danish?"

"Dutch, by way of England, as I understand it."

"Fascinating. I've really gotten into all that online research about genealogy. My family's from Scotland by way of Philadelphia. You know, you can check out everything online now. You really ought to give it a try."

"Doubtful," George said. "But thanks anyway."

He glanced over his shoulder at the line of passengers waiting to check their bags and felt embarrassed. He couldn't care less about genealogy, and here he was, holding up the line while someone rattled on about it. George's brother had been bitten by the genealogy bug a few years earlier. He was always sending e-mails about this or that relative he'd discovered. George felt pretty certain the entire business wasn't much different from weather forecasting or day-trading stocks—a huge waste of time and money.

Carol would say, "Have you read Hugh's latest e-mail? You're related to a famous buccaneer!" Why was it, when it came to genealogy, nobody was ever related to a milkman or butcher? It was always dukes and earls and Founding Fathers and famous outlaws. What were the chances?

George boarded the plane and nestled in to his seat. As the flight to Panama and Guayaquil reached altitude, George considered opening either a movie or book. However, he again lost himself in Carol's questions. Why had this Ecuadorian businessman sought him out? Were there no qualified website developers in Ecuador or the rest of Latin America? What were the chances he would be selected out of all the consultants in the United States?

He flattered himself by thinking his websites were so much better than anyone else's, but was that really true? What would provoke a man a continent away to pay a $5,000 retainer and provide a round-trip airline ticket worth $900 to a total stranger? Besides, with the Internet, the work could have been done long-distance without him even traveling to Ecuador.

Maybe Roberto Ordóñez was the old-fashioned type. He knew he needed to have a strong web presence but still preferred dealing face-to-face. That had to be it. No online video conferencing for this man. What else could it be?

One Month Earlier
Thursday, 1 December
2:18 p.m.

"Hello?"

"Señor d'Hout?" The accent was so thick that in spite of the fact the man spoke English, George could barely understand him.

"I'm sorry. I think you have the wrong number," George said impulsively.

"Hor-hay d'Hout?" the voice came back. "*Lo siento.* I'm sorry — Gee-orge d'Hout? Of Houston, Texas? You are a consultant, no?"

Adjusting his ear to the thick accent and a tinny sound on the phone that made it sound like the voice was coming from faraway, George answered, "I'm a consultant, yes. Who is this? How can I help you?"

"*Soy* Roberto Ordóñez— I am Roberto Ordóñez *de* Guayaquil, Ecuador. I am familiar with you and wish to hire you. You travel for the right price, yes?"

"Let's slow down a second. Yes, I do travel, but first I would require quite a bit of information about your business. I need to make sure I'm the right person for the job."

It sounded to George like the phone was being covered on the other end. Two people were speaking in muffled voices. "Hello?" George said. "Are you still there?"

More muffled sounds. Roberto Ordóñez came back on the line. "Your services are highly recommended, and I am prepared to pay you fifty thousand dollars for two weeks of work. Can you be here in early January?"

"I'm sorry. I don't believe I heard you correctly. Could you repeat that?" George felt his pulse race. "What did you say?"

"I will also send your airline ticket," Ordóñez continued. "You are coming in January. Do not let me down, as I am trusting you to do your part." The line went dead.

It occurred to George he was surely the victim of a ridiculous hoax. One of his friends or a client was pulling a stunt. Did the fellow say he was calling from Ecuador? It might even be something his brother Hugh had arranged. Hugh had said something not too long ago about Ecuador. What was it?

It didn't matter, he decided. This was clearly a gimmick or a gag. Not a very funny one, however. Somebody needed to bone up on his or her pranks.

Wednesday, 14 December
5:19 p.m.

George convinced himself the entire affair was a silly stunt. He had completely dismissed it by the time a large envelope arrived at his home bearing Ecuadorian postage. "What in the world is that?" Carol asked.

"Some guy called a few days ago from Ecuador. I thought it was a goof," George said. He used a letter opener to slice into the large manila envelope. He turned it over so the contents spilled out on the kitchen bar. Carol swiveled on a stool. A check drawn on an Ecuadorian bank fluttered onto the countertop. So did a sealed envelope and a flight itinerary. It was for a flight departing Houston for Guayaquil on January 5.

Carol picked up the check and dropped it just as quickly. "Did you rob a bank?" she almost yelled. "What are you doing with a check for this much money? There must be some mistake. This is for five thousand dollars, drawn on the Central Bank of Ecuador. It says it's a retainer. For what? A treasure heist?"

George related the earlier telephone conversation and how he'd dismissed it. Carol said, "This is a scam of some kind. You know, one of those 'I will give you twenty thousand dollars if you will just send me five hundred dollars first' kind of things. You need to either send it back or just throw it away. There's something wrong with this whole thing. Who sends a check for that much money to someone they've never met for work they've never even inspected?"

George shook his head and shrugged. He opened the inner white envelope. He dropped the contents next to the check and airline itinerary. It was a business card that simply read ROBERTO ORDÓÑEZ GONZALEZ. Below that were the words GUAYAQUIL, ECUADOR, and a phone number.

"Where is Ecuador?" Carol asked. "It's in South America, right? Or is it one of those countries in Africa? I never can keep that stuff straight."

"I'm pretty sure it's on the west coast of South America. Somewhere around Colombia and Peru, I think."

Pulling out his iPhone, George accessed the Internet. He found the international calling code for Ecuador. He dialed it, along with the number on the card. The phone made a series of clicks. George didn't know whether they were rings or a busy signal.

"*Dígame*," a man's voice answered.

"Is this Mr. Ordóñez?" George fairly yelled into the phone, as if the great distance between Houston and Guayaquil required it. "This is—"

"Señor d'Hout," the voice replied, "I have been anticipating your call. I trust everything is satisfactory. Has the check already made its way to you? That is very quick, no?"

"I'm holding the check right now, or rather my wife is," George said. "We just received it. This is a great deal of money. You don't even know my work."

"That is the point, señor. Your reputation and work are for all to see on the Internet. Is that not the point of our, how you say, our *era de la informacion*...Information Age? I want you and the knowledge only you possess. You will be here in January?"

"Knowledge only I possess? You certainly have a lot of faith in me."

"I want you for two weeks. Can I count on you, Señor d'Hout?"

"It seems we need to visit for a bit first. There are a lot of good web site designers out there and—"

"If I wanted any of them, I could have them, no? This is very good money, Mr. d'Hout. I expect the information you provide me and your great help will more than make up for what I am investing in this operation. Do we have an understanding and an agreement?"

George stared at Carol for a moment. She wrinkled her brow and frowned.

George spoke into the cell phone. "I will see you in January, Mr. Ordóñez."

He heard Ordóñez say, "Beautiful, no? January, yes."

Clicking off the phone, George looked into the questioning gaze of his wife.

"Why did you say yes?" she asked. "Shouldn't we have talked about it?"

"While I was talking to him, I realized something," George said. "If it's a scam, the check won't clear. At least I wouldn't think it would. I'll talk to David up at the bank and explain the whole thing. Maybe he can hand carry it through the process. If the check turns out to be a fake, they can let me know. We won't do anything regarding the money until we hear that it clears. If it does, we can transfer it to a savings account and then hold it in case the deal is fishy. That way we can return it, if there's something wrong, or I get there and decide not to take the job."

"George, there is something wrong with this."

"We're in a for-profit economy, right?" he asked her. "This is the kind of deal everybody is looking for. I landed it. I'd think you'd be proud of me, at least a little bit."

He flashed Carol a wounded look. She said, "I am proud of you, with or without this deal. I just don't trust mystery mail from strangers halfway around the world. Especially when they include checks for five thousand dollars marked 'retainer.'"

"If it's not legitimate, I'll get on a plane and fly right back," George said. "Then I'll return his retainer, and that will be that. At best it's a golden opportunity. At worst it'll make a great story one day."

"I won't tell you not to go, but between now and then, will you at least see what you can find out about this guy? That way maybe you can get an indication if he's on the up-and-up."

CHAPTER 2

Sunday, 5 January
2:42 p.m.

When George asked friends about Panama—the first stop on his journey—a mixture of blank stares and horror stories greeted him. There were tales of a bleak, overgrown wilderness with a humble landing strip and a sad airport terminal. One client insisted in 1990 he'd been on a flight in which Panamanian soldiers actually boarded the plane, waving machine guns in passengers' faces. In angry Spanish they'd asked who was trying to smuggle goods in or out of the great Democratic Republic of Panama.

The client told the story with the flourish of a Scout leader relating a well-worn ghost tale to a bunch of tenderfoots around a campfire. "It was right after US troops had stormed the place," he explained in conspiratorial tones, as if more soldiers might storm the office building at any moment. "You remember how our forces went in there and had a big shootout with Manuel Noriega's people before arresting him and bringing him back to the United States to stand trial for—what was it?—drug smuggling? After the gunfight at the airport, the Panamanians refused to clean up the blood that was all over the place. They wanted us to see it, to be horrified."

George was no tenderfoot. He listened politely but skeptically. What about the airport in Guayaquil? The only people he could find who knew anything about the place were those who used it as a jumping-off point for a trip to the Galápagos Islands.

"*Ecuador* means 'equator' in Spanish," a friend from George's church said over lunch one day. "Debbie and I went there a couple of years ago. Honestly, the airport in Guayaquil was like any airport in America. In fact, if anything, clearing customs was faster there than anyplace we've ever been, especially in South America."

"How was the weather?" George asked. "I'm going to be there in January."

"Since it's on the equator, I'm not sure they have summer and winter, like we do. You'd have to check on that. I think most of those countries right on the equator just have dry seasons and rainy seasons. Perpetual spring is what the travel brochures said. To me, Guayaquil was about like Houston, just a little more run-down. It *is* a third-world country, after all."

"More run down than Houston? Doubtful," George said. Both men smiled.

His friend had a thought. "You do know their official currency is the US dollar, right? Not having to find a cambio to get your money exchanged is pretty convenient."

"I don't know whether that's good or not," George said. "No chance to get a favorable exchange rate."

***

Now that he was in Panama with a two-hour layover, he found the airport was a very comfortable facility with all the modern touches, including several American fast-food restaurants. If there had ever been angry Panamanians waving guns, that time had long since passed.

Among the pleasant surprises, George found he was able to connect to the Internet, though the search engines were all in Spanish. For the umpteenth time he typed in "Roberto Ordóñez Gonzalez Guayaquil" to see what popped up.

This time his roll of the dice came up sevens, no doubt because the search engine was working from different data than his searches in the United States. Roberto Ordóñez Gonzalez had to be a very popular name in Latin America, simply based on the number of websites he discovered.

It seemed Roberto Ordóñez Gonzalez of Guayaquil—if the references were all dealing with the same person—had his fingers in many pies: construction, excavation, historical preservation, and work with governments on projects of historical significance. However, George couldn't be certain whether the websites were dealing with one person or twenty. Nowhere could he find a picture of Señor Ordóñez.

A voice on the airport intercom announced in Spanish that flight 301 was boarding for Guayaquil. He clicked off his MacBook, gathered his bags, and joined the mob surrounding the boarding area. Three times the gate clerk reached for her intercom to request, first in Spanish and then English, that passengers form one orderly line. It did no good. If anything, the request made people press even more for the boarding gate.

When George reached the attendant, she told him in broken English that he couldn't board the plane because he hadn't had his passport checked upon landing in Panama.

"Where do I do that?" George asked. "*Donde? Donde*, right? Where?"

The gate agent pointed to another line a few feet over. "Get it checked and come back. But hurry."

Moving to the second line, George thought, "I'm not missing this plane, even if I have to run down the tarmac and jump on board."

However, the passport verification proved only a formality. Soon George was back in the boarding line. "I think it's part of their one-hundred-percent employment plan," a man in front of him said.

"Possibly," George answered. Small talk with strangers, whether in grocery stores, in airport lines, or at shopping malls, was something he avoided at all costs. Therefore, he never made eye contact with those who tried to converse out of the blue. On airplanes, he made sure his body language indicated "leave me alone" to those around him.

Standing in the boarding line for the second time, George thought Guayaquil must be a very popular place to elicit this kind of crowd response. The nearby American made another stab at engaging George. "Big time on the playas this time of year. Summer for them, you know. Everybody wants to go to Ecuador now that so many places in Mexico are dangerous. You headed for the beach?"

"Doubtful," George said, avoiding eye contact. "Consulting work." Then the crowd surged forward, and George couldn't hear anything else the fellow said. During the flight, George was surprised to find Copa served complimentary beef and chicken sandwiches as good as anything from restaurants in the States. Further compounding his favorable impression was the nonstop congenial service. The flight attendants were helpful but never intrusive.

"Wonder what the word for 'incredible hospitality' is in Spanish?" George thought. "They really know how to take care of people."

He turned back to his laptop and opened a downloaded travel video on the history of Guayaquil. While he didn't particularly enjoy history, he did like knowing enough about where he was going to converse intelligently with clients.

His brother, Hugh, liked to say, "Everything is history. If it isn't now, it soon will be." It occurred to George that it was too bad Hugh wasn't on this trip. He'd really get a bang out of an opportunity like this.

The video displayed pictures of the Guayas River and its many islands. The narrator explained that during Spanish colonial times, shipments of silver and gold made their way up the wide river from Bolivia into the port of Guayaquil.

The narrator said, "Since there was no Panama Canal, there was no easy way to reach the Pacific from Europe. One option was to sail through the dangerous waters of Tierra del Fuego. Another was to sail to Panama, hike some thirty miles across mountains at the narrowest point along the isthmus, and then catch another ship on the Pacific side.

"Because of the difficulty of reaching the Pacific from Europe, the Spaniards considered the west coast of South America their private domain. After the subjugation of the Incans by the conquistador Francisco Pizarro, Spanish ships sailed freely up and down the coasts of modern-day Colombia, Ecuador, Peru, and Chile. They would load and unload their treasures, which were then toted by slaves to the east coast of Panama for the long trip to Spain."

Suddenly the documentary's musical score took a somber tone. "For those few daring pirates who were brave or foolhardy enough to aim for the Pacific side of South America, whether by Tierra del Fuego on the tip of Argentina or by sailing around the world via the Orient, Ecuador held rich treasures.

"Imagine the Spaniards' surprise when ships sailing under the black flag of pirates suddenly appeared at the mouth of the Guayas River with guns aimed at the poorly defended port. Surviving documents tell us pirates attacked the city, looting it and killing innocents on at least four occasions. Among the most vicious of these cutthroats was George d'Hout, the Dutch sea rover who captained men-o'-wars with both English and French crews. Another pirate infamous in Guayaquil's history was—"

George hit the pause button. He backed up the video and listened again. Indeed, the narrator said George d'Hout. "Hey, I'm famous," George thought, "or more likely infamous."

He hit play. "Another pirate who preyed on Guayaquil was the Flemish buccaneer Edward Davies. Captaining a stolen thirty-six-gun ship called *Bachelor's Delight*, Davies and d'Hout led their men in small ships to the mangroves outside Guayaquil. Stowing their landing craft, they marched into the city at night, taking most of the province's leaders hostage before anyone could sound an alarm."

An even more somber tone. "What happened next constitutes one of the great mysteries of the period. Historical records show that the pirates demanded they be taken to the treasure of Francisco Orellana. Legend says the treasure of Orellana might have been as much as a half-million dollars in silver, pieces of eight, and precious stones."

Flutes trilled a haunting tune. "Many believe when Orellana returned to Ecuador from exploring the Amazon, it was with huge shipments of cinnamon, which he sold in Ecuador and Peru for great profit. He also claimed to have plundered the Amazon's legendary women warriors. However, when Orellana returned to Spain in 1543, he had little in the way of monetary wealth to show for his efforts."

Again the music went somber. "It is held by some that Orellana didn't want to give the Spanish Crown its portion of his ill-gotten gains, so he hid it somewhere in Ecuador, possibly Guayaquil. In 1545, Orellana returned to Ecuador, again via the Amazon, which he entered from the Atlantic. However, this time the indigenous peoples were ready. Following multiple attacks, the survivors of the expedition made their way to Quito. Orellana was suffering the effects of multiple wounds from poison-tipped arrows. In his dying days he demanded to be reunited with his treasure at 'the four rivers.'"

The flutes sounded foreboding notes. "There are many theories regarding which rivers constitute the four to which Orellana was referring. However, that is a mystery that may never be solved. Adding to the difficulty is the fact that literally hundreds of rivers flow into the Amazon throughout Ecuador."

The video transitioned between artists' renderings of Orellana and modern pictures of the Amazon basin. From there it next segued to recreated scenes of pirates planning their attack on Ecuador.

The narrator continued. "When d'Hout and Davies attacked Guayaquil, it was with knowledge gained from an escaped slave who had seen the Orellanas Treasure and knew where it was hidden. After the raid on Guayaquil, the two leaders of the expedition, d'Hout and Davies, disappeared, never to be heard from again. When Spanish warships overtook the *Bachelor's Delight*, Davies and d'Hout were not among the crew. Members of the pirate crew who were captured went to their graves insisting that Davies and d'Hout, along with the treasure, had disappeared and never made it onto the ship."

The video continued working its way into Guayaquil's modern history, but George wasn't listening. His mind kept replaying what he'd just heard.

In fact, when the plane touched down near midnight at an airport even more modern than the one in Panama, George realized he had invested no time in preparing to meet his new client. "Don't want Mr. Ordóñez thinking I'm a pirate trying to steal his money," George thought." When I get to the hotel, I better get down to preparing for our meeting."

After collecting his luggage, George got into the customs line. When he had previously traveled abroad, going through customs had often been an aggravating ordeal. *Open your bags. Explain why you have this. What is that?*

In Guayaquil, however, the process seemed almost painless and routine. The agent never asked to see inside his luggage, nor did he even ask how long George planned to stay in the country. When his passport was stamped and placed back in his hand, George grabbed his suitcase, placed the strap of his carry-on over his shoulder, and stepped toward the group of people making their way down a long white hall out of the airport.

Going about twenty yards, George was suddenly aware of a white door on the white wall to his right. A uniformed officer stepped out. The officer appeared so quickly that George almost ran into the man before he could stop with his two bags.

"Por favor, billete de abordaje con su registracion," the officer said in a flat tone, indicating he didn't intend to be messed with. He held out his hand, apparently expecting George to put something in it.

Looking over the shoulder of the officer's brown uniform, George watched as everyone else who had been on the flight continued on.

The guy who tried to talk to George earlier about South American beaches came into view behind the policeman. He made eye contact with George as he sailed by. Smiling way too much, he said in a theatrical whisper, "Who did you make mad? Good luck, buddy." He then winked and made a clicking sound with his tongue.

George brought his eyes back to the officer's shoulder, counting the number of stripes on his uniform to determine his rank. The officer repeated his earlier request.

"No entiendo mucho espanol," George said. I don't understand much Spanish. George attempted to indicate he was perfectly willing to cooperate, if he just knew what was desired.

Another uniformed officer stepped out from behind the unmarked door. "You name?" he said in broken English. "Also you baggage checked tag."

"Of course, I checked my baggage when I was in Houston," George said. His voice betrayed the fact he was very tired from an all-day airplane trip and that he suspected he was being harassed.

"You name?" the second officer repeated.

"George d'Hout."

"From?"

"Houston, Texas, in the United States of America. Is there a problem? *Problema?*"

"*Sí.* You not give us proof this is you *maletas.*"

"My what? Here is my passport. Is that what you want?"

"What will help is you proof of ownership."

"My name is on my bags. Is that what you mean? Just look at them. I'm George d'Hout. If you open the big bag, you will see a blue T-shirt on top. My shaving kit is on the bottom with an electric beard trimmer. What more proof do you want?"

"*Su boleto, señor,*"

George felt his temper growing short. However, he knew better than to lose his cool at any airport. And certainly not one where he barely spoke the language. As he pondered his next move, he saw a young man just under six feet tall with thick, slicked-back black hair; a simple shirt; black jeans; and black, pointy-toed dress shoes. The man was coming upstream against the now-dwindling crowd of *touristas*, who were leaving customs and heading out into the night.

The young man stopped, appraised the scene, and then stepped gingerly toward the guard who spoke some English. In hushed tones, the two whispered back and forth for a few moments. Then the young man turned to George. "Señor d'Hout?" he asked.

George nodded, wondering what new, unfathomable problem was about to confront him.

"You are to come with me, *muchacho*," the young man said.

"I'm not going anywhere. I haven't done anything wrong." In his head, George could hear his wife's voice uttering a thousand I-told-you-sos that he never should have come on this trip. Now, before he could prove her wrong, the airport police had singled him out for no good reason.

"You do not wish to go to your hotel?" the young man asked. "Señor Ordóñez sent me to escort you. I am sorry you have had trouble, *muchacho*. They only wished to see your luggage claim check. Apparently you have misplaced it. I have assured them, based on the word of Señor Ordóñez, that all is appropriate and there is no irregularity."

The young man took George's luggage from him. "*Con su permisso*," he said, hoisting the smaller bag over his shoulder and rolling the other toward the exit. "My name is Juan Pacheco. I work for Señor Ordóñez."

"Señor Ordóñez must be a pretty powerful man if two guards will let me go at an airport simply based on your say-so that Mr. Ordóñez wants it done," George said.

Juan walked slightly ahead, but George thought he recognized a bit of a smile creep across the face of the younger man. "*Muchacho*, Señor Ordóñez has many interests and is a busy man. He desires you to be welcomed to our country with the greatest of hospitality. This is a very gracious country, and we do not want a misunderstanding over a misplaced baggage claim check to spoil your evening or your stay."

George followed Juan Pacheco out into the tropical night air. Lush plants were everywhere, reminding him of the airport in Miami, Florida. The humidity was thick, even by Houston standards. A large crowd was waiting for the arriving passengers, but Juan cut through them with a manner suggesting he was used to getting his way, or at least his boss was.

Looking out at the distant parking lot, George saw large groups of people piling into the beds of pickup trucks at various spots. There were also groups of five and six people at other parking places and along curbs, folding themselves into compact cars built for no more than four.

"We have a shuttle waiting, *muchacho*," Juan said, continuing his brisk pace. "I will personally see you to your hotel and give you instructions on preparing for your work with Señor Ordóñez." Juan stepped to the curb, reached out his right arm, and lowered his index finger as if he were tapping a key on a keyboard.

An unmarked black van at the end of the driveway flashed its lights and pulled toward the pair. George felt a sudden pang of concern. "Is this the hotel shuttle?" he asked.

Juan seemed to read his mind but never turned toward him. "*Muchacho*, you are a guest of Señor Ordóñez. He felt it would be rude not to have someone personally meet you. He was otherwise occupied with a very important transaction, or he would have come himself."

Juan's near-perfect pronunciation made George wonder if the young man had studied in the United States. Juan appeared to be about twenty-five with an eye for how he carried himself. He dressed to simultaneously fit in and stand out. It was a gift not many people possessed. If his parents were well-off, it would make sense he had recently returned from the States and that Ordóñez had hired him because of his education, style, and bi-lingual abilities.

The van stopped in front of them. The driver hurried around to open the passenger door for George. At almost the same moment, Juan opened the rear doors, and George could hear the suitcase and carry-on being placed in the storage compartment.

As George moved to step into the van, the driver said, "You are famous, no? George d'Hout. 'Dee-haw'—almost like our word for 'to flee.' I have heard Señor Ordóñez and his compadres say your name many times."

The man was much shorter than either George or Juan, perhaps only five feet tall, but he was stout like a wrestler.

Juan was suddenly right there. "Your job is to drive, not to talk, *muchacho!*" Getting into the passenger seat, Juan turned to George, who sat on the first row in the back of the van.

"*Lo siento*. My apologies, Mr. d'Hout. Miguel is new with us. He was hired because he can drive well and speaks *un poco* English. However, he is still learning when not to speak."

"What does he mean when he says I'm famous? Nothing could be further from the truth."

"Nothing at all, Mr. d'Hout. He is confusing you with another man by the same name from our past."

"The pirate George d'Hout?"

"You know of this man?" Juan asked, glancing at George from a mirror on the sun visor. "He is a relative, no?"

"Doubtful," George said, "though I really couldn't say. My brother is the one who is into all that."

"Into all that? What do you mean?"

"Family history. Genealogy. You know, all the famous dead relatives."

"Your brother—" Juan contemplated. Then he seemed to have an epiphany. "Of course, it would be natural for brothers to have different concerns and then share them when they come across areas of mutual interest. My brothers and I are the same way. You and your brother are close, no?"

George attributed his suspicion to fatigue from the all-day flight, , but his impression of Juan was quickly changing from suave man Friday to incurable busybody. People who made small talk, in George's mind, should all find other hobbies. All George wanted to do was get to his hotel, check in, and get ready for bed.

He also needed to text Carol, as agreed upon, just before he called it a night. His previous plans to work on his presentation for Ordóñez would have to wait until morning. Thinking of how tired he was made George yawn.

As his ears cleared from the yawn, he heard the end of Juan's next remark. "Many families pass these things from generation to generation."

"I'm sure that's true," George said, not having a clue or even caring what Juan had rattled on about. "How far to the hotel?"

"*Cinco minutos, muchacho,*" Juan replied, again staring at George in the visor mirror. It was as if he was trying to get a sounding on the gringo, to look past the conversation and see something deeper. Then in English Juan said, "Five minutes. While we have this time, let me pass on instructions from Señor Ordóñez, which he expects you to follow as his guest and temporary employee. First, you are not to discuss with anyone why you are here."

George thought, "That will be easy, since I don't have a clue myself."

"Second, you are to wait at the hotel until Señor Ordóñez or his representative comes for you, as I have tonight. Under no circumstances are you to leave with anyone else."

George frowned. "Who else would I leave with? I'm on a business trip to work for your Mr. Ordóñez, not on a vacation."

"*Muchacho*, I am only passing on the instructions as they were given to me. Third, our business dealings are confidential. Before we begin, you will sign a binding agreement to that effect. Until that time, however, you are still expected to hold to the terms. Señor Ordóñez will ask if I made all that very clear. Your answer?"

George was used to signing such agreements in the United States. He nodded toward the back of Juan's head.

"One final thing," Juan added. "When Señor Ordóñez asks that this not be discussed with anyone, he means anyone, including your fine family, until it is determined their help or advice would be needed."

"I don't keep secrets from my wife, and I don't appreciate any suggestion that I won't exhibit the highest ethics in our—"

"Perhaps the stress of the day has caused you to misinterpret something I have said," Juan fairly cooed. At that moment George realized the van was coming to a stop along Avenida 9 de Octubre in front of a large hotel. Before either man could continue, a bellman opened the side door and indicated George should step out. Another hotel employee opened the back of the van and removed George's luggage.

Juan and Miguel made no move to get out. Juan simply rolled down his window and said something in Spanish to the two bellmen. Then he glanced at George with a large smile. *"Buenas noches, muchacho,*" he said. The window went back up, and the van rolled down the block.

The head bellman stepped into George's line of sight. "We offer our highest compliments to you and will do all in our power to make your stay pleasurable," he said in English, as if the speech was rehearsed but he wasn't entirely sure what the words meant. "Please follow me to registration. Señor Ordóñez has arranged for you to have our best room. And the other gentleman will be in the room next door, for your mutual convenience."

"What other gentleman?"

The first bellman looked confused. The extent of his English had just been exceeded. Another bellman stepped in. "The other gentleman who arrived just earlier. He came in on the same flight, but Mr. Ordóñez insisted on private transportation for each of you. I believe the registration desk said you were on the same flight, according to their records."

"Who was it?"

"Ironically, it is another man with a name like yours."

"I'm not following you," George said.

"*Otro descendiente de un pirate.* Another descendent of those who raided Guayaquil. The pirate Edward Davies."

"Doubtful," George said. "It's late, and I'm very tired. Show me to my room, please."

CHAPTER 3

Monday, 6 January
1:28 a.m.

George sent a text.

> Carol, all is fine. No problems with flight. Ordóñez sent man to pick me up at hotel. All checked into room. How r u doing? I miss u.

Less than a minute passed before her reply.

> Don't care if phone calls are $2.99 a minute. Invest it in letting me hear ur voice.

George got up and walked across the floor of his ninth-story room. He looked out the window. Guayaquil's skyline spread out in a panorama of steeples, bell towers, high-rise apartments, office buildings, and the inky blackness of the Guayas River. Even at this late hour the contrast between emerging economy and third-world poverty was unavoidably obvious.

The horns of taxis tooted below him. It was a cacophony reminiscent of junior high orchestra warm-ups. Though the hour was late, and it was a Sunday night turning into Monday morning, Guayaquil was still a busy place.

George knew he needed to call Carol, but he also knew if he did so too quickly, his voice would betray his irritation. He was second-guessing the wisdom of his decision to travel to Guayaquil. He smiled when he remembered how he had taught her to pronounce it—why-I-kill. There were a couple of times tonight when he had wanted to wrap his hands around some throats.

Staring out the window, he followed the dark shape of the Guayas River snaking across the eastern edge of the city. Lights from distant Santay Island flickered in the blackness. It was odd that this was the most important port city of Ecuador, yet it wasn't really on the coast. To reach it from the Pacific Ocean, one had to sail into the Gulf of Guayaquil and then up the Guayas River.

The documentary said the river was deep enough for larger Spanish ships to sail up the main channel and dock right at the entrance to the city. However, according to the video, for the pirate d'Hout to have tried such a move would have been suicide. Cannons from the city would likely have torn the ship and its crew to pieces.

For pirates, stealth was even more important than strength. Every cannon or musket ball fired was one less available for the next scrape. Economy was the name of the game in that day. Or at least that's what the video said.

George remembered hearing somewhere, perhaps in the documentary, that sugar and rice fields had since replaced most of the ancient mangroves along the river. The area was also now famous for growing bananas, cocoa for chocolate, and a variety of other commodities that provided a great deal of Ecuador's gross domestic and foreign product. Carol had specifically asked George to buy some Ecuadorian chocolate to bring home from his trip.

George shook himself from his contemplations brought on by exhaustion. He reached for the cell phone lying on the bed. He dialed the access code for the USA, followed by the area code and number. On the first ring, Carol picked up.

"This has been the longest night of my life, waiting to hear from you." she said. George didn't have to worry about her picking up on his distress. Hers was running circles around any irritation he might be feeling. "What took you so long?"

"Didn't you just text?" George asked in his most innocent schoolboy voice.

He could hear her breathe out. "OK, you're right. I forget how far these texts have to travel to reach you. I'm sorry. I've just had this nagging feeling all day that something was wrong. Are you all right?"

"Here I am, safe and sound," George said. "The only thing wrong is I miss you."

"What do you think of this Ordóñez fellow?"

"I haven't met him yet," George said. "He had some sort of meeting tonight...Actually I guess we're now well into the morning...and couldn't pick me up. He sent a driver and an escort."

"An escort?"

"Not *that* kind of escort. Don't be silly. One of those man-Friday types, I'm guessing. He was a nice enough guy, but he kept calling me *muchacho*. That was pretty annoying."

"If I've been worrying all night, and the worst thing to happen to you is being called *muchacho*, I got the short end of the stick," Carol said. "What time are you meeting Mr. Ordóñez?"

"You know, I don't believe he told me."

"That's not much of a man Friday if he didn't tell you what time to be ready."

"He said not to leave the hotel until he came."

"Well, that won't work," Carol said. "How are you going to go for your morning run? I can't remember the last time you missed it. That's more important to you than coffee."

"I'm counting on the fact that when he said not to leave, he didn't mean at six or six thirty a.m."

"Have you had a chance to chart your jog? I don't want to worry about you getting into any bad areas."

"Actually, I believe there is probably some type of area to run along the river. I was just looking at it out of the window."

"How's the hotel?"

"Not bad. Easily a three-star by US standards."

"Any idea what it's costing Mr. Ordóñez to put you up?"

"No, but it looks just like a hotel for business travelers in the United States. If you've seen one, you've seen them all."

"That's good, though, right?" Carol asked. "You could be staying in a place with screens on the windows, headhunters outside, and mosquitoes and bedbugs for roommates."

"You know, I didn't get to see much of the city because it wasn't that far from the airport to the hotel, but it appears really nice. Hard to believe how much history there is here. This place was an established city before the USA was a glimmer in George Washington's eye."

"Since when did you become a history buff?" Carol wanted to know. Then she cut herself off. "I just realized we're busting the budget to make small talk. You're good, right?"

"Right."

"You're madly in love with me, right?"

"Right."

"You have your Bible on your MacBook and will read it tomorrow before your run, right?"

"So far, I'm batting a thousand."

"You'll text tomorrow evening to kill the worry bug that lives inside me?"

"Text or call?" George asked. "One is fifty cents. The other is two ninety-nine a minute, not that you're not worth it, of course."

"Just text, but get your full fifty cents' worth. You miss me?"

"Right again. Love you, honey. Good night, or should I say, 'Good morning'? Bye." The phone went dead.

George had been staring out the window during the entire conversation, mentally plotting his morning jog: four blocks toward the river and the huge monument he could see at the river's edge, then right four blocks toward the docked ship. Looked like one of those full-masted jobs from a few centuries ago. Then back through the city to the hotel.

If he got up at six, followed his morning routine of reading and drinking coffee, and then went out for his jog, he could surely be ready to meet Mr. Ordóñez by eight.

Setting the alarm clock on his smartphone, George disrobed, jumped into the shower, and enjoyed the hot water running over him. When his head hit the pillow, he fell asleep almost instantly.

Monday, 6 January
7:45 a.m.

George's run down one of the streets, Calle 9 de Octubre, had been interesting, as had been his realization that the monument he had seen shining in the night commemorated the meeting of South American liberators Jose San Martin and Simon Bolivar in Guayaquil in July 1822. They were as important to South Americans as Thomas Jefferson and Ben Franklin were to people in the United States.

When George turned back toward downtown, he came across Parque Seminario, a city park inhabited by hundreds, possibly thousands, of iguanas. When one tumbled out of a tree just as George passed it, he thought he was a goner. Usually nothing stopped his runs. However, an entire city park teeming with iguanas in the trees, on the sidewalks, throughout the grass, and even climbing up on benches was a sight he had to pause and appreciate. The reptiles ranged in size from a few inches to the giant as- seen-on-TV varieties.

"Wow," George thought. "I really am in South America. Cool."

Running in downtown Guayaquil reminded him of attempting to run in downtown Houston. Streets were clogged with cars and taxis, and sidewalks were just as jammed with businesspeople. However, both the streets and sidewalks were far narrower than those in Texas. George trotted down Calle 10 de Agosto onto 6 de Marzo and back to the hotel on 9 de Octubre. High school Spanish hadn't equipped George with an understanding of why every street seemed to carry the name of a day and month. Upon further review, however, he decided the naming wasn't any more or less creative than cities that began with First Street and crossed them with avenues A through Z.

On his way upstairs after entering the hotel, George saw a bellman he thought might speak English. "Tell me about the street names," he said. "What's with all the days and dates?"

"I believe you would say that for us it is like you naming streets Fourth of July and Twenty-Fifth of December. Because we have much more history due to the age of our cities, we have many more dates to commemorate. *¿De donde eres?* Where are you from?"

"Houston, Texas, in the United States."

"That once belonged to the Spanish, yes? We had a revolution against Spanish rule. Did you see the great statue at the end of our *avenida*?"

"I did. Very impressive. Sort of reminds me of some of the statues we have in Washington, DC."

"What year was your city founded?"

"I don't really know."

"Guayaquil was founded in 1538. It is a very old, very important city, yes?"

"Hugh would love this," George thought on his way upstairs. "Every street has its own history and genealogy lesson. How come nobody ever names streets after geometric theorems or accounting terms? Something that's interesting. Tax Shelter Avenue.

Now *that* would be the street to live on—or maybe Pythagorean Theory Drive."

Having found what passed for his own unique sense of humor, George felt better about the entire venture into Ecuador. He showered, washed his slightly curly, graying hair, and wondered if he should have gotten a haircut before coming on the trip. He also used the clippers from his suitcase to trim a few stray hairs in his salt-and-pepper beard. Then came the matter of selecting clothes.

George had always heard that people in Latin America took a very casual approach to attire. However, the businesspeople he had seen this morning on the street dressed much more formally than he was used to in Houston.

He passed on the Panama-style shirt and khakis he had intended to wear with loafers. Instead he went for a more conservative button-down shirt, dark slacks, and dress shoes. He hadn't packed a sports jacket or tie, so Mr. Ordóñez would have to cut him some slack.

As he finished dressing, George thought he heard the door nearest his room open and close. Since there was no peephole, he waited a moment to quietly slide his door open and see what his neighbor and supposed fellow businessman looked like.

The man was entering the elevator; George could have sworn it was the same smarmy guy on the plane who'd wanted to strike up a conversation. He was also the one who had made a smart remark when customs had detained George.

"Great," George thought. "So I'll be taken around by '*Muchacho Juan*' while having to put up with everybody's best friend— what was his name? Oh yes, the other pirate, Edward Davies."

Instead of carrying his MacBook down to breakfast, George decided to spend a few more minutes in his room. He tried to go over what he would say to Señor Ordóñez. However, since he didn't even know the specifics of the job, he found he was wasting his time speculating rather than actually planning anything of substance. With that, he decided he might as well be officially introduced to the man he was now thinking of as Smarmy Eddie the Pirate.

Stepping into the elevator, George pushed the button to go to the floor marked CAFÉ. He exited the elevator on a floor featuring an elaborate breakfast area complete with a huge buffet, tablecloths, and real dishes that looked like what George would expect at a five-star restaurant. He looked around for the person he thought was Edward Davies.

As he scanned the restaurant, a hostess came over. "*La mesa?*" she asked. George reviewed all his knowledge of Spanish, which unfortunately took less than a minute.

"Table?" he asked back.

The young woman nodded.

"Yes, but I am looking for a man. *Otro hombre.* Alone. *Solo.*"

"*Sí, señor,*" the woman said, leading George to a table away from the other diners. "Señor Knight, *su huésped.*"

She walked away, leaving George to face a man in a worn Panama hat, crumpled shirt, khaki pants, and hiking boots. He was approximately forty, but his worn face and hardened hands made him appear much older. He had an air of eccentricity that made it unclear to George whether he was a rich man who was slumming or a poor man who had somehow afforded a hotel far beyond his means. One way or the other, he was not the man George had seen at the airport or in the elevator.

"My guest?" Knight said. "What an excellent surprise. To what do I owe the privilege?"

"I'm afraid there's been a mistake," George said, backing up a step. "I'm in town on business and was told I was to meet someone else. I'm sorry to trouble you."

"But clearly this other man isn't here, so until he arrives, I insist you join me. My work requires me to spend all my days with Ecuadorians, speaking only Spanish. It's good to hear some American English. From Texas, if my ears serve me correctly."

As much as George had instantly taken a dislike to *"Muchacho* Juan" and Edward Davies, he was instantly drawn to this Knight fellow. "You're correct with your guess. Houston, Texas. Here doing some consulting work. My name is George d'Hout. And you?"

"William Knight. Here doing an archaeological expedition. Been here for so long, I'm starting to feel like this is home."

"Archaeology? So is it *Dr.* Knight?"

"The PhD kind, yes, but down here most people say 'professor' instead of 'doctor.' Who are you consulting for?"

As the words were about to leave George's mouth, he remembered what Juan had said about confidentiality and caught himself. "Roberto Ordóñ— Actually, I haven't even met the person yet. I start work today. With the Internet and our global economy, you never know where you're going to go or who you're going to work for." Trying to change the subject lest he stupidly violate his terms of employment before he had even started, he said, "Tell me about what you do."

"I will. Ecuador is one of the smallest countries in Latin America. You probably know this, but most people don't. The whole country is about the size of Colorado. You have all kinds of history here. Amazing history. People have inhabited this place for eleven thousand years. But, for the most part, it's never been excavated. Not really. Not with a serious, scientific intent. There's an incredible story to be told here."

George was instantly sorry he'd asked. Knight said, "When the Cañari people began to create great civilizations, they were one of the few examples in the world of a matriarchal society. They were led, even into battle, by a queen. Have you ever seen a Cañari? They're really a tiny people. Less than five feet tall in many cases. But square and strong as oxen. They built great cities..."

The professor launched into an animated twenty minute monologue on Incan and Cañari history. When he came up for air, the professor said, "Am I boring you, Mr.— ?"

George suppressed a yawn. "No, not bored at all. Very interesting. Please continue."

Before he did, Professor Knight made the same arm-extension-finger-tapping motion toward a waiter George had seen Juan make to hail the van. *"Por favor, café para mi amigo,"* Knight said. "Would you like your coffee black, Señor d'Hout? George nodded.

"Café negro," the professor said. *"Para Señor d'Hout.* Now, where was I? Cañari, Incas, Spaniards. You've heard of Atahualpa, the great Inca chief?"

"Sorry, I'm not sure I have," George said. "Probably too much football and baseball on TV and not enough of the history channels."

"I don't mean to offend," the professor said, "but you're much better off without them. Lies and damn lies. Popular tripe. They always tell the third-grade version of history. Never the really interesting, complex stuff. Anyway, once the Spaniards had the run of the place, they began turning the indigenous people into slaves. Nothing so surprising there, I suppose. Before the Spaniards, one tribe was turning another tribe into slaves all over the place. Most great cities of the ancient world were built on the backs of slaves. It is both a tragic and a glorious story."

The waiter arrived with George's coffee, black as pitch in a shining cup of fine china. Without pausing in his story, the professor signaled permission for the coffee to be set down.

"*¿Crema?*" the waiter almost whispered. Cream?

"*Solo negro*," the professor reminded the waiter in a voice that sounded like he was talking to a child. The waiter ducked his head and slunk away. Professor Knight continued his story.

"When the Spaniards saw the way the Incas were sacrificing virgins and llamas and first one thing and then another, they were horrified. Came in the name of the cross and all that. At Ingapirka they found a place where thousands of llamas and hundreds of virgins had been sacrificed in the name of feeding the sun god, Viracocha. Well, that would never do, would it?"

The professor proceeded to give the entire history of the Inca and Cañari peoples of Peru, Bolivia, and Ecuador, from then until the present day. George listened politely but kept glancing at the breakfast buffet.

Once when the professor paused to sip his coffee, George said, "This is all very interesting. Uh, have you gotten your breakfast yet?"

"As a matter of fact, I have not. Let's go check out the buffet, shall we? Have you had your first guinea pig, Mr. d'Hout?"

"You're kidding, right?" George asked as they walked toward the buffet. He looked around, seeing a massive variety of carbohydrates cooked in every imaginable fashion. They were surrounded by scrambled and poached eggs, a white cheese, crispy bacon slices, ham, and fruit of every color, size, shape, and texture imaginable. Many of them George had never seen before.

Professor Knight said, "Kidding about guinea pig? Well, yes and no. It is the unofficial national dish in Ecuador. The guinea pigs here are huge. At least twice as big as the ones you buy for the kiddies back home.

"They kill them by crushing their skulls in their hands in one giant clap. Then they boil them, clean off the skin, gut them, and roast them on a stick whole. Run the skewer in one end and out the other, if you get my meaning. The poor things all look like they are screaming when you see them."

George felt his stomach turn just a bit. The professor pressed on. "They are called *cuy*. Not that different from eating rabbit. Go ahead, Mr. d'Hout, and get yourself some breakfast."

"Think I might just have fruit."

"One thing you need to learn about Ecuador is they have the finest fruits and vegetables in the world." In spite of the *cuy* story, there was something in his manner George found endearing.

However, for just a fraction of a second, George got the mental picture of a spider weaving a web. On the other hand, if Knight had been one of his college professors, he might have developed a much greater appreciation for history.

"This man is trouble," he heard his wife say, *"in the same way Ordóñez is trouble."*

"Doubtful," he thought, "on both counts."

Professor William Knight continued. "You have eaten carrots and cabbage and potatoes and bananas all your life. However, when you eat Ecuadorian food, your taste buds will know what they were created for. It will be as if you are eating for the very first time.

"In the United States, you get flavor from food by adding seasonings. With Ecuadorian food, you get flavor from the foods themselves. It is like plucking fruit from the Garden of Eden. Here there are no added chemicals and hormones. The food is natural, the way it tasted in the rest of the world before all the mass production of farm products. Think a potato doesn't have much flavor, Mr. d'Hout? Eat one from Ecuador. And the fruit? Only pineapple eaten fresh from the fields in Hawaii comes close to what you will experience when you eat fresh fruit here."

The professor's explanation of the fruits and vegetables was as calming as the description of the *cuy* was disturbing. George determined he would try his best to enjoy his first Ecuadorian meal. His plate included bits of everything offered. As he tasted each fruit, vegetable, and meat, Professor Knight provided a play-by-play on the history, cultivation, and social importance of it.

The fact that there was no guinea pig on the buffet also helped allay George's fear.

During a discourse on the merits of yucca, whether used in bread, baked, roasted, or fried, George glanced down at his watch.

Monday, 6 January
9:05 a.m.

"Oh my gosh," George said, interrupting the professor. "I'm terribly sorry, but I'm supposed to meet my client, and I really ought to be downstairs. I'm going to have to excuse myself."

"If you must," the professor said, "but if your client knows Guayaquil at all, he will know to come and find you up here. The lobby of the hotel is much too small to contain many people. Everyone meets their party here. But go if you must. It's been a great pleasure talking to you."

"Where do I pay?"

"This excellent breakfast is complimentary. One of the many reasons I choose to make this hotel my quarters. And I will cover the *propina* for the commendable service by the waitstaff. Have a profitable day, Mr. George d'Hout."

George wiped his mouth and laid the napkin on his plate. As he walked off, he heard the professor say, "By the way, Mr. d'Hout, if you have an extra few hours, I'd love to show you my work. You think yuccas and potatoes are interesting? I deal in the real nitty-gritty of human history. All the bloody stuff you like in movies and books. You're invited to come out and get your hands dirty one day. I'd love to have an extra person helping. Here's my card. Call me anytime."

"Unfortunately, doubtful," George said, trying not to sound disinterested. However, he was thinking, "Go participate in an archaeological dig or run a pin through my eye. Hmmmm. Tough choice."

George had to admit there was something mildly intriguing about the professor's offer. Just not *that* intriguing.

Out loud George said, "Only in town a few days, and then it's back to Houston. Thanks for the invitation, though."

Stepping into the elevator, George heard the professor say, "The invitation is an open one, Mr. d'Hout. The kind of thing you could take a personal interest in. Make a lifetime impression."

CHAPTER 4

Monday, 6 January
11:20 a.m.

George couldn't remember ever having been stood up before. Maybe once in high school, but if so, he couldn't remember by whom or what the circumstances were. Numerous hotel employees invited George to return to the restaurant upstairs, promising they would summon him when Mr. Ordóñez arrived.

Carol texted once, asking how the meeting was going. George didn't respond. He couldn't believe the whole thing was a sham. Why? For what purpose? Even if Mr. Ordóñez was tied up in another meeting, wouldn't he have sent Juan, Miguel, or both?

And though George still had the original business card Ordóñez had sent him, the number he dialed wasn't answered. He borrowed the phone at the front desk because he didn't want to use his own. International calling fees were outlandish, especially if he had to return the $5,000 because the job fell through.

After his fourth time of borrowing the desk phone, the concierge suggested there was a phone store several doors down. Tourists, the concierge explained in broken English, often bought disposable phones and calling plans to use in-country for under a hundred dollars.

George thanked the man for the suggestion and returned to a chair he had staked out in the tiny lobby. His only thought about money was that in twenty-eight years as a consultant, he had never had to keep a retainer for work that wasn't done. He hoped the whole situation wouldn't get legally sticky. Carol would just love that, and legal issues would quickly eat up the retainer fee. "Probably just easier to return the money and wash my hands of it," George thought.

Having looked at every newspaper in the lobby, trying to make out the stories written in Spanish as best he could, George was now thumbing through tourist brochures that featured all the places he wouldn't be seeing: Baños, the Playas, Ingapirka, Quito, the Amazon, Cajas National Park. The list went on and on. For a little country, Ecuador sure had a lot to offer.

The elevator doors opened and closed dozens of times while George impatiently waited for his client to show up. He even quit looking up, knowing either Juan or Mr. Ordóñez would be coming in from the street. Therefore, it startled him when he heard the elevator door open and someone call his name.

"Mr. d'Hout."

"Yes?" George looked up.

It was the professor. "Are you already back from your meeting?"

"Unfortunately, my meeting hasn't begun yet. My client didn't show."

The professor glanced at his watch. "Well, the good news is, in forty minutes the hotel bar opens. It's behind those double doors over there. It will remain open until such time as you no longer care whether your client shows up or not."

"Thanks, but I'm really not much on—"

"Just a suggestion. And like my suggestion to join our dig, it is an open one. Have a profitable day."

With that, Professor Knight was out the door. George watched through the large front window as the professor stepped out of the hotel, dodging the nonstop parade of pedestrians. A bellman opened the door of a rather banged-up Renault, which the professor slipped into. He tooted his horn twice, and glided into the stream of traffic.

The front of the hotel was wide as if to give it a very large, roomy look from the street, like a shoe box turned sideways. It seemed like the rest of the hotel might go back quite a ways. Out of boredom, George got up and explored the small space one more time. He had missed the double doors to the bar until Professor Knight pointed them out. What else had he failed to notice?

As he tried the doors to the bar, a voice behind him said, "The bar *no está abierta ahora*."

"Not open?" George said. He looked at the clock on the wall. "Right. Still thirty minutes to go."

"You drink," the employee said. It was not a question but an invitation.

"Doubtful," George answered, "but thanks."

As time crawled by, George felt the muscles in his neck growing tighter and tighter. Embarrassment coupled with disappointment presented him a tremendous headache. He would have to face Carol with the news that she had been right all along. It didn't bother him she was right. He could be at home right now, working on another project or…

Suddenly, George realized he was obviously more tired from the trip than he had previously been aware. He could be working online on another project! What an idiot. Why was he wasting an entire day when he could be online, getting another task knocked out? There were several client websites that needed updating. One client had called before Christmas to say there was a link that appeared to be dead. It was no big deal, the client had said, and George could get around to it at his leisure. What better time than now?

George checked the paper case of his key card for the hotel's Internet access code. He clicked on his laptop and entered the code. Suddenly the afternoon flew by. He was in his domain again, regardless of the fact he was three thousand miles from Houston. For the millionth time, the thought flickered through his mind, "What did people do before the Internet?"

Monday, 6 January
6:02 p.m.

Over the next seven hours, George became a fixture in the lobby, something people stepped around, like a table or chair. He could have gone to his room to work, but the distraction of the cars and people outside was rather entertaining when he looked up. Further, there were complimentary hot teas in the lobby, something his room couldn't provide. The bar opened right on time and got progressively busier throughout the afternoon. With the doors open, the bar made the hotel's main floor seem three or four times its previous size.

"Clearly the social center of the place," George thought.

The only annoying thing about the entire afternoon was the fact the TV in the bar was turned up way too loud. However, because it was in Spanish, George had been able to tune it out the way he had ignored the tooting of horns and other street noises. George remembered the client with the horror stories from Panama saying that one of the differences between the United States and South America was TV volume.

The client had said, "In a sports bar in the US, they have the volume turned down, and they're usually playing music or something. In Latin America, the volume is full throttle."

The client had conspiratorially insisted there were political reasons for this. "Back when there was a revolution a week in those South American republics, one of the things people did to keep from being overheard as they plotted and planned was to turn up the TV's volume to drown everything else out."

"Doubtful," George thought. He said aloud, "But wouldn't that just mean you had to talk louder? It seems like a zero-sum game."

"There was a lot of bugging of public and private places," the client had insisted. "When you turn up the volume of a TV or radio, the background noise becomes so great, it's impossible to eavesdrop. Loud TVs and radios just became a habit."

George thought Carol wouldn't last long in this lobby. She was very noise sensitive, to the point that long periods of loud noise made her feel sick. His brother, Hugh, ever the walking game of Trivial Pursuit, had pointed out the words *noise* and *nausea* come from the same Latin root. It had been during a family cruise to Alaska. They had been listening to a 1970s cover band, and Carol was saying it was about time to head back to her and George's cabin. She had heard all the live music her ears could stand. Hugh announced significant discomfort caused by too much noise was well documented throughout human history as a cause for migraines.

He explained that was why police often piped loud music into homes or buildings they were surrounding during a standoff. Carol joked, "I'd have the shortest crime spree in history if they did that to me. I sure couldn't stand it for hours on end. I give up!" She raised her hands in mock surrender.

Now, thinking about Carol and her quirks made George suddenly homesick. He texted,

Miss u.

Fifty cents for two words, but it was worth it. In three or four minutes his smartphone vibrated with her reply.

Miss u 2. How did ur meeting go? Still working?

He texted back.

Will call later.

"Well, that was a dollar spent," George thought, ever frugal.

A voice interrupted his two-track thought process about texting Carol and tweaking the client's website. "You seem to have made a base camp here. Building up strength to climb the stairs to your room? They have an elevator, you know."

It was Professor Knight, whose disarming manner instantly made an otherwise smart-aleck remark seem harmless.

"Still holding out hope my client will show up," George said. "But I've gotten a lot of work done. And besides, the tea is free down here."

George reached out to shake the professor's hand but noticed both hands were in his pockets and he made no effort to remove them. "Need to wash up a bit before I go shaking hands," the professor said. "It wouldn't do to get you all dirty. Tell you what; I will go and clean up. Then we can retire to the bar, and you can tell me all about your work. I was Mouthy

Milly this morning. This afternoon, I want to learn about you and your profession."

Having nothing else to occupy himself with and tired of working on the laptop, George agreed. Maybe the professor could provide him with some leads for new clients. George hadn't done much educational web developing, but who knew? Maybe this could work out after all.

The professor turned, pulled his right hand out of his pocket long enough to punch the elevator button, and disappeared behind the closing doors. George thought his hands were clean enough, except for what looked a bit like brown mud or maybe flecks of brick-colored paint. "For an archaeologist, he keeps pretty tidy," George thought. "But he probably supervises a lot of other people, rather than actually doing the dirty work himself."

Watching the professor, George realized he had failed to keep a lookout for Edward Davies. However, such a gregarious man would be unable to walk by without saying something to George. He had certainly been a jabberbox in the airports in Panama and Guayaquil.

When the professor returned, he was in a different shirt and pants. They seemed as wrinkled and field worn as the ones he'd had on earlier. George also noticed the professor was wearing the same boots, though he had clearly tried to clean them. There were streaks along the sides and tops where a rag or towel had been run across them.

"Profitable day other than the snafu with your one client here?" the professor asked.

"Got some work done. Things that needed to be completed. You?"

"Spent the day fund-raising," Professor Knight answered. "You know, this kind of work can't exist without lots of financial backing. It is the lifeblood of what we do. Therefore, as much of my job is looking for funding as it is actually being in the field. Dreadful business, really. But important."

George thought the professor had said earlier his hands were dirty from being in the field. Maybe he'd misunderstood. Or maybe the professor had taken some potential donors out to a site. That actually made perfect sense.

Finding a table as far from the TV as possible, George and the professor sat down. The lounge was 90 percent full. A quick survey of the large room revealed the usual mix of businesspeople debriefing after a long day, rack-rate Romeos trying to ply women with alcohol and sweet talk, and fellow travelers making conversation with people they would probably never see again.

"Hey," George thought, "I'm making small talk! Have been every time I see this professor guy. Carol won't believe it." Whatever personal development advantages came from meeting the professor wouldn't match the ire Carol would unleash when she learned Ordóñez never showed up. Again, George's irritation and embarrassment welled.

"Everything all right?" the professor asked. "You look a little tense."

"I am," George said. "I can't believe my client didn't show up, didn't call, didn't do anything. Seems just flat-out rude."

George rubbed his temples, trying to ease the vice grip of a stress headache. Maybe a run later tonight would help him feel better.

The professor was unwinding in a different way. "Even people who don't like beer like Ecuadorian beer. Nothing heavy like those European lagers. You must try it. I'm buying. It's called Pilsener. Made right here. Delightful, really. A lot of people complain it's too watery, but I think it's actually pretty good. If you don't care for it, they also have another brand called Club. I believe it's made with corn. How's that for a different take on making beer?"

"To be honest, I really don't know much about beer," George said. "My father was a pretty heavy drinker, so I chose to never take it up."

"Never?"

"I guess you'd say I'm the least committed social drinker ever to make the social scene," George said. Inside he smiled at his clever turn of a phrase. His brother, Hugh, would appreciate it, if he remembered the remark long enough to relate it to him. Carol would just think it was corny. Like the Ecuadorian beer.

The professor seemed to miss the remark or not be amused by it. Changing the subject, Knight said, "Something I must tell you about Ecuador—all of Latin America, really—is that you need to learn the phrase *tranquilo*. It literally means 'to be quiet,' but the way it's used down here means the same thing as 'chill out' in the United States.

"When I first started coming down here to South America—I believe it was in Paraguay—I waited three days for a bus that was supposed to take me to the next town. Can you believe it? Three days! I was doing some work at an old Guarani Indian site that had just been discovered at the edge of a forest. Too far to walk, and I didn't have a car. So what did I do? I waited."

George nodded that he was listening. The professor plodded on. "An old Guaraní kept seeing me looking at my watch. *'Tranquilo,'* he says to me. *'Disfrutar de la vida.'* It means 'enjoy your life.' I put away the watch and for three days I just walked around observing. It taught me more about Latin America than years of reading books. I decided during that trip I would never let anything keep me from making each day profitable one way or the other."

"Good advice," George said. In spite of the fact the professor had promised to listen instead of talk, he was again rattling on and on. But George didn't mind. This professor was quite a character. It was like spending time with his brother, Hugh. George was convinced this professor was one great guy.

CHAPTER 5

Monday, 6 January
9:17 p.m.

After Professor Knight finished off three more beers in the hotel bar, the archaeologist suggested a place nearby that offered good food with a wonderful ambieance.

"It's called Café Aroma, and it's down by the river in a simply beautiful park on the Malecon Dos Mil. The restaurant is actually outdoors, but it's covered, and there is a perfect little pond with ducks and a delightful assortment of South American flowers and trees. It really is an impeccable place to eat. And the *lomo res* is very serviceable when washed by the right beverage."

"*Lomo res?*" George asked.

"Beef tenderloin," the professor said. "You find it everywhere down here."

"You're not trying to sneak in *cuy* on me, are you?"

"Believe me, if you are confronted with *cuy*, you will know it." The professor was right about Aroma Café. George had a wonderful *jugo fresas* to drink along with his tenderloin sandwich. The *papas fritas* were the best french fries George had ever eaten. There was a natural flavor to the potatoes George had never tasted before. Carol often said fries were a good excuse to eat salt and ketchup. But these fries were amazingly flavorful all on their own.

While the professor asked a few questions about George's business, he spent most of the time explaining South American customs, geography, and culture. During a discussion about the importance of the Guayas River to the area, Knight said, "I guess someone told you that you are not the first George d'Hout to frequent these parts?"

"Actually, I have heard that. My predecessor was a rather unsavory type, from what I've learned."

"I think there is a lot of misunderstanding about pirates," the professor countered. "Sure, there were some pure outlaws and highwaymen among them. But a great number of them were men who had no other choice. Others were privateers doing what they did for king and country."

"We all have a choice," George said, realizing too late that his remark had too sharp an edge to it.

"Perhaps," the professor said. "Or maybe until we are in a similar situation, we really can't say how we would react. Maybe we would do the same thing they did. After all, the Incas stole the treasures of the Cañari, and the Spanish stole it from them. So the pirates were just the latest in a long line of thieves.

What's the problem? Who really owned what? Who can tell? It comes down to one of those possession-is-nine-tenths-of-the-law situations."

The professor continued. "There is a really interesting site you ought to see, for the sake of your long-lost relative. It's not too far from here. It's on the north end of the Malecon Dos Mil where we are right now. You just follow the river north a few hundred yards. That will lead you to Cerro Santa Ana, a peak with colorful houses all the way to the top. The hill was the site of a fort that defended— or attempted to defend— the city from pirates like your relative. Today there's a lighthouse up there and a great view of the entire area."

"You keep saying 'my relative.' We have the same name, but not every John Smith is related. I know the genealogy crowd wants to make everyone think they're all related to kings and famous inventors, but I think life is a little more pedestrian than that."

"Have you ever researched it to find out?" the professor asked.

"You're actually the second person to ask about that. My brother, Hugh, is the guy who enjoys that kind of thing. Honestly, I don't care that much. Don't get me wrong; I would surely help the genealogists develop their websites, but the actual research on which ancestor married the sultan of Siam doesn't do it for me."

"So are you and Hugh close?"

For a moment George thought he was having an episode of déjà vu. First there was a history lesson, then genealogy, then a conversation about Hugh and whether the two of them were close. "Hugh lives in Midland, out in West Texas. He teaches at a community college, edits textbooks, and instructs some classes for a couple of online universities. His hobby is historical research and genealogy. He says it's more wholesome than cable TV and cheaper than liquor, so for him it's a pretty good vice."

Back in his hotel room later that evening, George was debating whether to text or call Carol. He had barely thought about Roberto Ordóñez or Juan Pacheco for three hours. But now that he prepared to call Carol, he anticipated her questions: When was he pulling the plug and catching a flight home? Did he need to contact their lawyer to determine how much, if any, of the retainer to keep? Would it be more ethical to simply return the whole thing, minus expenses, and forget he had ever heard the name Roberto Ordóñez?

Breaking his chain of thoughts was a ring of the room telephone. He picked it up and felt a surge of expectation. "Hello?"

"Señor d'Hout, this is Miguel. Señor Ordóñez asked me to contact you. He is very sorry you kept waiting." Silence came next, followed by muffled conversations in the background. "You services still needed, and he expect you to wait for him. ¿Entiende?"

"I understand, Miguel, but I really need to speak to Mr. Ordóñez."

"Good. He look forward to talking to you as well. *Buenas noches.*"

"No, Miguel, I mean I need to speak to him right—"
Click.

George felt his headache returning. "*Tranquilo*, d'Hout," he said to himself. "This isn't the USA, and they don't play by your rules. You are being paid good money to—"

Again the phone interrupted his thoughts. This time it was Carol texting.

> Well?

He texted back.

> Couldn't believe it. Ordóñez was a no-show. Got a lot of work done on other accounts. He called and said it would be 2morrow.

> R u serious? What a jerk.

> I was reminded by a fellow here that the byword is tranquilo. It means relax. Things happen in their own good time.

> No they don't. 2 weeks. If he's a no-show 2morrow, u need to be a no-show by Wed. Love u. R u ok?

> Have learned a lot about Ecuador. Will even put Hugh on notice with what I've learned.

> Hugh called today 2 talk 2 u.

We are now up to $4. I love you. Will call if there are problems.

Love u 2. Miss you very much.

That made it $4.50.

Tuesday, 7 January
6:10 a.m.

George left the hotel for his run, reviewing his plans for the day. If Ordóñez showed up, all would be fine. George could determine whether he was the right man for the proposed job. If Ordóñez didn't appear, George figured he would use all his powers of persuasion and Internet ability to find the man's house. He would simply take a taxi and see him in person. What was the saying? If the mountain won't come to Muhammad, then Muhammad must go to the mountain.

Speaking of mountains, as George reached the end of the riverside park known as Malecon Dos Mil and the beginning of Cerro Santa Ana, he stared at the lighthouse at the top. Pretty good workout, he thought. He jogged toward the wide row of stairs to his left. The houses were painted a variety of pastel colors and reminded him of some neighborhoods in San Francisco, California.

However, the ascent reminded him this was still a very poor country. Underfed dogs spied him warily from under shrubbery. They all had a wilted look, as did some of the children. Several men sat in their undershirts, looking out screenless windows as he huffed by.

"*Buenos días,*" He nodded, continuing to climb. Most just stared at him. One, he was pretty sure, offered to sell him a beer. Before seven in the morning? Was the guy joking?

At the top of Cerro Santa Ana, George enjoyed a 360-degree view of the city. Next he jogged around the lighthouse, examined ruins from a fort that dated to the time of the pirate d'Hout, and looked inside a lovely little church. Feeling himself cooling down and growing worried he wouldn't get his best workout if his heart rate dropped too much, George jogged in place.

"Let me see," he thought, "South is that way, so that's the direction from which d'Hout's men would have come up the river. They would have docked their boats in the mangroves late at night and snuck into the city. Wonder if the people here kept dogs back then. Did they start barking? Did anybody have a clue what was happening before the attack? How many people did d'Hout and Davies kill? Or were they really Robin Hood types? That's sort of what the professor implied."

Once he was back in the hotel room, George drank his coffee and read the Bible on his MacBook: "Do not be deceived: God cannot be mocked. A man reaps what he sows. Whoever sows to please their flesh, from the flesh will reap destruction; whoever sows to please the Spirit, from the Spirit will reap eternal life. Let us not become weary in doing good, for at the proper time we will reap a harvest if we do not give up."

"Do the right thing and don't give up," George summarized aloud. "I can do that…with a little help." Then he thought about how aggravated he was with Ordóñez. "Amend that," he thought. "With a lot of help!"

At breakfast, he again joined the professor. "You know," George said, "I never even asked what university you work for. How long are you down here? Do you have students assisting? I was really rude not to seem a little more interested in your work. *Lo siento.*"

Knight made no eye contact. He stared at his coffee. "No apology necessary," he said. Was it distraction in his voice or annoyance? "You are a businessman, and your interest is money, not academics. We of the ivory-tower set need you, but you do not need us. Or at least that is how most people perceive it."

"I certainly didn't mean that," George said. He wondered why he seemed to be getting off on the wrong foot with Professor Knight this morning. Yesterday the chemistry seemed so good.

"I would love to sit and chat," the professor said, looking at his watch. "However, my own business summons me. I must be at the excavation site very early. It is a long drive. Since my funding sources are here, it is here I must keep my base camp. Will you excuse me?"

"Of course," George said. Then he added, "I doubt I can make it, but is the invitation still open to visit your dig?"

The professor stopped in his tracks, fingering the keys in his pocket. "I have hit a bit of a snag," he said. "We are, as the saying goes, between a rock and a hard place. Of course, that is a space normally reserved for geologists. I will let you know."

"Maybe he's not mad at me," George thought. "Maybe he really is having some trouble at the dig. Besides, that's not my problem. I need to find Ordóñez and get on with the reason I'm here."

CHAPTER 6

Tuesday, 7 January
10:00 a.m.

Unfortunately, Tuesday was a carbon copy of Monday. George stewed in the small lobby, not that it helped. Trying the phone number on Ordóñez's card, he got no answer. His commitment to *tranquilo* expired in record time.

He asked the concierge, "Do you have a Guayaquil phone book? A, how would I say it, *libro de telefono?*"

The concierge looked at George as if he had lost his mind. "*La tienda teléfono es por la calle.*"

"*Tienda?* A store? Not the telephone store. A telephone book."

The concierge again looked lost. Apparently no one who spoke English was on duty. There were seemingly also no bilingual tourists nearby who could help translate. "My high school

Spanish teacher is somewhere laughing at me right now," George said, only furthering the concierge's exasperated expression.

"*No importa,*" George told him, not sure whether that was a real phrase or he was reduced to making up words.

Walking away from the desk, MacBook in hand, he decided it was time to do what he would do if he were back home: conduct an online search and start tracking down addresses. He heard taxis were cheap in Ecuador. It was time to find out.

Cross-referencing via three online mapping and address programs, George entered the name Roberto Ordóñez Gonzalez and the phone number listed on the business card. The number rang and rang, but no one picked up. "It would be easier to get on the first plane back to the United States, but now I'm mad," George thought. He was going to give this inconsiderate fraud a piece of his mind before he sailed the friendly skies back to Houston.

George got eleven hits on his search. Then he looked up the United States consulate, which turned out to be nine blocks away on the same street as the hotel. Walking to the consulate, George formulated his plan. He would tell the consulate he was considering moving to Ecuador and wanted information on good neighborhoods. Since their job was to keep Americans safe, surely the consul would be more than happy to help. Since chances were better than average that Roberto Ordóñez lived in a very nice neighborhood, it would help him to reduce his search even further to houses in the right part of town.

At the consulate, the only hitch was the person on duty wanted to give George a forty-minute lecture on the potential dangers of living overseas. The man pointed out that US relations with

Ecuador were dicey at best. Current Ecuadorian plans to formalize ties with Iran could make matters worse.

George said he understood and simply wanted to show the man a list of ten addresses, neatly plotted on a Guayaquil map, and ask which ones were in the safest neighborhoods. The consulate officer informed George that he couldn't make real estate recommendations. George answered he knew that, but maybe the man could just show George where the "right people" lived.

After another thirty minutes with the consulate officer, George had narrowed the list to five addresses. The officer suggested George might try the local tourist information office in the Banco Pacifico Building. George felt like a bloodhound on the trail as he again took to the streets. He walked instead of taking taxis, deciding to save his money until he needed it to get to the outlying areas where Roberto Ordóñez probably lived.

At the tourist office, the woman on duty spoke perfect English. She told George she knew Texas very well, having attended Texas Tech University in Lubbock. She'd majored in hospitality management before returning to her homeland to work in the tourism industry. Her eyes told George she was excited another "rich American" was looking at buying real estate in Ecuador. She volunteered to him that she knew several excellent brokers who would be happy to help him.

George said he wasn't to that point yet. He just wanted to look over the properties he was considering. For George, the whole thing felt a bit like being in a spy movie. The feeling was as foreign to him as eating guinea pig. By his own estimation, he was a rather uninteresting website consultant. He liked to jog and loved his wife. But Roberto Ordóñez had sent him on a wild-goose chase, so by golly, he was going to grab the goose by the throat.

Walking out of the tourism office, George felt a certain elation. With the help of the woman, he had narrowed the list of addresses where Roberto Ordóñez Gonzalez might live down to two. Both were in an exclusive neighborhood known as Samborondon.

Now it was time for phase two of his plan. Stepping to the curb, George mimicked the motion he had seen from *Muchacho Juan*. He held his arm out in front of his body and made a tapping motion in the air with his index finger.

One of the cabbies driving by blinked his lights at George and pulled over to the curb. "Samborondon," he said. The cabbie just stared.

"¿*Dirrección?*" the cabbie asked.

"North, I believe," George answered. *"Norte."*

The cabbie said, *"Dirrección,* not direction," in broken English. "Address. You not speak Spanish?"

"I'm terribly sorry," George said. *"Lo siento."* He was a guest in this Spanish-speaking country. As a guest, he believed he had an obligation to try to speak their language. However, until a month ago, he had no clue he would need Spanish like he needed it now. In the back of his head, he heard Carol telling their daughter when she was younger, "If you wait to learn something until you need it, you won't have it when you need it." Their daughter, all of thirteen, had simply stared at her mother as if she had lost her mind.

George thought, "Carol shouldn't have wasted the advice on her. I was the one who needed it." He made a commitment to begin Spanish classes as soon as he got back to the United States. "Of course, that probably means my next foreign client will want me to go to Bangladesh or Beijing."

The cabbie was still staring. "You speak English, yes?"

"Yes."

"Address?"

"Oh, yes. Sorry. It's right here." George showed the taxi driver the first address. As they drove through the city, George's mind ran along three parallel tracks. On the first, he was thinking about exactly how he was going to confront Robert Ordóñez. What would he say for maximum sting with minimum backlash?

On the second track, he considered what he would say if Mr. Ordóñez had some very solid reason for his delay, but wanted George to continue with the job. Would George be able to muster enough *tranquilo* to accept the delay and put his annoyance aside? Especially for the balance of the fifty thousand dollars?

Finally, what if it turned out that Ordóñez was a total fake? Should the police be summoned? Would they even care if Ordóñez was attempting to perpetrate some type of scam? George realized he knew almost nothing about the Ecuadorian justice system.

The neighborhoods were getting much nicer as the cab motored on for half an hour along Via Perimetral and Avenida La Puntilla, past a number of very nice restaurants, discos, and office complexes. The schools were growing progressively more upscale, as were the grocery stores, as they neared the Samborondon community.

The deep chasm between the very rich and the very poor also widened, with all traces of a middle class erased. High-dollar SUVs replaced taxis as the main vehicles. In Guayaquil, light-skinned gringos drew hopeful looks. Would they spend money? When one approached Samborondon in a taxi, the upscale inhabitants didn't give the vehicle or its passenger a glance.

On the outer edges of Guayaquil, George saw junkmen pushing carts, in which they collected scrap metal and recyclables off the sides of the road. There were also old women leading haggard milk cows as they grazed on every bit of public grass they could find. In Ecuador, owning a cow definitely didn't imply that one owned the land on which to graze it. But in Samborondon, the junkmen and cowherders disappeared. They were not welcome in this area.

Looking at the back of the driver's head, George continued his three tracks of thought. But they all derailed simultaneously when the cab pulled to a stop. The large, walled property had a very simple For Sale sign resting well inside a seven-foot iron fence that surrounded the property. Simple, but elegant.

The driver said, "Very nice. You going to buy?"

"Doubtful," George answered. "I wonder if someone lives there. If he does, I very much want to talk to him."

"I wait for you," the driver said. George stepped out of the cab. The fence and the house behind it had an intimidating aura about them. The gate was locked. George couldn't find an intercom system or bell to ring. "You rattle the lock," the driver said out the window. "*Fuerte*. Real loud. Let them know you here."

George tried it. Just as he was about to give up, a small woman in a simple dress moved past a window toward the front door. George heard her struggling with several locks. Finally she managed to get the door open. *"Usted no tiene una cita,"* she said. *"No hay nadie aquí para que vea."*

George looked sheepishly at the woman, then at the taxi driver.

The driver said, "She is just housekeeper. She says you don't have *cita*...a, a—how you say?—appointment. Nobody here for you to talk to."

George looked back at the small, dark-skinned woman. "Roberto Ordóñez? *Aquí?* Is he here?"

Tears rolled down the woman's face. She crossed herself. *"Muerto,* señor. *Tambien,* Señora Ordóñez."

"'Muerto'? Doesn't that mean like 'Day of the Dead' or something?" George asked the cabbie. "Are they out celebrating the Day of the Dead?"

"It means they are dead, señor. This lady is in mourning. She was their servant and has probably lost her source of income. Probably she is living here until someone buys the place and casts her out."

George looked at the woman. *"¿Muerto?* How long?"

The cabbie yelled toward the house, *"Señora, le acompaño en su sentimiento. ¿Cuando murieron?"*

"Tres meses," she answered. *"Que murió en un accidente de tráfico."*

George understood. Three months. It couldn't be his Roberto Ordóñez.

"Not the place I'm looking for," George said. To the woman he ducked his head in apology and said, *"Lo siento, señora. Lo siento.* I'm sorry."

Sliding back into the cab, he said, "I have another address. Don't think it's far from here. Let's go."

"But you not even look at the house," the confused cabbie said. *"Creo que le gusta.* It was very nice."

"Not the right address," George said. "Try this one."

He showed the cabbie the second address, and they pulled away. The tiny, distraught woman watched them drive off. She wiped her face with a dirty, white piece of lace she was clutching.

The taxi turned, first left off the main road and then right into a very exclusive neighborhood. This was George's last shot at finding Roberto Ordóñez.

CHAPTER 7

Tuesday, 7 January
4:41 p.m.

The house matching the address on George's paper was one of the most alluring he had ever seen. Like most of the finer properties in the Guayaquil area, it was surrounded by a large iron fence topped with spikes. There was a gate, but it stood open. The driveway was long, perhaps two hundred yards. It was adorned with a spectacular hand-laid patchwork of red-and-beige bricks, creating the effect of a maroon checkerboard pattern that wound around to the back of the house and trailed out of sight. There were no vehicles visible and no sign of life at the house.

Check that. This was not just a house. It was an estate.

"Drive on in," George said.

Nothing. The cabbie just sat there. George repeated his instructions. Then, thinking perhaps the cabbie was even more smitten by the property than he was, George said, *"Adelante."*

The house was glazed red brick with a shimmering green tile roof. It almost glistened in front of them. Nothing was out of place, as if the residence was from some fairy tale. At any moment Hansel and Gretel might emerge. A large bay window framed in white lattice was on the left side of the house, indicating perhaps a dining room or study.

The second floor featured a simple window with woodwork trimmed in white-and-green shutters; the green was just a shade darker than the tiles on the roof. In the middle of the wide front of the house were white double doors. Across the roof were three sets of windows indicating three additional rooms, besides the one over the dining room or study. The house reminded him of a colorful twist on Fred MacMurray's residence on *My Three Sons*.

Along the front of the house, opposite the bay windows to the far right side, was a covered porch. It featured an assortment of hanging baskets bursting with tropical flowers. The porch ended on the right side of the house at a portico. The driveway appeared to wrap all the way around the home. No cars were in sight, but they might all be behind the house.

The property seemed very familiar to George and yet very foreign. What was it?

"I need you to pull on in," George said again.

"I let you out here," the driver said. "I have been too long and need to get other riders. Three dollars, plus three more for such a long way."

"Actually, I am going to pay you to just wait here, and then you can drive me back to town. This is way too far to walk, and I doubt there are many other taxis out this far."

"Sí, and I need to not be this far, too," the driver said.

George stopped focusing on the house and turned his attention to the cabbie. The man was genuinely concerned. "What's wrong?" George asked.

"Got to get back to town," the driver said. "You come or stay? Three dollars. Not three more for the long way. Just three, and you go so I can go."

"Sir, I have been trying for some time to meet this man, and I'm finally here. I don't need to be ditched with no ride back into the city."

"No me quedo aquí," the cabbie said. His voice was growing anxious. It was as if he could see something heading his way and must avoid it. His ability to speak English seemed to vanish as his anxiety rose. The man's dark eyes were focused on the property as if he were a deer that just heard twigs snap. Were they the footsteps of an approaching hunter?

George knew from his experience as a runner that when things began to tighten up, the best thing to do was relax. He took a deep breath and let it out slowly. He quietly said, "I'm sorry, but what is your name? *¿Como se llama?*" He tried to sound as if he were talking to the man for the first time, taking things back to square one.

"Mateo," the cabbie said. His eyes never left the house.

"Mateo, *mi nombre es* George. *Mucho gusto.* I am new in Ecuador and need you to tell me what you think is wrong. If there is a cause for concern, I need to know what it is."

The calmness in George's voice had its desired effect. Whatever spell the house had cast on Mateo was momentarily broken. The cabbie looked into the rearview mirror and made eye contact with George.

"It is too quiet, and this gate should not be open," Mateo said. His voice took on a high, strained tone. "This is not an Ecuadorian *casa*. Not built right. Gringo *casa*. But gringos have *muchos empleados*. Many helpers—how you say?—employees. Why the gate not closed?"

Mateo looked again at the house, searching every inch for signs of life. "Very dangerous for a house this *rico*, this rich, to leave gate open. *Gente mala*—bad people, robbers—love houses like this."

"Mateo, people might leave their gates open at houses like this in the United States. They probably just forgot to close it. There's a simple explanation."

"*Aquí no.* Not in Guayaquil. Something bad happen. Here you not leave gate open like this. You see anybody? We sitting here ten minutes. *Ninguna persona* come to see what we doing. That not how you do it in Ecuador. Not Guayaquil. House like this have two, three people working in it. *¿Donde estan?* Where are they?"

George said, "Honk your horn. Let's get the housekeeper to come out."

Mateo complied with three short blasts. Honking horns in the United States meant something was wrong or someone was angry. George had already figured out in Guayaquil, honking horns could mean many things: "Watch out, I just passed you." "I'm about to pass you." "You need to pass me." "Someone else is passing you." "There's an intersection up ahead; I'm entering the intersection." "I just left the intersection." "Someone someday might enter the intersection." "Pedestrian ahead." "Pedestrian behind." Or simply, "Hey, how you doing?"

At this moment, it apparently meant "Please ignore us." The house sat quietly, undisturbed. Like a graveyard. George listened for any sounds. He heard none, not even birds singing from the variety of tropical trees on either side of the wide drive. There was not even a breeze. The place was completely still, completely quiet. George looked past the house toward a small banana grove. It sat off to the right of the house inside an expansive, gated yard. As he watched it for any sign of life, he became aware of a drop of sweat rolling down his forehead and into his eyes. It might be January, but Guayaquil was in the middle of the Southern Hemisphere's summer.

"Just stay right here," George instructed. "I have come a very long way to have a moment with this man. If he is in there, I'm going to find out. If he isn't, I will see if I can find where he is."

"I thought you looking to buy house," Mateo said. "You lie."

"I am looking to do business with this man," George said. "That is the truth."

George exited the cab and gave Mateo a ten dollar bill from his front pants pocket; it was an exorbitant sum for a taxi ride in Ecuador. George hoped it was enough to make Mateo stay. George fixed his eyes on the beautiful house. He squared his shoulders and quickly walked up the neat drive. Looking at his feet, he noticed every brick was perfect.

There wasn't a trace of tire rubber or leaked motor oil on them. That meant either no one had driven on them, or the owner of the house had them steam cleaned; that would be quite a job on a sprawling driveway like this.

Nearing the house, George observed the tiles of the roof. They were the same *U* shape as used on other traditional Ecuadorian structures, but all those had been a rusty-red color. What must it cost to have special tiles made in the color of your choice? Maybe not much, since the cost of living in Ecuador appeared considerably lower than in the United States. However, if this job had been done in the States, it would have cost a bundle.

George noticed the porch railing was a latticework design, and the front doors were...What was the term Carol would have used for this style? French modern? It certainly wasn't the Spanish colonial style that dominated everything George had seen in Guayaquil. Mateo was right; the house seemed very out of place, as if it had been lifted from a design magazine in the United States and planted in the middle of the Ecuadorian coastal plains.

The front porch was accessed by a wide, fan-shaped set of steps. They were red tile that matched the front of the house. George looked at each step carefully, making sure he didn't trip. How ridiculous to finally find Ordóñez and then make a fool of himself by tripping. He could just imagine the man, some rich, eccentric fruitcake sitting inside the front room having a good laugh at the dumb gringo's expense.

George wasn't much at telling people off, but he planned to change that today. Stepping toward the front entry, he looked for a doorbell. Then George noticed something odd. There were double doors, and the right one actually stood open about four inches. The impression was that someone had tried to close it, but it hadn't latched properly. Perhaps.

"Hello? *Hola?*" George fairly yelled into the opening. He glanced back to make sure his safety net, the taxi, was still there. It sat just outside the gate. Mateo was staring at him, his arm resting on the window frame of the taxi door.

One thing had changed, though. George noticed the vehicle had been turned around as if ready to head back to town in an instant. It bothered George that, as he had walked toward the house, he hadn't noticed the sound of the taxi turning around. Not very observant.

"Hello?" George said again. He let the toe of his right shoe touch the bottom of the open door, so it could be nudged further open. Six inches. Eight. Enough to stick his head inside.

"*¿Hola?*"

Nothing. The picture in George's mind of eccentric Roberto Ordóñez sitting inside, laughing at him, burned George to the core. George's foot finally opened the door enough to step inside. Then George remembered what Mateo had said. Robbers? What if he was walking in on a burglary or home invasion?

"In the middle of the day where everyone could see?" George thought. "Doubtful. Besides, if it was burglars, they would have heard me and been long gone by now. There are no sounds, certainly not any footsteps of burglars running."

Suddenly, that changed, but just a bit. A creak?

Maybe.

"Hello?"

George took another half step into the entry hall. He was careful not to touch anything. Then he paused. What if he was perceived as the burglar? Might he be shot? He stopped cold. Maybe he was the one who would scare the people inside the house, instead of the other way around.

He gave his eyes time to adjust from the direct sunlight of the outdoors to the interior of the house. Light streamed in from large windows and the open door.

The first thing he noticed was the walls of the front room. They were painted a pale yellow, with a chair rail painted white to match the doors running the length of the room as far as he could see. A traditional Spanish coffee table sat to his left inside the large room about four feet away. Just on the other side of it...

There was someone lying on the floor. A man. Dark hair, tan shirt. George couldn't see the face, just the top of the head and the body past it and...and blood. George's heart raced.

He didn't notice the blood at first because it had seeped onto a red tile floor. But there was definitely blood.

George immediately thought of a serious car accident he had come across several years earlier outside of Houston. He had been the first person on the scene, and the woman behind the wheel was bleeding profusely.

It wasn't blood like cutting your finger. The color was a deeper red, as if life itself were pouring from her body. George had heard the EMS workers later say the woman "bled out" before help arrived.

That was the color of blood George saw now.

He stepped closer, trying to assess the situation. He still couldn't see the man's face, but the skin on his arms was ghostly white, like the underbelly of a dead fish. George also couldn't determine exactly where the blood was coming from. Was the man alive? Dead? Somewhere in the middle?

Most likely dead. Something just told him so. Simultaneous thoughts ran through George's mind. "Feel for a pulse" and "Don't touch anything." Two complementary thoughts came right behind: "Get help!" and "Get out!"

Where was the household staff? Or maybe this guy *was* the caretaker. Had he fallen and hit his head on the coffee table? With no one around to assist him?

"Of course, that explains everything. Get the guy some help." George stepped quickly back to the door to summon Mateo and the taxi. Had they passed a hospital a few minutes earlier? Wasn't there one just a little way down the road? Mateo could help George load the guy into the taxi. They would get him to the hospital. George wouldn't be in trouble; he would be a hero.

He turned and reached the front door in four steps. Squinting into the blinding daylight, George looked down the long drive. It couldn't be. The taxi was gone.

Suddenly, from another part of the house, George heard what he could have sworn was the sound of a gun being cocked. Maybe it was a heavy lock being turned. The sound was at once subtle and undeniable. It demanded his attention and made his adrenaline again race. Then again...*Click.*

George thought of robbers. Mateo had sensed danger. George should have listened to him. What if the burglars were real? What if they were aiming a gun at him *right now*?

Taking the six steps off the front porch in two bounds, George decided he must get out of there. Otherwise there might be two bodies lying on the red slate tiles. He ran down the drive back toward the open gate. His head jerked in every direction, and his mind worked to will Mateo and the taxi back. Looking down the street that ran back toward Guayaquil, George saw nothing except an old mestizo woman walking hand in hand with a child. He started to run up to her, but when she saw him she ducked her head and scurried with the child in the other direction.

"Got to get help or get out, but I can't stay here," George thought. He picked up the pace of his running. A very nice SUV passed him. He thought he had seen it earlier on the drive to Samborondon.

The woman driver looked at him. George thought her face carried a disquieted expression. What was a gringo doing running down the street in a golf shirt, khakis, and loafers? He looked even more out of place than the red house with the green roof and the dead body. The woman gave George a long look, then turned her eyes back to the road.

"Don't draw attention," he thought. "Or maybe I should be flagging down help. Why am I even here? Why didn't I listen to Carol and stay away?

As he thought about Samborondon, it occurred to George the subdivision might not even be within the boundaries of Guayaquil. Was Ecuador like the United States, in which small-town law enforcement was inevitably compared to Barney Fife of *The Andy Griffith Show*? If Samborondon had its own little police force, how would the people deal with a gringo wandering into a house and finding a dead body? Despite their best intentions, would the language barrier and their limited resources allow them to do a truly competent job?

His mind's eye pictured some Ecuadorian policeman slapping cold, steal bracelets around his wrists and continually saying, *"No entiendo Ingles."* I don't understand English. George would try to explain how he had come upon the man lying in a pool of blood in the house at Samborondon. *"No entiendo Ingles, gringo,"* the imaginary policeman said again. *"Muy mala situacion."* A very bad situation.

Why hadn't he listened to Carol and stayed in the United States?

Carol! That was it. He would get to a place with Wi-Fi and e-mail Carol. This was an affluent area. Surely a coffee shop or restaurant with Wi-Fi couldn't be that hard to find. Or maybe he should just call her on his cell phone…Suddenly George did a quick inventory of what was—or rather wasn't—in his hands. He felt totally naked.

He had set his MacBook Air down on the seat of the taxi. When he had climbed out of the cab, he had done so with the full intention of finding Mateo waiting for him. The house and the eerie quiet had so distracted him that he had walked away from the cab and left his $900 computer sitting inside.

No wonder Mateo had taken off. This was probably the best day the driver had experienced in a long time—a ten-dollar fare and a top-line American tablet as a tip. "What an unbelievably crappy chain of events," George thought.

He felt the sensation to panic. Then he took a deep breath and made himself relax. "Assess," he said to himself. "Assess." He breathed in slowly and out deeply. "You know Mateo's name. You can describe the taxi because you were in it a long time. What was the name on the registration certification? Mateo what? Did it start with a C? Maybe Cordones? Something like that. That can help track him down."

He determined not to run from the scene; it would only draw attention. "This isn't America," he thought. "You aren't a citizen. You don't have rights, only privileges. Get help. Check for a cell phone signal and call Carol." He looked down at his phone. No bars.

"Get to where Carol can be reached. Let her know I'm okay. Have her check on flights leaving Ecuador. Time to cut losses and get the heck out of Dodge. First get to the American consulate and ask what to do. Explain everything and get their advice."

George thought about how far he was from the central part of Guayaquil. "Get a ride. You can't walk all the way back to downtown Guayaquil. Besides, more cars are passing, and people are staring. If this is indeed a crime scene, the last thing you need is to be told you can't leave the country while an investigation is pending. Pray."

George thought of what Carol often reminded him: "You always remember to pray; you just do it last, instead of first."

He would have to recall that sooner next time. "Doubtful," he told himself.

Making it back onto the main road to Guayaquil, George noticed there were no shoulders on the highway. He could ruin his loafers by walking in the mud and matted grass off the paved surface, or take his life in his hands and walk on the edge of the road. He chose the former, deciding the shoes could be replaced. In fact, a lot of things would need to be replaced—the MacBook, the loafers, his self-confidence in his ability to make good decisions.

He wished for his running shoes and athletic gear. He knew it was within him to cover the distance back to town. If he were in running gear, no one would have thought twice about him running. But that wasn't the case.

He picked up the pace and reached into his pocket for his cell phone to check for a signal to call Carol. The first thing his fingers touched was a piece of paper. He fished it out and squinted at the white card in the bright sunshine. It was the card Professor William Knight had given him.

"Call me anytime," the professor had said. And the professor had a car. Maybe, just maybe, Professor Knight wasn't at the dig. Even if he was, it was getting late in the afternoon. Maybe the professor would be passing this way as he headed back to central Guayaquil.

Knight said the dig was at the foothills of the Andes Mountains. George could see them in the distance. He would call Knight first. No matter how good Carol's advice or comfort was, she couldn't provide a ride back to downtown Guayaquil. That was what he needed more than anything else right now.

A tanker truck roared by, leaving a strong diesel and exhaust smell. George stepped back from the road, grasped his phone in one hand, and began pushing numbers with his thumb as his other hand held the professor's card. It was the first time in a very long time George hadn't considered the cost before making a phone call.

Even in the United States, the cost of phone calls would occur to George as he dialed a number. Though his calling plan had included free nationwide long distance and unlimited minutes for several years, he always checked himself before dialing a number. "What's the cost?" he would ask himself. Then he would remember the plan. "No problem." How could he be so good at the economy of money and so bad at the economy of discernment?

The phone made the same sound George had heard previously, something between an American-style ring and a busy signal. On the third one, the professor answered. *"Bueno."*

"Professor? This is George d'Hout. I met you at the hotel, and we talked and had dinner."

"Of course. You are calling to take me up on my invitation. You wish to join our little expedition into the riches of Ecuador's past. I suspected you would find the invitation too good to pass on. How delightful."

"Professor, I had a cab take me to an…an appointment… and the cabbie ended up leaving me. He also drove away with my laptop in his taxi. I'm kind of stuck out in the middle of nowhere. I was wondering if there was any way you could—"

"He stole your computer? That's dreadful. I guess this just hasn't been your day, has it? How did your appointment go? Did you meet with...what did you tell me his name was? Roberto Ordóñez? Did you find him?"

"Professor Knight," George said, trying not to sound desperate, "is there any way you are close enough to come pick me up?"

"Of course, of course," the professor said. "Can you give me, say, twenty minutes?"

"I'm at Via Aurora just north of Via Perimetral, where it enters Samborondon."

The professor said, "I happen to know the area. There is a very fine little *tienda* near there that sells a beverage called *ciruelo* made from plums and *ishpingo*. Have you ever had *ishpingo*, Mr. d'Hout? It's a very fine local spice. Why don't you order us a couple of *ciruilos*? They will be ready by the time I arrive."

George felt his temper rising. He reminded himself Knight knew nothing about what he had seen at the red house or how terrifying the experience had been. Besides, the professor's eccentric charm was what made him seem so interesting, even when he was discussing things George didn't care about.

"I think I can find it. The name of the place?"

"Honestly, I don't think it has a name. Not one that I recall seeing, and I'm very good at details. Have to be good at names in my line of work. However, the fellow who will be preparing your beverages knows me. You may speak my name to him and then say, '*Dos ciruelos.*' Then you may rest in the knowledge that you will be well cared for."

"Thank you, Professor Knight. I'm in your debt."

"Careful, Señor d'Hout, or I may take you up on it one day." The professor laughed and clicked off the phone. George knew he felt better when it occurred to him to wonder how much that conversation had just cost him.

He found the store and a small table in the back. It sat next to a makeshift stand where the proprietor had set up his workstation. George sat in a cramped corner surrounded by groceries and watched the man put together the drinks. Though Professor Knight had played them up as some magic concoction, they were really just squeezed plums and vodka.

Out came a dried bit of plant the color of a hazelnut. It was the size of a garlic clove. George figured it was the *ishpingo*. It was grasped tightly and then squeezed until it began to crumble. The proprietor opened his fingers to let it fall out into the *ciruela*.

A smell somewhere between cinnamon and allspice wafted past. George found the sensation quite pleasant. Finally, the *ciruela* glasses were held over small candles to gently warm the concoction. Watching this impromptu laboratory procedure gave George something to focus on besides the dead body and his missing MacBook. In a minute, the glasses of *ciruela* were too hot for the proprietor to hold in his bare hands.

The man set the two glasses in front of George without a word. George watched the tiny bits of *ishpingo* drift toward the bottoms of the two glasses. He thought they were an appropriate metaphor for his entire trip. He had been lured under false pretenses, he'd discovered a dead man, and he'd been robbed of a computer.

"These drinks'll be very expensive," he thought.

"*Para usted y el profesor,*" the proprietor said. "*¡Salud!*" George nodded absently, not sure what the words even meant.

George watched the drinks. If he stared hard enough, perhaps the professor would appear sooner. Just when impatience was about to drive him back out onto the street, Knight appeared. True to his word, he arrived just shy of the twenty-minute mark.

The professor strode into the *tienda* like he had just won the customer-of-the-month contest. He was effusive in his praise of the drinks, the man who made them, and the privilege of being in Ecuador. George felt like he was riding a roller coaster, from the horror of an hour ago to the festive atmosphere of the professor's arrival. But, like all roller-coaster rides, George felt his gut tighten at the apprehension of what would come next.

The professor planted himself in a chair, the history of *ciruela* and *ishpingo* as certainly in his mouth as were his teeth. George launched a preemptive strike. "The moment we finish our drinks, I need you to take me to the American consulate. It's on the same road as the hotel, so it won't be out of your way at all."

The professor sat back, holding up his *ciruela*, and stared at it as if it were his first high school crush. Then he focused on the ceiling and downed the drink in one gulp. His eyes came back down and focused quizzically on George.

"You do? Really? I have generally found the American consulate to be a huge pain in the rear parts. Why would anyone intentionally talk to them? Or do you have to?"

George was resolute. "I can't really get into it, but yes, I need to speak to them. It's very important."

"I see," the professor said. "Well, drink up. All in one gulp, or you will offend our friend, the owner. I didn't make that up either; it's a well-documented fact. You can check in any of the books on Ecuadorian culture. And if you offend him, it's okay for you, because you may never come back in here. But what about me?"

"You may have mine," George said. "I don't drink."

"So you are unsatisfied with offending our host; you want to offend me, too? And I put my afternoon on hold for…for what?"

George felt like a very bad day was only getting worse. His one acquaintance—friend?—had just been offended. How else might he screw up the day? Without another word, he drank up. The drink was sweet and spicy and mildly warm. What was all the fuss about? It tasted like juice with cinnamon in it.

But when George looked back toward Professor Knight, he believed it must have been very important to take that drink. The professor's offense had melted, replaced by the warm sunshine of affection for a fellow American in a foreign land.

George stood and reached in his pocket to pay for the drinks. The professor put his hand on George's and said, "My suggestion, my *cuenta*. My bill."

Two one-dollar coins were produced, and the professor laid them on the small table. He turned to leave, George in tow. "*Gracias, mi amigo*," Knight said. He led the way outside toward the Renault. Climbing in, he reached across and lifted the door lock.

George got in and put on his seat belt, not knowing whether such precautions were mandatory in Ecuador. As the car started, the radio carried the voice of a Spanish language broadcaster. The professor listened for a moment. His face grew solemn. He turned to George and asked, "How much Spanish do you speak?"

"Very little," George confessed. "Embarrassing but true. If people here speak slow enough, I can make out some words. But when they are talking like that guy, I'm completely lost."

"So you didn't understand what was just said? Seriously?" Professor Knight asked.

"Sorry, no," George said. His pulse raced a bit. "Why do you ask?"

"It's a repeat of the report I heard driving over here. It caught my attention, and I wanted to discuss it with you before anyone else did."

George felt his face turning red. "What do you mean?"

"Didn't you tell me your employer here was Roberto Ordóñez?"

"I don't honestly remember." He stuttered a bit, remembering Juan's injunction. "I must have, since you know. Why?" He felt like a schoolboy who'd been caught doing something wrong but wasn't ready to confess anything. After all, he had nothing to confess.

"First, you should know the news here is not like the news in the US," the professor said. "The press doesn't enjoy the same freedoms. There are no nonstop news channels. It's more like the United States before cable TV. Don't get me wrong; there are endless channels from all over the world—maybe more than in the US—but not all the news channels. People are more cautious here of offending the powers that be. Call it what you want, but that's the situation."

"I don't understand what you're trying to tell me," George said. "What does it have to do with me and my employer?"

A solemn face grew more so. "I'm telling you to make this point: when there's a news flash here, it's quite a thing."

"I'm sorry, but I'm not following you, Professor Knight. Just tell me what you're telling me." The tension strangled George like a rope.

"Mr. d'Hout, you told me you had an appointment, and I believe you indicated it was with Roberto Ordóñez. You called because you said you were stranded. Something happened apparently. It was something less than desirable. You said your taxi driver ran out on you. I have never heard of that happening here. Not one time. Taxi drivers here pride themselves on their professionalism and service."

Knight drew in a long breath. "As I was driving over here, there was a news story. The police just found a man dead at his home. The man was named Roberto Ordóñez."

It felt like someone just punched George in the stomach. "How?" he gasped. "How could police have already found him? I just left him not an hour ago."

The professor shrank back against the door of his car. His hand reached toward the handle. "Mr. d'Hout, I barely know you, but you don't seem like a killer. Are you going to hurt me? You asked me to come here, and I did. Have I made a serious mistake?"

George worked to control his breathing. Was this what it felt like to hyperventilate? He searched the professor's eyes. The man seemed genuinely afraid. "Professor, I walked into a house and found a man on the floor. I went back to get the taxi driver. My plan was for us to take the man to the hospital. The taxi driver was gone. I heard something that sounded like it might be...I don't know...like a gun cocking."

George paused and gulped air. "So I got out of there. I called you as soon as I could. That's all that happened. If we can find the taxi driver, he can verify a timeline. He can also verify there is no way I could have done anything. I stepped into the house, saw the body, and turned around and came out. The driver can verify that."

"I thought you said the driver took off."

"He did, but he saw enough to know I didn't kill anybody... Well, I think he did. I don't know. He told me he thought there might be robbers in the house."

"George, I thought you said the driver left. How could he know there were robbers in the house if he left? And I thought you only saw the dead man. Now you're saying there were robbers. I'm going to ask you again, and I want you to tell me the truth; what do I need to do so you don't hurt me? I am not a hero. I have done what you asked. I don't want it to cost me my life."

George stared out the car window. He had no idea what to do. He understood why the professor was skeptical. And if he couldn't convincingly describe what happened to a friendly audience, how would he ever persuade the police?

"I don't know what to do," George said. "I didn't kill anyone. I just went out to the house, and he was there bleeding on the floor."

Professor Knight said, "I'm not sure why, but I'm going to believe you. But again, what you just said sounds like a contradiction of what you told me a few minutes ago. I am very concerned for you."

"That's why I need to get to the consulate. They can tell me exactly what I should do."

"George, I want to say this in the most fitting way I know. You are making another mistake. Maybe it comes from singing one too many verses of 'God Bless America' at baseball games. You seem to believe there are nothing but red, white, and blue angels waiting to help you at the consulate. Those people are there for one reason: to protect the interests of the United States."

Knight watched as his words sank in. "They don't care one iota about your interests. If you go to them, they will turn you over to the police in a heartbeat. The last thing they want is to be portrayed in the Ecuadorian media as helping a killer avoid justice. There are already a lot of people in Ecuador who don't trust the United States. The consulate knows that. The first thing they are going to do is turn you in."

"So I should just get out of the country as quickly as possible?" George asked.

Knight said, "I've been reluctant to bring this up, but the news said there was someone who fit your description, right down to the clothes you're wearing, leaving the scene. George, they described your hair color and length, your beard, your height. Well, everything. Whoever talked to the police was a very observant person. What I'm saying is, I'm afraid if you try to leave the country, you will be spotted at the airport and arrested."

George could feel sweat running down his face. His hands were trembling. "As I was leaving, there was a woman who drove by in an SUV. The taxi had taken off, and I was trying to get down the road quickly, so I was running."

Knight considered, started to say something, stopped, and started again. "There is another option. You said you didn't do this. Is that right?"

"Professor, I did *not* do this. I walked in and found Roberto Ordóñez dead on the floor. That's all. Then I left."

Knight weighed his words. "Then here's what I think should happen. If you didn't do this, obviously someone else did. The police must have the chance to catch the person or persons who did, and without the red herring of you as a suspect."

"Red herring," George repeated. He considered this.

"Further, the Ecuadorian police are sure to see an American as a nice scapegoat, especially since, as I said, relations between Ecuador and the United States aren't all that good right now. However, if you are out of the way, so to speak, you wouldn't risk arrest. What's more, the police could focus on finding the real criminal or criminals."

"But where? The hotel is on a very busy street. Besides, if my description is being broadcast, the hotel staff will know it's me in a second. They might have already called in a tip that they have a guest fitting that description."

"George, I have been engaged in projects all over this part of Ecuador." His voice was that of a counselor, a loving parent, a patient friend. "There is a very fine city about three hours from here called Cuenca. I mentioned it earlier. It's very ancient and beautiful. Most important, it's out of Guayaquil. I have access to a house there, right on the Yanuncay River in a very quiet residential neighborhood. There is a market around the corner where we can keep you stocked with food until this thing blows over or the real crooks are found."

"What will I tell Carol?"

"Nothing! If you do, you'll scare her to death. And there's nothing she can do for you right now. Why panic her for no reason? You just have to stay out of sight so no one matches you to the description being broadcast. Cuenca is a very good place to do that."

The two men sat in silence. Then the professor snapped his fingers. "You can tell her you are working there, if you like. I even have some things you can look into, if you need a distraction."

"I don't want to worry Carol, but I won't lie to her. Besides, the man who was supposed to pay me is now dead."

Knight said, "True enough. The main thing is to keep you out of sight. What I'd like to do is drive you out to our dig site. It's empty by this time of evening. You can stay there. Give me your room key, and I will quietly get your things. Of course, that's provided I can safely do so. Then I will come back and get you. We can drive to Cuenca. Is that acceptable?"

"What other choice do I have? Thank you, Professor."

CHAPTER 8

Tuesday, 7 January
11:06 p.m.

George very nearly paced a hole in the floor of the hut where the professor left him. It sat on the edge of a banana and cocoa field. The professor said he had used the hut, with the absentee plantation owner's permission, during some excavation work at the foothills of the Andes two years ago. It sat two miles off the main road that led into the mountains. Knight had said the banana crop was nowhere near ready for harvest. No cattle grazed anywhere close to the site. Hence, it was a perfect hiding place.

When he returned from the hotel with George's clothes stuffed in a duffel bag, the professor said, "Look at this place. It's the very type of hideout your predecessor, the pirate, might have used when ducking both the Spanish and his own crew."

"Honestly, that kind of stuff is the last thing on my mind right now," George said politely but firmly.

"I completely understand. But the irony, the irony. What are the chances history might literally repeat itself so brilliantly?"

George couldn't ignore the remark. "I haven't stolen anything. I haven't done anything wrong. I simply walked into a situation, and now I don't know what to do."

The professor took an apologetic tone. "Of course, of course. My mind was just racing across a rather bizarre idea. Wouldn't it be something if one desperate George d'Hout hid the treasure and another desperate George d'Hout found it? A simply amazing idea."

"Like I said, I couldn't care less about that. Professor, I appreciate all you've done for me, but I need some time to think and..." George stopped. He had been rifling through his things. When Knight returned from the hotel, he reported no one had given him a second look as he walked into the hotel. Why should they? He was a regular guest. No one was in the hall on George's floor, for which the room key granted access.

So the professor had walked into the room, put George's things in one of his own duffel bags, and departed again. No problem. George looked through the bag again. "Did you pick up my cell phone charger?"

The professor looked confused. "Honestly, I don't remember. I got everything in sight, like you asked me. I was working very quickly before I was detected by anyone. I got really spooked when I heard a loud noise from the room next to yours. It sounded like someone was having a party or a brawl in there."

"Next to mine? I believe that was Edward Davies, another man Roberto Ordóñez had apparently hired to come down here from the States."

"Another pirate? What are the chances?"

George was too tired and aggravated to respond. Then he changed his mind. "You heard the man next door? Did you see him?"

"As I said, no. But I don't know the first thing about this sneaking-around business. I'm not sure what you have dragged me into but——"

George continued methodically digging through his clothes and toiletries, which all appeared to be present. Where was the charger?

"My phone is almost dead, and without the charger, I can't call Carol on my phone."

"As you have noticed, I'm sure, there isn't even a hint of a cell phone signal out here. You are simply going to have to save that for tomorrow."

"Could you drive me to where there's a signal tonight? I can at least let her know I'm alive."

Knight said, "George, I wasn't going to bring this up, but I saw two police cars back on the main road. There was a roadblock. Of course, they let me right through, but I could identify myself and honestly tell them where I was today. With your things sitting in the trunk of my car, however, I was as nervous as a cat."

The professor looked as if he might cry. "They looked and just saw clothes, you know, so they let me right through. But if we go out searching for a cell phone signal and run into that roadblock, or another one, all you're going to find is handcuffs... or worse. This isn't the United States, you know. They have their own ways of doing things down here."

George looked at the floor. Knight pressed on. "And to compound the situation, I will probably be arrested, too. I guess you'll be saying, 'Thank you very much for helping me in my hour of need, Professor. For your trouble you will now be deported out of Ecuador, and your life's work will be completely in ruins.'"

George didn't like melodrama, even from the man helping him out of a tough spot. "Carol will be worried sick," he said.

"If your cord doesn't turn up, I can call her on my phone once we are safely on the road to Cuenca...or text her or whatever you would like. Tomorrow. I don't have a signal either, not out here."

Wednesday, 8 January
3:16 a.m.

Carol d'Hout sat on the edge of the bed, her bare feet hovering just above her house shoes. She had texted and retexted George. She had broken down and tried to call, even though she knew he would be upset about the cost.

She paced the house, sat in the study praying, and flipped through all 189 television channels three times. Infomercials, violence, and reruns. She didn't want to see any of them. She wanted to see her husband. She called again. Straight to voicemail. Texted again. Waited. No reply.

Now she held a sudoku puzzle book in one hand, a pencil in the other. But she couldn't concentrate. A tear ran down her cheek. Why hadn't he called? This wasn't like him. She was going out of her mind fretting.

"George calls. He always calls," she said. "Something is wrong. Something is very wrong."

Opening her laptop, Carol waited for it to pick up their wireless signal. She propped up pillows at the head of the bed and drew up her knees with the computer resting on them. She typed the name of the hotel and "Guayaquil" into the search box. The hotel's website popped up, along with a picture of the front lobby and reviews from previous guests.

Clicking on the site, she found the phone number. She opened another search box and found the country code for Ecuador. She entered the numbers on her cell phone and waited. After a long silence, the phone rang, like an elongated busy signal.

"*Dígame,*" a voice answered.

Speaking slowly and clearly, Carol said, "Do you speak English?"

"*¿Ingles?Lo siento, no,*" the voice answered. "*Mi jefe habla Ingles. Un momentito.*"

Carol waited and did what she knew George would have done in this situation: counted the seconds to determine the financial damage. A quarter century of marriage had taught her not to say, "It's only a dollar or two. No big deal."

When they were first married, she'd used that line a few times. George had responded, "Seconds make minutes. Minutes make hours. Hours make days. Days make weeks. Weeks make months. Months make years. And what is a year? Lots of seconds all added together."

It was a saying his father had taught him. There was no doubt the lesson had taken; George was nothing if not a good steward of his time and money. His only fault, as far as she could tell, besides her millionaire pie, was that he always remembered to pray...too late.

She wondered what prayer-worthy situation he was in now. It had to be something. She could tell it in her gut. Wives knew when something was wrong. She wondered whom she could call if the hotel was no help. Maybe her brother-in-law, Hugh.

Of course, George would just die when he realized she had called Hugh in the middle of the night. But it was George's own fault. And if Hugh spent years teasing him about it, maybe that would serve as a reminder he shouldn't go trotting off halfway around the world and forget to call.

But simple forgetting didn't account for why he wasn't answering his phone. Unless he didn't have it. Maybe he'd left it somewhere, or it was in his jacket pocket, vibrating away. And what if the jacket was in his hotel room's closet, where he couldn't hear it?

Carol felt a little silly for worrying. Or maybe the phone had died. It wasn't like there was a cell phone company on every corner in Ecuador...was there? She had to admit she really didn't have the faintest idea.

But if he couldn't call, he could e-mail, right? Unless his MacBook had died, too. Or he was lying in a ditch somewhere after being robbed and left for dead.

A voice in her ear brought Carol back to the moment. "Allo? Dees id dee manahar."

"George d'Hout's room, please."

"Our rooms are for dee rent, yes? Yes. What night you arreeving?"

Carol wanted to take out all her annoyance and worry on this man. But he was trying his best. And his English could run circles around her nonexistent Spanish. She repeated herself, only louder.

No good.

She swallowed her frustration and spoke as if talking to a child. She remembered Hugh's admonition that if someone doesn't understand you very well, slow down, enunciate, and give his or her ears a chance to get a toehold. Most people try to explain, or they talk faster because they are excited. Just slow down and be very clear.

Okay, Hugh, here we go:

"George…d'Hout's….room…He's…a…guest…in…your…hotel…Call…him."

Contemplation on the other end of the line. "You want to call hee's room?"

"Yes."

"Jees dial dee hotel phone number an theen the room number deerect. Thank you for calling. Eet's okay to do dat."

"No! I want you to dial it for me."

"What room number, please?"

"I don't know. George…d'Hout…is…the…guest." Carol wanted to tear her hair out. She remembered a credit card commercial in which a man named "Peggy" was equal parts incompetence and willful obstruction. But this wasn't TV. Carol was pretty sure the guy on the other end of the phone wasn't named Peggy either.

"He es staying at what hotel?"

"He…is…a…guest…at…your…hotel. Please…ring…his… room."

"Reeeng?"

"Please…call…his…room."

"What you want me to say to heem?"

"I…want…to…talk…to…him…Please!"

"Oh! Hold for minute." Silence. Then more silence. She heard three clicks and thought she had been disconnected. But then there was a buzzing sound, as if the call had been transferred to his room. Finally. One ring, two, three, four…Then came the hotel voice mail in Spanish. He didn't answer. Again.

Carol hung up and tried not to cry but with very little success. She felt sick. Some husbands might go a couple of days and not call or text, but not George. That wasn't their relationship. Something was wrong.

Not knowing what to do next, Carol checked e-mail and Facebook. Maybe George was sick and stuck in the bathroom. But surely he could at least send a quick message. After all, computers were his life.

Carol first opened their Facebook page, then another window for e-mail. As she toggled back and forth, a small message popped up in the bottom right-hand corner of the screen. At first she thought it was from George.

> What are you doing up this time of night?

It was Hugh. Good ol' Hugh! If George was the king of husbands, Hugh was the grand champion of brothers-in-law. She toggled back to Facebook and responded, telling him what was going on. Hugh responded.

> That's not like him. How you doing?
> I'm up at almost 4 am. You tell me.
> What do you want me to do?
> Help!
> You want me to call the hotel?
> How's your Spanish?
> :)

Carol remembered Hugh loved to say he was the one in the family with the birthmark on his forehead that read GEEK. He considered it a badge of equal parts honor and embarrassment. He'd said, "It's like the lightning bolt on Harry Potter's forehead, only without the magical powers."

She sent him the link to the hotel so he could see the phone number. He messaged back.

> Give me a few minutes. Was working on some family history and lost track of the time. Stay online. Calling now. Will let you know.

An eternity passed. Finally Hugh messaged again.

> Calling you now on your cell.

Hugh reported that though he was able to talk to the desk clerk, he'd had no success reaching George. Carol looked for something to say that wouldn't make her cry. "What did the hotel people say?"

"The guy rang the room. No answer. I asked if George was still checked in and he said yes. I asked if anyone had seen him. He said he wasn't sure. I described George. He hadn't seen anyone of that description, though I have to admit they probably think all gringos look alike. It's the same pseudoxenophobic phenomenon causing some Anglos to think all Latinos or blacks look alike."

Carol said, "Did you happen to—"

"Send someone up to check his room? I did. They knocked, but no answer. I even convinced them to go in. Told them he needed regular shots of insulin, and he could be lying there in shock. I know it was a lie, but otherwise they weren't going in the room."

"What did they find?"

"That's where I don't know what to make of it. They said his suitcases were there. So was his phone charger, but they didn't see any clothes."

"What do you think it means, Hugh? I'm just sick with worry."

"One of the guys I go to church with is an FBI agent. I'll call him in a few hours…let the sun come up first. I'll ask him what the next steps should be."

Carol's fears weren't put to bed, but at least she didn't feel so alone. Maybe she could get a couple of hours of sleep after all.

"I'll call as soon as I talk to my buddy in the FBI. Get some rest."

"You too," Carol said.

"No can do. I've got two weeks before classes start back up, and I'm in a lull period right now." He explained his wife Brenda was visiting relatives and he was "footloose and fancy free."

Hugh said, "That means almost nonstop research time. It's like Christmas just keeps going on and on."

Carol and Hugh said good-bye and hung up. Carol set the cell phone and laptop on the side of the bed where George normally slept. However, she didn't close the computer. In case a communication came through, she wanted to make sure she didn't miss it.

CHAPTER 9

Wednesday, 8 January
6:32 a.m.

It was the longest night of George's life. Howls, chirps, growls, and calls of a thousand varieties saturated the blackness. Was it insects, frogs, monkeys, birds, all of the above? No idea. It was an unnerving concerto that reminded George he was a long way from home.

What would Carol think when he didn't contact her? Eventually, she would call. It would ring six times and go to voice mail. She knew he never failed to contact her when traveling. Once, his phone even fell down an aiport toilet just as it flushed. The phone had made two circles around the bowl and taken a sudden dive, disappearing forever into the Cleveland sewer system.

Even then, George had used his computer to e-mail her with the news. When George got back and they went to the phone store, she told the clerk he was replacing his last phone, the Turd Talk 2000.

Looking out the window of the hut at the surrounding banana orchards and listening to the sounds of the nearby jungle, George said, "Professor, remind me how people stayed in touch before the age of cell phones and laptops. It seems like a thousand years ago."

The professor said, "The fellow who inspired Daniel Defoe to write *Robinson Crusoe*—a pirate named Alexander Selkirk—had to go four years without talking to his family. It seems they all survived the ordeal. Have no fear; your wife will be fine."

That was easy for this smug bachelor to say. He'd never met Carol. He had no idea that her worry had gone from a hobby to a professional pursuit many years ago.

She knew it was wrong to worry, but couldn't seem to help herself. Once, in an effort to reform, she'd printed off two Bible verses and taped them to her bathroom mirror. The first was "Be anxious for nothing, but in everything, by prayer and supplication with thanksgiving, make your requests known unto God. Philippians 4:6." The second was "Remember, it is a sin to know what you ought to do and not do it. James 4:17."

To tease her, George had added a third verse: "The spirit is willing but the flesh is weak. Matthew 26:41." The next morning, he found her reply: "But with God, all things are possible. Matthew 19:26."

At one point there were so many back-and-forth verses posted on the mirror, Carol had trouble putting on her makeup or curling her hair. That was the kind of relationship they had—knowing each other's weaknesses and flaws but never using them as a point of accusation. The professor also didn't know they were perhaps the tightest married couple in the entire state of Texas. For their twentieth anniversary celebration, Hugh and Brenda had flown to Orlando to meet them for a few days.

During a trip to an amusement park, while George and Hugh were off seeing which one would be the first to throw up on a roller coaster, Brenda said to Carol, "You realize, I hope, that you and George are our marital role models. There have been a couple of times when we were ready to chuck it in. But we decided if you guys could do it, so could we."

Brenda continued. "Hugh says talking to George makes their dad's death a lot easier. You know how they do, trading their dad's pearls of wisdom back and forth. That means so much to Hugh. Things like 'The most important thing a person can be is teachable' and 'If you're going to be married, take the time and effort to make it a great marriage.' And 'For just a little more, you can fly first class.' In spite of their dad's trouble with alcohol, he really was an amazing father. Hugh still misses him terribly. I think that's why he's so into genealogy. It makes his dad seem closer."

Now the mosquitoes in the banana grove were thick, their buzzing incessant. The meager, holey netting on the unscreened windows did little to keep them at bay. Further, they didn't seem to bother the professor. "I take sulfur tablets," he explained during one of George's slapping fits. "Doctors in the United States say it hurts your liver. All I know is mosquitoes don't like the taste of it. They stay away."

"Got any of those sulfur pills?" George asked.

"I do. In my hotel room in Guayaquil. Also at the work site. Here? No."

George tried ignoring the mosquitoes. However, the nagging thought of yellow fever, encephalitis, dengue fever, and the other wonderful gifts the winged fiends carry put him back on slap patrol. He imagined arriving back in Houston and saying, "Hi, honey, I'm home."

Carol would say, "Did you bring me anything?"

"I have two souvenirs: West Nile virus and malaria." It was about as close as George could come, under the circumstances, to a sense of humor.

The professor said, "George, I strongly recommend you dress as unlike yesterday as possible. They are looking for a man in loafers. Wear tennis shoes. You get the idea. And do you have a baseball cap? If you have any dirty clothes, wear those."

"I just got here Sunday night. No time to get anything good and smelly"—he sniffed his underarms—"except me."

He sniffed again. "Say, where's the shower?" He was only half kidding. He opened his deodorant and was getting ready to apply it.

"That's part of the problem with the mosquitoes," the professor said. "That deodorant is scented. I can smell it. So can the mosquitoes. It attracts them."

Then Knight said, "If all goes well, we'll be in Cuenca, up in the Andes, by tonight. Insects aren't nearly such a problem up there. Go ahead and apply it, if you choose. But there might be some benefit, if we are stopped, of not smelling quite so American, if you take my meaning."

George did, but he couldn't resist putting on at least one dab. He remembered Hugh saying when he taught junior high that warm days and thirteen-year-old armpits were a lethal combination. "You feel like you're a goat herder instead of a teacher," Hugh had joked.

George restuffed his things in the professor's bag. He looked around to see if there was anything to eat. The professor, still wearing the clothes he'd arrived in and smelling just a bit goatish, said, "For breakfast, we have bananas, bananas, or perhaps bananas. The only question is whether you want them green, green, or very green?"

"Yellow isn't an option?"

"Ecuador is one of the world's leading exporters of bananas. But the good people in the US, China, Russia, and Europe like them yellow when they arrive. That means they have to still be green when they're harvested. You want a yellow banana; there's plenty in the market in Guayaquil. But as I stated earlier, like cell phone coverage, it comes with quite a price."

George grimaced. "However, never fear," Professor Knight said. "We are driving to Cuenca today. There are several places along the way to stop and grab a little something." Knight walked out to the Renault, where he retrieved a map and a white capsule. "In the meantime, here is a very good multivitamin. There is some water in the backseat in a bottle."

After taking three large swigs of water and washing the pill down, George walked up to the professor. They both stared at the map.

"Let me see," the professor said. "If I were a policeman, where would I set up a roadblock?" Looking up at George, he explained,

"We are about here, near Delia." He pointed a calloused hand and dirty fingernail at a spot just southeast of Guayaquil. He traced the orange highway line farther southeast.

"We need to get into the Andes, which is quite a jump in elevation. From sea level to over eight thousand feet; that's two thousand five hundred thirty meters. At Boliche, we need to make a decision. Do we go south through the rice fields and over the mountain at Luz Maria? Do we swing way south all the way to Machala and totally outflank them? The other direction is heading in a circular route north, sort of sneaking up on the Andes through Zhud."

George stared. No comment. No clue.

The professor thought for a minute. "Going south, we might blend in with all the gringos heading to the playas for some beach time. However, gringos are famous for heading to the beaches, so that might be the first place they look. And if we go straight over the mountain, the visibility is almost zero due to all the cloud forests up there. The trip is beautiful, but the rock slides and two-lane mountain roads with no guardrails make it...interesting."

The professor paused and looked at George. Was he expecting some input? George just shrugged.

Professor Knight pressed on. "It seems to be a national sport for Ecuadorians to go as fast as possible on those mountain roads and then try to pass on a blind switchback. The nice thing about an accident like that is you don't have to worry about walking away from it."

Silence filled the hut, except for the buzzing of mosquitoes around George. Finally, the professor said, "I'm thinking it would be better to go the northern route. It takes us into the Cañar Province, which is very—shall we say—'pristine' compared to the Guayas Province where Guayaquil is. And the provinces here—think states back in the US—are infamous for not cooperating. So the sooner we can get out of this province, the better. Also, if they think you might head to Cuenca, they will block the main road through Cajas National Park. I believe what we are doing is what some might call a back-door maneuver."

Throwing everything in the car's trunk, George and the professor climbed into the Renault. The professor turned to George. "I do have one other thing to ask. If I am caught cooperating with a murder suspect, it would be disastrous to my career. Should such a thing happen, do you mind saying you were hitching a ride and I simply picked you up?"

"Of course," George said. "I will do anything I can to help you. You're a godsend."

"I'm not sure the Lord agrees with that," the professor rather snorted. "He and I have not been close over the years." A cynical laugh.

"Maybe that's about to change."

"I rather doubt it." The professor slipped the car into drive and headed toward Cuenca."

Wednesday, 8 January
7:36 a.m.

As the pair reentered the highway and turned west, George pulled his smartphone out of his pocket. No bars. "You have anything?" George asked.

Professor Knight fished for a moment for his phone, which was in his shirt pocket. He glanced down. "No. Don't have a signal either. Drat."

Before he could put the phone away, however, it suddenly began to vibrate. He looked sheepish.

"Maybe I spoke too soon."

"*Dígame*," the professor said. He listened, glancing at George every now and again. The professor seemed embarrassed to be on such a long call while someone was just sitting there. After a few minutes, the professor said, "So you really think you have it? At what price?"

The professor listened more. "I see. I see. *Claro*," he said. Then he began speaking very quickly in Spanish—much too quickly for George to even attempt to keep up. "Well, that is good news," he said, returning to English. "I am currently en route to the place in Cuenca. Yes, the one by the river. Keep me informed. Yes, I have it with me, so if we need to dig, I am prepared with my field gear and equipment."

George didn't recall seeing any field gear in the car's trunk. He glanced into the back seat. Nothing there. Knight hung up and slid the phone back in his pocket. "Do you believe in coincidences, George?" he asked.

"I guess so."

"We were doing a dig not too long ago at Pumapungo."

"I think you mentioned the place."

"Well, when the conquistadors went there centuries ago, they pretty much tore the place apart. The Incas were such amazing stonemasons and builders; they didn't need mortar. Can you imagine such a thing? Their work is very close to architectural perfection. They would also terrace their settlements. On the first layer were the peasants. As the community was built up, the higher social and political figures would live quite literally above their inferiors."

Another history lesson. George settled in. Professor Knight pressed on. "At the top of the hill was the local chieftain and any representatives of the supreme king, along with the military leaders. You get the idea. Well, the fourth level, or the one just below the top of the hill, was quite simply called 'the Fourth Level.' It was the place of death. Kings were buried on the Fourth Level, deep inside the mountain. But Incas didn't believe death was the end of things, only a transition. In the next life you would need the same things you needed here."

He looked to see if d'Hout was following his tale. George nodded, so he continued. "That's why when an important leader died, they would kill dozens of his servants and a bunch of llamas. When the leader was reborn into the new life, he would have...how should I put it most bluntly? ...He would have all his stuff."

George hadn't slept well, and this story was sending him straight to Nodsville. Suppressing a yawn, he said, "That's really interesting. Now, how does this tie in with what we are doing?"

The professor kept talking. It seemed like his voice was getting farther and farther away. George couldn't keep his eyes open even another second. So much for that multivitamin the professor gave him doing any good.

CHAPTER 10

Wednesday, 8 January
10:27 a.m.

Carol didn't realize she'd fallen asleep. She was dreaming about looking for George, but the dream seemed real. He was in a room. She was in the next room but couldn't get to him. "I don't like this dream." She thought through the fog of sleep. "I want a different one." Through the wall she heard George say, "Help me, honey. I need you to help me." She was instantly afraid he was being hurt in some way. There was a vibrating electric sound. Not good. Not...

She looked around. The buzzing came from her cell phone. "Hello?" she said, trying to catch the call before it went to voice mail. "Hugh?"

"Yes. I've been making calls all morning," Hugh said. His voice wasn't relaxed or reassuring. Carol knew she was transitioning from an uncomfortable dream to a possibly worse reality. "My friend, Van, from the FBI said when people go missing overseas, unless there is strong evidence of a crime, the assumption is they don't want to be found."

"That's ridiculous."

"He said there are hundreds, maybe thousands, of people who do it all the time. Running off from a bad marriage, having a midlife crisis, escaping debts, that kind of thing."

"But you and I both know that's not George. We are almost completely debt-free—"

"I know, Carol. I said that to him. He said, 'Well, maybe he wants to go out and create some.'"

"Some what?"

"Debt. You know...fast living, being reckless."

Carol laughed.

Hugh did, too. "Van was just being a law enforcement agent. He doesn't know George. But he did say one thing of real value. What we need to do is contact the State Department in Washington and report George missing."

Carol's laugh turned into a gasp. There was something about the sound of it that made her physically hurt. Hugh said, "Van doubts they will do anything until he's been missing for a week or two. One or two days equals a lot of manpower and money spent trying to track down somebody who was never really missing. He said it happens all the time. A guy is having so much fun, he doesn't even realize his cell phone isn't turned on. He did have some questions, however."

"Go ahead."

The Ecuadorian Deception

"First, he wanted to know why George was down there. It was a website consulting job, right?"

"Yes, for a man named Roberto Ordóñez Gonzales."

"What's this man's address and phone number?"

"No idea. We had a card with his phone number on it, but George took it with him. Oh, Hugh, I will go out of my mind if I don't hear something."

"I know, Carol. I feel the same way. So what I did was call the US consulate in Guayaquil. I found their number online. I talked to the consulate officer and told him I've been trying to find my brother. I made it sound like he had been missing several days rather than several hours. Here's the good news; he said George had actually been in their office."

"Oh, that's wonderful! Where is he now?"

"Carol, you didn't tell me you guys were thinking about moving down there."

"What? We aren't considering moving down there! This was a two-week business trip. I didn't even want George to go, so I'm sure not considering moving down there. What are you talking about?"

"The consulate officer said George came in with a list of addresses and wanted information on which ones were in the best neighborhoods."

Carol's head was spinning. "I think the consulate person got George mixed up with someone else."

"That's what I thought, too. But the more we talked, the more I realized it had to be George. The MacBook Air laptop, the way he was dressed. The officer even said the person he talked to was memorable because a couple of times he answered questions with the word *doubtful*. He said he'd never heard anybody do that before. Who do we know who uses that word like he invented it?"

Carol laid her head back on the pillows and stared at the ceiling. She clutched the phone so hard her knuckles turned white. Looking for real estate? This was all pure nonsense. "What do we do, Hugh? This is ridiculous."

Hugh continued. "The consulate officer said he recommended a real estate broker to George because they aren't allowed to comment on anything having to do with choosing one property over another. I called the lady, and she also described George to a T. She said he had a map and seemed very serious about finding a place. She thinks he had it narrowed down to two or three."

Carol uttered an involuntary whimper. Maybe she was still dreaming.

"Carol, let me ask you a very serious question that Van Williams of the FBI asked me. Are the two of you doing okay marriage wise? Are you absolutely sure this wasn't all a plan by George to run away and start a new life? If it was, they say there's nothing we can do but let him go, or go down there and try to get him back."

Tears gushed down Carol's face. She was mad and embarrassed. She felt like crawling into a hole and dying. This was supposed to be a simple business trip, a very lucrative deal. Easy and breezy. Come work for Mr. Roberto Ordóñez and—

"Hugh!" Carol yelled into the phone. "I know how we can start to look for him. He was working for this man named

Roberto Ordóñez. The guy contacted him out of the blue and wanted his help on a project. He sent a five-thousand-dollar retainer. Isn't that a clue maybe he was kidnapped or something? Isn't it a place to start?"

She heard Hugh exhale. "Carol, I could call Van Williams back. But when I tell him I think my brother was kidnapped, only this time the kidnappers paid us for the privilege of taking him, I think we may get laughed at."

Carol didn't laugh. What was even remotely humorous about any of this? Her husband was missing. She was going to do something about it. "Hugh, I guess the only thing for me to do is to fly down there."

"Let's think about that. You speak even less Spanish than George. How is all this going to happen? What will it look like? What are steps one, two, and three? Besides, it's only been a few hours since you've heard from him. We have to give it some time. George isn't missing yet. He is exhibiting untypical behavior, but that doesn't mean anything is wrong."

Wednesday, 8 January
1:49 p.m.

Carol got up from a fitful nap, brushed her hair, and threw on a jogging suit. She checked her phone, along with Facebook and e-mail. Maybe George had tried to make contact.

Still nothing.

She made herself hot tea. The phone buzzed from the bedroom. Carol sprinted back through the house, angry she'd left it so far away. She glanced at the name as she raised it to her face. "Hugh, what have you found out?"

"You said George was working for a man named Roberto Ordóñez. Did I write that down correctly?"

"Yes. Did you find something?"

"I called the consulate and the real estate broker back. The first thing I learned was they were both very busy and didn't appreciate being disturbed. I probably shouldn't call the consulate officer again unless I'm offering him a promotion to be an ambassador someplace. Anyway, I bounced the name Roberto Ordóñez off them both. I asked if there had been anything in the news about a Roberto Ordóñez."

"And?"

"Here's what I learned. There was a news story today about a Roberto Ordóñez who called the Guayaquil police with a really weird case. He wasn't home at the time, but apparently some taxi driver was trying to break into the guy's house. The gardener beat the guy nearly to death. Then the cabbie pulled a gun, according to the news story. The gardener took it from him and ended up killing the cabbie with it."

Carol's heart skipped a beat. "Hugh, they are sure there's not some mistaken identity, right? The man who was shot isn't George, right?"

"Both of them seemed pretty sure it was a taxi driver. I don't remember his name. Mateo, I think. That would be Matthew in English. They said they found some things in his taxi, which was parked behind the house. It made them think the cabbie had stolen from other houses, too, or maybe from a passenger. One of them was a MacBook Air."

Carol let out a gasp. "George was carrying a MacBook Air. Do you think it's his?"

"I have no idea. And don't know how to find out, short of going down there. If George doesn't turn up in a few days, do you want me to go down there?"

CHAPTER 11

Wednesday, 8 January
5:30 p.m.

George awoke to what sounded like cannon fire. He looked around, trying to figure out where he was. He was in the Renault, which motored up a steep mountain curve. The sky was gray. Angry clouds looked like swirling butterballs. They levitated seemingly inches from the Renault. Outside the car, everything was still lush and green. But it had changed hue from mantis and mint to emerald and shamrock. George instantly thought of Ireland. Wasn't he still in Ecuador? He yawned and stretched.

The clouds ceaselessly changed shape and shade. What didn't change was how fierce they appeared. Looking around, George saw the shape of the ground was different than when he'd dozed off. It reminded him of motoring through a giant plate of spaghetti and meatballs. Hmmm, a giant plate of *green* spaghetti and meatballs. Now that was an appetizing picture. He would have to work on his descriptive terminology before he talked to Carol.

Another cannon shot. "What was that?" he asked, groggy, alarmed.

Professor Knight said, "Thunder. The storms come rolling through this part of the Andes about five every afternoon, regular as clockwork. We are up high enough that the storms actually roll up the mountains from the valleys below."

George tried to wake up. He felt...drugged?

The professor was off on another verbal adventure. "For the indigenous people who lived here and didn't understand anything about meteorology, it must have scared them half to death. Every afternoon, the angry god Llapa made a personal appearance, throwing lightning bolts at them. Come to think of it, I have five college degrees, and it still gives me the willies."

George thought the archaeologist was like a music box. Lift the lid and the music plays and plays and plays and...

"And it's not the kind of thunder you hear in most of the United States. It's just BANG!" George jumped. The professor smiled. "If you ever wanted to cover up a killing, just wait until this time of day. Thunder and lightning and murder, all in one easy moment."

George shifted and sat up. "I didn't kill Roberto Ordóñez," he said. "Besides, the weather was completely clear in Guayaquil and Samborondon that day."

"I didn't mean anything. I was just discussing the climate and weather patterns. They can play havoc with a dig, I will tell you. The good thing is the workers, whether they be Cañari or Incan..." He was off on another diatribe.

George looked out the window and saw a large white church gleaming like an elongated pearl. It was set into the side of a mountain like a diamond in a ring.

"That is the Virgin of the Rock Church," the professor said, though George didn't ask. "The area is known as Biblian. It means 'of the Bible.' The church is built right into the side of the mountain. Let me tell you something about these people. You may think they are the salt of the earth or the biggest superstitious fools who ever lived. The choice is yours.

"Back in 1894 there was a terrible drought, and the people came together to call on all the powers that be, both Catholic saints and the native gods. They heard there was a miraculous statue of the Virgin Mary that could make it rain. But the statue was in Spain! That's almost six thousand miles from Ecuador, before the days of jet travel. The money was carried from here to there, and the statue was carried back. Lo and behold, they prayed and, according to legend, the statue made it rain."

George kept staring out the window at the church. "And they say God can't be bought." The professor laughed. "Oh, I'm sorry. Are you Catholic?"

"No, but I am a Christian."

"Good for you," the professor said. Something about Knight's manner struck George as condescending. Knight pressed on. "So the first time I went to the church, I expected to see this giant statue. Turns out the little thing is somewhere between a Beanie Baby and a Barbie doll. Tiny, really."

Trying to change the subject, George said, "Any sign of police?"

"Around the statue? No, it could probably be stolen without much effort."

"What? I mean on the roads while I was asleep."

The professor looked momentarily baffled. Then he stared ahead and said, "Fortunately, no. No signs of police. How did you sleep?"

"I feel like I was drugged. What a nap."

The professor glanced sideways at George and said, "When we stopped for gas at Tambo, what did you think of the forest?"

"Tambo? I don't know what you're talking about."

"When I stopped to get gas. I came back to ask if you wanted anything to eat. You weren't in the car. I came back a few minutes later, and you were back in the front seat asleep."

George sat up and rubbed his eyes. "Professor, the last thing I remember is getting in the car this morning. When I woke up, we were looking at this Biblian place and discussing Catholic statuettes."

"Have it your way," Professor Knight said, "but if that's true, how did I get a full tank of gas? I even asked you if you were going to text or call your wife since there was a pretty good cell signal there."

George straightened farther. He reached for his phone. It wasn't there. "Stop the car, Professor. Now!"

He fired a menacing look at Knight, causing the archaeologist to almost run off the road as he stamped the brakes. "All right, all right. I don't want to go over this again," the professor said. "I am not your enemy. Please don't hurt me."

"I don't want to hurt anyone, but I don't have my phone! Let me look for it." He felt both front pants pockets, reached around in the seat, and bent over to check the floorboard. Nothing. By this time, the professor had pulled over to the edge of the road. George climbed out, half expecting the professor to use it as his opportunity to speed away and summon help. However, he sat on the side of the ascending mountain road with the engine idling.

"The last time you had it, you were using it in Tambo," the professor said. "What did you do with it after that?"

"Professor, one of us is crazy. I have no memory of using a phone. I have no memory of a place called Tambo. If you are so sure it's there, let's go back."

"I'm not sure it's there. I merely said that was the last time—"

"Let's go back!" George thundered. He decided if Professor William Knight wanted to be afraid of him, he would use it in his favor. "I'm not going to hurt you, but I do need you to do what I say."

"Okay," Knight said. "You are in charge. Just don't hurt me." He clenched the steering wheel, checked the rearview mirror, and did a U-turn back down the mountain.

As they drove back toward Tambo, the professor reached in his shirt pocket for his own phone. Steering with one hand and dialing with the other, he then put the device to his mouth and ear.

George expected that Knight was calling the police. But what if he was? What could George do about it? George listened, but couldn't understand anything.

"Este es el profesor. Me han sido retrasado en Tambo. No voy a ser capaz de asistir a la reunión de esta noche. El dinero será destinado a otra persona."

The professor listened to a voice on the other end and then said, *"No lo puedo. Lo siento. Lo siento."* He hung up the phone and stuffed it back in his pocket.

George said, "I heard you saying you were sorry. Is everything okay?"

"When I realized I was going up to Cuenca," the professor explained, "I called some of the board at the Catholic university there. I wanted to arrange a meeting. You know how it is, or perhaps you don't, when you have to live on begging for grants."

George had no idea, so he sat silently.

Knight said, "Anyway, I agreed to meet several of them at this wonderful steak place called La Parrilla. They said they would listen to my grant request for the archaeological work I'm doing. It could have meant another year's funding."

"Could have meant?"

"Of course, nothing is certain. They would still have to take it back to the entire board. The biggest problem will come the next time I want to approach them. You know the old saying. Stand me up once, shame on you. Stand me up twice, shame on me."

"I believe it's 'fool me once.'"

"I don't want to fool you at all," the professor said. "I have tried to be very kind to you."

George didn't explain. "What do you mean, 'could have'?"

Knight said, "We're going back to Tambo. I can't make it in time for my grant appointment. It means I'm losing a great deal of money."

If he was trying to make George feel guilty, it worked. But d'Hout had already lost his MacBook. He wasn't about to lose his cell phone, too. If he did, he would be totally cut off from Carol. "Are there cell phone stores in Cuenca?" George asked.

The professor kept his eyes on the winding mountain road. His voice was curt. He was clearly miffed. "Cuenca has half a million people. There are easily as many cell phone stores there as in a similar-sized city in the United States. Actually, that's not true. I'm reasonably sure there are more. But I have already called and canceled. They will have their dinner, just not with me present. I can only hope your cell phone is still there."

"Doubtful," George said. "Can I use your cell phone to call my wife? I will be happy to pay you whatever it costs."

"Not possible," Knight said. "I don't have international service. In-country only."

George stared out the window at some of the most beautiful countryside in the world. Giant trees, flowering vines, and deep shrubbery melded into a panorama of splendor. It didn't make him feel any better.

Wednesday, 8 January
6:39 p.m.

Darkness had fallen over Tambo. The professor was using the light from his own cell phone to search for George's. The pair also incorporated the help of two station attendants. They had greeted George like a long-lost friend. However, try as he might, he had no memory of the gas station or the men. How could he have just been there and have absolutely no memory of the event? The thought was unnerving.

The men wore coveralls with the name of the station on the left side above the heart. George tried to tell them he had misplaced his telephone. They smiled like they would at a child or an insane person.

The professor laughed along, saying, "*Su esposa se está divorciando de él. Se puso muy borracho la noche anterior. Perdió su teléfono y me dice que ya está aquí.*"

"These are really nice people," George told the professor. "What did you tell them?"

"That you tried to call your wife, and then you misplaced your phone, and we need their help to find it."

"This is the worst week of my life," George said.

"I know something that could make it immeasurably worse," the professor said. "Welcoming the coming days in an Ecuadorian jail."

One of the station attendants walked up. *"Estábamos discutiendo y no recuerda que perdio algo allí. ¿Era el teléfono?"*

"What did he say?" George asked.

"That we can search for the phone all we want, but they heard a puma in the brush over there. They just want us to be careful."

"A puma? This close to town? Doubtful."

"This is not some state park from back in Texas, George. This is the real thing. If they say there is a puma hanging around here, you can take it to the bank. Wandering into the brush in the dark is roughly the equivalent of suicide."

George tried to clarify. "I never said I was going to. I just want to find my phone. Why would it be in the brush? If I dropped it, it should be right here, somewhere. You don't think one of them stole it, do you?"

"In Cañari and Incan societies, there are three things that get your head chopped off: lying, cheating, and stealing. The Cañari are almost pathologically honest. Even when it works completely against them, they will tell you the absolute truth. Are you accusing them of stealing, George? If you are, that's a very serious accusation, and I need to tell them."

"You don't need to tell them anything," George said. "I have lost my MacBook Air, now my phone. I saw my client dead on the floor. I'm running from the police. And now they say a puma wants to eat me."

The professor's face softened. "I completely understand, but let's not make a bad day worse by turning into puma chow."

Both station attendants walked toward the professor with quizzical expressions. The older of the two said, *"¿Seguro que no quieres que busquemos el teléfono?"*

"No," the professor said. *"No, pero gracias. Mi amigo esta muy confuso de la cabeza."*

George beamed a little. "I heard the word *confused*. Something about being confused. I remember that from high school Spanish. My teacher used to say I was perpetually *confuso* when it came to learning another language."

"I told them you were just confused about where the phone is," the professor said. "If they find it, I know they will call me. They have my number."

George said, "They can use my phone. That's one bill I will gladly pay."

George walked over to the two men and said, as if speaking to a child. *"Mucho peligro de la puma.* Much danger from the puma. You be careful."

As they climbed into the car, the two men stared in stunned silence. The professor said to them, *"Te dije que es delirios."* With that, the car motored off again toward Cuenca.

George turned to the professor. "I know you have to be careful driving in the mountains, but I do hope you can get to your appointment in time to save things a bit. We're only about forty minutes behind schedule. Remember all the *tranquilo* stuff. Surely they can be *tranquilo* for forty minutes."

"I have already moved on," Knight said.

"You can even drive straight to the restaurant. I will either wait in the car or just go in and get a different table. They won't even know we're together."

"You are a kind soul, Mr. d'Hout. We will see what happens when we get to Cuenca. It could prove very profitable. We will see."

Wednesday, 8 January
8:00 p.m.

Carol jumped when the phone rang, as did the two women from her church who had come over to keep her company. Checking the name on the display, she held the phone to her ear. "Hugh, have you heard anything?"

"Sort of. The consulate officer in Guayaquil called. He didn't want us to freak out if we heard the news and got the wrong idea."

"What news? What idea?"

"I've checked online and haven't found anything yet. However, he said the Guayaquil media is reporting the body of an American was found floating in the Guayas River. There was a bullet hole in the chest and another in the head. Apparently the guy had been tortured, too. But Carol, it is *not* George. They don't know who it is, because he didn't have ID on him. But it's not George."

"If he had no ID, how can they be so sure?" Her voice quavered.

"Apparently the guy had several tattoos indicating he served in the US Navy. Another one had the name of a wife or girlfriend. Anyway, it's not George."

"Do they think this is a political thing? Something aimed at Americans?"

"I asked the same thing. While the government of Ecuador can sound pretty anti-US at times, we send them more tourists than any country in the world. Also, they export a lot of fruits and flowers our direction. Bottom line, they may not love us, but they certainly don't hate us. No reason to believe Americans are being targeted."

The thought of the dead American, whether it was George or someone else's husband, deeply upset Carol. She started to shake and cry.

Her friends came and stood by her, putting comforting hands on her shoulders. "Hugh," Carol said, "is there anything else?"

"I'll keep you updated," he said. "By the way, George didn't fly down with anyone else, did he?"

"No, of course not. He's a one-man operation. You know that. Why?"

"The consulate just asked. He said he talked to an Ecuadorian federal prosecutor who is monitoring the case. They took the victim's picture to all the airlines to see if anyone recognized him. They are also reviewing surveillance video to see if they can find where the guy entered the country. If he flew in, they should be able to spot him."

"And?"

"A customs official thought he recognized the picture. The victim spoke to someone they were detaining. The detained man was trying to leave the airport with bags. There was a hubbub because the guy couldn't prove they were his."

Carol said, "I still don't—"

"The guy they were detaining was George. They thought he was stealing other people's luggage."

The weight of everything overpowered Carol. She sank to the carpet of her living room, a puddle of tears and anger. Her friends followed her to the floor. One of them took the phone.

"Carol's kind of a mess right now. Is your name Hugh? And you're her brother-in-law? Well, Wendy and I are here with her, so I'm going to let you go. We won't leave her alone. If you need to call back, my name is Kathy. Know that we'll be right here with her."

CHAPTER 12

Wednesday, 8 January
9:25 p.m.

On the way to Cuenca, the professor placed a number of phone calls. On some he did all the talking, completely in Spanish. On others he listened, said only a word or two, and then hung up without even a good-bye.

"Networking," he said to George. "A constant need to network."

George thought this professor must know half the people in Ecuador. Then something occurred to him. "You never mentioned which university you're associated with."

"That's true," Knight agreed. "And with so many of them dropping their archaeology programs, the list of prospective universities I might want to teach at in the future is quickly dwindling. It is amazing when you think that nine programs have been shuttered in just the past decade. One a year. Why? Less history? Less interest in history? Hardly."

"What is it?"

"Quite simple, really. Lack of funding. Business programs produce businesspeople. They generate millions and then give back to their alma mater. I bet you give back thousands to the school you graduated from, George."

"Doubtful."

"If I sound indignant, I'm not, George, because it takes money to make things happen."

"And the school you are on faculty at?"

"Business schools produce businesspeople. Law schools produce lawyers. Medical schools produce surgeons. And archaeology schools produce people who use the term 'genteel poverty' their entire lives as a polite synonym for the truth. They are poor."

"I haven't known you that long, Professor, but with your knowledge and experience, couldn't you write a book? Host a TV show? Something?"

"To borrow a phrase I have heard you use several times, doubtful. When is the last time you picked up a book on archaeology?"

"True, but I'm not a good acid test for your theory. Now my brother, Hugh. He's cut from a different cloth."

Professor Knight cleared his throat. "I must meet this brother of yours. Especially if he's buying what I would love to sell."

"Actually, you are in associated fields. He's a teacher, too. However, his passion is teaching for a community college and a couple of online universities."

The professor made a sort of snorting sound. He moved his mouth as if dispelling something unpleasant tasting.

George realized telling a full-fledged professor he was an "associate" of a man who taught online classes might have been unintentionally offensive. He clarified, "You are both in the business of education." It didn't help, but it did cause the professor to fall morosely quiet. There was something to be said for that.

A persistent mist was making it hard to see out the windows of the car. The Renault's wipers smeared the moisture around, rather than actually pushing it away. George sat quietly as the car followed the curves of the road left, then right, then left again.

After twenty minutes of trying to make out lights or towns or outlines of mountains through the inky, cloudy darkness, George heard the phone in the professor's pocket vibrate. The sound reminded him again of his stolen MacBook and missing iPhone.

"*Dígame*," the professor said into the phone. Someone appeared to be giving instructions.

Finally, the professor answered, *"Veinte minutos, mas or menos."* George understood. Twenty minutes, more or less.

"So we're near Cuenca?" George asked.

"We are," the professor said. He was still clearly irritated at being compared to a teacher at a community college and online university. George thought to himself that academic types had egos like a warehouse full of fine china: expensive, extensive, and fragile.

George decided to push ahead. He wanted to know when there would be an opportunity to call Carol. "So what's the plan?"

"Thanks to our doubling back for a phone—which I knew wasn't there to start with—my meeting has been canceled. However, it has come to pass that we are going to be meeting with a man who is funding some research on…"

The professor's spirits appeared to brighten. He was at least making a show of optimism. "Actually, it may be the most wonderful coincidence," he said, sounding like the person George had first met in the hotel dining room.

"The man I am meeting with is…his name is—" Professor Knight stumbled a moment, like he was trying to remember. "His name is Roberto, but I can't recall his last name at the moment."

"Roberto?" George said. "I don't like that. The last guy I was supposed to meet was named Roberto. He's dead."

"If you depleted the Latin American countries of their Juans, Robertos, and Miguels, there might not be many people left," the professor said dismissively. George was surprised. All three names he'd rattled off were people George had actually met. That surely proved the truth of the professor's statement about their popularity.

George tried to make out the time on his watch. Normally he would just check his smartphone, but, well, that wasn't an option, was it? "Are we going to be able to find a restaurant still open?"

"Roberto has taken care of all that," the professor answered. George thought the professor seemed relaxed again, almost like he was in charge. Was the man afraid of George or not?

George said, "All I know is, I'm starving, and I must call Carol. After she hugs my neck through the phone line, she will try to wring it for leaving her worrying so long."

"Mr. d'Hout, I find your doting attitude toward your wife so...sweet. Dinner will be in front of you by eleven, along with a refreshing beverage that will make you forget your previous woes. How long have you two been married?"

"A quarter of a century," George said. "After this, it may take the next twenty-five for her to let me out of the house without a leash."

"Being married compared to being a pet dog," the professor mused. "How charming."

"Say what you will, but we have a great marriage. I'm the most blessed man in the world. I just need to call her."

The town of Cuenca unfurled before and slightly below them as they began a descent into the Tomebamba Valley. The professor said, "*Tomebomba* means 'the valley of knives,' a native term describing the stone protruding from the ground, which produced excellent axes. That made it a leading sacrificial center."

In spite of the darkness, George could tell the peaks and edges of the rock outcroppings had indeed become more stark, replacing the rolling spaghetti and meatballs of the earlier journey.

A distant rushing sound began to intrude on their conversation. George felt the hairs on the back of his neck stand up. He was unable to identify the source. The professor saw him looking around.

"The four rivers of Cuenca have joined just below where the road now runs through the mountains. This valley was carved thousands of years ago by that confluence," he explained. "The next stop for these waters is the Amazon River. The highway was built through the valley and above the river. No telling how many pitiful Indian laborers died building it. They still lose several people a week who get too close to the waters and fall in. Children, mostly."

"That's terrible. So the rivers are fast?" George said.

"Fast enough to wash this car and all traces of us away in a matter of moments," the professor answered. His voice made it clear there was something about that kind of power he liked very much. "A few weeks ago a car drove over the edge with three children and their grandfather in it. Dozens of people saw it happen. It was on a Sunday afternoon. Do you know where they found the bodies?"

"No idea." George shrugged.

"That's because they haven't. The car, yes. The bodies, no. The gods of these people are stern, unforgiving. None of that grace business. You either toe the line or pay the price. They found themselves in the river. They died. You have to appreciate that kind of simplicity."

"Not me," George said. "I want a God with all the grace in the universe at his disposal. Otherwise we're all doomed. If I get what I deserve, I'm in trouble. Just ask my wife."

"We all get what we deserve," the professor said. Again his voice changed. George thought of the book *Sybil*. Who am I talking to now? Just as quickly, he dismissed the thought.

The professor said, "I'm just hoping I deserve a lot."

George didn't answer. Instead, he looked into the dark valley at the sparkling pinpoints of lights. "Like a million stars, a brilliant constellation," he said.

"God, grace, and constellations," the professor said. "You are quite the poet, George."

"Doubtful. Just trying to keep the glass half-full. Not easy. But it is beautiful out there."

As the Renault motored into Cuenca, George gave a thought to his appearance. His beard could quickly devolve from close-cropped to caveman. His clothes and sneakers weren't exactly the latest in going-out apparel, especially since they would be dining with one of the professor's potential benefactors.

"So, this place we are going to...?" George began.

"That has changed as well."

George decided the professor must be a magician or psychic. How could he have made so many detailed plans with George missing them?

"We are dining at a place in *cuidad centro*, the heart of the old colonial city. It's called Tiesto's, and it is simply the best food you will ever taste. Roberto has us a private table where we can talk. Actually, he will talk, and we will listen."

The professor just listen? George was going to have to see that to believe it.

Wednesday, 8 January
10:31 p.m.

The Renault bounced along the cobblestone roads of Cuenca's central city. High walls decorated with small balconies, flower boxes, and brightly colored shutters above narrow stone walkways on either side of the streets gave a slightly claustrophobic feeling. Very different from the vast expanses and wide streets of Houston.

"When you described it as a colonial city, that really fits," George told the professor. "May I borrow your phone? I will be happy to pay you back, whatever the cost, but I'm calling my wife right now."

"No international calling plan, remember? Let's get inside first. After we have made our introductions and had something to eat, I'm sure there will be time for all that phone business later."

Three doors down from where the professor stopped the car, George recognized two sets of words on a business. The first was CLARO, the name of one of the large cell phone companies in Ecuador. The second was INTERNET CAFÉ. Amid all the beauties of Ecuador, this was the best thing he had seen.

"Do what you want," George said. "I'm contacting my wife."

PART TWO

CHAPTER 13

Wednesday, 8 January
10:32 p.m.

George didn't know much Spanish, but he did know three magic words: *Open* and *How much*. "*¿Abra?*" Open?

"*Sí.*"

"*¿Cuanto cuesta?*" How much?

"*Ochenta centavos por hora para el Internet. Veinticinco centavos por minuto en los teléfonos,*" the bored mestiza said, barely glancing up from her own computer screen at the checkout counter. It looked like she was on Facebook.

Eighty cents for an hour of Internet? Is that what she'd said? It didn't matter. He was paying, whatever it cost. Along the walls of the cramped business were clear fiberglass cubicles. Half held telephones; the other half were computers. On the wall of each cubicle were dialing instructions in Spanish, English, German, and Portuguese.

Each device was attached to a digital readout that allowed both the attendant and customer to see exactly how long the customer had been connected and what he or she could expect to pay. George thought of the meters on taxicabs. Then he thought of the taxi that had taken him to Roberto Ordóñez's house and what he'd found there.

Grimacing, he looked for an open phone booth. However, a variety of brown-skinned young people had taken all of them. None looked as if they were in any hurry. There was an Internet booth open. George decided he would use e-mail as the quickest way to communicate.

He logged on to his e-mail account and quickly began to type.

> Carol, I am doing fine. Phone lost, MacBook stolen. I am ok, but haven't been able to call. There is a man from the United States who is helping me. I am in no harm and trying to get home as soon as I can. I love you!!! George.

Hitting "send," George hoped against hope that Carol was online at that exact moment. He needed to get her advice. But he didn't want to say too much until—

Everything in the Internet café went dark. People shrieked in anger and alarm. Even the meters measuring how much each customer owed went out. Total blackness. Where were the emergency generators? George sat still, waiting for them to kick on. People bolted from their booths and headed out the doors into the night.

"A nice little break for those finishing up their conversations," George thought. "Lots of talk and no cost." Then he felt foolish waiting for emergency power. This wasn't San Francisco or St. Louis or Houston; it was Cuenca. He could probably sit in the darkness for a while or get up and simply leave like the others.

The only real question was, had the message gotten to Carol? Did she know he was okay? When the power came back on, he would find out.

"What do I owe?" he asked into the darkness. "*¿Cuanto cuesta?*"

"*Nada. Ya cerramos. Buenas noches.*" Nothing. Good night.

She shooed him out and reached for heavy steel doors that rolled out of the ceiling. They clanked over both the front door and windows. The street was quiet. Streetlights were still on, though. The power outage hadn't affected them. Odd.

George walked back toward Tiesto's, half expecting it to be locked as well. There was a solitary man about George's height standing in the shadows a few feet from the front door. Other than the solitary figure, the streets appeared completely abandoned. No sign of the other customers from the Claro store. The shadowy figure watched George approach. As George got closer, the man turned on his heels and walked in the opposite direction. There was something familiar about him. There was also something large in his right hand. It reminded George of a large pair of clippers. The man ducked into an alley. George heard footsteps hurrying on cobblestones, then nothing.

"Great," George thought. "Now the place is closed, the professor is gone, and I am stranded. It just keeps getting better." However, the door opened right up at George's touch. As he stepped inside, the exotic odors of cooking meats and vegetables captivated his senses.

Candles resting in the middle of their tables illuminated two or three groups of customers. A cooking area lined the restaurant's stone back wall. In the candlelight, George imagined this was what it had looked like to have dinner in some cozy Cuenca inn five hundred years ago.

Whatever they were cooking, it smelled incredible. George scouted around for the professor. Tucked in a small corner of the establishment was a table for four. The professor sat with his back against the wall. George could see the back and head of thick black hair of the man he supposed was Roberto.

"I guess the power outage hit here, too?" George said. "Or is it always this cozy in here?"

Knight and the other man exchanged glances. The professor said, "The outage...yes, but people in Cuenca are very used to this kind of thing. Hardly even an inconvenience. The real question is, did it come before you could communicate with your wife back in the States?"

"To tell you the truth," George said, "I'm not sure. It was just as I hit the 'send' button. I guess I'll have to wait until tomorrow to see."

"Well, you certainly didn't have much time to compose a message," the professor said. "I don't think I could get out 'Hello, this is Bill' in the time you were gone. What were you able to tell her?"

"Just that I was okay and not to worry."

The man with his back to George listened politely. He now stood, turned, and said, "Hello. I'm Roberto. What would your wife have to worry about? You are in the most beautiful place on earth and in the company of excellent hosts."

The professor stood and held his hands out. "George d'Hout, allow me to introduce you to Roberto Ordó…I'm sorry. Just Roberto. He is considering underwriting a very special project in which I believe you will take more than a casual interest."

"Doubtful," George thought. "All I care about is getting home to Carol." Aloud he said, "*Mucho gusto*." Glad to meet you.

"The pleasure is all mine," Roberto said. His accent was thick but understandable. It reminded him of…whom?

In spite of the long nap, apparently so deep he didn't remember waking up to text Carol—something really wasn't right about all that—he still felt in a fog. Roberto was talking to him, and though he had been looking the stranger in the eyes, George wasn't listening.

"So the amazing thing is you and your pirate ancestor have wandered into the same place. I have no doubt he is a relative of yours. And the mystery this pirate began…Professor Knight tells me that you might be able to help him solve. Beautiful, no?"

George said, "I'm not sure I follow what you're saying. I apologize, but I am very tired and have had a very difficult last few days."

The professor jumped in. "You remember us discussing the pirate George d'Hout?"

"Yes, and Edward Davies, I believe."

"Davies was one of the pirates, but our focus for the moment is on d'Hout. He stole a great deal of treasure from Guayaquil, and it has never been recovered."

George said, "Perhaps it *has* been recovered. Maybe the people who found it simply didn't tell anyone. You know, dig and depart. No one the wiser."

"We would like you to play a bit of a game with us," Roberto said. "I am a businessman. The professor is an archaeologist. And you are a descendant of the famous pirate."

George held up a hand in protest, but before he could speak, Roberto cut him off. "This is a game, Mr. d'Hout. It is not—how you say—real life. And in a game, we can make up any rules we wish. So, for the sake of the large amount of money Professor Knight wants me to invest in his endeavors, please indulge in my rules. Beautiful, no?"

Beautiful, no? The phrase was as irritating as the now-vanished Juan's constant use of *muchacho*. Speaking of Juan, George was eager to get back to the Internet café tomorrow and place an anonymous call to the consulate in Guayaquil. He would suggest that authorities consider Juan as suspect number one in the murder of the other Roberto.

It was a great relief to George to know there was a place in Cuenca where he could telephone or access the Internet. And being safely out of Guayaquil, there was little or no chance for police or anyone else to trace the call. All he needed to do was cool his heels and tolerate these guys until tomorrow. Then he could straighten this mess out.

"Your rules," George said. "Go ahead."

"So what we must determine is this," Roberto said, bending his head conspiratorially toward the other men. The professor followed suit. George declined to participate, maintaining his previous posture and tone.

Speaking quietly, Roberto said, "We have some documents that have taken many years to procure. They are authentic, you may rest assured. The first is a letter seeking credit. It was written by George d'Hout in 1689 in the Caribbean. In and of itself, it is only worth a modest sum to collectors or perhaps some museum.

"But if we can fully come to terms with the content of that letter, it will be worth a very great fortune. Let me say, Señor d'Hout, that many men have killed over lesser amounts of money."

The professor, still leaning in, said, "And this might interest you even more, George. One of the methods used to verify the contents of the letter, in which d'Hout speaks in specific terms about where the treasure of Orellana is hidden, was to cross-reference certain key passages with other documents left behind by him and Edward Davies. They match perfectly."

George spoke. "What's in this letter?"

"Not yet," Roberto said. "First there are three very simple rules. There is a great deal of money at stake, and we cannot have someone else get to the treasure first. Not when we are this close. Therefore, I must insist you follow the rules. That is fair in any game, no? And if someone fails to follow the rules, they are out of the game, yes? You agree to follow the rules?"

George made a mental note that when doing business with Ecuadorians, you first had to go through a litany of mind-numbing rules. Every culture had its annoyances, and this was one of them. Or was that just true with rich guys named Roberto?

"I am a man of my word," George said.

George saw the veins stand up in Roberto's forehead. "So when someone says to stay..." Roberto stopped. His nostrils flared just a second. He took a breath and smiled. "That is good. So we have an agreement. All in or all out. And you agree to be all in. I have your word."

"It is very late," George said. "Do we simply want to delay this discussion for another day?"

"I would prefer to give you some things to sleep on," Roberto said. "It is simply amazing what our dreams, our subconscious, our hidden memories, can reveal when we give them time to ponder."

Candlelight flickered against the walls of the restaurant. Low conversations murmured in the background, and a bed of quiet Andean folk music came from some hidden stereo. It was mildly hypnotic. George suppressed a yawn.

"The professor tells me you know of d'Hout's attack on Guayaquil," Roberto said. "You know about the treasure of Orellana, how your relative stole the treasure with Edward Davies and then disappeared?"

George nodded that he was following, so the man continued. "The treasure had been snuck out of Guayaquil by Davies and d'Hout and brought here to Cuenca. They were going to sneak the treasure out the way Orellana brought it in, along the

Amazon. Only then did the two men realize a huge problem. The rivers here are narrow, treacherous, and incredibly fast. Any boat they might launch would be shattered in a very short time.

"But the treasure was too heavy to continue hauling by land, especially when Spanish authorities would soon be hot on their trail. Their plan was to conceal the money, escape into the rain forest, and then come back for it later."

Knight said, "That brings us to d'Hout's letter attempting to secure credit. He wrote this letter, seeking certain funding for an expedition to go back and get the hidden treasure. The crew would dock quietly in the mangroves outside Guayaquil, keep the boats hidden, come here to Cuenca, retrieve the treasure, and take it back to the coast.

"This is where it gets very interesting. How could d'Hout and Davies make sure they secured their boat and crew without divulging exactly where the treasure was? After all, if they revealed the location of the treasure, anyone might come and get it. They said in all the world only the two of them knew where the treasure was."

"What about the mestizos who helped them?" George asked. "They knew."

"You have very keen powers of observation," Roberto said.

George thought, "Doubtful, or I wouldn't be in this mess."

The professor answered, "Six sets of eyeballs were included with the letter seeking credit. Those who received the letter were to suppose those were the eyes of the mestizos who had been forced to carry the treasure and help to hide it. As Roberto said, people have died for this treasure. It is worth a great deal."

George thought to himself that if Roberto and the professor really believed such a treasure was still hidden, especially with d'Hout and Davies telling people it existed in letters, they were crazy. "Grow up, for heaven's sake," he thought. He wondered if they also played Dungeons & Dragons and attended Renaissance fairs dressed in period garb. Sheesh.

The food was delivered. It was a meal epic in both portions and taste, a sumptuous collection of gourmet Ecuadorian cuisine. There was grilled beef in a chimichurri sauce, sautéed fruits and vegetables served with Amazon spices, and for dessert, the chef handcrafted a passion fruit ice cream and chocolate mousse pie. When each man spooned his way into the fruit-shaped dip of ice cream, real passion fruit poured out from the center.

Once the dessert had been cleared and fresh cups of coffee were served to each man, George said, "Let me ask you again, what makes you think I can help? Or do you just need another hand on the dig?"

"Oh, you are hardly just another hand," Roberto said. "You are the linchpin. Fate has brought us all together in a miraculous way. I can hardly believe our good fortune that you happened to be in Cuenca at this time."

"Neither can I," George said. "I'm sure you have a beautiful city, and I appreciate the fact you would like to find this treasure, but frankly I'd just as soon be back in Houston."

Roberto looked stern. "All in or all out, Mr. d'Hout. Remember? There must be some truth to the stories I hear from your country about people having a commitment problem. You have already agreed to be all in."

George wasn't going to engage this man in a verbal sparring match over such an absurd topic as buried treasure. "My apologies," he said. "Of course."

Roberto said, "The fact is, your ancestor apparently wrote a letter that has come into our possession. He was trying to get back to the Andes to claim his treasure. In the letter he is seeking a marque of credit to command a ship. In the letter he is attempting to give as much information as possible, so as to legitimize his claim. By the same token, he doesn't want to say too much, because he doesn't want to give the treasure's location away."

The professor again leaned in. "George, do you see? He never secured the credit. He never came for the treasure. It is still here! We also have found the last will and testament of d'Hout, which is clear evidence that at the time of his death in 1702, the treasure had still not been retrieved."

"What about Davies?" George asked.

"Also in 1702 Edward Davies returned to the area from Philadelphia, where he had settled. He had heard that someone found the treasure in Cuenca and took it to the Cocos Islands to rebury it."

Roberto said, "He found the Cocos Island treasure but upon inspection determined it was not the treasure he and d'Hout had hidden here in Cuenca. As of his death in 1716, the Cuenca treasure had still not been found. And in his will, Davies included a rather cryptic line. It echoed something in the will of d'Hout. I suspect it is something, as a member of the d'Hout family, you know very well."

"Doubtful," George said.

The professor said, "Both men included in their wills the line, 'The place where the treasure is hidden is a place my family shall know as well as they know their own names.'"

George's eyes were diverted toward a back wall. Candlelight glistened, creating elongated shadows. Listening to Roberto and the professor go back and forth, with the music in the background, was intoxicating. George had that drugged feeling again. Fighting off another yawn, he said, "That's it? That's your clue? The family would know where the treasure was hidden as surely as they knew their own names?"

Roberto said, "So it only makes sense that a direct descendent of d'Hout might be an excellent resource in searching for the treasure. You do know your name, yes? Therefore you can help us. Beautiful, no?"

George protested. "So you think two families would know a secret like that for hundreds of years and never do anything about it? Nobody thought, 'Hey, some extra milk money would be nice. Let's go to Cuenca and have a little family reunion and treasure hunt'?"

It wasn't like George to be so direct. But he was getting so terribly sleepy, and these two men were annoying him. What a ridiculous story. What a waste of—

"Señor d'Hout, are you all right?" Roberto asked. "You don't look so well. Are you going to pass out? Professor Knight, would you summon—?"

Blackness. Sweet sleep had come at last.

CHAPTER 14

Thursday, 9 January
12:03 a.m.

"Hugh, this is Carol. Sorry to call so late, but—"

"I can tell you have news. What is it?"

"I just heard from George! I can't believe this, but the lovable idiot got his MacBook stolen and then proceeded to lose his cell phone."

"How did he contact you?"

"E-mail. Wanted to let me know he's all right. I am so relieved! And now I'm going to brain him just as soon as he gets back here. I've aged ten years over this."

"Did he use the hotel's computer? Why did he wait so long to make contact? What else did he say?"

"The answer to all those questions is, I don't know. But at least he's safe. I'm going to call my friends Kathy and Wendy and let them know. They said it was okay to call at any time."

"Keep me updated," Hugh said. With that, he hung up. While Carol called her friends, Hugh made a call of his own.

When the phone was answered, he asked in Spanish for the room of George d'Hout. The desk clerk said Señor d'Hout still hadn't come back to the hotel.

"*¿Cuantos dias?*" How many days?

"*Dos o tres...No se.*" Two or three...I don't know.

"*Gracias. Buenas noches.*" Thank you. Goodnight.

George hadn't been at the hotel in two or three days? Hugh weighed what to do next. Maybe George was okay. Then again, maybe someone just wanted Carol to think so. But if that was true, why? If it was a kidnapping, the person responsible would want the family to know he was in peril so they could start putting together a ransom.

Certainly, though, something was still amiss. George had left his hotel room empty without checking out or indicating to Carol that he was relocating. On the other hand, maybe his client had extended the hospitality of a room at his home, and George hadn't felt like he could turn it down. In that case, keeping the hotel room would have been a safety net for George, especially if the employer was paying for it. Now that sounded like his brother.

Since Hugh knew Carol was still up, he decided to call her back, requesting every shred of information she had about George's employer. Something still wasn't quite right. If Hugh had to call the consulate again, he wanted all his information readily available.

When Hugh called back, Carol cut him off before he could ask her any questions. "I know you're going to think I'm ridiculous," she apologized, "but Hugh, the more I think about it, the more I can't get past the sensation that something is still wrong. Would you mind calling the—"

"Already done. I wasn't going to mention it until I had more information. Since you are directly asking, the person at the hotel front desk said it appears George hasn't been in his room for the last couple of days. I just don't know what to think. Did he say how the MacBook was stolen? Maybe that will give us something to go on."

"No. And the lost phone is bothering me, too. Other than several years ago in Cleveland, George has never lost anything. It was back when cell phones were still pretty new, and George thought it would be cool to have one of the flip phones because it reminded him of *Star Trek*.

"The thing was so small, it slipped out of his hand and went straight down the toilet. But even then, he couldn't wait to get in touch with me and let me know what was going on so I wouldn't worry."

Hugh thought about the situation. Carol filled him in regarding everything she knew about Roberto Ordóñez.

"So you say George never could find anything substantive about the guy? What line of work is he in?"

"Don't know. At the time I thought that was really strange. But if they have cabbies going around breaking into houses and that kind of thing, maybe Ecuador is really dangerous. In that case, affluent people would have to go the extra mile to protect themselves."

"Actually," Hugh said, "from what I've read, Ecuador is one of the safest countries in South America. How they manage it, being lodged between Colombia and Peru, I have no idea. Anyway, get some rest, and in the morning, we'll start back in on whether to be relieved or furious with dear George."

"I choose option C," Carol said. "All of the above."

Thursday, 9 January
7:45 a.m.

Hugh felt like a bit of an idiot, but he dialed the number anyway. He knew lawyers, law enforcement officers, and physicians hated it when friends abused the relationship by trying to get a free consultation instead of going through proper channels. Surely, since this was a one-off situation, Van Williams would forgive him.

"Hugh," Van said, "heard anything else on your brother?"

Hugh told the FBI agent everything he knew about Roberto Ordoñez and their concerns about George's safety. "Suddenly he sent an e-mail he was fine. But the e-mail said his phone was lost and his MacBook Air was stolen."

"So you've heard from him," Van said. "That's great. Case closed."

"I don't know how exactly to explain it, but I guess it's what you law enforcement officers would call a hunch or a sixth sense. This just isn't in my brother's character. Something is very wrong."

Van said, "Actually, when people disappear, that's what we hear one hundred percent of the time. If it were in character, people wouldn't be calling us."

"That makes sense," Hugh said. "What I'm trying to determine is what steps I need to follow to make sure my brother is safe. You said I should call the State Department. Do I also need to hire a private investigator or head down there or what?"

"You said he e-mailed."

"He did e-mail, but then I called the hotel. They said he hasn't been seen in several days. Also, I might let you know that I called the American consulate down there. The city is Guayaquil. The consulate officer said there were two shooting deaths in one day and that one of them was apparently an American. The consulate told me the victim might have even been on George's flight. But no word on George."

"So I can keep track of the score on this," Van said, "do you happen to have the name of the guy on his flight who was killed?"

"Last time I heard, they hadn't identified him. They knew he was an American because of his tattoos. US Navy."

"Let's get back to the guy your brother is supposed to do work for. Ordóñez, right? What line of work is Mr. Ordóñez in?"

"No idea. He was very mysterious, according to my sister-in-law. He said something about wanting some Internet work done, but other than that, he said he would fill in the blanks once my brother arrived."

"Your brother works on websites, right? I need you to speak to your sister-in-law and get a list of his clients. Make it as complete as possible. Also a list of anyone he is about to do work for, in case someone is trying to use your brother to hack into some websites."

"Sure," Hugh said. "You think that's it? They want him for his knowledge about some websites?"

"No idea. It's just the first lead we have to follow."

"I'll get back to you with that."

"Sure. It also could be some kind of money-laundering operation. It's possible they're looking for a person to be their American connection. It's just too early to know."

Hugh asked, "While you're running down those leads, what can I do? The idea of George getting involved in some international criminal enterprise or running off to South America is something I just can't buy."

Van said, "You could do your own Internet search and see what you can find. However, it's possible the name is fake. If the guy is flush—and it sounds like he is—and he is hell-bent on getting a connection in the United States, it may be money laundering. He sends money to an unsuspecting party; the party handles it and disposes of it. If someone is going to go to jail, it's usually the stooge."

"My brother, the stooge."

"If George really does fall completely off the map, remember to call the State Department, and they will request Ecuadorian officials to look into it. When someone from another country disappears in our nation, the FBI is sent a BuDed lead."

"A what?"

"A high-priority lead. State Department sets a 'Bureau deadline' or BuDed to gather information, and we report back to headquarters on the missing person. BuDeds take a lot of time and inevitably lead to a dead end. As I said, there is always the assumption that if someone goes missing, it's because they don't want to be found."

The two men exchanged small talk and discussed mutual friends. Then, as Van was saying good-bye, he paused. "You know,

I do know a guy with Immigration and Customs Enforcement, an ICE agent. He's completely fluent in Spanish and recently took a temporary duty position at one of our embassies in that part of the world. Let me see if I can get in touch with him and put out a feeler. If a guy named Albert calls you, that's him."

Hugh thanked Van and hung up. If talking to the FBI was supposed to make him feel better, it hadn't worked. Of course, that was because Van had told him the truth rather than what he wanted to hear.

CHAPTER 15

Thursday, 9 January
9:04 a.m.

"Señor d'Hout. It is me, Miguel."

George tried to wake up but felt groggy. Where was he? Who was that? Someone was whispering in his ear. "Señor d'Hout, I don't have much time. Wake up."

"Hmmewho?" It was more a grumble than words.

"You are in danger," the voice in his ear said. "They killed the other man because he wouldn't help them. He told them to go to hell, so they killed him. You must help them, or you will die."

George pulled back from the voice to try to focus on the face. Miguel? The driver Ordóñez had sent to pick him up?

The room was cold and damp. Gray light, as if it was cloudy or rainy outside. George rubbed index fingers into both eyes. He mumbled, "You were with Juan Pacheco at the airport. You worked for Roberto Ordóñez? Was it Juan?" As he spoke, George worked to sit up. Miguel was holding George's shoulders and trying to stay close to his ear.

"You must not tell him anything about this, or he will kill me and my family," Miguel whispered.

From somewhere there was the sound of a door creaking open and closing. Miguel said, "They were meeting, so I came to warn you. Do not betray me."

With that, Miguel was out the door of what appeared to be a little girl's bedroom. George sat up and looked around. How did he get here? Where was he?

The head of the bed was against a large picture window, and outside were large trees. Pink, frilly curtains lined the window. The door was along a wall to his right next to some posters of puppies and kittens thumbtacked to the wall. Opposite the bed was a wall of built-in shelves and cabinets.

George listened. It sounded like someone outside the room was descending wooden stairs. From somewhere below him came the sounds of a conversation in Spanish. Then George heard a voice. The professor? "Is he awake?"

"I watched him, like you said. You came out at just the right time. He is starting to wake up."

"Did he see you?"

"No, Señor Knight. I was very careful."

"It's Professor Knight. Now get out. You have work to do."

George heard a door open and close and then what sounded like two heavy locks being bolted. There were more steps. He lay down and pretended to be asleep. Nothing made sense. Miguel from Guayaquil here with the professor? Why was the professor giving orders to a man who worked for Ordóñez? Did that mean the professor was somehow in on Ordóñez's murder? And how did George get into this house, this room? Again he felt as if he'd been drugged. All thoughts were interrupted by the sound of footsteps on the stairs.

"George," he heard the professor call, "it's a beautiful day, and we have much to do. Coffee is downstairs. I will see you in ten minutes. Your clothes are in the bedroom, and your shaving gear is in the *baño* at the head of the stairs. Dress very casually, as we will be outdoors and perhaps getting dirty."

George's head was spinning. In danger? From Roberto, the professor, or someone else? Were they still in Cuenca? If Miguel was here, where was *Muchacho* Juan?

Then another thought occurred to him. If the professor was in on it, had he actually been the one who murdered Roberto Ordóñez? Had their meetings in Guayaquil been pure staging rather than coincidence?

Looking out the window, George saw that the house he was in was across the street from a city park. In the middle was a fast-moving river lined by large trees. There was also an old man in the park walking a milk cow on a leash. George wondered if he was hallucinating.

Everything out the window was painted in shades of green and gray, the combination of low clouds and large cottonwoods, eucalyptus, and palms. It was dark and beautiful and forbidding.

As he hurriedly dressed, George longed to go for a run. He was in the right clothes for it. If there was an opportunity, he was prepared to run all the way back to Guayaquil, jump on a Copa Airlines flight, and get out of Ecuador.

Escape. He could do that. Just step out the front door for a breath of fresh air and never look back. Take off and keep going. But in order to pull that off, George knew he must act as if nothing was wrong. He didn't know whom to trust, so playing dumb seemed the best option. Appear to trust everyone, do what they ask, and look for an opportunity to get away from all of them.

George walked down the wooden stairs to the first floor, listening to them creak beneath his feet. At the bottom of the stairs, he looked around. To his right was a large table cluttered with papers. Professor Knight walked out of the kitchen with a mug in his hand. He held it out to George.

Taking the cup of coffee, George said, "Seems like a nice house. Yours?"

The professor said, "We are merely borrowing it due to its location. When we step outside, you will notice we are across the street from the Yanuncay River, near where it meets the Tomebamba River. It was from somewhere very close to here that Davies and d'Hout began following the rivers to their intersection with the Amazon. It was somewhere near here where they hid their treasure until they could return."

Knight picked up his own cup of coffee from the large table. He sipped it as George looked around the first floor. The kitchen was off to the right. Walking past the front door, which had two heavy bolt locks on it, George saw an enclosed patio behind the kitchen. The table sat in an open dining room, with the great room past that.

The stairs were opposite the great room, and on the other side of those a bathroom and two closed doors. "Bedrooms?" George asked.

"We are guests here," the professor said, "so I have kept my curiosity focused solely on locating the treasure, not what happens behind closed doors. You may want to follow a similar path." It seemed to George that the professor had two personalities. The one he was displaying now was not the friendly one.

George decided to change the subject. "I don't remember coming here last night."

"You must still be suffering the effects of exhaustion and stress. Roberto and I had a difficult time getting you here. But that is all in the past. Now is the time to work toward a profitable day."

"How exactly does that happen?" George asked. "Are all the treasures you find property of the Ecuadorian government or a university or…?"

The professor ignored him and walked to the large table. He stared out a huge picture window past a large iron fence with barbed tops. George followed the professor's eyes, thinking the barbed wire at the top of the fence reminded him of homes he had seen in other parts of Latin America, like Mexico and Honduras.

Knight was looking across the street and in the direction of the Yanuncay River. He then looked down at the table. It was square and of a light-colored wood, with two chairs tucked under each of the sides. The two chairs on the side where the professor stood had been pulled back to give him plenty of room.

Spread out on the table were several maps: Cuenca; the Azuay Province, of which Cuenca was the capital; and a topographic map of the area. On the maps were a variety of marks and writings. George saw several dates written at various places on the map with the word STARTED. Most of them had Xs below them and ending dates for excavation on the site.

George noticed that the house where they were was highlighted on a street map and sat just a couple of blocks from the confluence of the rivers. The professor looked up to see George studying the maps.

"If staring at this map revealed the secret, we would have found the treasure long ago," the professor huffed. "What we need from you is some recollection. What did your ancestor mean when he said the d'Hout family would know the location of the treasure as surely as they know their own name?"

"I can tell you the absolute truth," George said. "If we had known something about a treasure like that, it wouldn't still be there, and I wouldn't be here. I would be in Nassau enjoying one of those drinks with an umbrella in it and asking my wife how we were going to get all the clothes she had just bought back to the United States."

Professor Knight stared at George for a long moment. In the uncomfortable silence, George asked, "Yes?"

"So," Professor Knight said, "we can assume when you say you will tell the absolute truth, you mean you will tell the most convenient truth?"

"What are you talking about?"

The Ecuadorian Deception

"Are you going to tell me you had no idea that when the pirate d'Hout wrote that letter about the location of the treasure, he was writing it to officials in Nassau?" Knight asked. "Freudian slip?"

The professor rested a hand on the table, never breaking his stare. "I think you know a great deal about the treasure. You should do all you can to assist us. We can...help each other."

George's mind raced. Of all the places in the world he could have named, how did he just happen to pick the one place the other d'Hout had gone after Ecuador?

George crossed his arms. "Remember when I told you my wife wasn't going to let me out of the house without a leash? You can add a muzzle to that. Professor Knight, I don't know a blasted thing about your treasure, this pirate ancestor, or anything else."

The professor's hand still rested on the table. He focused an icy stare at George. In response, George rested both of his hands flatly and matched him glare for glare. "I want to go home. That's all I want. Tell me what I need to do to make that happen. Or just open the door, and we will each go our separate ways."

So much for playing along. George was sick of the professor and his seesaw personality. He would just leave and take his chances.

One of the two bedroom doors behind George opened, and a familiar voice said, "Hey, *muchacho*, we are just getting started. You don't want to go now. I'm sure of it."

It was Juan Pacheco from Guayaquil. What was he doing here? George watched him dip a hand into a pocket and pull out a pistol, pointing it straight at George.

Thursday, 9 January
11:13 a.m.

Hugh's phone sat on the desk next to his computer. It began to vibrate. "Hello?"

"My name is Albert, and I was asked to call you. Tell me what you know about Roberto Ordóñez."

"Did Van ask you to call me?"

"Quite frankly, I need to ask the questions for the time being."

"Okay, so the mystery deepens. Look, if you know anything about my brother and what happened to him, I'd really appreciate it if—"

"Tell me what you know about Roberto Ordóñez."

"Only that a man by that name contacted my brother, offering him fifty thousand dollars for two weeks' work. My brother went to Guayaquil, Ecuador, to meet him and now has dropped off the map. Well, actually, he did contact us, but there's something not right about it. He's not at his hotel, and we don't know where he is."

"You don't trust your brother? His wife is jealous and fears there's another woman? What's the source of your suspicion?"

The questions made Hugh feel foolish and accusatory. "My brother...he shouldn't have taken the job. Now he's in Ecuador, but the hotel says he hasn't been there for two or three days. He e-mailed once to let us know everything is okay, but there's still something fishy."

"With all due respect, you still haven't told me anything of substance. What line of work is your brother in that captured the attention of Mr. Ordóñez? Let me guess—director of acquisitions for some museum specializing in Latin American relics."

"Definitely not." Hugh laughed. "He's is a freelance web developer. He stays as far away from history as possible. I'm the history guy in the family."

"Does your brother design historical websites? Perhaps some dealing with archaeology? Or does he do any work for auction houses or museums?"

"Look, my brother doesn't give two hoots about history. Why are you asking these questions? What does my brother's disappearance have to do with archaeology?"

"As I said, Mr. d'Hout, I need to be the one asking the questions. At what hotel was your brother staying?"

Hugh gave Albert all the information he had, including what flight George had arrived on and exactly what he told Carol in the last e-mail. He also filled Albert in on what he'd learned from the consular officer in Guayaquil.

"So you have no way of contacting your brother?" Albert asked.

"I can send an e-mail to his account, but he told his wife his MacBook was stolen. I have no idea how he contacted her, since he apparently didn't use the hotel computer."

"I can't promise anything, but I'll look into the matter. Mr. Ordóñez, if this is the man I believe it is, he is known to us. He deals in black-market relics and historical objects of great value. He has a number of businesses that front for this endeavor. If your brother has gotten mixed up with this man, he has made a big mistake. Should you talk to your brother, you should caution him to get away as quickly as possible. I've told you more than I should, but you need to know in case your brother contacts you. He's very likely in danger and needs to be aware."

The line went dead.

Thursday, 9 January
11:25 a.m.

For over an hour, George had been sitting in one of the light-colored chairs at the mystery house in Cuenca. Professor Knight accused him of lying regarding what he knew about the pirate d'Hout. Juan suggested repeatedly that if George didn't voluntarily cooperate, there were other ways to make him talk.

The fear in George was rising. He worked hard to control his breathing so he didn't hyperventilate. Now that he knew the score, if either of the men gave him the opportunity, he would take his chances with his fists. But with Juan's pistol touching George's temple just beside the right eye, that didn't seem like much of a possibility.

"There's something you should know, *muchacho*," Juan said. "The dead man you found at the house outside Guayaquil...I did that. After you saw him, my *muchacho* Miguel and I drove him to the Guayas River and let him go swimming. He needed to get some water, after all the fluid he lost."

Juan leaned in to George's ear. His breath was an acrid mix of peppers, sausage, and cigarettes. "That man was a smartass. He was uncooperative. He joked when he should have been serious. Are you going to be a smartass?"

"Doubtful," George said. He stared straight ahead. "However, once you have the treasure, you're just going to kill me. I think that much is clear. What's my incentive to help you?"

"A lack of torture before you die," Juan said. "But it's up to you. Some people like screaming until they believe they will go insane, begging me to kill them. Your choice, *muchacho*."

The professor intervened. "George, I think we are being premature in believing that death is the only way this can end. The simple fact is, Juan here works for Roberto. If you impress Mr. Ordóñez, I mean Gonzales, I think there is a better-than-average chance he might even let you become an employee."

"So this man really is Roberto Ordóñez," George said. "You accuse me of lying, but this entire thing was a setup to get me here. You've wasted a lot of time and money to bring in someone who can't help you."

"And you are wasting your last days by making me angry, *muchacho*."

The professor said, "Juan, step back with that gun. Don't put it away, but step back. We don't want a repeat of the little accident that prematurely ended our interview with Mr. Davies."

George stared at the professor in disbelief. "You mean the dead man was Edward Davies, the guy from my flight? The man in the next room at the hotel? You killed him?"

"I didn't kill anyone," the professor said. "We were having a very nice conversation, in which Mr. Davies was displaying his wit. The next thing I knew, Davies, who had been sitting in a chair just like you are now, was on the floor in a pool of blood."

"But I thought that was Ordóñez," George said. "You even told me it was."

Professor Knight shook his head. "No, you *assumed* it was. We didn't expect you to arrive when you did, so we stepped into another room. You came in and assumed it was Ordóñez."

"But the police roadblocks?"

"A bit of poetic license to encourage you to stay off your phone and accompany me to Cuenca," Professor Knight explained. "What is absolutely true is I require your help in finding this treasure that your ancestor hid. If you do not, your wife will never see you again."

"This is absurd! Completely absurd." George tried to stand, but Juan dug fingernails into his shoulder and the pistol into his temple, forcing him back into the chair.

The professor suddenly had an idea. "You told me your brother knows a great deal about your family history."

"Certainly more than I do, but I won't do anything to lure him down here, the way you did me. You can go straight to—"

"Mr. d'Hout," Professor Knight said. "Such language. I have no desire to lure your brother down here. But I'm sure he would love the opportunity to save your life."

Turning to Juan, the professor said, "You and our friend, George, are going to walk down the street to the Internet café. When you reach it, have Mr. d'Hout e-mail his brother. You must be in the cubicle with him to see every word he types."

Facing George again, the professor said, "You are to explain only that you are working on a project for a client. Let him know you have come across your family name here in Ecuador. Ask him to search all family records for information on where the treasure is. Use whatever means necessary to encourage him to put his best effort in this. But under no circumstances are you to tell him about our little clambake or the fact that you feel somewhat intimidated by Juan's gun."

Again Professor Knight faced Juan. "If you need to, kill him. We'll explain to the police that we have found the man who murdered Edward Davies and killed the taxi driver."

"What?" George wanted to know. "What taxi driver?"

The professor said, "I believe you told me the taxi driver absconded with your MacBook. In fact, he was still waiting for you when I stepped up to the cab and was able to persuade him, via one of Juan's guns, to pull around behind the house from the side entrance and leave you stranded."

"Doubtful," George said.

"But true, nonetheless," Knight insisted. "The cabbie was very uncooperative, so Juan had to kill him. I believe that was about the same time you called, asking me for a ride back to Guayaquil. Didn't you think it was strange I was able to reach you so fast after you called?"

"I did think it was an interesting coincidence," George said. "Now I just feel like a moron."

The professor made a tsk-tsk sound with his tongue. "You are certainly no moron, George. You used all your powers to locate Mr. Ordóñez's house before we were ready. You were quite the eager beaver. We believe you can do the same in locating the treasure. It's the reason you're still alive. And you may thank me for that. I reminded Roberto what a good little detective you were in finding his house."

George said, "I shouldn't even be involved in—"

"You will feel much better when the treasure is found, and you realize you can either split some portion of it or you can suffer the same fate your pirate ancestor inflicted on those who helped him hide it. Are you ready to run a little errand and get your brother, Hugh, to help us on our game of lost and found?"

George's mouth moved, but no words came out. Then he said, "You are going to take me in as a partner? Is that the latest work of fiction you're asking me to buy? Doubtful. Besides all that, you're risking my life and substantial jail time for yourself on a rumor. Buried treasure? C'mon. We're not children. This is ridiculous."

Juan's pistol pressed hard into George's temple again. George tried to lean back, but the pistol continued to press between his right ear and eyebrow. "You just messed up for the last time, gringo!" George heard a click and thought it must be Juan's finger releasing the safety. He braced himself for what was about to happen.

The professor said, "That's fine, Juan. We're all right. George is speaking out of ignorance. He has not seen what we've seen."

Turning to George, he said, "This is not a request. It is an empirical sentence. You are to listen as if your life depends on it. What I tell you will certainly educate you. It may also, if you are as smart as I hope, save your life."

With that, the professor pulled a map of western South America out from the clutter on the table. He opened it and moved it so George could see the section on Bolivia. "We are here," he said, pointing to Ecuador, "and this is Bolivia. It was the site of our last dig, and it was very productive—so productive that Juan and I were on an extended vacation for over a year. Then we came back and continued working on our current project, which has been an interest of mine for more than a decade."

He pointed to Cuenca and then traced a line southeast to La Paz. "In 1767, the Jesuits were expelled from South America. They had accumulated such wealth, they were actually a threat to the Spanish authorities."

George had a so-what look on his face, which Knight ignored.

"The Jesuits helped the people of the Sacambaya Valley, a really forsaken little dot on the map. But a spot that happened to be rife with gold and silver mines. They turned a small mountain of gold and silver into a stunning collection of statues, church ornamentation, and sacramental chalices. Before they left, the Jesuits hid their treasure from the Spaniards, who would come in very short order, hunting for it. While the priests had taken a vow of poverty, the mother church had made no such commitment."

"They just left it all there?" George asked. "Doubtful."

"The Spanish were watching every road and route of escape," the professor said. "There were two options: hide the treasure and hope to come back for it later or let it fall into the hands of the Spanish authorities, who were operating at cross-purposes from the church."

"Wouldn't the Indians—Incas or whoever they were—have simply waited until the Jesuits left and dug the treasure up?" George asked. "Then they could have been rich or used the treasure as a bargaining chip when the Spaniards arrived."

The Ecuadorian Deception

The professor said, "This is where your slight grasp of history is showing, George. How well did such a plan work for the Aztecs or for Atualpa, the great Incan chief? The indigenous peoples were simply outgunned. But there was another issue."

Juan stepped forward. "What is the most death you have ever seen, *muchacho*?"

George ignored him. Juan pushed the gun harder against his temple. "I have been to a couple of funerals," George said.

Juan sneered. "When the Spaniards arrived in the Sacambaya Valley, there was no one there. No one. The area was completely abandoned, or so they thought."

The professor said, "Whether it was a mass suicide or mass murder, all the people who had helped the Jesuits hide the treasure were dead. The Spanish blamed the Jesuits, and the Jesuits blamed the Spaniards. Both sides also said it could have been a mass suicide. The bottom line was the treasure was hidden, and there was no one among the indigenous population to be bribed or tortured into telling where it was.

"In 1928, the Sacambaya Exploration Company of Great Britain, using the very latest in technology, invested countless lives and dollars into finding the treasure, which the Spaniards could never locate. They also brought hundreds of guns and rounds of ammunition to defend them in getting the treasure safely back to London.

"They didn't find the treasure, Mr. d'Hout. Several of their leaders ended up in jail or dead at the hands of the Bolivian military, which didn't appreciate this little army invading their country without so much as a 'please' or 'may I?' The failure of the

Sacambaya Exploration Company convinced the world that the entire story of Jesuit treasure was a myth. In the 1930s another attempt was made. Again, nothing."

Professor Knight began tracing his finger around the Sacambaya Valley. A gleam appeared in his eyes, like a proud parent recounting the day his son won the science fair.

"The world said the treasure was only a myth. But I found it, right about here," he said, jabbing his finger at a spot south of La Paz along the Sacambaya River. "Señor Ordóñez financed our venture. Juan and one of our former colleagues named Tomas provided some very important labor management. I pored over maps, and had countless conversations with indigenous peoples in the area. I found it, Mr. d'Hout. I found it.

"You see, I find what others cannot. Why? Because I never give up. If blood must be spilled in the cause, so be it. But I never give up."

George looked squarely at the professor, trying to see if this was just one more lie. "I suppose this is true, like the police looking for me because of a murder I didn't commit, right? Or maybe like a taxi driver who didn't really desert me but was killed. I am no longer up for recruitment, Professor. I am at your mercy because of that gun. You don't have to keep lying."

The professor sat down in the chair next to George. "Look into my eyes, George d'Hout. The Sacambaya treasure was real. It is real. Just as the Orellana treasure here in Cuenca is real. We will find it, and you will help, just as key people in Bolivia assisted us. Or we will put a bullet in your head right now. Your choice."

Juan took a step closer and again raised the gun. "Well, *muchacho*?"

George knew his only chance was to stall. "What do you want me to do?"

The professor stood and stared at the maps, refocusing his sights on Cuenca. "'My descendants shall know the location of the treasure as surely as they know their own name,'" he repeated. "Where is that treasure, George d'Hout?"

"I'm not the history guy," George said. "You wanted me to seek assistance from my brother. Where's the phone?"

"Actually," the professor responded, "you and Juan are going to one of those delightful little Internet cafés. There is one around the corner. You are going to very carefully e-mail your brother, Hugh, and tell him you've stumbled on a mystery and want his help. Make it sound like great fun, but get his help. George, your life depends on it. If you don't believe me, just ask Edward Davies."

CHAPTER 16

Thursday, 9 January
11:36 a.m.

"Van, there's a guy on the line who says his name is Albert Pujols. You want me to——?"

"It's for real." FBI Special Agent Van Williams smiled. "He's Albert Pujols, just not the baseball Albert Pujols."

"Okay. Line three."

Van picked up the call. "Albert, did you talk to Hugh d'Hout?"

"Yes, and it sounds like your friend's brother has crossed paths with a relics and antiquities smuggler named Roberto Ordóñez Gonzalez. He operates out of Guayaquil but has a web of associates all over South America. According to intel reports, it's estimated Ordóñez has removed sixty-six million dollars' worth of native artifacts and treasures out of Ecuador, not to mention what he's done in Bolivia, Peru, Paraguay, and the list goes on."

Van said, "I recommended you because I knew you were working in South America. Then I ran Ordóñez's name and saw ICE had an open case on him. If the Ecuadorian authorities know where he lives, why don't they arrest him?"

"Ordóñez is rich and slippery," the ICE agent answered. "He's been accused before, but the charges never stick. Or he bribes his way out of trouble. He also has friends in key positions within all levels of government."

"How did ICE get involved?"

"If someone is bringing artifacts worth hundreds of thousands of dollars into the US, Uncle Sam wants to make sure everything is properly cataloged and the customs duties and taxes are all paid."

"Where are you at on it?" Van asked.

"We haven't gotten a lead on Ordóñez in quite a while," Albert said. "From what we know, he buddies up to middle-class families in nice neighborhoods, offers to lease their houses, paying exorbitant amounts. He's also been known to use strong-arm tactics to force the homeowners to help him. He's used that tactic to create a network of hideouts all over the place, but with no paper trail. It's all cash, and it's all under the table. There are rumors he has even linked many of these houses with a series of tunnels that could stretch on for a pretty good ways."

"You buy that?" Van wanted to know.

"There's actually a tradition of tunneling that goes back hundreds of years," Albert said. "You ever been to Paraguay? The priests there had the Guarani Indians dig hundreds of miles of tunnels as escape routes from Spanish slave hunters."

"How deep do they go? Is it like mines where they had to pump in air?"

"Nothing like that," Albert explained. "Might only be fifteen or twenty feet below the surface. Just enough to allow them to move around covertly."

"How many people does Ordóñez have working for him?" Van asked.

"His enforcer is a guy named Juan Pacheco. He was educated in the US. When he's not providing muscle for Ordóñez, it's believed he sells his services to Latin American drug cartels. Really gets his jollies torturing people. But the whole thing is held together by the guy who actually locates the treasure, a real slimeball named William Knight. The two met at Arizona State University. Ordóñez was sent there for college by his family. Knight was a student as well. Great mind but apparently completely devoid of morals or ethics. He got drummed out of the anthropology and archaeology program at ASU for unethical behavior. Because they are student records, we don't know what 'unethical' means. However, I suspect it was stealing artifacts. He's pretty much the modern-day incarnation of the conquistadors. Take what you want and kill who you need to."

Another question came from Van. "You anywhere close to Guayaquil, where you can look into this thing?"

"Not allowed to answer that. But if you hear from Hugh d'Hout or George's wife, I need you to call me on this number and keep me updated."

"Hugh told me there was a dead American found in the Guayas River. Is it connected?"

"Quite possibly," Albert said. "These guys have a pretty set pattern. They study up on hidden and lost treasure mythology, determine which stories are credible, convince people to help them, and after they find the treasure, begin a process of disposal—first of witnesses and then of the artifacts. The problem for us is that there are hundreds, maybe thousands, of those stories down here. So there's no way to figure out which one Ordóñez, Knight, and Pacheco might be working on."

The ICE agent added, "There is an interesting note here that may provide a clue to what Ordóñez is going after. I didn't realize this until I was doing some background work on stories about lost treasures; I was trying to think like the bad guys. It seems George d'Hout has the same name as a pirate who stole a very sizable treasure in Guayaquil back in the sixteen hundreds. d'Hout was partners with a guy named Edward Davies. Everywhere those two went, they left a path of death. Bad customers."

Van said, "It sounds to me like if you don't find our modern-day George d'Hout and stop Ordóñez and his buddies, that trend is very likely to continue."

Thursday, 9 January
11:45 a.m.

The professor finished rattling on about a lost treasure from Bolivia and his claims of archaeological invincibility. George stood to walk out the front door. However, he was redirected, at the point of the pistol, back toward the closed door he saw when he first descended the staircase. It had once been a bedroom, but all the contents of the room and closet were shoved into one corner and a single mattress was now in the center of the room.

"Welcome to Miguel's room," Juan said. "He used to have all that stuff everywhere, but we moved it for him. It reminded him too much of his wife and children. You know, they are taking a little vacation right now, courtesy of Señor Ordóñez, so that Miguel can let us use his house without any trouble. If he is a good little Cañari, he may get to see them again one day. If not..."

"That's enough for now," the professor said. "Mr. d'Hout gets the idea. We don't take kindly to those who choose not to dedicate themselves fully to the cause, just as soon as we tell them what the cause is."

George said nothing. He tried to glance back at Miguel and get a read on the small man's face, but when he did, Juan shoved him toward the closet. So this was Miguel's house? These animals had taken control of it and abducted the man's family in order to secure his cooperation? George suddenly wasn't just thinking about escaping. Now he was thinking about gaining control of Juan's pistol and using it to end this madness.

"Open the closet door," Juan said, "and then lift the wooden hatch in the floor." Once he did, a narrow stairway appeared, leading into the darkness below. George watched as the professor descended. A light was switched on. Cryptic shadows replaced the blackness. "Now your turn," Juan said. *"Vamanos."*

George gingerly descended ten steps. At the bottom, the professor warned George that he also had a weapon and instructed him stand still "like a good fellow without tricks or guile" while Juan came down." The weapon he held was a large sword of gleaming silver with a golden hilt.

"If you attempt to escape or overpower me, two consequences will be effected," Professor Knight said. "The first is, you will never get to see the treasure of Orellana that your ancestor so ably hid. The second is, you will die by a sword found at the Sacambaya Valley and dating back to the time of the Spanish invasion, proof positive that I was telling you the truth."

George took a slight step back, raising his hands to indicate he had no plans to do anything but cooperate. As he did, his right heel bumped the final step leading down from the bedroom closet above. "So why all the cloak-and-dagger stuff?" George wanted to know. "Didn't I hear the front door earlier? Why not just go out that way and leave your escape route hidden from me?"

"An excellent question," the professor said, glancing up to see Juan begin moving down the stairs. "But first, George, will you be so kind as to move five steps to your right so Juan can come down unimpeded?"

Juan reached the tunnel floor. Knight said, "The house belongs to Miguel. He lives here. He comes and goes, and the neighbors see him and say hello. However, the neighbors have been told his wife and daughters are visiting family in the countryside. It is unclear when they will return. They are actually a guest of Mr. Ordóñez at one of his other properties in another city. If Miguel wants to see them again, he will do nothing to raise suspicion."

The professor gestured with the sword and said, "This was a very nice job of building a basement and underground pathway leading all the way to the Yanuncay River. It was done almost entirely by Miguel so we may come and go, and no one is the wiser about our presence. It is amazing what people can accomplish when they are sufficiently motivated. He was given three months, or his family would be killed, one at a time, for every week he went over. You have never seen such a—how shall I say?—busy beaver."

With Juan at the bottom of the stairs, the professor leaned the sword against a far wall of the tunnel. The air was moist and moldy. The smell of fresh dirt was overwhelming in the tight space.

"George," the professor said, "you will lead the way, followed at a fair distance by Juan. I will bring up the rear. When you get to the end of the passage, you will stop, kneel down, and cover your head with your hands. If you make any move to get up while

I am opening the next door, Juan will shoot you. Do not scratch, do not flinch, and do not tremble. If you do, you will die."

George obeyed, walking for what seemed like half a city block. The claustrophobic tunnel reminded him of a trip to some wild caves he and Hugh had taken their families to in New Mexico.

"Miguel dug all this?" George asked.

Juan said, "Cañari Indians are very strong, *muchacho*. He is Cañari. I am Inca. We are faster than the Cañari, but they are often stronger than the Incas. When the two work together, they are a formidable team. But Cañari have simple minds. They need direction."

"I don't think team members take wives and children hostage," George said, continuing his walk. A single strand of wire, hung around bent spikes driven into the ceiling, connected the string of lightbulbs.

George took note that if he had the opportunity, he might grab the wire and yank. If he could envelope the tunnel in darkness, he might have a chance to take the gun from Juan, get past the professor, and escape. On the other hand, the passage was so narrow. If Juan immediately fired the pistol, there was no doubt he would strike George. It was too risky for now.

Once they reached the end of the passageway, George did as instructed, hearing but not seeing the professor open a hatch. There was a sudden roaring sound. The river. They had walked underground all the way to the river.

The professor exited first. Then George came out, squinting in the light. They were under a bridge and hidden from view of the cars passing above. The hatch looked just like one of the large stones used to construct the bridge. Even if passersby saw the hatch, they probably wouldn't recognize what they were seeing.

Then Juan came out, his pistol back in his pocket. For a second, George thought this was his chance to run for it. He looked around for which way to go. Then he realized Miguel was standing near a tree beside the river.

"I wouldn't," the professor said. "Miguel is very strong. If you force him to choose between killing you and sacrificing his family, I believe the family will win, hands down."

The idea of fleeing left George as quickly as it had arrived. The river bisected a city park with walking paths on both sides. Eucalyptus and balsa trees grew beside giant cottonwoods. Carnation plants grew as tall as some of the trees. Their pink and red flowers bobbed in the breeze. Under different circumstances, George might have thought this was one of the most beautiful spots on earth.

Moving his eyes past the river in what he thought was a southerly direction, George saw a huge peak with houses clinging to the mountainside all the way up. At the top was a white Catholic church, its steeple aiming toward heaven.

From the river George was led on foot several blocks to the Internet café. He followed the professor's instructions and sent an e-mail to Hugh. He intentionally didn't ask to write Carol, hoping both Hugh and Carol would take that as an indication something was dreadfully wrong.

George also hoped four men traipsing through the streets of Cuenca in the middle of the afternoon would strike someone, possibly a policeman, as odd. Unfortunately, as George surveyed the distance from the hidden passage under the bridge to the Internet café, it occurred to him a large number of people in Cuenca relied on either public transportation or walking.

At least three different groups of men loitered in the park, making George and the three bandits fit in rather than stand out. Another man was fishing with a net from the riverbanks. George watched him draw the net out of the water, pulling three large trout along with it.

"In this world," the professor observed, "there are fishermen, and there are fish. I am a fisherman. And we are about to land a very large catch."

Entering the Internet café, Miguel took a position by the door, apparently to watch for authorities or in case George made a run for it. Juan entered the computer booth with George, sticking the gun into his ribs as soon as the attendant wasn't watching.

The professor, meanwhile, slipped into the next cubicle and began doing his own furious typing. Whatever message he was sending, it was energetic. George pulled up his e-mail account and tried to decide what to say.

"You are not writing a speech," Juan hissed. "Get on with it."

"It's hard to concentrate. Please put the gun away. If you make a mistake, I don't want to be smeared all over this computer terminal."

"The only mistake is you talking instead of writing," Juan said. "*Vamanos, muchacho.*"

George kept the e-mail as sparse as possible. He also attempted to use words that sounded unlike himself.

> Hubert, remember when you regaled me with tales of those you believed to be our kin? Especially a pirate? Being so close to the source of those tales, pray tell me more. I love history and wish to be fully informed. George Robert d'Hout.

Juan watched him compose the message and said nothing. As George went to push the "send" button, he was nudged with the pistol. "Now, creative writing time is over, *muchacho*. Cut the crap. You think I can't read English? You think we are new at this? Amateurs? Rewrite the message, keep it simple, and get it done."

George deleted the previous message and wrote,

> You told me about some famous family members. Want to know everything about the pirate d'Hout. Everything. Please write ASAP. George.

"Better," Juan said. "Now send."

George obeyed and watched the screen go back to his in-box. There were six messages from Carol. George ran the mouse over to log out, but he was again nudged in the ribs. "Carol wants to hear from you, George," Juan said. "Tell her you are doing good. Tell her you miss her."

"She will want to know why I haven't called."

"Tell her you are completely overrun with work and that you will call in one week."

"One week?" George thought. "So that's how long I have before they plan to kill me."

He followed the instructions, not answering any of the questions Carol had asked. He also didn't sign in his customary manner with the words "I love you," hoping that would also be a clue something was wrong.

Juan indicated to Professor Knight that they had completed the task. The professor also logged out, paid the attendant, and the foursome walked back to the park.

"Couldn't we have just used a computer or phone at the house?" George asked. "Doesn't this increase the chances I will escape?"

"There are no phone lines, cell phones, or computers at the house," the professor said. "No electronics in the house also means no prying eyes from service technicians. Nor will you have the opportunity to alert anyone by reaching a computer or phone when no one is watching. Mr. Ordóñez is very protective of his privacy. Whenever he adopts a new location, that is always directive number one."

"What's next?" George wanted to know.

"You hope your brother responds to the e-mail quickly," Juan said. They were back at the park and George was instructed to sit on the ground a few yards from the raging Yanuncay River. Juan idled a few feet from him, his right hand in his pocket. The professor was sitting on a tree stump. Miguel stood on a bridge about forty yards to George's right as he faced the river.

"Beautiful, don't you think?" the professor asked. "Makes a man forget his troubles. All the greenery, the power of the river, being in this valley surrounded by the Andes. Can you think of any other place you'd rather be?"

George thought about telling the professor where he wanted him to go, but changed his mind. Instead, he calculated his options. Knocking the gun from Juan's hand might work if the *muchacho* got close enough. The professor didn't seem all that strong or fast, but it was hard to tell. Juan, on the other hand, looked like a human jackrabbit. Even in George's current state of physical fitness, outrunning Juan might prove impossible.

Then there was Miguel. Outrunning him wouldn't be a problem, since the man was almost as wide as he was tall. Besides, wasn't Miguel his ally? After all, it was the Cañari who woke him to warn him about the danger he faced. However, when it came down to it, would Miguel be willing to possibly sacrifice his family and himself to let George get away?

The professor was staring at the river but addressed George. "Thinking about how to escape? Don't take your eye off the ball, George. You need to be using the full powers of that analytical mind to determine where the Orellana treasure is located. Look around. Drink it all in and then impress us. I know you can do it. You certainly impressed me when you knew the pirate d'Hout had composed his letter in Nassau."

George surveyed the scene, without a clue where the treasure was buried. *My family will know as surely as they know their own name.* Maybe a family crest held a clue. Or perhaps a coat of arms. George suggested that to the professor.

"If they held any clues, I would not have troubled you, George. You can do better."

"I don't even know for sure where we are or what I'm looking at," George said. "Give me a place to start."

Knight's face changed. The nice professor reemerged, spewing trivia like volcanoes spew lava. "Back that way, in Cajas National Park, is where the mighty Amazon's headwaters are located. You follow the Yanuncay another quarter of a mile or so, and it merges with the Tomebomba. A little past that the northernmost river, Milchichig, and the Tarqui all merge and flow toward the Amazon. This is where d'Hout and Davies came, thinking they would take a boat out of here. As you can see, that would not be possible on such rough waters."

George surveyed the surroundings. The river was maybe twenty yards wide, strewn with huge boulders. White water rushed and crashed its way along. Past the river, George looked at the neighborhood. "How old are these houses?" he asked. "They look pretty new."

"Keen eye," the professor said. "You are correct. This is the newer part of the city."

"So this isn't exactly where d'Hout and Davies were. Where was the city in 1687?"

"Over your right shoulder," Juan said. George turned and looked down Avenida Suarez. Colonial Cuenca sat at the top of a plateau like a sparkling jewel. The Tomebomba River flowed around it like pearls adorning a lovely neck. How had he not noticed it before now? He'd been so concerned with a possible route of escape, so consumed with the thought of being shot or of never seeing Carol again, that he hadn't looked up to see the gleaming colonial city on top of the mesa.

At the center of the colonial part of town, towering above all other buildings, were the three turquoise domes of the Cathedral of the Immaculate Conception. It seemed everywhere George looked there were church steeples.

"So the city was up there? Was that also where the Inca and Cañari cities were?"

"You are beginning to restore my faith in you, Mr. d'Hout," the professor said.

"Then why are we down here? If these pirates dumped the treasure way out of town in the middle of a field, we'll never find it. Seems more likely they were led into town and found some kind of a landmark to bury it by. Otherwise, how could they come back for it?"

"If you think you are going to escape in the bustle of the *cuidad centro*, the central city, you are very mistaken," the professor said. He waved at Miguel, who nodded back. Miguel then walked to the corner and made the motion to hail a cab. Instead of a cab, however, it was a private security vehicle with SEGURIDAD ECUADOR written on the door.

"What you see," Juan said, "is that Mr. Ordóñez has reserved for us the services of a private security firm. They will help make sure you do not escape. And these men are licensed by the government. Many of them are also on the payroll of the police department. It is such meager pay, however, that they must supplement their income with the very generous offerings a job like this provides."

Juan watched the effect his words had on George. "They carry shotguns. They have been told you are an American fugitive who was released into protective custody. You are here to help solve a crime of which you have direct knowledge. But you are a detestable human being who has hurt women and children. These men have never met you, but they do not like you very much, *muchacho.*"

The professor smiled. "What was that science fiction show? It had a line I liked very much…Ah, yes. 'Resistance is futile.'"

George felt a pang of hopelessness crash against him like a wave against the rocks. Just as quickly, he watched it retreat. He said, "You didn't watch the end of the show? The resistance won."

Juan stepped very close to George. The gun emerged from his pants pocket. With one quick motion, he used it to punch George in the ribs. George tried to catch his breath, but nothing happened. Juan smiled and leaned in close. To an onlooker, it appeared the Inca had just told a joke that made George double over in laughter.

The pain of the blow crystalized thoughts in George's mind. This wasn't a goof, a joke, a bad dream, or a situation that was simply going to work itself out. If George didn't do something drastic, he was going to die.

While still doubled over, trying to catch his breath, George felt another mouth close to his ear. The professor said, "I think sufficient time has passed for us all to take a little walk back to the Internet café. We will hope brother Hugh is on the ball with his response."

CHAPTER 17

Thursday, 9 January
2:15 p.m.

Hugh was trying to call Albert on his cell phone. At the same time, caller ID on his landline indicated Carol was trying to reach him. He quickly picked up the phone and held it to his left ear, while he pressed the cell phone to his right.

"You get one, too?" Hugh asked. Without waiting for her response, he said, "Something is really wrong. No question. I'm calling a federal agent who can help. I'll call you back in a second."

Before Hugh could hang up, he heard Carol say, "Make one other call as well. Pray!"

At that moment, he heard Albert's voice in his right ear. "Yes?"

"I just heard from George," Hugh explained, detailing word for word the content of the e-mail as well as specific ways it varied from what George might have written if he'd been left to his own accord. "It seems we're right. George has gotten tangled up with some bad characters. But these people have the wrong guy. George can't help them. Maybe I should go down there."

Albert spoke slowly and calmly. "Mr. d'Hout, that's not a good idea. They, George, and I need you right where you are. I can hear the distress in your voice, and I completely understand. But what you do next is crucial. Therefore, let's just slow down and talk about this."

The ICE agent asked Hugh, as quickly as possible, to compose an e-mail that included everything he could recall about the pirate George d'Hout but to send it to Albert's e-mail account, not George's.

Albert said, "After I have looked at it, I will call you back and tell you any changes you need to make. It may be that I will have you send the information just as it is. The main thing is this: don't, under any circumstances, intentionally or accidentally, send or forward your brother any of our correspondence. Make sure you send him a completely new e-mail. Are we clear?"

Hugh said he understood and got to work on what he could remember. He quickly accessed his files, a couple of websites he often used for research, as well as an online family tree he'd created.

He wrote,

> George d'Hout. Family name variously spelled Hout and Dhout. Birthplace: unknown. Ancestry: Dutch. Approximate year of birth: 1645.

The Ecuadorian Deception

> Approximate year of death: 1702. Prior to death, believed to have settled in Shillingstone, Dorset, England. Married. Wife: Eliza. Profession: privateer, pirate, buccaneer. Most noteworthy achievement: infamous for raid on Guayaquil, a port city in what is now Ecuador, 1687. Treasure never recovered. d'Hout disappeared. Whereabouts of treasure unknown. d'Hout possibly settled in Nassau for a short time before sailing for Dorset following Guayaquil incident. Family members also located in North Petherwin, Devonshire.

After a minute or two of consulting online sources, he added,

> Wife Eliza was believed to have had two children. One did not survive to adulthood. Surviving child (first name unknown) also a seaman. Eventually settled in Quebec, Canada. Descendants immigrated to U.S. via Michigan.

Hugh searched his memory to see if there was anything else known about their ancestor. He'd invested almost six years tracing their family tree back as far as the pirate. The research hadn't been easy. The family name was spelled in a variety of ways, including Hout, Dhout, Doubt, and—for some puzzling reason—Huff.

The occasional pronunciation of their last name as "doubt" had led his brother, George, at every opportunity to make a very private play on words, answering "doubtful" to questions. No one ever laughed, which was fine with George.

Hugh read over the information and hit "send." While he was waiting for a reply from Albert, he called Carol. "What did he write you?" he asked her.

"Nothing, really," she said. "Just saying he was doing fine. I know that's not true. Why would he say that? What's going on?"

Hugh recounted George's e-mail asking for information about their pirate ancestor, as well as his conversations with Van Williams at the FBI and with Albert Pujols, the ICE agent. He told her he was following Pujols's instructions. He also told her it was likely George had gotten involved with men conducting illegal activity regarding lost treasures.

"Should you get the American consulate in Guayaquil involved again?" Carol asked. "Do they have officers or agents who could look into it?"

"I don't think so," Hugh said. "They are there for diplomatic purposes and to do paperwork regarding visas. I think criminal investigations are out of their line of expertise."

As Hugh hung up after talking to Carol, an e-mail arrived from Pujols.

> What more information do you have about this lost treasure? Begin checking immediately. Remember to contact me first before sending on any information. Will continue working from this end.

Hugh copied and pasted the content of his original e-mail. He read it over and hit "send." Then he did what the ICE agent had requested. Researching the lost treasure, he reflected on what he'd earlier told Carol; Ecuador was as safe or possibly safer than the United States. He said to himself, "For George, that's doubtful."

Thursday, 9 January
2:48 p.m.

"It is a beautiful day," the professor said. "So beautiful, in fact, it would be a shame to waste it. Let's all stroll back to the Internet café and have a little look-see at what dear Hugh has sent."

"He might be at work," George said. "He might not be able to send anything until tonight. Or he might not even check e-mail if he's busy."

"That would be lost time, and your hourglass only has so much sand in it," the professor said.

Leaving the park and walking back to the Internet café, George saw the security patrol car a block away. It crawled along, keeping its distance, but always with a clear line of sight on the four men. Miguel meandered along, also a block away in the opposite direction. George watched as the Cañari reached down to pet a stray dog he saw napping on a sidewalk.

As they passed a small corner store, George said, "Can someone step in and buy me some water?"

"Let's all go in," Juan said. "Only you don't need water. You need something stronger. We will get three Pilseners. Water is for women."

The professor reached into his pocket and pulled out a handful of quarters to pay for the beers. As they left, George said, "I wanted water."

"Drink it," Juan said, "or I will lean in very close to you and tell you another funny story. Kind of hard to drink beer when that happens, yes?" Any pretext of kindness on Juan or Professor Knight's part was dissolving into gleeful sadism. George didn't need to provoke them. He wanted a bottle of water, not a confrontation. He held the bottle of cold beer to his mouth and took a sip.

As he took another drink, it occurred to him that the professor and Juan had made a tactical error. In their desire to force him to do something he didn't want to do, they'd provided him with a glass bottle. If they had given him water, it would have come in a harmless plastic container.

Now George drank the beer more quickly but slowed his pace to the Internet café. He was formulating a strategy. If he made a break for it, it had to be with some planning. He would get only one shot at escaping, so he couldn't be too hasty.

Juan almost ran into George when his stride slowed. Juan didn't have a free hand. One was in his pocket, holding the pistol. The other embraced his beer. He simply nudged George with the beer, sloshing some on d'Hout's clothes. "*Muchacho*, we aren't on a picnic. Get moving."

Now the idea of a glass bottle in his hand appealed to George. "This beer is pretty good," he said. "I like it."

"We will mention that at your funeral," Juan said. "Move it. *Vamanos.*"

George took a moment to glance out of the corner of his eye, trying to get a bearing on where Miguel and the security guards were. Nothing he did, however, seemed to escape the professor. "Yes, they are all still there," Knight said. "And you are still here."

Before they entered the Internet café, all three men finished their Pilseners. The professor dropped his empty bottle into a trash can just inside the door and gestured for George to do the same. "Not quite through," George said. "Good to the last drop and all that."

"You're not drinking coffee," the professor said. "And you're not keeping a glass bottle. How stupid do you think we are? Drop it in the trash." George complied.

Walking inside the Internet café, George noticed there were no other customers. The earlier ritual repeated itself. Miguel appeared after a couple of minutes to stand watch at the front door. Juan was in the booth with George. Knight worked furiously in the next one.

"Why doesn't the attendant notice how weird all this is?" George thought. "If she would look up every now and again, she would plainly see that something isn't right about this."

But the attendant didn't look up. Whatever she was doing on her own screen, it absorbed all her attention. George asked, "Can I please just call home for a minute and hear Carol's voice? I will even pay for the call. You can listen. I won't try anything. I want to get back home to her."

The professor thought for a moment and said, "You really love her, don't you?"

A mixture of loneliness, despair, and anger welled inside George. He didn't answer, but he did meet the professor's eyes, attempting to indicate he had no guile in his face, only a desire to speak to his wife.

"You know, love is a very powerful emotion," the professor said. "Look at Miguel. He doesn't care a thing about helping us. However, love for his wife and children has driven him to be a very able assistant. Are you going to be a very able assistant, George?"

"I have done everything you've asked," he replied.

"We really haven't asked very much of you so far," Professor Knight said. "Send one e-mail? Did you find that an imposition?"

George could tell the mercurial professor's anger was rising again.

"I didn't find it an imposition," George said. "I am doing what you ask. May I call my wife?"

"George," the professor said, "listen to yourself. I believe you are trying to use psychology on me. Being a university man myself, I have to appreciate that kind of tacit approach. Therefore, the answer is…no. Get in the booth and check your e-mail."

As George did, he found himself mentally stepping back. It was time to assess what set the professor off and what pleased him. Otherwise, as they moved closer to either finding the treasure or realizing it was a myth, chances were good that George would catch a bullet.

Thinking about it, he realized he needed to keep the conversation focused not on himself, but on the treasure. That would accomplish two purposes. First, talking about history and archaeology seemed to please Professor Knight. Second, it might provide George clues leading to discovery of its location.

And the professor indicated there might be an opportunity for George to "buy in" to the gang. If he could do that, he might find a way to reach the authorities and get help.

Inside the cramped booth, George pulled up his e-mail. Juan reached over to hit the "print" button. "Professor, there's a *respuesta*," Juan said. He reached over the clear wall of the booth and handed the page to Professor Knight, who pored over it.

"A very knowledgeable brother," he said. "Good. He'll be useful."

The professor stepped out of his booth and opened the door to the one George and Juan occupied. It felt comical to have three grown men inside one cramped booth. What a farce; but no one was laughing.

"Here is how you will respond," Professor Knight said. "You need to know everything your brother has learned about the treasure. Your ancestor wrote that your family would know its location as clearly as you know your own name. Where is that information kept?"

After George typed the message, he looked at Juan and the professor. They both nodded, so George hit "send."

"We will now pay for our time online and retire to the house," the professor said.

George piped up. He didn't have to fake his conviction. "No," he said. "We are here to find a treasure. We aren't going to find it at the house. I want to see the city. Not the new city but the city from 1687. If we are going to find this thing, let's find it."

Professor Knight searched George's face. "Why, Mr. d'Hout," he said, "I do believe you are coming on board with our little team. How delightful."

Thursday, 9 January
3:17 p.m.

Exiting the Internet café, Professor Knight walked over to Miguel and said something George couldn't make out. Miguel, in turn, walked a half block down the narrow street to the security vehicle. Whatever the professor had said, Miguel passed it on dutifully. The men in the vehicle gave a half wave to the professor, as did Miguel.

The security car rolled off in one direction, and Miguel headed in the other. Knight rejoined Juan and George. The professor said, "We are going to take advantage of this beautiful afternoon to walk down Avenida Suarez into *el centro*, the city center. But don't fear. Miguel and the gentlemen with all the guns will be watching. When we get to city central, we will stroll up the stairs to the top of the mesa. That will put us on *Calle Larga*, Long Street. It was once the southern boundary of the city. From there I will lay out for you Cuenca in 1687."

The professor looked for a long moment at George. "And wouldn't it be the nicest thing if you, in return, told me where the treasure was?"

"Yes, *muchacho*," Juan said, nudging George's bruised ribs. "Nice."

George thought, "If I get the chance, *muchacho*, I'm going to stick that gun where the sun doesn't shine and give it a good twist."

Aloud he said, "Nice. Absolutely."

Thursday, 9 January
3:20 p.m.

Albert Pujols closed his laptop and walked into the office of Consul General Vicente Noboa. The ICE agent knew things were tense among members of the diplomatic corps in Ecuador currently, and Noboa was unlikely to be an exception.

Recently information was leaked by someone to the Ecuadorian government that the US ambassador to Ecuador made private allegations of corruption among members of Ecuador's law enforcement community. Of course there was corruption. Everyone knew it. But you didn't want to get caught saying it. Getting caught made you persona non grata or PNG as diplomats and spies termed it. While a new ambassador had been installed and formal relations were on the mend, everyone attached to the diplomatic corps was on pins and needles, both to avoid further problems and to find out who leaked the information.

As Albert introduced himself, Noboa closed the door to his tiny office. Albert said, "I will try to be brief. I was sent down by the embassy in Quito. I've been working on a case involving the smuggling of Ecuadorian national treasures and antiquities out of the country for sale to collectors. What I am telling you is strictly confidential. Lives are at stake."

"Crap," Noboa thought. "Just what I don't need." He kept a poker face and said, "Really? Hmmm. I take it you have already informed the Guayaquil federal prosecutor you are in the area."

"That is the SOP," Albert said. It wasn't a yes or no. Just an acknowledgment of standard operating procedure.

Albert asked, "Do you know the name Roberto Ordóñez?"

"I don't think so."

"What about George d'Hout?"

"No, I haven't...wait. d'Hout? Isn't that the famous pirate?" Noboa thumbed through some papers on his desk. "And there was another man named d'Hout in here the other day. Said he wanted to buy a house. Was asking my opinion about certain neighborhoods."

"Which ones?"

"There were a number of them." Noboa kept shuffling through papers. "I told him we don't make recommendations like that. I suggested he contact a real estate broker."

"Was that it?"

"He showed me a map of the city. Had questions about specific addresses and areas."

Albert said, "Maps? Like that one on the wall behind your desk? Show me which areas and neighborhoods. I also need you to write them down for me."

"You know, I really try not to get involved..."

Albert smiled. He didn't have time to waste on a bureaucrat. "Here's the situation: that American floating in the river the other day; in all probability, he was killed by a criminal named Robert Ordóñez. When d'Hout came into your office, he wasn't trying to buy real estate. He was looking for Ordóñez, who he thought had stiffed him on a business deal. He had no idea how dangerous Ordóñez is."

"That wasn't very smart, was it? You don't go looking for trouble." Noboa smiled. A lot of smiles passing back and forth.

"Actually, I do," Albert said.

"You do what?"

"Go looking for trouble. It's my job."

More smiles.

"And I'm very smart. Hopefully smarter than this guy Ordóñez." Silence. Smiling back and forth. "Can you do it now?" Albert asked.

"What?"

"Make that list of neighborhoods d'Hout was asking about." Albert stood, turned toward the door, then back to Noboa. "I will be back in a couple of hours to pick it up, along with the address of that real estate broker."

Albert left the consulate and walked down the street to the hotel where George was registered. However, in Albert's line of work, walking never involved a direct path from point A to point B. Instead, he did a great deal of window-shopping along the congested streets, using reflections in the glass to check for anyone who might be following him. No apparent tails. Good. But you never know.

On the flight from Quito to Guayaquil, Albert had studied a map of the city. People standing on street corners reading maps stood out. Standing out was the last thing Albert wanted to do.

His impeccable Spanish, though carrying a definite Tex-Mex accent, helped him fit in. However, any prolonged conversation would lead an astute listener to ask him, *"¿De donde eres?"* Where are you from? His accent made it clear it wasn't Ecuador.

At the hotel, porters held open the double doors. One of them spoke to Albert in faltering English, meaning he instantly recognized Albert as a foreigner. Albert hated it when that happened.

He answered in Spanish, acting as if he wasn't sure what the man had said. Also in Spanish, he told the desk clerk he was looking for a friend of his, George d'Hout. The desk clerk responded that no one had seen Mr. d'Hout, though he was still checked in at the hotel.

Albert asked if it appeared George's things had been removed. The desk clerk summoned the manager. This time Albert took a different approach, saying George was both a friend and fellow employee.

"Then you must work for Señor Ordóñez," the manager said in Spanish. "But you have never been introduced to us. Odd."

"I am new to Señor Ordóñez's employment," Albert said.

The manager seemed surprised. "Then your timing is perfect," he said, "since Señor Ordóñez is at this very moment upstairs having coffee in the hotel's restaurant."

CHAPTER 18

Thursday, 9 January
4:30 p.m.

Hugh was chomping at the bit to dive into his files, both electronic and paper, on the pirate d'Hout. However, no sooner had he gotten off the phone with ICE Agent Pujols than his wife, Brenda, called.

"Your brother has disappeared in South America, and you didn't let me know?" Brenda asked. "Were you going to wait until I read it in the Pittsburgh paper?"

"Sorry, hun," Hugh said. "Hopefully Carol told you I called in the Mounties. I got Van Williams on the line, and he connected me with an ICE agent."

"ICE Agent? Is that something you made up? It sounds like something from a GI Joe movie."

"They're real," Hugh assured her. "The guy won't tell me where he is, but I'm pretty sure he's stationed somewhere in South America. I can't prove it. Just a feeling. Besides, there is something about the background noise when I talk to him. I haven't nailed it down, but it definitely isn't domestic."

Brenda said, "You're the one who ought to be the secret agent. You really think this is going to be okay?"

"I honestly don't know. And I will head down there if I need to. I already offered, but Albert Pujols told me to man the computer here."

"Albert Pujols? Like the baseball player? You're pulling my leg."

"Same name, different guy," Hugh assured her, "and he's given me some research I need to do. Time is of the essence, so I'm going to let you go."

After telling Brenda he loved her, Hugh hung up and dug in. Following 9/11, when the CIA was ramping up its international espionage units, Hugh had considered applying for a job. Research and jigsaw puzzles were his two favorite hobbies. What more could a good spy need? Apparently to be ten years younger.

Hugh realized he was too old to be hired for such a position. He explained to Brenda, "The federal government passed anti-age discrimination legislation, but one of the few employers to whom it doesn't apply is the federal government. No wonder there are so many people fed up with Washington."

No time to think about that now. It was crucial to find clues that might liberate George from his captors. Within an hour,

Hugh had numerous electronic files open. Even more paper files were scattered across the desk and floor of his home office.

He began frantically typing notes that could quickly be copied, first in an e-mail to Albert and then to George.

> The pirate d'Hout learned of treasure from a former slave named Manuel Boso.
>
> Boso learned of it while in the service of an official in Guayaquil.
>
> Boso sent to slave auction. While on board ship, liberated by pirates.
>
> Attack on Guayaquil: April 1687.
>
> Three hundred pirates vs. 200-man defense force.
>
> Leaders of Guayaquil had previously hidden treasure.
>
> While waiting for the city to be ransomed by authorities in Quito, d'Hout "persuaded" locals to reveal location of treasure. Also learned about Orellana's route from Atlantic to Guayaquil via the Amazon.
>
> Spanish *audiencia* paid the ransom, fearing the pirates would kill every person in Guayaquil if they didn't.
>
> Edward Davies and George d'Hout left Guayaquil, hostages in tow, to try and learn if ransom was forthcoming.

A few days later, it was realized that Orellana's treasure was commandeered by d'Hout and Davies and their Indian hostages. The two men and their hostages disappeared.

Rest of pirates finally abandoned city with 100 sacks of flour and 10,000 pesos.

Under new leadership, they vowed to kill d'Hout and Davies when they found them.

The new pirate leadership had them separate and go different ways to (1) search for the missing treasure and (2) work to evade Spanish warships, which were heading that way to rescue the city.

Conjecture: Since Orellana left via the rivers feeding the Amazon, it makes sense Davies and d'Hout would attempt same route. Would explain why neither pirates nor Spanish ships found any sign of them.

Thursday, 9 January
4:51 p.m.

The walk into the colonial section of Cuenca had been fascinating, in spite of the circumstances. Or maybe because of them. George drank in history as if his very life depended on it. Where would pirates hide a treasure?

Along the street called Calle Larga, George marveled at the huge Banco Central building, which sat squarely on top of the ancient Cañari and Inca site forming Cuenca's foundation. A large archaeological park was behind the bank. George, Juan, and the professor examined it from outside an iron fence.

The remains of the Incan village sat on a terraced hill. The professor explained that the most important military and government officials had lived at the top. Below that was an area known as the Fourth Level. Carved into the hillside was a huge Incan graveyard, where the top echelon of society had been placed for their journey to the afterlife.

Below that, along the terraced hills, were the merchants and farmers. On the lowest rung, figuratively and literally, were the workers who tended fields of cabbage, squash, corn, beans, and a variety of medicinal plants. Past that were all manner of fruit trees including mango, avocado, oranges, and limes.

"Is this really the way it looked when the Incas ruled?" George asked.

"Very close," the professor said. "Very close."

"Those trees, they seem very manicured. The whole thing is more like a garden than a working farm. Tell me how it would have been different in the Inca period," George said.

"See those men over there?" Professor Knight said, pointing to several gardeners. "They are Incas. Slender, strong nose; distinct profile."

"It is a regal look, *muchacho*," said Juan, who stood nearby, preening just a little. George pretended not to notice.

Knight continued. "In all probability, they are working the very same land their ancestors have worked for hundreds of years. The only difference is who is at the top of the hill calling the shots. It was the Cañari, then the Incas, then the Spaniards. Now it is the bank."

George looked through the bars. "What is that area over there in the grove of trees where those ladies are kneeling?"

The professor said, "Some religious something or another, probably dedicated to the Virgin Mary. The priests who accompanied the conquistadors into this land did a very thorough job. The Indians converted from their pagan ways, or they were killed. So today Ecuador is ninety-five percent Catholic. And they are very pious. You can just see a statue of the Virgin Mary in that niche in the stone wall. It dates back to the earliest days of the Spanish occupation. It is still venerated. Outside of the churches, that is one of the most revered places in Cuenca...for the superstitious."

George looked past the Incan ruins to the modern bank at the top of the hill. A dozen guards wearing body armor toted automatic weapons, shotguns, and more gadgets on their belts than Batman. "Those bank guards preparing for war?" George asked.

It was not just the way the guards were outfitted that caught George's eye; it was also the sheer number of them, as if they knew someone was about to wage war on the institution.

"Have you not heard?" Juan said. "It is rumored there are bad people in Ecuador—people who steal and shoot and kill. They are just being careful. When there is a bank robbery in Cuenca, it is a—what you call?—humdinger."

Juan thought that was funny. George had two thoughts that weren't funny at all. The first—he could try to get the little group as close as possible to the bank guards, then drop to the ground and scream like crazy that there was a robbery. Then he would count the seconds to see how long it took for a bullet to strike him. Surely Juan would pull his pistol and be killed, but probably not before he murdered George.

The second thought he voiced. "So what if the treasure is buried under that building? For that matter, it could be hidden under any of these buildings." He pointed down the long street leading into the heart of the city.

The professor didn't look where George was pointing. Instead, he watched the bank guards the way a rat watches a hawk. "Then I will personally be very disappointed, as this will appreciably diminish my standing with Roberto Ordóñez, and his patronage is very important. And Juan will be disappointed. The last time Juan was disappointed, someone died. Miguel will be disappointed because he knows until we find this treasure, he will not get his family back."

George was growing weary of the professor's bombasts. Unaware of George's irritation, or perhaps egged on by it, he continued. "Your wife will be disappointed because you will be dead. And, as a final bit of icing on a very disappointing cake, I can promise you one of us will go to all the trouble of traveling to the United States to find your brother Hugh, and we will kill him, too. That means his family will be disappointed. So let us hope your very negative thinking about this entire situation does not pan out."

Juan chimed in. "*Muchacho*, if I am disappointed, I will kill you slow. I learned with Edward Davies not to let my temper get the best of me. There is no suffering that way. Just—poof—you are dead. What fun is that? No matter how disappointed I am, I will kill you extra slow to make up for hurrying too much on Davies."

The thought of his wife back in the United States, no doubt worried out of her mind, along with the threat against Hugh, sent a wave of anger and sadness through George like an electric charge. He worked to refocus on the treasure. "Professor, if you were attempting to narrow down the locations, based on what you know, where would you think is most likely?"

It was not the right thing to ask. "If I knew where it was," the professor said, moving very close to George, "I wouldn't need you, would I?" He was suddenly angry, nearly spitting the words. It was enough of a display that the bank guards, who were half a block away, even took an interest.

"I'm trying to help," George said. "You know this isn't my thing. But I'm trying to help and…"

Juan also moved in close. There wasn't much foot traffic on the street, but George thought those who were around might finally be noticing that something didn't seem quite right. They looked twice, then looked away. One man didn't look away quickly enough, and Juan gave him a withering glare. Then Juan turned back to George and was less than an inch from his ear.

"*Muchacho*, you shut up," Juan said. "You think but don't speak. He turned to Knight. "Professor, this is all a ruse to draw attention or find a way to escape. Let's walk him back to the house."

"I have a better idea," Professor Knight said. He signaled to Miguel, who had noticed the momentary commotion from his post a block away. The professor held up his index finger and made a circling motion. Miguel nodded.

The Cañari man, in turn, jogged off, and in a moment the security vehicle made an appearance, slowly rolling down the street toward Juan, the professor, and a concerned George.

Dark clouds were rolling toward Cuenca from the mountains. A large storm was building. George could see lightning in the distance and hear the cannon-shot thunder beginning to march toward the city.

When the security car pulled up, Knight instructed, "*Dale a mi amigo un paseo.*" The guard in the passenger seat sprang from the vehicle, opened the back door, and shoved George inside. The security officer climbed in after George, elbowing him hard to move over.

Two women who bore every indication that they were American tourists turned a corner and witnessed what was going on. George heard one say, "Do you think that man is okay? What are they doing to him?"

George considered yelling for help. However, he feared if he did, the outcome would be his death, along with that of both innocent tourists. The professor's demeanor suddenly made a 180-degree turn that startled George.

"Ladies," he called out, "I am with the embassy in Quito. These policemen are helping us apprehend a criminal who is wanted in the United States and here in Ecuador. I'm sorry you had to see that. Have a very profitable day."

As the security car sped away, George watched the two women hurrying off, flushed with excitement, because they had witnessed the apprehension of what they thought was an international criminal. As the car turned a corner, George saw Miguel walking up to Juan and the professor. Then they were out of sight. The storm clouds continued to build, turning the day from blue to gray.

The two security guards were speaking in a quick, clipped Spanish. Whatever they were discussing, George was pretty sure it wasn't good. He looked at the door, noticing the knob on the old-fashioned manual lock had been removed. Past it, the sky was as dark and roiling as his emotions. Were they taking him out to be executed?

George thought about Carol and wished he could hold her. He was greatly relieved their faith taught that death was not the end.

The driver looked at George in his rearview mirror. "*Muy mal*," he said.

George knew those words. "Very bad." To what was the security guard referring? Him? The professor? Something that had happened or something that was going to happen?

The guards had the same sadistic smiles George had seen on Juan. Apparently they were a prerequisite for getting hired by Roberto Ordóñez. George watched to see where they would go. It appeared they were driving in circles or just cruising residential neighborhoods. All the houses, from the richest to the poorest, sat behind large walls or fences of barbed wire.

As melancholy gripped George, a taxi pulled up beside them. Juan, the professor, and Miguel were inside. Apparently those in the security vehicle had been killing time, waiting for the three men to catch a cab. The taxi pulled in front of the security vehicle, and the two cars motored back to the bridge by the Yanuncay River.

When they reached the park, both cars pulled over to the curb. Professor Knight stepped out of the taxi. He glanced around, then walked up to the passenger door of the security team. He was smiling. Maybe his anger had subsided in the intervening minutes.

"Doubtful," George thought. Large drops of rain were falling, but no one seemed to notice.

"Get out very slowly," the professor said. "You have been a bad boy. And bad boys don't get their supper."

"What are you talking about? I did everything you asked. I…" George felt a sharp jab in his hip. He turned to see the security guard holding a syringe, the contents of which had just been deposited through George's running pants.

"Maybe going through the clothes, it didn't completely get me," George thought. It was the last thought he had that night. The world went black.

CHAPTER 19

Friday, 10 January
7 p.m.

Hugh was beside himself. He hadn't heard from George or the ICE agent Albert Pujols in over twenty-four hours. Calls to Albert's number went straight to voice mail. Both Carol and Brenda were calling frantically, wanting updates. Several times during the day, Carol insisted that Hugh call Van Williams, seeking his advice about what to do.

Hugh begged off, saying he was going to give Albert time to do his job. Staring at his laptop, Hugh thought his powers of telepathy must be improving. A message popped up from George's e-mail address.

> Hey, *muchacho*, we never know how much more time we have. I am dying to know something

very important...Our pirate said family members would know the location of the treasure *as surely as we know our own name*. What does that mean? Not much time to get an answer right. Very important. George.

"Muchacho?" Hugh said aloud. "What's George been smoking? There's no way he wrote this. 'Our pirate'? George wouldn't call him 'our pirate.'" Clearly, someone else was accessing George's e-mail. That meant George wasn't around to compose the letter himself. Was he dead? A hostage?

Hugh dialed Van Williams's home number. When Van answered, Hugh said, "This thing is accelerating, and I don't know what to do. Someone is e-mailing me and claiming to be George, but it's not him. The way the e-mail is written, everything about it, says it's a fake. I've tried calling Albert, but he's not picking up. He could be on another case, but I truly believe my brother's life is hanging in the balance. What do I do?"

Van slowed Hugh down and asked him to recount the events since they last spoke. He asked him to be very clear about exactly what had been said during discussions with Albert. Van said, "I want you to forward me all the e-mails. I'm going to make a couple of calls. Stay by your phone, and I'll get back to you."

First, Van called his supervisor, the special agent in charge of West Texas, to bring him up to speed on what had started out as some help for a friend. It now appeared to be something more.

The supervisor reminded Van that come Monday, this little episode was going to earn him a lot of extra paperwork. "Thanks," Van said. "If we can get this George d'Hout out of Ecuador alive, it will be worth it. By the way, Congress is always telling us we need more interagency cooperation. Does this count?"

"Get this guy back alive, and we'll talk about it," his supervisor said.

Locating the after-hours number for the embassy in Quito wasn't easy, but Van finally waded through all the protocols and got someone with authority on the line. He identified himself as an FBI agent and explained he was concerned about the welfare of an ICE agent on temporary duty in South America.

"Of course, I can't say if Mr. Pujols is known to us," the voice on the other end of the phone said. "I'm also not in a position to comment on any case to which he might currently be assigned."

"I understand that," Van said, "but there's got to be someone who can get a message to him."

"I will give you the number of someone who could possibly help. Tell him what you told me and explain that this is time sensitive."

The voice gave Van the cell number for Vicente Noboa, an employee in the consular office in Guayaquil. The first two times Van called, it went to voice mail. Van texted the number with a simple message:

FBI. Top priority. Pick up.

He called back, and on the first ring, a mildly annoyed voice said, "It is after hours. I will be happy to talk to you Monday. I get into the office at—"

Van interrupted. "You are about to have more American bodies floating in the Guayas River." He identified himself and explained he had previously talked to the embassy in Quito. "I'm trying to get a message to a man named Albert Pujols."

Noboa said Pujols had briefly come in the office on Thursday, asking some questions. Noboa suggested that the ICE officer could be anywhere, since Guayaquil had a very energetic nightlife, and it was the weekend. "He's probably up at one of the little places on Cerro Santa Ana," Noboa said. "Are you in-country? You should really check out—"

"Where do you think Agent Pujols is? Where was he heading after he left your office?"

Noboa suggested that either the real estate broker, to whom he'd referred George d'Hout, or the hotel where d'Hout had been staying were better targets for these questions.

"We have a situation," Van said. "I need you to go to that hotel and find out if Albert is or was there."

"This is not my line of work," Noboa protested. "I'll give you the numbers and let you call them yourself."

"Unfortunately, my Spanish isn't up to where I could competently do that. Therefore, I'm relying on you."

Noboa let out a guttural, exasperated sound.

"Just find out if he went there. Also, see if you can get the real estate broker on the line. Find out if she's seen him. Be extremely casual, but find out what's going on. If you locate Albert, have him call me immediately. He knows the number."

"Do you have the agent's cell number?" Noboa asked. "Why can't you call him yourself?"

"His phone is off or out of commission. Otherwise, I wouldn't be bothering you."

Noboa said something in Spanish that sounded like he was swearing. Van said, "If I haven't heard from you in two hours, I'm going to call back to Quito and tell them you aren't cooperating. At least two lives are at stake, including Agent Pujols. Feel free to call the embassy and get their permission, but once again, this is important."

Friday, 10 January
8:40 pm

Noboa and his wife were hosting a dinner party for several prominent Guayaquil couples. He made his apologies and excused himself with a promise to return promptly. He drove through the evening traffic to the street named 9 de Octubre. He left his keys with the bellman, walked inside the hotel, and asked to speak to the manager on duty.

He described Albert and asked for help quizzing all persons on duty. Had any of them seen him in the last twenty-four hours? "He is new here and has gotten lost," Noboa said. "He has a very important family. They are insisting we check on him."

"He has important friends, too," the manager said in Spanish. "One of them is Roberto Ordóñez. He came in yesterday while Señor Ordóñez was here for a meeting. He asked if Señor Ordóñez had been around. He was also asking about your Mr. d'Hout."

"And?"

"We told him that as it turned out, Señor Ordóñez was in the dining room at that very moment."

"What happened?"

"He said he would be back in a bit but had an errand to run first. However, another associate of Señor Ordóñez, a Señor Pacheco, overheard the conversation and insisted they go see Señor Ordóñez at once. So both men joined him in the restaurant."

"Did this man I am seeking leave with Señor Ordóñez?"

"They talked for a very long time, and then they left. It seemed there was some strain between them. Several times your man tried to leave, but apparently the others wanted everyone to depart at the same time. If they come back, do you want me to contact you?" the manager asked.

"That won't be necessary," Noboa said, "as long as we know he is safe and in good hands. I will file my report. And please do not disturb any of them regarding this incident. They are important men and might be angry with us if we interrupted their get-together."

Noboa walked into the humid evening. He was sweating profusely. He was not cut out for this kind of work. He walked down the street and rounded the corner, pulling up short and taking out his cell phone.

"*Soy Vicente Noboa,*" he said. "*Necesito hablar con el Señor Ordóñez.*" Though it happened from time to time, Noboa hated getting involved in these kinds of situations. And someone would pay for making him get involved in this one.

Friday, 10 January
9:25 p.m.

Roberto Ordóñez and his new friend sat at the large square table with Professor William Knight at the house in Cuenca. In a few minutes Juan Pacheco joined them; he had been taking care of "personal business" at a nearby Internet café. Miguel watched the scene from the kitchen.

Albert, still groggy from the stab of a hypodermic needle back in Guayaquil, looked down at his hands, which were tied to the arms of the chair.

"I believe we have been very civil to this point," Ordóñez said in Spanish. "However, my patience is reaching an end. Why were you looking for me and for George d'Hout?"

"It's all very simple, as I told you before. I work for the embassy in Quito. We had a missing person's report, and I am running it down. However, you are getting yourself into some hot water. You drugged me, brought me here, took my phone, and are holding me against my will. All I want is to find Mr. d'Hout and leave."

"You told the hotel people you worked for Señor Ordóñez," Juan said. "That's not just looking for a missing American. That's looking for trouble. So you found it. And you are about to find a bullet if you don't tell Señor Ordóñez what he wants to know."

At that moment, there was a loud clanking on the iron gate outside the front door. Everyone inside involuntarily jumped.

Juan reached for his pistol. Miguel looked out the front window. "It is my next-door neighbors," he assured everyone. "That's all."

"Go out and speak to them," Ordóñez said. "Juan, go with him. Make sure everything is very friendly and that they go on their way without the slightest hint of trouble."

The gate clanked again, and Miguel and Juan opened the front door and went outside. Turning back to Albert, Ordóñez said, "If you know who I am, as you apparently do, you also know people who cross me have a way of disappearing. You were very foolish to—" There was a buzzing sound. Ordóñez looked at the professor.

"Not mine," he said. "I know your rules about cell phones and electronics. You packing?"

Ordóñez pulled a phone from his pocket and laid it in front of Knight. "Answer it."

The professor did as instructed, listening for a moment, but saying nothing. Then he handed the phone back to Ordóñez. "It's important."

Ordóñez took the phone and listened. "Yes, he is here with us now. Yes, the situation is under control. Thank you for letting me know. I don't believe any more will come of this. We should resolve it all tonight. Yes, you will be well compensated for your consideration. Thank you." Ordóñez hung up. He looked at Juan, who was coming back inside. "What did the neighbors want?"

"Said they hadn't seen Miguel's wife and kids for a while. Wanted to catch up on family business. Just chitchat. They invited Miguel and me to join them for a cookout on their patio."

"I believe you both will be otherwise occupied," Roberto said. "We need to dispose of this man. People are looking for him."

"It turns out a lot of people who disappear have fallen into the river," Juan said. "You a good swimmer, Mr. Busybody?"

The professor said, "Are we going to use the tunnel? We certainly can't take him out the front door. Not with the next-door neighbors out there."

Roberto said, "Juan, get Miguel back in here. Have him go down into the tunnel and make sure Mr. d'Hout is not in the way when we come down. We will then exit through the hatch to the river, and our friend will get a swimming lesson."

"Look," Albert said. "Okay, so I stretched the truth a little. I was just trying to find this guy. You just said he was downstairs. Let me have him, and we will take off. No questions asked."

"There are already too many questions being asked," the professor said. "But very soon, you won't be one of those asking them." Knight turned to Ordóñez. "You have his phone? If he's some type of law enforcement, they can trace it."

"Already taken care of. It was disposed of in Guayaquil. If they look for him, the signal will lead them there."

"And our guy at the consulate knows what to say if more people come looking?"

"Shut up, you idiot," Ordóñez barked.

"It's not a problem," Knight insisted. "Who's he going to tell? This guy is on a one-way trip to the Amazon via the Yanuncay River."

Miguel and Juan reentered the front door. Miguel closed it behind him. He fiddled with the lock so it rattled but left it unbolted, hoping no one noticed. Ordóñez told him to go downstairs and check on d'Hout.

Miguel entered the bedroom, opened the trap door in the closet, and descended the ten steps. George was down there, bound and lying against a wall. He squinted at the light streaming in from above. Then Miguel turned on the string of lights leading down the tunnel to the river. George turned his eyes from the glare of the naked bulbs.

Looking back up to make sure no one was near the trap door, Miguel leaned in close to George and said, "There is a man trying to find you. They have him and are going to kill him. There is nothing I can do about that. But while they are taking care of him, I am going to help you get free. You must run with all your might. If you are caught, it will mean my death, too, and the death of my family. I cannot risk that. We will make it look like you surprised me. But if you are caught, I will have to kill you myself. I don't want to, but you must understand. It is my family."

Miguel reached for the sword Professor Knight had shown d'Hout earlier, releasing it from its scabbard. George fell back.

"No," the Cañari whispered, "I'm not going to stab you. I am moving this so it is close by. It is how they will think you got free. Then they will blame the professor and not me. Be ready to go at a moment's notice."

Heading back up the steps, Miguel went to assure Roberto the way was clear to bring their guest down through the tunnel and to the river.

George had a pleading look on his face. His hands and feet were bound, but there was also a chain around his waist. "What about the chain?" George whispered.

"It's run around your waist and fastened in the back, but it's not locked. I did it myself. At the proper time, you will just unhook it."

"What's going on down there?" Juan called from the large room.

"I told the gringo to stop talking to me. That is all."

At the table, Juan reached over and cut loose the binding on Albert's wrists. The agent stood up, rubbing his hands. "You don't have to do this," he said.

Roberto responded, "In that case, I guess we better reconsider. Professor, what do you think?" Knight laughed.

"And you, Juan? Do you think we have to do this?" By way of answer, Juan reached out, grabbed Albert by the shoulders, and suddenly pulled them together. As he did, the Inca raised a knee and lowered his forehead, so he slammed into both Albert's crotch and head at the same time.

Albert crumbled back onto the floor. The ICE agent's face was covered in blood and he gasped to breathe. "Sorry, Señor Ordóñez, but I just had to do it," Juan said. He watched Pujol's obvious pain. It made him laugh. . "How you doing, *muchacho*? Did that feel good? Want one more?" He raised a foot to kick Albert, but one look from Roberto made him lower it just as suddenly.

"Your point is made," Ordóñez said. "He must be able to walk. It is quite a little stroll through the tunnel and to the bridge. Now, Miguel, get this man a towel to wipe the blood before too much more gets on your wife's lovely floor. Speaking of lovely, how is your wife these days?"

Juan laughed again. "Hope you were watching this, you Cañari dog. If you ever think about crossing us, remember this could have been your little wife getting this. You cross us, and the next time you speak to her, it will be standing over her grave. But she won't be lonely, *muchacho*. Your daughters will be there, too."

Miguel's hands began to clench and unclench. The veins in his thick neck stood out. "You wish to say something, *muchacho*?" Juan asked.

For a moment, Miguel met Juan's stare, but then he bent his head and focused on the floor. He turned and walked into the kitchen, picked up two towels and walked back, kneeling in front of Albert's blood-covered face.

His vision still blurred, Albert felt something touch him. He grabbed the towel and curled into a fetal position, expecting another blow at any second.

"Please, Mr. Embassy Man," Roberto said. "We are not animals. Well, actually Juan is a bit of an animal. Nonetheless, we need you to get up. We are going on a little hike."

Miguel helped the agent to his feet. Albert staggered a bit and tried to focus his eyes. He took longer to do this than he really needed, though the pain racking his body was quite real. Stumbling, he looked at each of the men's shoes, then up a bit toward their belts to see who had a gun or knife.

Only Juan seemed to be carrying a weapon. The Inca was standing a few feet away, flexing his muscles like he might strike again at any time. His face was a mask of sadistic pleasure.

While wiping his own face, Albert glanced at Knight and Ordóñez. Both were dangerous in their own ways, but neither one appeared to be a particular physical threat. So it was Juan whom Albert must concentrate on when he made his move. After what had just happened, he was happy to focus on Señor Pacheco.

Roberto Ordóñez led the way to the bedroom as if he were leading a parade. Then he disappeared down the steps, followed by the professor, Albert, Juan, and finally Miguel.

Ordóñez said, "Juan, if the river is loud enough, feel free to deposit a bullet in his forehead. On second thought, put it under his jaw and shoot it up through his brain, so if he is eventually found, the authorities will wonder if it was a suicide. If the river is running quietly, simply incapacitate him and throw him in. Just make sure he is unconcious, so he drowns before coming to."

Juan smiled at Albert and pushed him ahead. "You love your work, *muchacho*? I love mine. Yes I do. And I'm going to love all over you before your swimming lesson." He pushed Albert again, who landed against a wall. The ICE agent put a bloody hand against the wall, attempting to get as much blood on it as possible. If he were unable to escape, at least he'd be leaving his DNA on this wall. Should the house ever be raided, it would provide proof he was here and evidence against his killers.

The group descended the steps into the underground tunnel. Albert held onto the towel and kept dabbing his face, trying to clear his eyes and look for any chance to escape. When he reached the bottom of the steps, which he very nearly fell down due to the intense pain still racing through his body, he noticed a man in a corner, hands and feet bound.

"So this is who I'm dying for?" he asked. "Can I at least see him for a second?"

"That won't be necessary," Knight said. "Keep walking."

Ordóñez led the group to the end of the tunnel. He stepped aside and gave Juan room to open the hatch leading to the secret entrance under the bridge. As Juan released the hatch, Albert suddenly bent over in agony. He shrieked, "My kidneys! I think you burst one!" Knight and Ordóñez stepped back to assess the situation. "Dear God! You busted a kidney! Ahh!"

The screaming filled the tunnel and made each man wince. Knight covered his ears and looked away. Juan reached to grab the agent and yank him through the opening. "In a few moments, your kidneys won't bother you ever again."

When Juan got within striking distance, Albert uncoiled both fists into the Inca's throat, knocking him backward. The gun fell from Juan's hand and clanked out the opening, landing somewhere under the bridge. At the same moment Albert screamed, "Get down! Gun!"

Ordóñez and Knight involuntarily ducked before they had time to realize it was a ruse. Albert reached up and yanked the string of lights loose, making the tunnel go black. He shoved Juan into the wall of the tunnel as hard as he could, then grabbed his hair and smashed him into it again.

Diving out the opening, Albert had no time to form a plan, no time to think. His body still ached, but his life depended on getting away. He sprinted to the left, running hard. The river's roar was so loud; he had no idea how close his pursuers were or if they were shooting at him.

Roberto pushed the professor out of the way and stepped around a dazed Juan to exit the tunnel. He looked to see which way Albert was running. Sticking his head back into the tunnel, Roberto screamed for Miguel. After a moment or two, the Cañari appeared. "Where were you? Never mind. Take my phone! Call our security people. I want three cars, two officers in each. Now!"

Along the river, Albert was scrambling through knee and waist tall grass, ducking and clambering first to the left and then to the right in case the men behind him were firing. He ran for what seemed like two or three hundred yards when suddenly he saw a police car, or perhaps a private security patrol, come skidding around a corner to his left, lights flashing. The car slid to a stop by the park, and two men jumped out, each holding a shotgun.

Albert dove into some tall grass, then raised his still-bloody head to see which way the uniformed men were going to come. He prayed they didn't cut him off. Then another car, another few hundred yards ahead, made any hope of evading these patrols impossible. The uniformed men all ran toward the river.

Albert looked to his right. The river, even in the darkness, was an angry mass of white water and fury. Behind him was Juan, and to the left and ahead of him were the armed men. No choice. He said a two-word prayer and jumped into the river. "God, help!" he cried as he fell.

CHAPTER 20

Friday, 10 January
8:26 p.m.

Noboa called Van Williams. "Here is what I know," he said. "Albert Pujols went to the hotel. I believe Roberto Ordóñez was at the hotel at the same time. Employees of the hotel said they visited for a few minutes. Very congenial. Then your Albert Pujols walked out of the hotel, telling everyone he was going back to Quito."

"Quito?" Van asked. "I don't think so. You said he told everyone. Who is everyone?"

"Look, this isn't my line of work. I left a dinner party at my home to find this out for you, though it is none of my business."

"The welfare of an American agent in the city to which you are assigned is none of your business? Again, who did he tell he was going back to Quito?"

"I don't know who he told. I am only repeating what the manager of the hotel said."

Van's years of experience with the FBI told him something was fishy about Noboa's story. However, he also knew Noboa was on the verge of hanging up on him. If that happened, he would be left completely in the dark.

"You're right," Van said. "I appreciate all you've done. I will make sure the people at the embassy in Quito know you went above and beyond."

"*Usted es muy amable*," Noboa said. "You are very kind. I'm sure you will be getting a report on the agent very soon." Noboa hung up.

Van, who thought he was very good at noticing small details, kept the phone to his ear, though the line was now dead. Noboa's last comment replayed in his mind. *You will be getting a report on the agent. On* the agent? Why not *from* the agent?

Friday, 10 January
10:41 p.m.

Slender, but not in particularly good shape, Knight huffed along the sidewalk near the river in the general direction he thought Pujols had gone. Roberto soon overtook him. Knight said, "If he follows the river, he could go for miles. He mustn't get past our men down there. Do you think he has Juan's gun?"

Ordóñez held up a pistol. "I have Juan's gun. And I will have Juan's hide if this man gets away." The thought of Albert's escape caused both men to pause and consider options.

"I am not worried that we will fail to find him." Roberto tried to assure the professor. "However, to be on the safe side, you are to prepare our package in the basement for shipping to our location in Bolivia. Also, you and Juan must be ready to move to Bolivia as well."

"And you?"

"As always, the less you know of my whereabouts, the better for all of us."

Miguel came up behind Ordóñez. "Your security team is arriving," the small, stocky Cañari reported. "Six guards in three vehicles."

"I see that," Roberto said. "You are turning into a very reliable assistant. But right now, the future hinges on finding this American agent. And we must make sure we don't fail. Go."

A movement behind him caught Roberto's attention. Juan was struggling along, his head as bloody as Albert's had been. He bent over to catch his breath. "It appears you were bested," Roberto said, dumping salt onto Juan's wounded ego.

"I will kill this man," Juan said. He wiped blood from below his left eye and reached down to rub it onto some grass.

"What you will do," Roberto corrected him, "is what I tell you to do."

Juan declined to make eye contact. Instead, he stared down the river. "Sure. Whatever you tell me. And what is that?"

Friday, 10 January
10:49 p.m.

Albert shivered in the tall grass near a cottonwood tree on the far side of the river. The water had been ice cold, but he managed to cross it without getting swept away. How? Nothing less than a miracle, Albert thought. He looked at the water, a raging, angry white foam of roaring fury. A miracle, no doubt. The water also cleared the agent's head and washed away most of the blood.

Past the river and across the park, Albert saw the security guards, backlit by houses. One of those houses was the one where George d'Hout was still a prisoner, but Albert didn't know which one. He was unconscious when brought to the house and only awoke to find himself tied to a chair at the large table covered with maps.

Clouds covered the moon, making it hard for the security guards to see. They avoided turning on their flashlights. The ICE agent suspected that meant two things. First, they were concerned with not drawing attention to their activities from Miguel's neighbors. Second, they were not absolutely sure he didn't have some sort of weapon. Men in the dark carrying flashlights made very easy targets.

Then another thought occurred to Albert. It could also mean they were operating with night vision goggles. If that was the case, he was a sitting duck. He wiped blood away from his eyes and dismissed the thought in favor of more hopeful options.

Though he'd worked hundreds of operations in his twenty-two-year career, this was the closest Albert had come to having the bad guys blow him away. And he wasn't out of the woods yet.

He moved from the cottonwood to an even larger cypress tree along the banks of the Yanuncay River. Maybe two hundred yards away on the other side of the river were the vague outlines of four men. The rushing water concealed Albert's heavy breathing and shivering as he looked for a route of escape. His legs and arms were scraped and bruised from where he had skittered, almost like a water bug, across the river, working to stay on top and not get pulled under by the sucking power of the rapids.

How had he made it? Looking back into the water, he almost couldn't believe what had just happened. He'd jumped into deadly waters, what rafters would label at least class four, without a life vest and had come out on the other side still alive. Hadn't Roberto and Juan agreed that falling into this river was a death sentence?

Albert thought, "Okay, George d'Hout, am I alive because somebody is praying for you or for me?"

Movement across the river drew Albert back to the moment. He raised his head and counted. At least nine people were over there, scouring the riverbank. How long before they thought to go back up to the bridge and cross over? When that happened, Albert's good luck might come to a violent end.

The blows to his forehead and crotch began to ache. Albert felt more than a little helpless. But there was no time for that. Hiding behind the cypress tree, he focused on what he always focused on when he was in a tight spot. "Stack one good decision

The Ecuadorian Deception

on top of another one. Keep stacking till you have enough blocks to see over the wall in front of you."

Albert kept low and moved toward the bridge. He needed to get past it if he was going to help d'Hout get free. Also, if he could hide out until morning, past the bridge was an assortment of retail shops where Albert could find a phone and call for help.

Looking back across the river, Albert saw Ordóñez had moved under a streetlight. The ICE agent wondered which house he had been held in.

How would he find the right house to rescue d'Hout? Bingo! Albert saw Miguel going back into a house in the middle of the block. Then he came running out excitedly, saying something to Ordóñez.

The clouds were still thick from the afternoon showers. Pujols could stay close to the ground, use the noise of the river to hide sounds, and run with relative ease. He headed for the next large tree. It was maybe only forty yards from Roberto and his goons, but across the river. The professor and Juan were peering toward the water but not seeing anything in particular. They seemed content to just stand there. Why weren't they coming after him?

Then Albert got his answer. Three more marked cars turned off Avenida Suarez, heading their direction. Just great. If the police in Cuenca were in the pocket of Ordóñez, his chances of actually getting out of the town alive were appreciably narrowed. He knew there were checkpoints at every road leading into and out of Cuenca.

Staring through the darkness, Albert realized they weren't police cars but more vehicles from a private security firm. That didn't make him feel any better. In Ecuador, private security forces were usually better armed than the police and worked with far fewer restrictions. These were no US-variety rent-a-cops. These guys were more like mercenaries. They didn't come cheap, and they meant business.

With the arrival of the extra security team, Albert now felt very close to death. He had to take more wild chances to get out of this alive. He considered jumping back into the river and letting the current carry him far away. However, he'd been in Ecuador long enough to know that when the rivers were full during January and February, the chances of surviving such a ride weren't good. He had pushed his luck once. Unless there were no other options, he would consider something else.

Looking back down the river and away from the house, Albert checked the progress of the security forces and Juan. They were almost to the location where he had jumped in. There were probably footprints where he'd slid in along the slippery bank of the river. Fortunately, when they saw the tracks, the men began looking downstream instead of back upstream toward the bridge.

That was the good news. The bad news was that Albert had reached the end of heavy cover. Between his position and the bridge was a clearing maybe seventy yards long on this side of the river. To get to the bridge undetected, Albert would have to slip down the bank toward the river, a drop of only about four feet. However, it would be slippery and make falling in the river a real risk.

Albert peeled off his shoes, knowing his best traction would come with bare feet. He quickly knotted the laces together and put the soggy shoes around his neck. If worse came to worst, they might even be a makeshift weapon.

The deep grass along the riverbank was cold and wet from a late afternoon rain. That also made it slick. Albert stayed hunched, keeping a low center of gravity. He didn't want his bobbing head to show above the exposed bank. He suddenly heard a shout, even above the din of the river, and his blood ran cold. He ducked and froze.

Friday, 10 January
10:46 p.m.

Miguel entered the house, looking back over his shoulder. Out the large picture windows, he could see Roberto and Professor Knight standing in the street. They watched as Juan and the heavily armed security guards continued their search. A sixth sentinel stood next to Roberto like a bodyguard. They were all scanning the park, looking for signs of the escaped ICE agent.

Maybe the next-door neighbors would call the police. They had gone inside quickly enough when it seemed there was some sort of trouble. On the other hand, calling the police as a preemptive strike against violence wasn't usually the way it was done in Ecuador. People usually let the cards play out and then brought in the authorities, if they were summoned at all. Since you never knew who might be on the take, minding your own business was usually a better option.

Roberto had sent Miguel inside because the Cañari thought he'd heard something and wanted to make sure d'Hout was still securely bound. Miguel took a last look outside, catching the silhouettes of three men under the streetlight. He opened the bedroom door, went to the closet, and opened it. He squatted and raised the hatch in the floor. Looking back, he realized he had left the door to the bedroom open.

He went back and closed it. Returning to the opening, he quickly descended the steps. George d'Hout lay at the bottom of the stairs, mere inches from the large sword. His hands and feet were still bound, and he still had the chain around his waist.

"I'm not going to harm you," Miguel said again. The tunnel was dark because the lights had been pulled down and disconnected from the wall. "Help me quick to get you loose."

Miguel grabbed the sword from its scabbard and raised it. George pulled back and curled into a ball. "Please!" Miguel said. "Do not resist me. We only have a moment. If you hope to escape, you must help me. Hold out your hands."

George did so. Miguel used the end of the sword to pierce the tape binding George's hands. "Pull against it," he kept saying to George. "If you fail, we will both die. My family is in great danger. Please, pull against it!"

"Numb. My hands are numb," George said, when Miguel pulled away the tape covering his mouth. "My hands and feet are numb from being bound."

"Don't talk. Pull!"

With Miguel puncturing the tape multiple times, George mustered enough strength to pull it apart. He then began to work on the tape binding his feet.

"No," Miguel said. "Let me do that. You unfasten the chain around your waist. It is not locked, just hooked in the back. Hurry!"

By the time George had contorted himself around to unfasten the chain, Miguel cut through the last bit of duct tape. Dizzy from lying bound in the dark for so long, George wavered and rocked when he tried to stand. He suddenly felt sick and landed on the floor.

Miguel said. "Get up. Get up! You must make your way to the end of the tunnel. Go!"

Half-crawling, half-running, George stumbled along after Miguel, who was still holding the sword. George fell again, and Miguel had to come back to help him to his feet.

"If it was your family," Miguel said, "you would not stumble. Choose to run instead of fall. Make yourself do this. Draw strength and make yourself do this. You must do everything I tell you. Everything."

They both tripped several times over the electric wire Albert had pulled from the ceiling. Glass popped and shattered under their feet when they stepped on light bulbs. Finally, they reached the end of the tunnel.

Miguel said, "Take this sword and use the pommel to hit me in the face. Do it hard. Make me bleed, as if you were viciously attacking me. Do not hold anything back."

"What if I knock you out? What's the rest of the plan?"

"You have never hit a Cañari, or you would not ask this. My head is hard, like the goat or the bull."

George took that as a personal challenge, rearing back and laying into Miguel with all his might. As he did, it occurred to him that if Miguel was wrong, he would be knocking out the person who could tell him how to escape.

The blow came, knocking the Cañari against the back wall. However, Miguel only smiled. "That was a good one," he said. "I am bleeding a lot. Good."

Miguel shook off the blow, the blood, and the bump on his forehead as if they were mosquito bites. "I am going to open the exit under the bridge. You will get out and hide. But you cannot stay there. You must watch out because Roberto has Juan and many security guards out there."

"They know I'm escaping?" George asked. Was he being set up again?

"No, the American who came for you has escaped. They are looking for him. He is hiding on the other side of the river."

"How do you know?" George demanded. "Have Roberto and the others seen him? He could be dead by now. I could be walking into another trap."

"That is true, but I do not believe it," Miguel assured him. "I saw him hiding by the river, but I don't believe the others saw him. I am sure of it. But he is now at a place where he is trapped. He will not make it to the bridge unless I can get back upstairs to tell them you have escaped. However, when I do, they will come straight to the bridge. If you and this agent are there…"

Miguel didn't need to finish the sentence. "I need you to hit me again," he said. "There is still not enough blood. Harder this time. Then wait a minute or two. I will run back to get Roberto and the professor. I will tell them you have escaped and then attacked me with the sword."

"Where do we go?" George said, feeling panicked. "I don't know where to go."

"You must travel fast all night. Follow the Yanuncay River upstream into the mountains. It will lead you to the Inca Trail in Cajas National Park. From there, avoid all roads, security, and police. Señor Ordóñez's influence is great, and you cannot trust anyone."

"Then what?"

"You will make your way to the Paper Tree Forest," Miguel said. "It is a land of great power. Very rugged and a good place to hide. When I have freed my family, I will come for you. Now hit me again."

"Paper Tree Forest? What's that?"

"You will see. But first you must get there. Now hit me."

George struck, feeling the scabbard dig into the skin on Miguel's forehead. He then turned and felt for the handle that would open the rock passageway under the bridge.

As Miguel ran back down the tunnel toward his house, George heard him say, "That was a good one. I am really bleeding now. Good job, Señor d'Hout! ¡*Buen trabajo!*"

George fought the urge to immediately try to escape. Miguel said to wait until he had time to distract Roberto and the others. In addition, whoever this agent was, he also needed time to get away. As George stood in the darkness, an idea came to him.

He had no doubt Carol was praying God would send angels to help her husband, wherever he was. Didn't the Bible teach that Michael was the archangel? And wasn't *Miguel* simply the Spanish word for Michael? George held the sword in his right hand. The sword of an angel named Michael. And if required, he would run it through anyone who tried to stop him from escaping.

CHAPTER 21

Friday, 10 January
8:49 p.m.

After weighing the pros and cons, Van decided to do something he had never done before. If he was wrong, he would bring a great deal of embarrassment on himself and his bosses. In addition, he would make a lot of people attached to the US diplomatic mission in Ecuador very angry. But he absolutely believed he was right. There was nothing left to do but ignore his hunch or follow it.

He picked up the phone and called the after-hours number in Quito again. "This is Van Williams, special agent with the FBI in Texas. I need to be put in direct contact with the man who supervises ICE agent Albert Pujols. It is a matter of life and death."

Ten minutes passed. He was finally connected to Dean Connors, who identified himself as part of the Diplomatic

Security Service. "I trust this is important," Connors said. "Talk to me."

Williams recounted everything in a manner as economical as it was complete. "I don't know the consulate employee in Guayaquil, but I am under a very strong suspicion there is something wrong in that situation," Williams said. "I understand the consequences of my allegations if I'm wrong. But I am asking you to please assume, for now, the worst. You have me to be the fall guy if this is wrong. That should give you a clear path to get some help to Agent Pujols."

"That's a problem," Connors said. "We are very lightly staffed here. I am the backup, and I am four hours away by car. There are no more flights to Guayaquil tonight. Any suggestions?"

"I'd suggest starting now," Williams said. "It's going to be a short night and a long drive."

Friday, 10 January
10:57 p.m.

George involuntarily held his breath and pushed on the stone escape hatch. The sound of the river greeted his ears, drowning out everything else, including his own thoughts. He tried to fight past the white noise of the roaring water and listen for anyone who might pose a threat. Believing it was now or never, George poured out of the hole, waving the sword in front of him like a talisman, hoping to ward off evil as he came.

As the sword cleared the hole and George was out just past his shoulders, he suddenly felt someone grab him in a terrific choke hold. He tried to wield the sword around to strike the attacker, but the person had a positional advantage. Instead, George drove his elbow into the dark figure as hard as he could, hoping to break some ribs.

The attacker only increased his hold on George, grabbing him by the throat so his air was immediately cut off. George imagined the consequences not only for him but also for Miguel's family if he was defeated. He had to overpower this threat.

The attacker was equally fierce, yanking George out of the escape hatch like a rag doll and pinning him to the ground. The man growled something in Spanish. George grabbed the arm around his throat and tried to release it enough to get some air.

"I'm an American," George gasped. "You can't do this. Please! This shouldn't be happening! I didn't do anything!" No good. His air was gone, and George was starting to black out.

Suddenly, the choke hold was gone. "George?" the voice said. "Crap. You're George d'Hout? Sorry. I came looking to help you, not break your windpipe. Didn't expect you to have a sword."

"We've got to go," George gasped. "They will be coming this way in a minute or two. We have to run now."

"They were all huddling back at the house. The little guy was screaming something, and they all went running back."

"He's telling them I escaped," George said. "We've got to hurry."

Both men bent low and headed off under the bridge upstream and away from Roberto and the others. From there, George took the lead, sword in hand, and scrambled up the embankment to the top of the bridge. He glanced back, but the wide bridge blocked his view of the house and the men in front of it.

"I need to get to a phone," Albert said. "We've got to get some help."

"Miguel said it was too dangerous. He told me how to get out of here, but we've got to keep moving." Two cars were driving by on Solano Street, and both slowed. Those inside the cars stared at the two men with a large sword running between the road and the river.

Albert said, "This can't look good. People in Ecuador are usually pretty slow to call the cops, but two guys with a giant sword might just do the trick."

George was already moving, heading down the opposite embankment, which put him and Albert on the opposite side of the river from Roberto's thugs. It felt good for George to be running, something he hadn't done for several days. Knowing that getting caught meant certain death added extra urgency to his pace.

Though he was sprinting, George found that the agent had no trouble keeping up. They might have been two members of the same running club, challenging one another to go faster. "Where are we going?" Albert asked. "I don't know this city at all."

"I don't either," George huffed, knowing he had a long run ahead of him. "But Miguel said we shouldn't trust anyone. Ordóñez has too many people on his payroll." George took a deep breath. "He said we have to get out of Cuenca. We are supposed to hide in the Cajas. Something called the Paper Tree Forest. He said he'd come for us and help us get out of here."

"The Cajas has got to be ten or twelve miles from here, and all uphill," Albert said. "You up for that?"

"Doubtful," George said, "but I don't think we have much choice." They continued running.

"When is he supposed to come for us?" Albert asked.

"Sorry, I don't know," George answered. "His wife and kids are being held hostage by Ordóñez. That's how Ordóñez got use of his house."

"It's a good thing we're running," Albert said, "or I think I'd be pretty cold. It really gets brisk up here in the mountains at night."

"I was thinking the same thing," George said. "We're following the river all the way into the higher Andes. Get pretty nasty up there?"

"Around freezing," Albert said. "We've gotta get some warmer clothes, or there won't be anything to rescue when Miguel finds us."

Suddenly, there was an explosion of sound. "Thunder?" George asked.

"The man-made kind," Albert said. "They're catching up. That was a rifle."

Albert looked around and realized they had allowed themselves to get between Ordóñez's men and some street lights luminating the river park. "Got to go faster," Albert said. "Gotta stay low. Hurry!"

As they ran, another shot rang out. Running as fast as he could, George momentarily lost his grip on the sword. He stopped to go back for it. Another gunshot. "Let it go!" Pujols ordered. "Run!"

George spotted what appeared to be a low spot in the river. Across from it was an old shed of some sort. He pointed and Albert nodded.

They splashed into the icy water, trying to get across as quickly as possible before they hit deep water and were carried away. George's feet felt instantly numb. Thinking about following the river all the way up into the Cajas, he knew he had made a mistake. One of the first rules for runners is to take good care of your feet. The second is to take good care of your shoes. George had broken both of these rules. He hoped he wouldn't live to regret the mistake.

When they reached the shed, George pulled on the door. It opened, and a large face stared at them. Both men jumped back. Then George managed a laugh. It was the cow he had seen being walked through the park. "Hide in here?" George asked.

"No, but leave the door open so they will think we are," Albert said. "It will slow them down. We need every second we can get."

The cow bellowed as George and Albert ran on.

Friday, 10 January
11:19 p.m.

Juan and a security guard named Pablo had taken the south bank of the river. The other guards had taken the north bank. As they moved forward, one of them saw a bit of light reflected off something ahead. He leveled his rifle and fired. It looked like a shed of some kind. "If they are in there," the guard thought, "they are as good as dead."

The guard was about to tell his compadres what he had seen. Another shot rang out. He felt peculiar. Then he looked down to find something warm on his shoulder. Was that blood? At that moment the puzzling feeling became excruciating pain. He had been shot.

An old man was on one knee between the cowshed and his ramshackle home, taking cover behind a ragged piece of sheet metal. "You won't steal my cow!" the man yelled in Spanish. "She is all I have. No you won't!"

The guards were about to open fire on the man, whose muzzle flash revealed his location. This would be easy. Juan took in the situation, yelled, and began running through the low spot in the river, Pablo right behind him.

"No señor, no," Juan cried. "We are here to help you. Someone else is trying to steal your cow. We are a security patrol. We are here to help!" Juan enjoyed a good killing as much as anyone, but if they weren't careful, there could be a bloodbath of people along the river tonight, without capturing the two who had escaped.

The other guards knelt next to their fallen partner. Blood poured out of his shoulder. He looked at the blood and vomited. The guard named Pablo reached for a walkie-talkie. He reported to the guard with Ordóñez what had happened. He also asked them to bring around one of the patrol cars.

"We've got to get him to a hospital," Pablo said.

Juan grabbed the walkie-talkie. "Roberto," he said, "I have the situation under control. Yes, a car would be good, but I have the situation under control."

Handing the radio back to the guard, Juan said, "Right now, I will take him down by the river to wash away the blood. The cold water will slow the bleeding. You all stay here and, with this good man's assistance, search around the property to make sure the thieves are not still hiding. Examine everything carefully."

Juan took the wounded man and helped him to his feet, leaning his head as far as possible away from the vomit.

One of the disgusting things about people who were seriously hurt was the way they lost control over bodily functions. Juan had seen people soil themselves, wet themselves, and, like this idiot, throw up. How embarrassing it must be to lose control. That kind of embarrassment would make death a welcome thing. Who would want to live with that kind of shame?

When they reached the river, Juan saw the low spot where Albert and George had obviously crossed. However, he moved farther away from that point, back toward the bridge. The water there was much deeper. He led the dazed guard to the edge. "It is time we put some water on that wound, *muchacho*. We must wash all traces of tonight's trouble away."

With that he took his pistol and smashed the back of the guard's head. Then he pushed the guard into the river. The sound of the rushing water covered a broken, startled cry. The guard sank under the water, surfaced, and then was swept hard by the current into a large, exposed rock. His head hit the rock and bounced backwards for just a moment. The head spun around and the eyes looked at Juan, then rolled back in the sockets. His open mouth took in large amounts of the icy water. In a moment the river carried him away.

"The river is good," Juan said to no one. "It washes away all the blood."

Juan looked back toward the other three security members. They were occupied searching the old man's property. When Juan reached them, Pablo asked, "Is the car here? Is he on his way to the hospital?"

"He's taken care of," Juan said. "Any sign of the two thieves?"

"They aren't here," Pablo said. "We even looked in the house."

"Who else is here with you tonight, señor?" Juan asked.

"My wife is inside," he said. "She is frightened by the guns. She is praying to the Virgin Mother to help us."

"No need," Juan said. "I will help you. Would you get her?"

Pablo and the other guards gave Juan a knowing look. "Do we need their help looking for clues by the river?"

Juan said, "Yes, I believe we do. But be very careful, because it can be slippery down there."

However, when the old man came back, it was with seven men and four women. "The people from the barrio heard the gunfire and came to see what was wrong," the old man explained. "They will help us search for the thieves."

"You are very lucky, señor," Juan said, "to have such helpful neighbors. Neighbors like that can save your life."

The guards looked at Juan, who gave a dismissive shrug. "We will go now," Juan said. "And here is something for your trouble." He reached into his pocket and pulled out a ten dollar bill, a huge amount for the peasant. "Let us say nothing about these thieves," Juan instructed the group. "They would give this good barrio a bad name."

The walkie-talkie crackled, and Juan heard the security guard with Roberto say they were to rendezvous at the street.

When they arrived, Juan updated Roberto and the professor. As he did, the security guard named Pablo looked around, confused.

"Where is Reynaldo?"

"Reynaldo?"

"My cousin, who got shot."

"Your cousin?" Roberto asked. "I had no idea." He and Juan gave each other a long look. This situation was spiraling out of control very quickly.

Juan said, "He is over by the river. The bleeding is much better, but we will get him and take him to the hospital. Come with me."

Roberto told the other guards they would all walk back to the house and leave the car for Juan and Pablo. As the guards, led by Miguel and the professor, headed back to the house on foot, Roberto said, "After your business is done with Pablo, meet me. We must discuss this neighborhood and what we do next."

Pablo had already started down to the river. They could hear him tentatively calling, "Reynaldo, we are coming. We will get you some help."

Roberto grabbed Juan's sleeve and pulled him in close. "I understand there is a serious risk of fire in this barrio. Do you think a controlled burn will bring this situation back under control?"

"It will." Juan smiled. There was always a bright side to every negative event. "I will attend to it."

"We have worked together a long time," Roberto said. "No situation has ever come this close to disaster for us. Rein it back in."

Juan turned toward the river. "Hey, Pablo. Hold up, *muchacho*. I am coming. I will show you where your cousin is."

CHAPTER 22

Saturday, 11 January
12:07 a.m.

Hugh sat straight up in bed. "I've got it! I know where the treasure is, or at least I can get them close."

His wife, Brenda, who had cut her trip to Pittsburgh short, sat up beside him. "Say that again."

"I know where the treasure is," he repeated. "The message said d'Hout's family knew where the treasure was like they knew their own name. He was being completely straightforward. It was so easy, no one could get it."

"Hugh, I've been traveling all day. I'm exhausted. Tomorrow I've got to get to Houston to be with Carol. We've only been in bed an hour. I'm exhausted. Can this wait?"

"Van Williams and the ICE agent said if I knew anything, I needed to communicate it to them and then to the people who are holding George."

"What if George is already dead?" Brenda asked. "I know it's horrible to say, but you said they were trying to imitate him in the e-mail. Maybe that's because he's dead. Whatever you do, don't say that to Carol. But it could be true. Do you want to help these monsters get the treasure after they've killed George?"

"You've already got George in the ground," Hugh said. "My brother is pretty good at getting out of trouble. I saw him as a kid. I know. We have to believe he's still alive and do all we can to help."

Hugh climbed out of bed and headed to his home office, Brenda behind him. He pulled up some of his genealogy files and read over them. "Yes, here's part of it," he said. "Now I need to find out for sure what Edward Davies is hiding."

"You aren't making any sense," Brenda said.

"It makes perfect sense," Hugh insisted. He typed in the name Davies and began to search databases on the name. "I'm right! Here it is. I can help them find their treasure. We will make it conditional. They have to release George first."

Saturday, 11 January
2:00 a.m.

By the time the volunteer fire fighters for southern Cuenca, known as *bomberos*, reached the six houses and multiple sheds along the Yanuncay River, it was too late. All of them were a complete loss. The sickening smell of burning hair and flesh indicated that the blaze had victimized more than just houses and barns.

The noise and bright dance of the flames had drawn people out of their homes. There were screams for help, but the fires were seemingly everywhere at once, and no one had a chance to escape. Even the animals were dead. Accompanying the smell of burning flesh and wood was the unmistakable odor of kerosene.

A tall man with Incan features loitered around the outside of the crowd. As the captain of the volunteer unit talked to his men, the tall man meandered up. "Hey, *muchacho*, did you hear that earlier in the night there were some men here trying to steal a cow?"

The captain turned to him. "How do you know this?"

"They were gringos," the tall man said. "One had a graying beard, curly hair, and was wearing a running outfit. The other looked Latino, but he was a gringo, to be sure. I am certain they were traveling together. They were both speaking English and were maybe drunk. Yes, I am sure of it. They were both quite drunk."

"You seem to know a lot about these two men," the captain said.

"I live down the street. I was looking for my lost dog, and the neighbors were all outside talking about the commotion these men were making and the threats they were hurling. The ones who were talking about it were people from these houses. Are they all dead?"

"So you were out here tonight?" the captain asked. "Can anyone vouch for you?"

"I can," said another man, stepping from the shadows. "I am Roberto Ordóñez Gonzalez, and I am personal friends with many here at the university in Cuenca as well as several in the Azuay provincial government. Your supervisor is Daniel Cabaza. I know him very well. Are there any other questions?"

"Señor Cabaza is not my supervisor," the captain said. "He is the head of the entire organization. My supervisor is—"

"His name is Jose Leon. As I was saying, Daniel Cabaza can vouch for me, and I can vouch for this man," Roberto said. "Are there any further questions?"

In Ecuador, having the right connections made the difference between power and impotence. Roberto made it clear he had power. The captain was too smart to continue asking questions of the Inca, though he instantly disliked and distrusted the man.

As Roberto and the Inca walked off, the captain asked one more thing. "These gringos," he said, "any idea which way they went?"

"I didn't see them," the Inca said. "I'm only telling you what I heard. I'm trying to help. But I believe people said they went that way." He pointed west toward the mountains, in the direction of the Yanuncay River's headwaters. "You can ask others and see what they know."

The two men walked back toward their secret tunnel entrance under the bridge. Making sure no one was within earshot, Juan asked Roberto, "What about this agent and George d'Hout? This is a serious matter. How did d'Hout escape?"

Roberto didn't blink. "That is a very good question, Juan. You are the one who bound d'Hout. You know how I feel about complications. They hurt our bottom line and threaten our business."

Juan felt a moment of fear. He wouldn't take the blame for this. If necessary, he would even kill Roberto to save his own life. He and Professor Knight would find some new businessman to front their operation.

"How was he discovered missing?" Juan asked.

"Miguel was afraid the agent might try to free him, so he went to the basement to check on him," Roberto answered. "When he went down the steps, he was attacked."

"By one man or two?"

"I asked the same thing," Roberto said. "He only saw one. But he said there might have been two."

"How strong is Miguel?" Juan asked. "Stronger than a man who has been bound hand and foot for over twenty-four hours?"

"You are suggesting Miguel let him escape?" Roberto asked. He looked at the ground as they walked. "If this is true, I will have no choice but to kill one of his daughters in retribution. I may also have to turn his wife over to my men for an hour or two."

"She is so ugly; it will be more of a punishment for the men." Juan laughed. When Roberto didn't join in, he stopped. "Will you force him to watch?"

"I believe it will be more of a lesson if he is forced to listen over an open phone line," Roberto said. "The imagination is always worse than reality, as bad as reality may be."

"Do you want me to begin preparations?" Juan asked. "We must have everything ready, including a way to restrain Miguel before he gets a hint of what is about to happen."

"Let's not get ahead of ourselves," Roberto said. "I know you very much want to find someone else to blame. Therefore, you are eager to make it Miguel's fault. And we have devised a fitting punishment for that transgression. What would be the fitting punishment if it turns out the fault is yours?"

Juan stopped. A vein in his forehead rose and seemed to throb. "It was not my fault," the Inca said. "Any man who says it is—any man—is questioning my manhood and my ability to follow orders to the letter. That man is challenging me to a fight to the death."

"I see," Roberto said. "Well, we can't have that, can we? Although I have always wondered who would win if it came down to a contest between you and Miguel."

Roberto began walking again. "The clouds are beginning to clear," he said, looking at the sky. "That means the temperature will begin to fall. We know the agent and George crossed the river. That means they are wet and will be very cold. Where do you think they are going?"

"I don't know," Juan said. "Perhaps you should ask Miguel."

"Back to that, are we?" Roberto said. "Incas versus Cañari. The battle that is older than Ecuador itself. Who will win? Or will one kill the other before there is a chance for a clean fight?"

Behind the two men, *bomberos* continued pulling more blackened, smoking bodies out of the smoldering ruins. But Roberto and Juan paid no mind. They had moved on.

Saturday, 11 January
2:06 a.m.

The smell of smoke, the glow of the fire, and the constant whine of sirens from fire trucks and ambulances sickened Albert and George as they hid under the Avenida Loja bridge nearly four miles from where they escaped. Dropping temperatures chilled them to the bone, but their attention was on the fires.

"You think it was some sort of accident?" George asked. "I mean, it's right where we came through."

"Roberto Ordóñez has gotten away with his business of stealing the treasures of South America and selling them to dealers around the world for a long time," Albert said. "We have always wondered how, and I guess now we know. Anybody who gets in his way is involved in an accident. But I can smell the kerosene from here. He's gonna have a hard time convincing anybody this was an accident."

It occurred to George that he had been running beside this man for several miles but had no idea who he was. "I'm George d'Hout from Houston," he said. "You?"

"You might say I'm a friend of your brother's," Albert said. "Hugh contacted an FBI agent, who contacted me. It happened I was assigned to a case a little over a year ago in which Ordóñez was a suspect. That was down in Bolivia. We got a tip he was working in Ecuador, so I was in Quito, following up on leads. If we can survive this, we won't have to prove Ordóñez has been illegally selling antiquities. We will have him on more serious charges. Murder."

"I still didn't catch your name."

"Albert Pujols," the ICE agent said, "but not *that* Albert Pujols."

"Good thing. I'm an Astros fan. *That* Albert Pujols has been killing us for years."

"I think there's been enough killing tonight. Let's see if we can prevent there from being more." Albert brought George up to speed on how Hugh and Carol had been working to find him after his disappearance. "I know you'd like to call your wife and let her know you're alive. I've got to get in touch with our Quito office and get us some help. That adds up to the fact we both need a phone."

"The Internet cafés will all be closed, won't they?" George asked. "Do we dare go up to somebody's house or flag down a policeman?"

"I don't think so," Albert said. "It's just too risky. As far as my agency or our embassy in Quito knows, the level of corruption in Cuenca is pretty minimal. However, Roberto has been able to fly under the radar both here and in Guayaquil. That means people are protecting him. We've worked too hard to blow it now by getting help from the one policeman in the entire city on Ordóñez's payroll."

Albert didn't hear any cars crossing the bridge. "What we need," he said, "is more clothing and dry socks. You ever rob from clotheslines as a kid?"

"Can't say I did."

"Well, where I come from, you weren't allowed to graduate from high school until you had proved yourself by lifting watermelons from the field and a few pairs of girlie underwear off a clothesline. Let's see if we can find something warmer than girls underwear, though."

Venturing out from under the bridge, George and Albert looked around. Large fences or walls topped by barbed wire, broken glass, or metal spikes surrounded virtually all of the houses in Cuenca, as they did across most of Latin America.

"We need to get down into *los barrios pobres*," Albert said. "The really poor neighborhoods. But we've got to avoid the cops, too."

Making a four-block loop but being careful to dodge any passing cars, the pair managed to set off four motion detectors on houses, disturb three dogs, and get too close to a Chevrolet Sail. Its anti-theft device screamed into the night.

George and Albert ran six blocks before stopping to catch their breaths. "I thought you said they wouldn't let you graduate high school until you pulled off a few thefts," George said. "Are you sure you didn't drop out?"

"Good thing I didn't go to high school here. These houses are better protected than most banks." Deciding it was their lot to be cold, and fearing the cacophony of alarms was bound to bring the police, they headed back to the river.

At Avenida Primera de Mayo, they prepared to duck back under a bridge and hide out. However, they found it was already occupied. "*Esta es mi casa. ¡Vete!*"

Albert's voice immediately took on a tone of reassurance. "Yes, this is your house," he said in Spanish. "We mean you no harm."

George didn't know whether to run or fight. He held back, waiting to see what happened. The person under the bridge was an old man. As Albert drew closer, he realized he couldn't exactly see the fellow, but he could certainly smell him.

"We are poor travelers," Albert said in Spanish. "We have gotten wet from the river. We need dry clothes. I will pay you for two warm shirts."

The homeless man declined, clutching a bag of torn and dirty clothes tightly to his chest. However, as Albert sat down and visited with him, hearing his stories of hardship and disappointment, the old man softened. George, meanwhile, stood shivering in the dropping temperatures and the breezes blowing along the river.

After another twenty minutes, Albert emerged with a jacket and a heavy wool sweater. "These cost me more than if I bought them new," he said. "The guy didn't have any socks, so that wasn't a possibility."

"Did you have to pay extra for the smell? This is wretched."

"Best I could do. Now let's get out of here. We've still got a long way to go."

"Okay, but I'm thinking since you bought these clothes, you get to wear them. I can barely stand the smell on you. If it's between wearing these clothes and being cold, I'm voting for the cold."

"Your choice. But if you change your mind, let me know. Me, I'm grateful to be warm."

In the distance, the whine of a car engine could be heard approaching. George and Albert exchanged glances and then sprinted for the next bridge. Getting caught wasn't an option.

CHAPTER 23

Saturday, 11 January
2:30 a.m.

Miguel kept pouring cups of strong Ecuadorian coffee as the professor and Ordóñez planned their next move. They were staring at a map of Cuenca. Juan was staring at Miguel.

"Here is the house, and here is where we lost them," Professor Knight said. "So that means they are following the river. Where do you think they're headed?"

"Why don't you ask Miguel?" Juan said, staring daggers at the Cañari.

At first Miguel ignored him. However, when Juan repeated the question, Ordóñez leaned back in his chair as if watching a sporting match. Miguel knew he had to respond.

"I was surprised by one of them," Miguel said. "I don't deny that. I'm ashamed. But you were surprised by the other one. Are you ashamed? Or do you merely wish to blame me, hoping others will forget how you also failed?"

In a flash Juan pulled the pistol from his pocket. The chair he was sitting on toppled backward, and he sprang out of it. "You son of a—"

"Stop!" Ordóñez said. "If you shoot him, I will have you killed. But not before you watch your beating heart being pulled from your chest."

Juan's hands trembled with anger as he released the safety on the pistol. "You will not accuse me of failing. No one says such things about me."

"Juan," Roberto repeated, "if you pull the trigger, you are killing yourself. Please re-engage the safety on your pistol, pick up your chair, and sit down. In fact, it is time for you to go to bed. You are very tired. When the sun comes up, we have to rectify a couple of mistakes. Get some sleep."

Juan's hands continued to shake. Normally, killing people made him feel better, and tonight he'd killed several. But he'd also let two get away. That was unacceptable. He must make up for it to save face and restore his place of superiority above the lowly Cañari, Miguel.

He put the safety back on and placed the pistol back in his pocket. "I will sleep for three hours, Señor Ordóñez. Is that acceptable?" he asked.

"An excellent idea," Ordóñez said. "You stay in the upstairs bedroom, and Miguel, you stay down here. That way we don't have to worry about someone straying into another room for some late-night vengeance. Professor, you and I have more work to do."

Miguel and Juan warily eyed each other until Juan disappeared up the stairs. Then Miguel turned back and said, "I am not proud of what happened. I hope you know that. But justice will be done."

"Justice," the professor said. "I don't think I like that word."

"Good night, Miguel," Ordóñez said. "We will see about all that tomorrow."

Turning back to the professor, Ordóñez said, "How did d'Hout escape? Juan has never had a prisoner escape before."

"I have been wondering the same thing. But I have also been thinking about cutting our losses before these men reach help. What is our timeline on leaving Ecuador? Where will you go?"

"That's the second time you've asked me," Ordóñez said. "And I told you. Where I go is none of your business."

The professor shot back. "Let's be clear. We are partners. I have found you riches beyond belief, and you have sold them for a hefty profit."

"If we are being clear, we can be clear on one other thing. You claim to be a famous archaeologist. But you rarely even soil your hands. You find those who know where the treasure is, and you make them tell you. Juan could do that. I could do that. Even Miguel could do that."

The professor said, "You are right that I don't know where the Orellana treasure is, but my method of finding treasure is much more efficient than spending years digging in the ground to find all the places it isn't. That's how the so-called *real* archaeologists do it. If they find one thing worth a page in *National Geographic*, their reputation is secured. I have found you an indecent amount of treasure. And yet my loyalty is only to you and to our partnership."

Ordóñez said, "At first light, we will have the security company—every car—out looking for this agent and d'Hout. We will place a five-hundred-dollar bonus on each gringo. That is as much as these security guards make in a month. They'll find them."

"And if they don't?"

"If they reach a phone, we are possibly in a great deal of trouble," Ordóñez said. "What time does the newspaper close up for the night?"

"I have no idea," the professor said.

Ordóñez made a couple of calls, first to the *bombero* captain and then to the newspaper pressroom. "You have a story to go with your pictures from the fire," he said into the phone. "It was two Americans who are responsible for so many innocent deaths. We need the entire city to be on the watch for them, yes?"

After gaining assurances he wouldn't be quoted and that his name wouldn't appear anywhere in the story, Ordóñez hung up. He tried to muster a smile. "What was that story you once told me? The one about the team of Frenchmen who wandered into Cuenca many years ago? I believe you said one of the men got a little too friendly with a native girl. What happened when the angry citizens found those men?"

"That was the Condamine Expedition in the 1730s," The professor said. "The arrogant French came to Cuenca and made themselves quite at home. Their arrogance didn't sit well—less so when it was learned that one of the men was, you might say, *courting* a prominent *Cuencana*. A priest, Juan Jimenez Crespo, denounced the immoral French from the pulpit."

The professor's eyes glowed with delight as he continued his tale. "When the annual bullfights began in August at the San Sabastian Plaza, the Frenchman, named Seniergues, was challenged by the crowd. He pulled a pistol and a sword and jumped into the ring, daring anyone to take him on." The professor paused for effect.

Ordóñez could almost taste the blood about to be spilled.

Professor Knight continued. "Instead of one person challenging him, the entire crowd attacked him with rocks, knives, and swords. The fool was brutally beaten and left for dead. The people of Cuenca don't like it when outsiders challenge them."

Ordóñez said, "And what of two gringos who come to town and set the houses of the poor on fire for their sadistic pleasure? What might happen to them?"

"I suspect they would never get a chance to be taken before the authorities, except to be fitted for their caskets."

"Get a little sleep," Ordóñez said. "We must be up by five a.m. to call all the radio stations and have them ask listeners to be on the lookout for these two Americans. We must be very specific about how they are dressed. We wouldn't want any of the tourists and expatriates here to be collateral damage."

"Heavens, no," the professor said. "Especially since I am one of those gringos."

Saturday, 11 January
3:16 a.m.

George and Albert continued to shiver as they made their way from bridge to bridge until they reached the edge of the city. There they continued following the river, though the going became painfully slow. The foothills were covered with thick straw grass and varieties of spiny cactus and yucca with razor-sharp needles. George believed he had found every one of them.

Gleaming in the night, a small white church stood on a nearby hill a little south of the river. Throwing large stones in the water and using them as a footbridge, Albert and George made their way across. The church perched on a small mesa. Around it were varieties of tall grasses.

"I think we can bed down in this grass and get some rest," Albert said. "What do you say?"

"I'm in, but how are we going to find a phone if we move out of the city?"

Albert sat down on the grass, trying to get as low as possible. "Unless I miss my guess, that fire is going to be blamed on us. Ordóñez will see to that. That means we are on everybody's list of least favorite people. If anybody died in that fire, it also means we're wanted for murder. We have to assume that at least some of those looking for us are going to shoot first and ask questions later."

"This just keeps getting better," George said.

"Just pray the first person here in the morning is a priest and not a grounds keeper," Albert said. "The priest is sworn to at least give us a fair hearing before calling the police."

George closed his eyes and tried to imagine himself with Carol back in Houston. "Don't quit praying, honey," he said. "I'm not out of the woods yet."

Albert looked over at George. "Okay," he said, "but you don't have to call me honey. We barely know each other."

George was too embarrassed to look at the ICE agent. "Sorry. Just talking to my wife." He looked at the sky. Clouds were rolling in from the mountains. The breeze went from unpleasant to downright icy. "Great," he thought. "All we need is rain." He closed his eyes and dozed off as large drops began to fall.

CHAPTER 24

Saturday, 11 January
4:08 a.m.

Dean Connors pulled onto Avenida 9 de Octubre in Guayaquil near the hotel where Agent Pujols was last seen. It was also where GPS indicated Albert's phone had been before the battery apparently went dead. Finding plenty of vacant spaces, Connors chose not to park right in front of the hotel. He wanted a chance to survey things before he himself was surveyed.

He had called Vicente Noboa as he was leaving Quito but reached only voice mail. "Vicente, this is Dean Connors with the embassy's Diplomatic Security Service in Quito. I need to speak to you ASAP. We have a situation. One of the temporary duty agents, Albert Pujols, has vanished. We are picking up a GPS signal in downtown Guayaquil near a hotel. If I don't hear from you, I may go there first. See you when I get to town."

Feeling under the seat of his car, he pulled out his pistol, a Sig P228, and tucked it in his ankle holster. It was strictly against policy for DSS agents to carry a weapon in Ecuador. Connors made sure everyone under his authority, including those on temporary duty like Pujols, followed that policy. He hoped it hadn't cost the ICE agent his life. It was a policy he was choosing to ignore.

Policy also dictated that Connors contact the federal prosecutor's office in Guayaquil to let them know he was in town. The late hour gave him some latitude to wait until morning to make the call. He was also wary of notifying the prosecutors he was in town for another reason. Evidence against Ordóñez, albeit circumstantial, had been delivered to the prosecutor's office multiple times. Connors was mindful someone in that office might be on Ordóñez's payroll and tip him off.

Even though he'd been out of the academy for over twenty years, anytime Connors carried a weapon, he mentally reviewed what he'd learned during his first day on the shooting range: correct grip, correct positioning, correct sighting. Kill what you're aiming at.

In his mind's eye, Connors saw Pujols as a prisoner. Five men were holding him. Things moved in slow motion: Allow yourself to be kicked. Fall over. Grab the pistol. Raise it and fire. Again. Again. Again. Again. Again. The shot order went from the man closest to Pujols to the one farthest away, eliminating threats based on the chances that they could get to the hostage and kill him.

The Ecuadorian Deception

Connors refocused on the street outside his car. He hoped none of that would be necessary, but if it was, it would be up to him to make sure whoever had done this paid dearly.

Looking outside the car in the predawn hours, Connors also considered where he was. Everything about Guayaquil was different from Quito: the humid climate, tropical plants and trees, even the ways crimes were committed.

It was no exaggeration to say people in Quito and Guayaquil didn't care for one another. Each city had its own Independence Day, and residents' senses of loyalty were often primarily dedicated to their city. In his orientation classes on Ecuador, Connors had learned that the cities of Quito, Guayaquil, and Cuenca almost went to war in 1822 because each wanted the country named after it.

Connors knew such rivalries could be useful in extracting information. He also knew that because he was headquartered in Quito, any enemies he made in Guayaquil were even more likely to want to do him harm.

Connors exited the car. Instead of walking straight into the hotel, he walked in the other direction, circling the entire block. He was looking for any doors or alleys where Agent Pujols might have been carried out of the building as a prisoner. None stood out to him. Like many colonial-style buildings, there were few back entrances.

That didn't mean there weren't underground passages, however. During the years of Spanish rule, the people of South America had become proficient, even gifted, at constructing tunnels to escape under the very feet of their would-be captors.

If there were tunnels from the hotel, they could lead anywhere. Connors took a deep breath and entered the front door of the hotel. It was time to finally put a knot in the tail of a certain snake named Roberto Ordóñez.

Saturday, 11 January
5:40 a.m.

Padre Eduardo Domingo couldn't believe what he was hearing. His radio was tuned to Cuenca's leading information and news station. The priest, almost sixty, had been born in Cuenca and considered it his God-given duty to serve the people of his hometown. He believed he was securing both for them and for himself a seat one day at the right hand of the Father. Listening to the radio each morning was, for him, a regular briefing on what those who were not as heavenly minded were thinking about.

Compared to other countries he had visited—Brazil, Argentina, France, and the United States—the emphasis on hard news was much less in Ecuador. However, that was fine with the padre. He firmly believed that filling one's mind with the things of this world left little room for meditating on the glories of the next.

Today, however, the news was nothing less than shocking. Two Americans were being sought in the deaths of almost a dozen *Cuencanos*, including two security guards who had apparently tried to stop a ghastly arson-fest along the banks of the Yanuncay River late last night. The guards' pummeled bodies were found by fishermen where the Yanuncay River passed the park known as Parque El Paraíso.

Padre Domingo thought it odd that so much was known about the arsonists, since they had apparently gotten away. What also flitted through his mind was how the arsonists had killed two armed security guards. He concluded that the answers were there, even if they weren't being reported on air.

The consequences of such diabolical acts stood to be extreme. Cuenca was a town that heavily relied on American retirees and vacationers for a steady infusion of cash. Though many in his parish worried Americans would bring their sundry vices with them to Ecuador, there was also the hope that as people from the US moved to a country with such established Catholic virtues, it might redeem them from the unsavory secular influences of the United States.

The church even offered deeply discounted Spanish lessons for new arrivals. Padre Domingo also invited retired American teachers to conduct classes in the poorer barrios on English, hygiene, and practical economics. It was a way of getting both the American retirees and the poor children into the church, where the Holy Spirit might begin a work leading to salvation.

The radio droned on about the arsons and the deaths of the two security guards. Padre Domingo stopped listening. He was thinking about the retirees and expatriate Americans he had met over the years. He smiled when he thought of Ben Jessup, the most cantankerous man he had ever met. Ben had taught math at some American high school before deciding he was sick of the United States and the liberal direction the country was headed in. The two men had met one day as Ben took pictures of a garden near the church.

When the priest said hello, Ben grumbled. When the priest offered to take a picture of Ben and his wife, Laura, in front of the church, the old man answered, "I always keep churches out of my line of sight and out of my pictures. God and I have a deal. I don't bother him, and he doesn't bother me."

From that moment on, the priest decided to strike up a friendship with the American. If he could reach this man, he could reach anyone.

Now the radio news intruded on the priest's thoughts. He murmured to himself, "Even hateful Ben Jessup would never stoop so low as to attack poor people, burning their homes with them inside. Only monsters would do that."

And if *Cuencanos* perceived Americans as monsters, the levels of retaliation might start a chain of events that would be devastating to thousands of people, as well as to the local economy. Padre Domingo said a prayer.

After shaving and dressing, the priest got into his car and headed to his favorite *panadería*, where he would make his usual purchase of two *pan dulces* and a black coffee to wash the sweet rolls down.

In the car he turned on the radio. A representative of the Cuenca Chamber of Commerce was assuring listeners that this was an isolated incident and begging them to be extremely kind to all Americans. The announcers then repeated the vague descriptions of the assailants, asking that no one approach them or try to take the law into his or her hands.

The announcer said, "There are two men. One is white with curly, graying hair and a beard. He is wearing a blue jogging suit and tennis shoes. The second man is Latino. He is wearing a long-sleeved shirt and khaki slacks. Both men are approximately five feet nine inches tall."

At the *panadería*, the same news was blaring. "Father, what would make men such devils?" Maria Zapata, the owner's wife, asked.

"There are seven deadly sins," the padre said, "but the first three—lust, gluttony, and greed—are, I believe, the worms that eat into the heart and lead people to commit the other four. You should pray for these men."

Padre Domingo held up three quarters, which Maria accepted and slid into a small bag under the counter. She said, "I'm sorry, Father, but I won't pray for them. I hope they die in their sins so they're punished forever."

The priest looked at the floor. "The sixth deadly sin is acedia," he said, "which is failing to follow through on our duties. It is our duty as Christians to pray for them and their souls. The seventh deadly sin is wrath, which is manifested in an unforgiving attitude."

Maria also looked at the floor. "My mind is made up," she said. "These men are evil. They deserve to die."

"You are correct," Padre Domingo said. "But I confess that by the standard of God's perfection, that could describe all of us."

"Once they are dead, I will burn a candle and ask for forgiveness. God will forgive me, won't he? Isn't the church required to forgive if I seek it and give penance?"

"You make delicious *pan dulce*," the father said. "We will leave it at that for now. And perhaps we will all find it in our hearts to forgive, even as Jesus has forgiven us. Have a blessed day." He walked out of the store and went back to his car.

On the drive up the winding road to the church, the priest wondered where the arsonists might be. Their actions were those of insane people, so logically determining their next moves would surely be impossible.

As he pulled up to the church, the priest looked over the rugged terrain along Cuenca's western edges. The arsonists might be anywhere. It was most likely they had forced their way into the home of some peasants and were holed up there. Fleeing the city would be difficult by road. All the ways out of town would be closely monitored.

As the father walked up to the front doors of the church to unlock them, he suddenly knew where the men were. Footprints in the wet grass and mud showed where two people trudged up the steep terrain and apparently headed toward the back of the church.

Padre Domingo considered his actions. He could get back in the car and drive for help. He could see if the men were in the church and confront them with the power of God to forgive and cleanse. He could—

He heard someone speak gently in Spanish. "Padre, we need your help." The voice was right behind him. Padre Domingo did not turn around. Looking at the front doors of the church, he said, "What is it you need, my son?"

"Someone is trying to kill us," the voice said. "There are two of us. I didn't want you to come inside and be startled, but we had to break a window in the back to get in. It was cold and wet outside, and we had to have warmth. My name is Albert."

The priest was surprised he didn't feel more scared. In fact, total calm washed over him. "Albert," he said, "why would someone want to kill you? What have you done?"

"I am a federal agent from the United States," Albert said. "I was attempting to rescue an American who fell into the hands of a criminal from Guayaquil."

"Albert is crazy," the padre thought. "He doesn't even know where he is." "This is not Guayaquil," Padre Domingo said gently. "You are in Cuenca."

No response.

The padre tried again. "There are stories on the radio today about some bad things that happened last night. Do you know anything about them?"

"Padre, I need you to step inside because right now I need to not be spotted. I will tell you everything I know. Then I will ask you to do the same. Please step inside."

The priest felt something nudge him in the back, perhaps a pistol. He unlocked the door and went inside. "Relock it please," Albert said. The priest complied.

A second man, clearly the bearded one described on the radio, was standing near the sacristy. Padre Domingo fixed his eyes on the man and began to walk toward him. Under his breath he said, "Father, forgive them for they know not what they do."

The sounds of their shoes on the tile floor echoed in the quiet of the sanctuary. The father's shoes made a sturdy tap-click sound. The unseen man's shoes, obviously wet from the dew and rain, squeaked a little.

When the clergyman reached the first row, Albert said, "Go ahead and sit down, Father."

Padre Domingo did as he was told, never taking his eyes off the bearded man. The American looked very much like a shivering puppy, wet and cold and alone. In spite of what the radio had reported, the priest saw no venom in the bearded man's eyes—only fear. He believed his initial appraisal had been correct. These men were crazy.

That meant they were not liable to God for what they had done. According to Catholic theology, those who couldn't help but sin were exempt from the consequences of such actions.

It also meant they were very likely to keep killing, since they lacked a clear moral compass to show them the horrors of their actions. "My sons," the father said, "the radio is reporting that a dozen people died in a horrible fire last night. It was along the Yanuncay River. What do you know about this?"

"We believe it was started by the men who are chasing us," Albert said.

"Paranoid," the priest thought. "Blaming their actions on others. So sad." He said nothing, only nodded.

The bearded man was either mute or didn't speak Spanish, because he hadn't said a word. Nor did he appear to understand much of the conversation. Albert continued. "I am taking out my badge and identification. I want you to look at it. We are not criminals. I am trying to stop the men who did this, and I need your help."

Padre Domingo took the badge and identification, realizing he had no way of knowing whether they were real or counterfeit. "I'm sorry, but I know nothing about badges," the priest said.

"I am a federal Immigrations and Customs Enforcement agent based in Quito at the US embassy," Albert continued in Spanish. He pointed toward George. "This man was lured down here under false pretenses by a gang of international smugglers. When he was captured, I was asked to come and look for him. This man is George d'Hout, and his wife back in Texas is very worried about him. We need to get to a phone so we can call for help. It will also permit us to convince you our story is true."

Not sure what to do or what to believe, the priest turned to his training. All good acts begin with charity. "Do you need something to eat?" he asked. "I have a *pan dulce* in my bag here. I had two, but I ate the other one on the way to the church. I am sorry, because you must be very hungry."

"Padre, would you hand the sack to George so he may inspect it?"

"Of course," the priest said. George looked inside and pulled out the pastry. He tore it in half and gobbled his portion down like a man who hadn't eaten in days. Then he put the rest back in the sack and handed it past the priest to Albert.

Padre Domingo followed the bag with his eyes. For the first time he got a look at Albert. In his hand was no gun, only an elongated rock he had used to trick the priest. Or did the crazy man believe the rock was a gun?

As Albert ate the other half of the bread, Padre Domingo said, "Were you going to shoot me with that rock?"

Albert swallowed and laughed, repeating the priest's words to George in English. George only managed a grim half smile. But Albert's laugh seemed to clear the air of much tension. However, Padre Domingo still believed his life was in great danger.

CHAPTER 25

Saturday, 11 January
7:15 a.m.

Dean Connors identified himself to the general manager of the hotel and asked if he had a moment to meet with him in private. Stepping from behind the desk, the manager ushered the American upstairs to a meeting room near where tourists and businesspeople were assembling for breakfast.

Connors reviewed with the manager all the events leading up to his overnight drive from Quito. The manager seemed transparent and eager to help, telling Connors he had instructed his staff not to touch the rooms until given directions by Davies, d'Hout, or Señor Ordóñez, who was paying for them.

Connors leaned forward in his chair. "Tell me about Ordóñez," he said. The manager was effusive in his praise of both

Ordóñez and his chief archaeologist, Professor Knight, who lived in the hotel but had been gone for several days.

"You have a copy of Professor Knight's passport on file?" Connors asked.

"Of course," the manager said. "That is the law."

"May I look at it, since I am with the embassy and he is an American citizen? Also, I believe your staff said one of my associates, Albert Pujols, was going back to Quito when he left your hotel. To whom did he say that?"

"You must be mistaken, señor," the manager said. "Your Albert Pujols did not go back to Quito. At least that was not my impression when he left with Señor Ordóñez."

"He left with Ordóñez?"

"Of course," the manager said. "I made that clear to the man from your consulate when he asked about it. I believe his name was Mr. Noboa. I am sorry there was a misunderstanding on that point."

Connors rose and moved back toward the staircase. "I believe I need to confer with Mr. Noboa on a couple of points. I may be back in touch. Thank you for your assistance."

As Connors reached the second flight of stairs, followed by the manager, he glanced down and saw Noboa standing at the front desk. Connors put a hand on the manager's shoulder and whispered, "Hold on a second."

The manager looked around questioningly but saw Connors staring at Noboa. Connors strained to hear Noboa say to the front desk clerk in Spanish, "Anyone claiming to be from the US

Embassy, call me at once. There is a gang of imposters, and we must deal with them correctly."

From the landing of the stairs, Connors said, "What if they really are from the US embassy?"

Noboa looked up and and all the color drained from his face. He rested a hand on the reception desk and stuttered two or three words. He stopped and tried again. "Dean, I got your voice mail, and I tried to call you back. When did you get here?"

One of Dean's hands remained on the manager's shoulder, and the other fished in his pocket for his phone. Glancing down, Connors said, "You called me back? Really? I don't see that on my phone. I think we need to—"

Noboa vaulted for the front door, grabbing a rolling luggage cart as he darted past. He turned it over and jammed the path to the door with tumbling suitcases and a jumble of hanging clothes.

Connors pushed past the manager, who said in Spanish, "What's going on here? This is a civilized hotel. This is not acceptable!"

On the street, Noboa frantically darted to the left. There was a casino two doors down from the hotel. If anyplace offered a chance to escape in the confusion of crowds, it was the casino. As he pushed by those going to work, Noboa shoved a woman, causing her to drop her bag of papers, which fluttered everywhere.

As Connors hit the street, the sounds of the startled woman and the sight of her papers in the morning breeze pointed straight to where Noboa had run. Connors cut hard left and then stopped. Where did this idiot Noboa think he was going to run? He had revealed himself as an enemy of his own government and a man who was probably aiding a smuggler responsible for stealing national treasures.

Vicente Noboa was, as far as Connors could tell, a man without a friend in the world, except possibly Roberto Ordóñez. Connors reached into his pocket and pulled out his cell phone. Calling the embassy in Quito, Connors asked to speak to the ambassador.

"Ma'am, it's my unfortunate duty to inform you that one of the employees of the Guayaquil consulate has apparently been providing substantial aid to a suspected smuggler," Connors said. He listened for a moment. "No, I haven't informed the consular chief yet. That will be my next call."

He listened again. "Yes, ma'am, it does appear, at least for now, this is tied to the death of the American a few days ago. It also appears tied to the disappearance of Agent Pujols."

Saturday, 11 January
8:02 a.m.

Above Connors, five stories up at the top floor of the casino's hotel, Noboa was also on the phone. "Roberto," he pleaded, "you must help me. The head of American embassy security is in Guayaquil. He knows I lied about Pujols. He's after me. If he catches me, that'll be it for all of us. I've helped you in every way you've ever asked. Now you must help me."

Roberto, sitting at Miguel's large square dining table in Cuenca drinking his morning coffee with one sugar and two creams, listened but said nothing. Noboa said again, "You've got to get somebody here to get me out of the city. My wife and children, too. We must escape. It's all over for me. You swore this would never happen."

"I believe what I said was, if you kept your head and never failed to follow my instructions, everything would be fine," Roberto said, measuring his words and his tone to convey no emotion. "When did you learn this man from Quito was coming?"

Noboa's panic had him almost to the point of weeping. "He called last night, but I didn't take the call. He left a voice mail saying he was coming. I went to the hotel first thing this morning to plant a story before he got there. However, he must have gotten there just ahead of me. Now I don't know what to do." The last sentence came out as a blubber of tears and dread.

Roberto looked across the table at the professor, who was instructing Miguel on exactly how he wanted his eggs this morning. "We are a little busy here," Roberto said, "so I am not going to be able to send anyone. But here is what I am going to do. I am going to give you two choices. You can do the chivalrous thing and kill yourself before you are captured, or I will have Juan torture your wife and family until they beg for death. And if you have somehow escaped the clutches of the Americans, you will get to watch the entire episode. Then I will allow the Inca to pull out your heart and eat it. If he does, you know what will happen. You will never get to enter the afterlife. Do they have the death penalty in America for betraying your country? No matter. Goodbye, Vicente."

Back on the street below, Connors was calling the office of the federal prosecutor with a request from the ambassador to help in the apprehension of Vicente Noboa. As the phone rang, it sounded like a bomb exploding on the street behind Connors.

Just as the security chief turned to look, a voice in Spanish said, "This is Captain Adolfo Stroessner. May I help you?"

"Hello, Captain Stroessner," Connors answered in Spanish. "This is Dean Connors with the American embassy. I am in Guayaquil and have just uncovered a smuggling plot involving one of our consulate employees. I was going to ask for your help in finding this man. However, he just fell into my lap." With that, Connors hung up the phone.

Men and women gasped in horror at the sight of Vicente Noboa, who had jumped from five stories up, caving in the top of a Volkswagen before amputating his own head on the convertible's passenger-side window. The head rolled a few feet from where Connors was standing. The body remained in the car. Connors stared at the scene, trying to process it all. With Noboa dead, he wondered where he was in trying to locate George d'Hout and Agent Pujols. Within five minutes, the flashing lights of a dozen police cars bouncing off the blood made it appear almost florescent.

Connors recalled a lesson he had learned when first arriving in Ecuador. The indigenous peoples had three ideals: don't steal, don't lie, and don't be lazy. In days of old, if you were caught committing these offenses, the punishment could be anything up to and including having your head chopped off. "Sentence served," Connors thought. "Now let's find out what you did with my agent."

Saturday, 11 January
8:03 a.m.

"We have never had this kind of trouble before," Roberto said to the professor. "You have gotten sloppy."

Professor Knight kept eating his eggs. Miguel was a few feet away in the kitchen, washing dishes and pretending he couldn't hear what was being said. Juan was out coordinating the search efforts of a dozen security vehicles.

Focusing on the eggs as if they were the finest things he had ever tasted, the professor said, "I have not gotten sloppy. You will recall that your lapdog, Juan Pacheco, is the one who started this downward spiral by killing Davies."

"Let me ask you something," Roberto said. His tone suggested he might be discussing his favorite vacation spot or the best book he had ever read. "What exactly do you do for this venture? You pose as an archaeologist, and I believe in your heart that is how you see yourself. But you do no excavations, and you wouldn't know the first thing about actually following a map or decoding a message. That is why you insisted I bring d'Hout here."

The professor wiped his mouth on a napkin, then began picking crumbs off the table around his plate. However, instead of setting them on the plate or in his napkin, he looked at Ordóñez and dropped them on the floor.

"There is a tempest on the sea of our plans, but I will not be the Jonah tossed overboard to supplicate an angry god. I determine where the treasure is so you can enjoy huge profits from the sale. That is what I do, Roberto, and I am quite unapologetic about it."

"So what you do is sort through fairy stories to determine which ones might be real, yes? Then Juan does the legwork to make people tell us what they know. I use my various businesses to ship the treasures out of the country. And again I ask, what is it you do?"

Ordóñez's voice was still unperturbed, but his eyes were burning a hole through the professor's face. Miguel watched from the kitchen. He believed the professor was on dangerous ground. It was possible that if Juan was here, Ordóñez would already have ordered Knight's death.

The professor watched Ordóñez for a moment but said nothing else. Then he took a deep breath and blew it out slowly. "What I do, Señor Ordóñez, is whatever I am instructed to do. If I have failed you, I can assure you it will never happen again."

"Thank you, William," Ordóñez said, using a name that seemed to startle the professor. "Miguel, where are we on locating the ICE agent and Mr. d'Hout?"

"I do not have a cell phone because you will not allow me to have one. May I have yours? Otherwise, how do you want me to contact him?"

Still sounding as carefree as if he were celebrating the first day of spring, Ordóñez said, "Miguel, I have had a very stressful morning, and it is barely eight. If you do not leave this house at once, find Juan, and bring back a progress report, I am going to vent my frustrations on one of your lovely little daughters. Beautiful, no? No."

The small Indian's acknowledgment was drowned out by a series of locks being unfastened and doors opening as the Cañari headed out to find Juan or one of the security cars. One day he would have his vengeance on these pigs, but not while his family was still being held captive at some undisclosed location. Reaching the street, he frantically looked up and down for some sign of Juan.

A security cruiser was a block away, and Miguel took off in pursuit. The two security men were cruising up and down in case d'Hout and the ICE agent circled back. Reaching the car, Miguel said, "Radio Juan. Señor Ordóñez wants an update."

One of the officers smiled and said, "I think there is good news. One of the cars is on the western edge of the city near the *iglesia* on the hill. He is looking with binoculars through the windows. It appears the two men are there."

At that moment, Miguel heard Juan speaking from a walkie-talkie. "You say the priest is in the church? With the two outlaws? Wait for my instructions, but do not let them leave."

The driver who had spoken to Miguel reached up and activated his radio. "Your little Cañari dog is here. He says Señor Ordóñez wants a progress report."

"I am in one of the cars. We are about twelve blocks away. *Muchacho*, tell Señor Ordóñez we have located the agent and George d'Hout. I will be there in a moment, and we will go conclude this business."

Saturday, 11 January
8:20 a.m.

Hugh d'Hout studied every map he could find on Cuenca. On his computer he had zoomed in on the southern edge of the original colonial city. He opened separate screens with a variety of topographic and historical indexes. His wife stood over his shoulder watching.

On the speaker phone, Carol also waited in silence. She felt like she was back in high school. It was one of those conversations in which both parties ran out of things to say but neither wished to hang up. She believed if Hugh failed in his quest, it could mean George's life.

In Carol's mind, George was tied up and gagged in a jungle hut. Dark-skinned natives with poison-tipped spears guarded him. She had never been to Ecuador, so picturing it accurately, or at least accurately based on where he really was, was impossible for her.

In trying to learn more about the country, Carol had stumbled onto a website dedicated to the lives of five missionaries from the United States martyred in the rain forests of Ecuador in 1956. Now, in her mind George was a sixth member of that party, captured by tribesmen and in danger of being their next victim.

"C'mon, Hugh," she muttered.

"What?" she heard Hugh ask on the other end of the line.

"Sorry. Nothing. How's it coming? Maybe we should be on video link. Not being able to see what you're doing is driving me crazy."

"Can't," Hugh responded. "I've got every computer, laptop, and tablet in the place fully engaged in helping me look for this."

"Tell me again what 'this' is," Carol said.

"The pirates wrote that the treasure was buried in a place family members would know as well as they knew their own names. Suddenly it came to me. They weren't being elusive or metaphorical. They were plainly telling everyone where the treasure was."

"And?" Carol said.

"If you can get him to tell you, you're doing better than me," she heard Brenda say.

"The names," Hugh said. "The meaning of the names is key to where the treasure is."

"That's as far as I can get," Carol heard Brenda say in an aggravated voice. "It's not a d'Hout character trait to be talkative."

"But it is a d'Hout trait to be smart," Hugh said. "I think I got it! Here's the thing: everyone thinks of pirates as common criminals. Many of them probably were, and some were worse than that. But a lot of the buccaneers were no dummies. Some of them, like Henry Morgan and William Dampier, were as bright as anyone you'd ever meet. Dampier was not only a sailor but a naturalist and geographer. His journals became best sellers when they were published. Davies and d'Hout appear to have been of that class, based on everything I know."

Brenda said, "Carol, the next sound you're going to hear is me strangling my husband if he doesn't tell us where the treasure is and how to use that information to help George."

Hugh relented. "Okay, here it is: *d'Hout* is Dutch. It means 'grove of trees.' *Davies* comes from the same origins as *David*, which means 'beloved.' They were telling the world that the treasure was hidden by a beloved grove of trees."

Brenda and Carol were both silent, completely underwhelmed by this revelation. "A beloved grove of trees," Hugh repeated. "Don't you see?"

"I've never been to Ecuador," Carol said over the phone, "but don't they have lots of trees there? And what are the chances that trees that were there in 1687 are even still standing? That clue is useless."

Hugh was unshaken in his conviction. "Like I said, these pirates were no dummies. They had to know this was an especially beloved grove of trees. Now I just have to figure out which grove." He turned to Brenda. "That's why I have all these maps pulled up and am cross-referencing them with original documents on the city of Cuenca. I have to find the beloved grove. George is counting on me."

Carol's voice came back. "Maybe you should just tell the ICE agent and the FBI. Then see if they think it's safe to tell the kidnappers. Maybe the people who are there can figure it out. They can go out and look for it."

"If the people who have George think I'm sending them on a wild-goose chase, it could be bad for him. Besides, I want the authorities to have as much information as possible. Since they don't know where George is being kept, their best chance of finding him is being at the treasure spot when the bad guys show up. We've come too far to let George get killed now."

On the other end of the line, Hugh heard Carol begin to weep. Brenda reached out and punched her husband in the shoulder. "I'm sorry," he said. "That just slipped out. It wasn't the right thing to say."

"But it's true," Carol said over the phone. "Oh, Hugh, I hope you're right. But what if…"

CHAPTER 26

Saturday, 11 January
8:22 a.m.

"Are you coming?" Roberto asked impatiently as he prepared to get in the car and go with Juan and a small army of security guards to the church where Pujols and d'Hout were sighted. Professor Knight stayed seated at the breakfast table, pretending to relax with another cup of coffee. He couldn't show how worried he was about his shaky position within the group.

In the kitchen, Miguel was putting away the last of the breakfast dishes. He also slipped two small paring knives into his pocket. When Ordóñez had taken over the property and kidnapped Miguel's family, all communication devices were removed, as well as anything the Cañari might use as a weapon.

The professor looked up from his coffee. "Juan is about to do what he does best. He is going to kill people. You are going to do what you do best, which is supervising the thing. Miguel is going to do what he does best, which is whatever you tell him. And me? I am going to do what I do best, unabashedly restoring your confidence in my unique abilities. I am going to go find the treasure."

Ordóñez eyed the professor. "Or you could be looking for an opportunity to escape before things get uncomfortable."

"Don't forget, Roberto, that you cleared over three million dollars in pure profit from our Bolivia adventure. Do not lose faith in me so quickly."

Ordóñez glanced at Miguel. "We are all going to do what we do best. Miguel, you are going to stay with my dear friend and trusted confidant, Professor William Knight, while he works his latest bit of magic. And if he makes the slightest move to try to leave us holding the bag, as the Americans say, you are to cut his throat with one of those dull paring knives you slipped into your pocket earlier. Beautiful, no?"

Both the professor and Miguel had stunned expressions, which they quickly tried to replace with nods of acquiescence. Sounds of cars pulling up outside broke the awkward silence. Juan exited the back of a security vehicle. A second one pulled up behind it. "What about going out the tunnel?" the professor asked. "What if the neighbors see you?"

"This is a matter of grave urgency," Ordóñez said. "If you don't understand that, you truly are of very little use to me." The professor shrugged and went back to his coffee and maps.

Outside, Juan moved toward the house, glancing up at the sky. Miguel stepped outside to assist with the locked gate, but

The Ecuadorian Deception

Juan produced his own key and quickly entered, moving across the tiled patio toward the front door.

"It looks like a nasty storm is moving in early today," Juan said to no one in particular. "That's good. I was wondering how we would hide the sounds of gunfire at the church. It appears God is going to do it for us with some thunder. Maybe the priest is not quite as holy as he wants everyone to think. God is using me as his angel of death."

Ordóñez was not amused. "Who said anything about the priest? The security guards are apprehending two wanted fugitives who murdered a number of innocent people last night. They will attempt to deliver them to the authorities, but when they try to escape, they will be killed. It will happen near the river to make sure the bodies wash away. Only, unlike the security guards, they will not be found. And the priest will be on the radio and TV, verifying that everything happened just that way. No accidents, mistakes, or sloppiness. Understand?"

Saturday, 11 January
8:39 a.m.

When Ordóñez's men first began surrounding the church, Albert sensed, more than heard, their approach. For the last forty-five minutes he had insisted that George and the priest join him in staying crouched behind the pews. "Am I your prisoner?" Padre Domingo asked.

"Right now, you are just a fellow caught in cross fire," Albert said. "I know you are excited about seeing Jesus, but I'd rather it not happen because of me."

Combining duck walks, crawls, and scoots, Albert and George stayed low, looking out the bits of odd-shaped clear panes peppered among the stained glass in the windows lining the church. Doing so, they made their ways past each of the Stations of the Cross.

"Those are good places to pray," Padre Domingo said as he watched them. "God will forgive you for whatever you have done."

"I know you don't believe us," Albert said, "but we weren't responsible for those deaths. The men outside right now were responsible, and they won't think twice about killing you, too."

Over an hour ago, Albert had asked about using a phone, but the priest told him there was none in the church, since it didn't contain an office. Padre Domingo's own phone had been no use since it had run out of minutes two days ago. "I have been meaning to go buy more minutes," he said, "but I didn't do it."

Now the priest wasn't sure whether that was a good thing or not. If the Americans were crazy, they might use the phone to summon more crazy people to their rescue. If they were telling him the truth, no phone might mean all three of them were about to die. "The greatest phone line of all is prayer," Padre Domingo said.

"Dial it up," Albert said.

George asked, "Albert, why aren't they coming in? What are they doing out there?"

"Probably waiting for Ordóñez. Last night was a total screw-up because Juan got too far out over his skis. We need to come up with something because when Ordóñez gets here, it's going to get bad pretty quick."

Turning to the priest, Albert resumed speaking in Spanish. "Padre, how old is this church?"

"It's the newest in Cuenca. It was built to minister to those on the west side of the city who could not travel to the churches farther away. It's still a very small parish because many people like going to the larger churches. They like to be reminded of how big God is and how small they are."

"What I need to know is this, are priests buried under this church like in some of the large cathedrals?" Albert had the seed of a plan, but it hinged on there being another way out.

"Catacombs?" the priest asked.

"Yes," Albert said. "I'm looking for a way we can get out of here. You, too. These men are international criminals. They will kill all three of us without blinking. I'm sorry we brought this to your doorstep, Father, but now we've got to find a way out."

The priest looked at the fourth Station of the Cross, which he was kneeling beside. The statue at the top of the foundation portrayed Jesus looking into the eyes of his mother, Mary. "What should I do?" he asked.

"What?" Albert said, glancing out a sliver of clear glass to see two security cars. The inhabitants were talking back and forth on their vehicle radios. Then the nearest car's door opened, and both men got out. They walked around and opened the trunk, removing two shotguns. "Time is getting short, Pastor. What did you say?"

George looked over to see the priest staring at the religious images. "I don't think he's talking to you," he said. "I think he's praying."

Murmuring, half aloud and half under his breath, Padre Domingo stared deeply into the eyes of the two figures portrayed before him. "I have been sworn to secrecy," the priest said. "Something like this could be devastating. What should I do?"

"Uh-oh," George said. He was positioned on the right side of the church. Albert was on the left. They had been moving in opposite directions, peeking out to see Ordóñez's henchmen. "Roberto just pulled up. There are two cars. Juan is there, too, along with four more of those security guards."

Roberto Ordóñez strolled out of the car, looking up toward the Andes Mountains surrounding the city of Cuenca. Albert could see Ordóñez talking to the guards, pointing to the mountains and the clouds rolling in over them and smiling broadly. Repositioning himself to follow where the men were looking,

Albert saw large, black rain clouds moving in quickly. Jagged lightning cut the sky and a rolling boom cascaded past the church.

※※※

"What a beautiful place, no?" Roberto said to no one in particular. "I can certainly see why our two friends were attracted here. Juan, you are right. There is a storm rolling in. I believe it will be here in less than twenty minutes. I love the rain. And the thunder and lightning will serve our purposes very well."

Roberto glanced at the small army of guards. "And who did such excellent work finding our two missing lambs?" he asked.

"It was Bartholomew," Juan said. He motioned toward one of the security guards. "*Muchacho*, come here and tell Señor Ordóñez how you found the two murderers."

Bartholomew explained how he and his partner, Enrico, had seen the priest drive up the one winding road toward the westernmost church and decided to follow. "We thought the men might be hiding out in the back of the car," he told Ordóñez. "Then we saw one of them come around from the back of the church. When they went inside, I could see through the front window, using my field glasses. The other one was inside as well."

"Outstanding work," Ordóñez said. "You will be richly rewarded. Juan, make note of it. This one gets extra in his paycheck."

Beaming, Bartholomew took his position by his partner, Enrico. "I told you working for Señor Ordóñez is better than working for the police."

Enrico said, "The police? They are the only people harder to find today than these two Americans. Have you seen a single policeman? Where are our compadres who work for the police force? They can't all work for Señor Ordóñez."

Juan was strolling toward the two men and heard their conversation. "*Muchacho*, you don't need to own all the dogs. You just have to know who holds the leashes. Are you ready to go in?"

Both men nodded. Enrico displayed his Remington 1000, showing it was loaded and ready for discharge. "When do we go?" Bartholomew asked.

"Señor Ordóñez is waiting for the rain and thunder," Juan said. "He's a smart one. Even the weather cooperates with his plans."

"That's because he would kill it should it refuse." Enrico laughed.

Juan did not join him. "Show respect," Ordóñez's lieutenant reminded the men. "Don't be too familiar. He can take care of you or me just as easily as he is taking care of these gringos. Never forget that."

Both security guards snapped to attention. "Just say when," Enrico said.

CHAPTER 27

Saturday, 11 January
8:41 a.m.

Dean Connors felt the phone in his pocket vibrate. He looked at the screen, then pushed the answer button. "Special Agent Williams," Connors said, "I was just about to call you. I am standing here with Vicente Noboa. Or rather, what's left of him. He saw me and panicked. He ended up taking a header from a fifth-floor window. I'm assuming that's a confession he was involved in this whole thing."

Van Williams acknowledged the information with a stirring in his throat but added no comment. "I've got you on one line," Williams said, "and Hugh d'Hout on the other. I am also linked to an FBI computer specialist. Mr. d'Hout gave him permission to piggyback onto his computer. We're trying to see if we can figure out where his brother and/or the suspects are transmitting from."

"What is your ETA on some insight?" Connors asked.

"So far the IT guy has determined that there's no effort underway to mask the kidnappers' transmission. He said it seems very straightforward. That's pretty odd for people who have done such a good job escaping detection in the past."

"What are they saying?"

"It appears someone is still masquerading as George d'Hout," Williams replied. "Hugh is an educator and used to identifying authentic-versus-fraudulent writing. Says the person on the other end doesn't frame sentences anything like his brother."

"Can anyone in the family hear our conversation?" Connors asked.

"No, I have the other line muted," Williams said. "Just listening as he reports what he is typing and what the responses are."

"And?" Connors wanted to know.

"The brother thinks he's figured out where the treasure is actually hidden," Williams said. He filled Connors in on Hugh's theory.

"Sounds pretty farfetched."

"Here's the thing: we've gone back and forth on the theory and how it will be received. The bottom line is that it probably doesn't matter where the treasure really is or if there is a treasure. We just need Hugh to lead the perps to a spot where the local authorities can make an arrest and you can liberate your man and George d'Hout."

"And where's that?" Connors asked.

"Near a beloved grove of trees," Williams said.

"You ever been to southern Ecuador?" Connors asked. "That's like saying the treasure is somewhere in Kansas near a wheat field."

"I understand. That's why we're hoping you can give us a specific grove of trees to send them toward. But it has to be a plausible spot. Hold it a second; the technician is telling me something."

Connors waited, watching a Guayaquil ambulance crew pick up various body parts Noboa shed when his throat encountered the windshield. Close to where Connors was standing there appeared to be a piece of an ear, or maybe it was an eyelid. It was hard to tell.

Guayaquil police officers were milling around with the crowd, asking people if they knew the man or had seen what happened. So far, Connors hadn't identified himself. Because Noboa was Latino, it didn't instantly dawn on anyone he might not be an Ecuadorian citizen.

An officer with lieutenant's bars on his uniform was gingerly inspecting the headless body that occupied the car's front seat. Connors watched him feel around in Noboa's pockets. He watched him pull out the wallet and inspect the contents. From the lieutenant's expression, it was clear he wasn't going to enjoy the rest of his day.

"Sergeant!" the officer cried out in Spanish. "*¡Adelante!*" Here, now!

The sergeant walked over, and the lieutenant bent down to speak quietly to him so the large crowd of gawkers couldn't hear.

The sergeant's eyes got big. Connors couldn't hear what they were saying, but when the view was unencumbered, he was a pretty good lip-reader.

"A consulate employee?" the sergeant wanted to know. "An American? That means murder, yes?"

"That's an interesting leap of logic," Connors said to himself. If the police were going to treat this as a murder instead of a suicide, it was all the more reason not to get involved and possibly detained. Then the embassy security chief saw one of the hotel bellmen making his way through the crowd.

Relying again on lipreading, Connors watched as the bellman looked over Noboa's clothes and said they looked like what a man was wearing a few minutes ago in the hotel lobby.

The lieutenant wanted to know if anyone was with the deceased. "He came in alone," the bellman said, "but when he saw my manager and another man, he ran away. Then the man who was with my manager ran after him."

Connors had seen enough. It was time to be somewhere else. As he ducked deeper into the crowd of gawkers, he almost forgot the phone on his ear. Then he heard Williams.

"Sounds like you're at the county fair," Williams said. "Can you hear me okay?"

"I'm having to make some tracks so I don't get tied up in the Noboa suicide investigation," Connors said.

"Our technician is going to make that easier for you," Williams replied. "It turns out you're in the wrong city."

"Don't tell me the transmissions are coming from Quito."

"He can't nail them down much more than this, but they are coming from a place called Cuenca. I believe it's up in the Andes Mountains. Hugh says it's maybe a couple of hours from your position on the coast."

"It is," Connors said. "Let me retrieve my car and start heading in that direction. I will call you in half an hour to get an update. I also need some direction on finding this beloved grove of trees."

"Right now I'm having Hugh play a bit of a cat-and-mouse game with the perps," Williams said. "He's asking them questions about the area as if he's trying to help them. When they write back, pressing for where the treasure is, he says they need to work together on it. So far, they're buying it."

"I hope for the sake of George d'Hout and Agent Pujols they don't stop," Connors said. "I'm at least three hours away from Cuenca, so you're going to have to give me some time. Also, I don't know anyone on the police force in Cuenca. I can't promise I can even get backup on this. Any idea how many bad guys we're talking about?"

"No idea," Williams said. "No idea in the world."

Saturday, 11 January
8:45 a.m.

Inside the church, Albert felt caged. "We are going to get out of here," he kept assuring George.

"Doubtful," d'Hout replied. "I just want to talk to Carol."

Padre Domingo listened to Albert and George's conversation. The priest's English was very poor. He picked up on only two or three words per sentence. But his attention was focused on how they were talking rather than on what they were saying. They appeared lucid and reasonable. There was nothing about their interactions with one another that gave the slightest support to his hypothesis they were crazy.

A loud rapping on the door of the church made all three men jump.

"Padre," Roberto Ordóñez called out in Spanish. "Are you all right? We are here to save you. Come open the door. If you don't do it right now, I am afraid you might be harmed in this ugly business."

The priest looked at Albert, then at George. Nothing.

Ordóñez called out again. "If you are holding the priest, you must let him go. Don't make this any worse for yourselves. If you kill the priest, we will be forced to kill you."

That was what Albert was looking for. "Padre, I hope you realize what's about to happen. They will come blazing in here and kill you, blaming it on us, just like they did last night. Then they will also kill us."

The priest's face became stern. "Enough," Padre Domingo said. "I have heard enough."

The priest crawled on hands and knees along the walls of his small church, peeking out from every vantage point to see who was surrounding them. He counted six private security vehicles but not a single police car. Odd, especially if these men were truly wanted by authorities, as the radio reported. Something was very wrong.

Ordóñez again pounded on the locked door. "We know there is a small break in a windowpane of a door in the back," he said. "But we don't want to defile this holy place. We are giving you a chance to come out, you outlaws. Have you no conscience at all? Release the priest so we do not have to come in with guns firing."

Padre Domingo crouched beside Albert. "You were right, Agent Pujols," he said. "There is a way out of here. It is not catacombs, but it is a secret passage. It is older than Cuenca itself and dates back to the time of the Cañari and the invasion by the Inca. Do you know about the Fourth Level?"

Pujols shook his head but repeated the question to George in English.

"The Fourth Level?" George said. "I heard about that when we were at the Inca ruins. It's the passageway for the dead to enter the next life."

Padre Domingo said in Spanish, "The journey to the next life for the Inca was a long one. The passages went on for miles.

They were also used as a way for the Inca shamans to move from place to place as if by magic, undetected by those walking above them."

"I saw tunnels like that in Paraguay," Albert said. "They were used by the Jesuits and their Indian charges to escape Spanish slave hunters hundreds of years ago."

"Exactly," Padre Domingo said. "The tunnels here must be kept a secret. The churches in the city sit on top of them. It would create chaos if people learned such things existed. There are other issues as well."

"C'mon, Padre," Albert said. "Time is short. What are you not telling me?"

"There are also stories that some of the passages lead to immense treasures," Padre Domingo said. "If people learn of these passages, how will we stop a destructive horde from ransacking our city and our churches?"

"Your secret is safe with me, Padre," Albert said. "With George, too. My word on it. Now, how do we get out of here?"

The priest slid back against the base of the fourth Station of the Cross, feeling between it and the wall. There was a slight clicking sound. Suddenly, a place on the statue base slid open. It was about the size of the door of a medium-sized doghouse.

"Slide in headfirst and reach up toward Jesus," the priest said. "You will feel a handhold. You can pull the rest of your body in and feel for a ladder going down. One at a time, you must go. It is very snug."

"How do we close it so it remains a secret?" Albert asked.

"There is another lever inside," Padre Domingo said. "I will come last and make sure it is done."

Suddenly, there was an explosion of sound near the front door of the church, as if someone had hit it with a battering ram. "Last warning," Ordóñez called. "We are coming, Father. Coming to rescue you!"

Albert slid into the darkness, felt for the handle, and pulled himself in. His legs dangled wildly for a moment, feeling for the ladder. Once he found it, he counseled George where the ladder rungs were and then scurried down. Next came d'Hout, followed by the priest.

As the priest pulled the lever, concealing the escape route, the sound of breaking glass and shattered wood chased after them. The sounds above them, however, soon disappeared. George could picture an infuriated Ordóñez angrily asking Juan and the security guards how they could have let the two Americans slip away again.

Counting rungs as he descended, Albert reached thirty before his feet found the floor. Total darkness. When George got to the bottom, he said, "Ask the priest how they were able to keep something like this a secret."

Albert translated back and forth. "You are a Catholic?" the priest asked George.

"Protestant evangelical."

"Then you may not have heard of a vow of silence," Padre Domingo said. "They allow our brothers in monasteries to contemplate the things of God, rather than waste their lives in foolish conversation. They also provide a wonderful work force of committed members of the church who know how to keep a secret. They just don't talk."

"Ingenious," Albert said. "Lead the way, Father. Let's get out of here and find a phone."

"We have quite a ways to travel," Padre Domingo said. "Do either of you have a flashlight? No? Then it is going to be even slower. There are no lights down here."

Taking the lead, the priest instructed Albert to put one hand on the minister's back and another along the wall. George was to do the same thing behind Albert. Like three blind men, they would make their way through the tunnel until they came to another opening.

"Without a light, how are we going to know where the next opening is?" George asked. Albert repeated the question in Spanish. In the dark, George waited for Albert's translation.

"That's a problem," Albert said. "We have to feel for the rungs. If we miss them, we could be down here forever."

"Or until the next priest uses a tunnel for a shortcut," George said. He wasn't overly concerned. "I guess we could just wait for Ordóñez and Juan to go away and go back the way we came."

"Not all the priests even know about the tunnels, according to the father," Albert said. "And those who do are sworn to never use them unless it is a life-or-death situation."

"It *is* a life-or-death situation," George said. "Ours."

Saturday, 11 January
10:15 a.m.

The professor's sense of victory was sublime. He had manipulated the idiot brother of George d'Hout about as completely as was humanly possible. Further, Miguel was able to report to Ordóñez that Professor Knight had gone to the Internet café around the corner, conducted his business, and returned without even a hint of desire to flee.

Miguel's loyalty to the professor was also enhanced when the professor offered to buy the Cañari a roasted guinea pig from the market they passed. Normally, the grilled *cuy,* cooked and served on a long stick inserted from mouth to anus, was reserved for special occasions like birthdays and religious holidays. However, the professor assured Miguel it was indeed a special occasion. They were about to make off with another long-lost treasure.

Making things even better for Professor Knight was the complete and utter failure of Juan and Ordóñez to capture the ICE agent and George d'Hout. In spite of the direct peril their escape placed him in, the professor believed he could extricate the treasure before d'Hout and the agent were able to get help.

Juan's dismal day enhanced Professor Knight's glee. The Inca had d'Hout and the agent cornered, and yet they had slipped away. Perfect. It was about time this idiot *muchacho* was brought down one or two pegs. The professor had to be careful not to gloat, however, since Juan's defeat was also Ordóñez's.

Instead, the professor gave the appearance of being the most concerned and sympathetic of conspirators. "What's our next step?" he asked.

"We still have guards at the church to make sure they don't get away," Ordóñez said. "They have to be hiding somewhere in there. We looked for catacombs, but there don't appear to be any. Maybe they are hiding in the walls or between the ceiling and the roof. You know how those churches are; the older ones are absolute labyrinths. Who knows? We looked but found nothing."

Juan smiled. "The good news is, it doesn't matter where they and the stupid priest are hiding. Tonight after dark, I have it on good authority that those two arsonists are going to strike again. And the church will burn, along with anyone hiding inside."

Now it was the professor's turn to smile. "Roberto, I certainly admire Juan's plan. However, there is a small problem. This is Saturday. In just a few hours, people will be swarming to the church for Saturday-night mass. You cannot burn the church tonight unless you want to kill fifty or sixty more people."

Juan's toothy grin disappeared. He glared at Knight, as if it was his fault today was Saturday. Miguel simply stood in the background near the kitchen and listened.

"Tell your men to slowly start pulling back from the church," Roberto said to Juan. "See if that lures them out. Everyone pulls back except for Enrico and Bartholomew. Do either of them have any family here?"

"No, señor," Juan said. "They are two of the ones we recruited upon the recommendation of an orphanage you generously support."

"True orphans or just abandoned? If they have brothers or sisters, do they contact them often?" Roberto wanted to know.

"Not very," Juan said. "They are supposed to send money, but most of the time they end up drinking it all away. Why? What do you have planned?"

"Go back into the church with them. Subdue them in whatever way you see fit. Make it appear the Americans killed them," Ordóñez said. "Start a good fire. Make it look like arson. Then get out of there and bring the security company car back here. Our arsonists have killed two more people and hopefully themselves, too."

"Do you worry you are unduly depleting your own forces?" the professor wanted to know.

"I am duly eliminating witnesses, should all of this not work out in our favor," Ordóñez said. "And I am turning up the heat, so to speak, on our two escapees. They will die, either by our hand or by the police. Beautiful, no? Now, where are we on locating that treasure?"

CHAPTER 28

Saturday, 11 January
11:19 a.m.

George kept waiting for his eyes to adjust to the darkness. However, the pitch-black tunnel shut out all traces of the light above. There was also no sound except their own breathing, words, and the shuffling of their feet in the stygian gloom.

"Any idea where this tunnel leads?" Albert asked in Spanish.

Padre Domingo ran his hands along the tunnel's walls. "It almost certainly leads back toward the colonial portion of the city. The tunnels were started by the Cañari, and then expanded by the Incas. Like the secret corridors under the pyramids of Egypt, their very existence was a closely guarded secret reserved for the holy men of the tribe. My understanding is the slaves who labored constructing them were always put to death to ensure their silence."

George gave Albert a nudge to indicate he wanted to know what was being said. Albert translated and George responded, "Any idea how far out the passages go?"

Following the same question-translation-answer-translation route, Albert repeated the priest's words. "At least as far as the two rivers running to the south of town and the one north of the city."

"I kept wondering how Miguel could have possibly constructed that tunnel from his house to the river bridge in just a few weeks," George said. "So it's possible he was just restoring an old tunnel that was already there."

Albert said, "Possibly, but don't underestimate the Cañari. They are truly amazing workers. Because they are so short, people tend to write them off. However, this entire part of Ecuador is a testimony to their abilities long before the Inca or Spanish came along."

Padre Domingo said, "If the tunnels truly date back to the Cañari's rule and were only taken over by the Incas as part of their conquest, they could run throughout the entire region."

The three men continued their blind trip down the tunnel. "Any spiders down here?" George asked. "Every movie I've ever seen with caves and tunnels also has spiders."

"Yes," Albert said. "The Ecuadorian orphan maker is rumored to be at least three feet tall." The ICE agent then repeated his words to the priest, who burst out laughing.

George didn't laugh. In the darkness, his imagination had a large canvas on which to paint a plethora of angry, venomous arachnids. "So, no spiders?" he asked again.

"No idea," Albert said. "But the great thing is that if there is one, it will eat me and the priest before it gets to you. Who says there aren't benefits to being last?"

Padre Domingo said in Spanish, "There is a serious matter we must discuss, since we have no idea whether we may be down here for minutes, hours, or days. That is the matter of the tunnel itself and what it may hold."

"Go ahead, Father," Albert said. "You talk; I'll translate."

"These tunnels are under both a heavenly protection and a curse. When I said earlier that they must remain a secret, I was not exaggerating. Legends that predate the arrival of the Spanish say these shafts run the length of South America. They were used to hide treasures and to spirit away those in danger."

Suddenly the priest stopped and turned, causing Albert to run into him and George to collide with them both. "I'm sorry, Padre," Albert said. "I didn't realize—"

"Listen to me!" the priest said. "You are still not listening. These passages are secret, and they must remain secret. Those who have spoken of them, who have disregarded the warnings, have been driven mad. They have suffered horrible deaths."

"Okay, Father, okay," Albert said, trying to reassure the old priest. "I am listening. You have my word. The secret of the tunnels is safe."

"What do you know of the Spanish conquest of the Andes?" the priest asked.

"Just what I learned in school," Albert said. "I know it was pretty horrible for the native peoples."

"There is a saying that the more one looks at food, the hungrier one becomes. That was true of the conquistadors. The more gold and silver they found, the more they desired. Their lust was unquenchable until they had gutted the entirety of the land. These tunnels are among the last of the unknown treasures. They hold many mysteries, many secrets. If the outside world becomes aware of them, a new kind of conquistador will come."

The padre continued. "They will call themselves tourists or adventurers, but they will crawl over us like ants and slowly eat away all that is ours. I have saved your lives, and in return you must keep this secret."

The priest turned and began walking in the inky blackness, leaving Albert and George to feel blindly to catch up. George asked, "You think he's regretting bringing us down here?"

"Whatever these tunnels were constructed for, the power of that purpose is still being felt hundreds of years later," Albert said. "What do the walls feel like to you?"

"I'm not sure," George said. "Maybe a polished wood. Hard to say. It could be stone, I guess, but it doesn't feel cold enough to be stone. Just cool, like wood."

"Have you felt any cobwebs or clutter on the floor?" Albert asked.

"No. In that regard, they remind me of some lava tubes my wife and I went spelunking in on the Big Island of Hawaii. Black and empty and endless."

"They just don't give me the feel of something that hasn't been used for years and years," Albert said. "They feel more like a mine shaft people trudge through every day."

"There is one difference," George said. "We toured some mines a few years ago in Colorado, near Ouray."

"Sure," Albert said. "I've done that, too. And one in Silverton. Even though it was summer, it was wet and cold in those mines."

"You got dripped on from surface water working its way underground, right?" George said.

"And here there's none of that. How can it be?" Albert asked the priest, listened for the answer, and then repeated it as they walked through the darkness. "He says it's because water would eventually destroy the integrity of the tunnels. That cannot happen because they are protected by heaven itself."

Behind them, a low rumbling and sudden thud shook the darkness. The sound was more felt than heard as it vibrated past them down the tunnel. George felt the hairs on his neck and arms stand up.

Albert involuntarily reached for his gun, which he wasn't even carrying. Every fight-or-flight mechanism within his body was on high alert. For his part, the father began praying aloud.

"My church, it is gone," the priest said in the darkness. "We just heard it die."

Saturday, 11 January
2:00 p.m.

Professor Knight was back at the Internet café, Miguel in tow. He had e-mailed Hugh d'Hout and was waiting to hear back. Outside, the air was thick with the wails of sirens and the howls of every dog in Cuenca. The siren blasts echoed off the surrounding Andes Mountains and revisited the city in mournful waves.

What had once been the Catholic church on Cuenca's western edge was surrounded by *bomberos* praying for another cloudburst to help them put out the fire. The flames burned so hot, they were catching the surrounding countryside on fire, threatening to create a wildfire running up the side of the mountain toward the Cajas.

Parishioners from all over western Cuenca rushed to the scene, distraught to see their beloved sanctuary going up in flames. "How could this happen?" they demanded of one another.

Others wanted to know where Padre Domingo was, since the parish car he drove was parked in the small gravel lot. Realizing the priest might be trapped inside, groups of women began crossing themselves and clutching the crucifixes around their necks to utter prayers.

Juan mixed with the crowd and, as he had at the fire along the Yanuncay River, was about to watch a rumor also burn red hot into forged fact. He turned to a man who was wiping away his wife's tears. They watched the futile effort to put out the blaze. "Did I hear someone say this was the work of those American arsonists?" Juan asked.

"If it is, they must die," the man said angrily.

"I'm pretty sure that's what I heard," Juan said. "The security guards who were looking for them went into the church during their search. That was the last anyone has seen of the guards. I hope they're okay."

The couple digested the news and immediately began asking those around them if they had heard it, too. Meanwhile, Juan slipped away and headed for the far side of the crowd. There he repeated his earlier remarks, this time to a group of distraught Quichera women. The women dispersed to ask others in the crowd what they had heard about the arsonists.

Juan knew by the time the rumor's two paths met in the middle of the crowd, close to where the commanders of the *bomberos* were huddled, they would be accepted fact. The story would be something everyone knew, though no one remembered how he or she first heard it.

As he got into the security car and pulled away, Juan flipped on the FM radio. An announcer for the station was reporting from the fire. Already the speculation regarding who was responsible was being broadcast across Cuenca.

"Even if this sets back tourism," the announcer said, "even if we never see another American, this outrage must be addressed. If you see the men described, they must be brought to justice."

"Good," Juan thought. "Make them hate Americans. Perfect. And when the professor finds the location of the treasure and shows us, he can be one more American for them to seek retaliation against. *Adios, muchacho.*"

Saturday, 11 January
2:44 p.m.

The total darkness of the tunnel was beginning to play tricks on George's mind. As he crept ahead, clutching an invisible shoulder with one hand and touching the wall with the other, he saw Carol ahead, summoning him onward. She was wearing the same outfit she'd had on the day she drove him to the airport in Houston.

"I'm coming," he said aloud. "Don't cry. I'm coming."

"What?" Albert asked. "Who're you talking to?"

George felt foolish. "No one," he said. "I guess this blackness is making me see things. I thought I saw..."

At that moment Padre Domingo suddenly sank before Albert, who went crashing over the top of him. George in turn sprawled across them both. The priest let out a cry of pain as Albert muffled a curse and George grabbed onto nothingness, trying to find a handhold.

Silence followed, but an agonizing moan soon pierced it. All three men froze, trying to assess what had happened. "My leg," the priest said. "I think it's broken. Dear God, it's bleeding. I can feel the blood."

Albert scrambled about on all fours, feeling in every direction, trying to figure out what happened and determine where they were. The wall was still to their right, and the floor was below them as it had been a moment ago. However, he felt a depression where the priest had fallen. Reaching around the priest, first with his arms and then with his legs, Albert determined that the space the priest had fallen into was about four feet deep and shaped like a semicircle.

George also felt around in the darkness. He felt the wall and realized that to the right of where the priest had fallen was another semicircle. Together, the two spaces opened to another space in the tunnel.

Albert pulled off his light jacket. "Padre, can you raise yourself back up to the floor we were walking on?" he asked. "I need to check on your leg."

The priest cried out in pain as he tried to put weight on the leg. "Are both legs hurt?" Albert asked.

"Just the left one," the priest said, unsuccessfully trying to hold back shrieks of pain that echoed through the black tunnels like howls from a banshee.

"Use the right one to lift yourself up," Albert said in Spanish. "George and I will help you."

The two men groped in the darkness, trying to find a way to get the priest out of the hole into which he fell. Once that was done, Albert began feeling along the leg. He reached the place where the priest's robe and the pants under it were soaked with the warm goo of blood. There was a tear in the pants, so Albert used the snag to tear the pants away.

Cries of pain again racked the priest. "Is the bone sticking out?"

Albert translated what the priest was asking and sought George's help to feel for any sign of a compound break. George felt queasy. As a runner, the thought of a broken leg was one of his worst fears.

Albert said, "I feel the bone. Not good. You've got a pretty bad wound here. I'm going to use my jacket to wrap around it and slow down the bleeding."

As he did so, George said he was going to check out the opening in the floor and wall where the priest had fallen. "Go really slow," Albert said. "Two of us can carry the third one, but if two people go down, we're in real trouble."

George felt his way back into the four-foot depression. The complete lack of light made every move agonizingly slow as he tried to make sure he wasn't about to bump his head or step off into another trench. What he felt was another passageway leading off at a right angle. After the initial drop, he had to walk hunched over, feeling his way, for four or five feet. Then he could stand completely upright.

"How are you doing?" Albert called. "I can hear your footsteps. Please stay close. We can't afford to get separated."

George answered, "This tunnel doesn't seem to be as high as the one we were in, but I can stand up. It's about as wide as my outstretched arms. The walls are rougher. It may be some secondary shaft, not a main walkway. What do you think?"

"I think I've never been afraid of the dark," Albert said, "but that's changing."

George said he was coming back toward the two men. "If the leg is really a compound break and we try to carry him without securing it, that bone could do some real damage in there."

"I was thinking the same thing," Albert said, "but we sure can't leave him here. Depending on how big a maze this turns out to be, and how long it takes us to get help, he could bleed to death. We can't leave anyone behind, period."

George said he agreed, and Albert translated their conversation to the priest.

Padre Domingo said, "You have a mission, my son. First, you must save our city from the madmen who are killing and burning. Then you must send help for me. In that order. I will not go with you. If I do, I might keep you from completing both missions."

Again Albert translated. As George and Albert discussed the ramifications of leaving the father behind, Padre Domingo said, "All my life I have looked forward to seeing Jesus. However, we don't know that today is my scheduled appointment. It would be rude to show up ahead of time. Therefore, if you don't mind, please hurry to get me help. Now go!"

Albert and George felt their way past the indention where Padre Domingo had fallen. As they were about to continue on, Albert had an idea. "We're both on the same side of the tunnel. What if the ladder leading out is on the opposite wall? We could go right past it and never know. We might have already passed one."

George said, "And if I am right behind you and we come across another one of those side passages, there's a good chance another one of us will be hurt. You want us to take opposite sides?"

"Yes, but we're going to have to stay at the same pace so we don't get separated. Let's try each walking sideways, with both hands feeling the wall. We need to kind of do a sweeping motion with our lead foot to feel for any other side holes before we fall into them. You okay with that?"

George moved to the far wall, and Albert stayed against the near wall as they continued the process of feeling their way through the inky darkness. Several times Albert called out in Spanish, "How you doing, Padre?"

The sound was so distorted by echoes when the priest answered that Albert couldn't understand what he was saying. But at least he was still alive and hadn't gone into shock. However, both Albert and George knew they were racing against time to get the padre help.

They traveled on for what felt like several hundred yards without finding anything, their pace growing gradually quicker and quicker. As they continued, it seemed that a rumbling sound was gradually growing above them. However, it was more a vibration they felt than a sound they heard.

"Any idea what that is?" George asked.

"Heaven only knows how far underground we are. I just hope it's not an earthquake. That would be a real capper on the day."

They continued moving forward and reached a point where the dim rumble seemed to be directly above them. "You think it could be a busy street?" George asked. "Maybe we're to the center of town."

"Only if we've been gradually going uphill and are pretty close to the surface," Albert said. "But I haven't gotten that impression. Have you?"

"To tell you the truth," George said, "I'm seeing my wife in the darkness. I think I hear things, and then I'm not sure. This total blackness is messing with me. It's also been a long time since I've had anything to eat. I'm kind of a mess, so my senses are probably messed up, too."

"Next time your wife appears to you, ask her to send help and show us the way out of here. Let's move a little farther and see if the sound stays where it is or moves with us. That might give us some idea what it is."

Continuing a few hundred more yards, the men agreed the sound stayed stationary. "What makes a continuous roar?" Albert asked.

"Jet engines, rivers, high winds, race cars, waterfalls…I don't know," George said, struggling for something that made sense.

"You mentioned water twice. There aren't any waterfalls that I know of in Cuenca. However, there are four rivers," Albert said.

"And the ones I saw looked like class-four rapids," George said. "They were certainly loud enough to make that kind of sound. But would the sound travel down?"

"Maybe not, but depending on how far underground we are, maybe we weren't actually under it. Maybe we were beside a bend in the river," Albert conjectured.

George had an idea. "We know there was a way into and out of the tunnel from the house where they held me. It was right beside the river," he said. "Think we could get that lucky?"

"I didn't feel anything as we passed it the first time," Albert said. "But I was so focused on the sound, I might have missed something."

"In this darkness, who knows?" George agreed. "Let's double back and find out. The priest can't last long."

Albert called out again in Spanish, "Padre, how you doing?"
Silence.
Albert yelled again, louder this time.
Nothing.
"You believe in prayer?" Albert asked.
"I had the thought earlier that my wife was probably praying for an angel to come and set me free, and here came Miguel. You know the archangel is supposed to be named Michael; that's Miguel in Spanish. Yeah, I believe in prayer."

"Can you pray and walk, or do you need to kneel down?" Albert inquired.

"Are you kidding?" George laughed. "I live in Houston. You ever been on the highways there? It's like a white-knuckle trip through hell. You better believe I can pray on the move."

"Do it," Albert said. They began backtracking toward the roar above them, hoping they had passed a portal leading out.

CHAPTER 29

Saturday, 11 January
5:15 p.m.

The afternoon thunderstorm cleared. Dean Connors sat in the back of the Coffee Tree Café, watching the light fade and the night fall on Cuenca. The café was moderately busy, a good mix of tourists and locals. They talked about the things they had seen on their tourist junkets outside the city and debated which of Cuenca's myriad churches offered the most architectural splendor. They also speculated about the nonstop wail of fire trucks in the distance.

Connors's cell phone was lying on the table next to his cup of coffee and sandwich, both of which were hot and delicious against the cold, rainy Cuenca afternoon. The phone vibrated.

"Ideas?" Connors asked.

Van Williams said, "My people say there are at least twenty Internet cafés in Cuenca. The connection lines there are rather antiquated by current standards, so they can't get a good fix on where the messages are coming from. That being said, their best guess is that they're coming from southeast of your present location."

"So my next move is?" Connors asked. "I don't know this city at all, so I'm totally flying blind here."

"Do you have any GPS that's working?" the FBI agent asked. "We could download coordinates to you."

"Actually, where the GPS says I am and where I know I am don't line up," Connors said. "Why don't I start heading southeast, and when I get to the approximate area, I can start asking people where an Internet café is. We can run them down one by one. I put in a call to my people, and they're re-checking for any known photographs of Ordóñez. They are also sending me the passport picture of one of his confederates, Professor William Knight, an American."

Connors explained that he had been about to see a passport picture of Knight at the hotel in Guayaquil when Noboa suddenly appeared and the brief chase ensued. "I was hurrying so fast to get out of there; I didn't go back to see the picture," he said.

His phone made a quick beep, indicating a text had been received. "I believe the picture just came in," he said to Williams. "Yes, here it is."

Connors promised to call Williams back when he reached the southeast quadrant of the city. Waiting for his bill from the server, Connors overheard a snippet of conversation at a nearby table.

"I can't believe two Americans started those fires," a middle-aged woman said to her dinner partner.

"This is one of the kindest cities on earth," the second woman said. "But the people today have been horrible. They're treating all Americans badly because of the actions of two maniacs."

Connors leaned over. "I'm sorry to butt in," he said, "but I just got to town. What's going on?" The women reiterated what they had heard on the news and from local gossip: two gringos, one white and the other Latino, were on a murder spree. The most recent victims were apparently two more security guards and a priest.

By the time the women finished, Connors felt certain the two Americans were George d'Hout and ICE agent Pujols. The descriptions matched perfectly. "And you say people are threatening to kill them?" Connors asked.

"The radio and TV stations are advising Americans to stay off the streets after dark," the first woman said. "It could get really dangerous. And since this is the weekend, when people start drinking, all gringos could be targets."

"That's just great," Connors said. "First, all the rain. Now this. And I was hoping to meet a couple of friends tonight."

"I hope they're not a white guy in a running suit with a gray beard and a Latino with a Mexican accent," the first woman half joked. "They may be in a pretty tough spot right now."

"No," Connors lied. "Nobody like that. You're right, though. I sure wouldn't want to be those guys right now. I wonder where they are."

"The radio says no one's seen any sign of them," the second woman said. "It's like the earth just opened up and swallowed them."

Saturday, 11 January
5:27 p.m.

After searching and re-searching the area closest to the sound, George and Albert moved on. There was no exit they could locate. They had now been sidestepping through the tunnel for several hours, and both were weary from thirst, hunger, and a lack of rest. George stopped and slid down the wall.

"If we get out of this, I'm sleeping with the lights on from now on," he said. "No more darkness for me."

"This is pretty frustrating," Pujols said. "We are wandering around in utter darkness while the priest is back there bleeding out or in shock. I don't think I've ever felt so hopeless in my whole life."

George could hear the irritation in the man's voice. He decided to scoot over to the other side of the tunnel to at least be close to the agent who had done so much to try to rescue him. When he did, he nearly fell right into another hole.

Letting out a gasp, George pulled back.

"What is it?" the ICE agent asked.

"Some sort of hatch or hole or escape spot, only it's right in the middle of the floor," George said. Albert moved away from the wall to feel it with his foot. Once he determined the hole's shape and width—it was a circle about three feet wide—he lowered his legs, trying to feel for any steps or rungs.

Initially, he felt nothing. He worked his way around the circle on his rear end, feeling with his feet as he did. Finally, he found rungs. "I'm going to try this," he said. "Stay close in case I need a hand getting out."

Albert descended the ladder cut into the walls of the downward tunnel, counting off fifteen rungs. When he reached the floor, he found that this section led in only one direction. "I'm going to go a little ways and see where this heads," Albert said. "Actually, 'see' is probably a bit optimistic. I'll just feel my way around."

"We have a deal," George reminded him. "You aren't allowed to get lost or go very far."

"Deal," Albert agreed. "And remember, you have a job. Keep praying."

Saturday, 11 January
6:04 p.m.

Night fell over Cunca. Miguel maintained his usual position near the kitchen in case Ordóñez or the professor wanted coffee or something to eat. For the last hour Ordóñez had been pacing around the living room. When Knight asked him about it, he said he was hoping for word of bodies discovered in the fire. While it hadn't come, neither was there any indication they had escaped the fire.

"Where are we on this?" he asked, watching the professor pore over maps and books at the large kitchen table.

"If you would let me have a computer here with an Internet connection, it would be much easier," Professor Knight said.

"Absolutely not," Ordóñez replied. "Computer and telephone signals can be traced. And that means they could be traced here. If you need to use the Internet, use it at the Internet café. That way no one can suddenly surprise us by following our signal."

"Then may I be so bold as to ask why you aren't worried about the phone you're carrying?"

"I paid a great deal of money for this phone with the assurance it was untraceable. A government official in Colombia secured it from the highest levels of their espionage service...not that any of that is your business. Are there any other decisions I've made that you'd like to second-guess?"

Professor Knight regretted bringing it up. Changing the subject was his best option. "According to the brother, we're looking for a beloved grove. Something in the old city that would have had a distinct significance. Beloved…beloved…What would be so important in 1687 that it would earn a special title of 'beloved'? Juan might have some idea, but he isn't here. What do you think, Miguel? What is of special significance? What is particularly beloved?"

Miguel was caught off guard. The city was beloved. The Blessed Virgin was beloved. And the oldest place where residents of the beloved city went to pray to the beloved Virgin was a spot that predated the Spanish settling of Cuenca.

When the area was Guapondeleg, a Cañari city, a special garden near the current ruins of Pumapungo had been designed for honoring the moon goddess. When the Spanish came, the indigenous peoples were informed that the area was now solely dedicated to the Beloved Virgin. The spot was on the grounds of the archaeological ruins behind Banco Central.

Miguel pondered his options. If he revealed his suspicions, Ordóñez might release his wife and family. On the other hand, if he was right and that was where the treasure was buried, did he really want to turn it over to these devils?

This was treasure the Spanish stole from the Indians and then English and Dutch pirates stole from the Spanish. If Miguel helped to return it to his people, he would be a national hero.

"Your ideas, Miguel?" Ordóñez asked. "I can tell that little Cañari brain of yours is spinning about as fast as it can. Why don't you let it cool off a while and unburden yourself of any thoughts?"

Miguel knew Ordóñez wouldn't want his current thought because it had to do with running a very long and sharp object through Ordóñez and watching his smugness turn to horror at the realization he was dying. "Patience," Miguel thought. "Get your family freed and then take care of your business with these men."

Ordóñez was looking Miguel right in the eyes. The Cañari knew some people, usually shamans, possessed the unique ability to use their eyes to travel inside another's mind. Roberto Ordóñez was certainly one of those. It was vitally important to Miguel that he do a better job of not traveling to the hateful places in his thoughts when talking to this man.

It was also important to tell him the truth, except when absolutely necessary, since this man had a frightening track record of discerning when he was being fed a line. "Beloved," Miguel pondered aloud. "Beloved. The church is beloved. Our families are beloved. The Virgin is beloved. Our history as a people is beloved."

There, he had given them what he believed was the secret, but he'd hidden it as the pirates had done. And, as with the pirates' clues, these evil men had apparently missed it.

"Enough wasting time," the professor said. "Otherwise our little friend here will begin to get nostalgic and try to run away."

"I can't have that," Ordóñez said. "He is supposed to watch you to make sure that isn't your idea."

Professor Knight looked back at the maps. "We must find this beloved grove, which Hugh d'Hout says holds the secrets. Roberto, can you get me into the archives at the Banco Central Museum? They keep all the oldest maps there. Perhaps one of them holds the key. Do you think a sizable and timely donation to the upkeep of the archaeological ruins might help?"

"An excellent idea, no?" Ordóñez said. "In the meantime, can you use the Internet café to assist your search?"

The professor nodded. "And I suppose Miguel will accompany me," he said.

"No," Ordóñez said. "I don't believe that would be a good idea. You two seem to be developing quite a little relationship. I believe it would be better for Juan to go with you."

"It makes no difference to me," the professor said. "Though once this is over and I have again proven my loyalty and my worth, we will need to have a serious discussion about how little respect and trust I am being paid."

"You are paid in money," Roberto said. "Our success doesn't hinge on your alleged gifts. They center on my prescient ability to know when to push forward and when to pull back, when to believe and when to doubt. And the more you question that ability, the more I question you."

Roberto reached into his pocket for his cell phone. He called Miguel over and said, "Walk some ways down the street and call Juan. Tell him I require his services at his earliest convenience. The others may stay out patrolling."

Thirty minutes later, when Juan arrived, a steady rain began to beat down on the city. Miguel was standing on his patio in front of the house, looking west. The glow of red lights from the *bombero* trucks made the low clouds glow. Juan breezed past Miguel with an unkind epithet for the Cañari people. Miguel thought, "When I have my revenge, you are number two, right after Ordóñez, and right before the professor."

The Cañari watched swirling low clouds mingling with flying ash and smoke from the church fire. As Miguel watched some of the ash pirouetting on the breeze, he thought of souls on a circuitous path toward heaven. How many more people would die before the treasure was found?

In a few minutes the professor and Juan emerged from the house, both carrying umbrellas. They climbed into the security car Juan was driving to head to the Internet café.

"Miguel," he heard Ordóñez call from inside the house, "why don't you come back inside. I'm lonely all by myself, and I wouldn't want you wandering away. You might get lost."

CHAPTER 30

Saturday, 11 January
9:45 p.m.

Dean Connors had been in troublesome situations before, but there was something in the air throughout Cuenca that told him he must be particularly careful. The glow of lights and the embers of the church fire reflected across the city. Though he knew rain was common in this highland area, Connors heard a radio announcer insist that this time it was the tears of God over the destroyed church.

His car trolled the streets for Internet cafés, watching those who entered and exited them. The car radio droned on with caller after caller insisting the Americans who had done this must be severely punished. There was no shortage of grisly suggestions how that punishment might be carried out. Others wondered whether "imperialists" should be welcomed in Cuenca any longer. Long subdued doubts and prejudices regarding the powerful United States and its citizens reached a tipping point and slid off into downright hatred.

"This isn't good," Connors said to himself. "If I get caught at the wrong intersection or by the wrong people..." He reached down into his ankle holster and took out his Sig P228, checking to make sure the aftermarket magazine he'd installed was ready to go with all fifteen rounds. After inspecting the gun, he tucked it down beside him in the seat of the unmarked embassy car. Even so, he realized that deadly force at this time wouldn't make things any better, no matter how justified it was.

Connors pulled the car over, just out of the glow of a streetlight at the corner of Adolfo Torres and Fray Carrasco streets. He watched some native women struggling through the rain with the last of their portable fruit stands, rolling them down the cobblestone streets toward some nearby home.

As he watched the women, he focused past them on a car marked SEGURIDAD ECUADOR cruising slowly down the avenue. These cars had been more common, Connors noted, than police cruisers, which surprised him. Perhaps their headquarters was nearby, because he had seen at least four different ones going past in the last several hours.

This one was different, however, because the two men inside didn't appear to be wearing uniforms. The driver, a hawk-nosed Inca, reminded Connors of a bird of prey. He even made eye contact with Connors for a moment. Connors watched the Inca's eyes glance from him to the license plates and then once over the vehicle, taking it all in. Connors used a common technique to get the man to look away. He began picking his nose. This worked, almost without fail. Doing something disgusting was a sure way to draw people's attention toward something—anything—else.

Once, several years ago, when Connors feared he was on the verge of being recognized as an American security official in Haiti, he'd resorted to stopping and urinating on a street corner. No one of any importance would have done such an uncouth thing, and the men following him pulled away just in the nick of time. It had worked again tonight; Connors saw the man in the patrol car mentally dismiss what he was seeing as of no consequence.

Nonetheless, Connors started the car and pulled away from the curb. In his rearview mirror he watched the security cruiser pull over near an Internet café. The two men got out. Because of the rain and their umbrellas, Connors couldn't make out the man exiting the passenger seat. Could it be Ordóñez or Knight? Hard to tell. He turned the corner and lost sight of the two men. He had to find a vantage point where he could observe them without being watched himself.

The rain intensified, and the temperature felt as if it had edged down around forty degrees Fahrenheit. For a country located on the equator, it was none too warm in Cuenca. But the rain was also a blessing. It made it easier to not be spotted from a few blocks away, provided he could find a place to park in the dark.

On the radio, the tone was edging toward mob mentality. A minister called in, reminding the people to be quick to listen and slow to judge. Other callers' angry cries for retribution quickly drowned out the priest's pleas.

Dean Connors stayed off the busier streets in favor of less-traveled neighborhood blocks, swinging back where he could catch a glimpse of the security vehicle every couple of minutes. Pulling over on a dark side street next to a large cinder-block wall, Connors dialed his cell phone. Van Williams picked up.

"I may have two of our suspects in view," Connors said. "They are in an Internet café now. Can you contact your technician and see if he's picking up any signals going to Hugh d'Hout's computer?"

"Our tech got off an hour ago, and the next one hasn't logged on yet," the FBI agent said. "Hold on and let me see if I can contact Hugh on another line."

In a moment Van Williams was back. "It may be your suspects," he said. "Someone claiming to be George d'Hout just sent an e-mail. Can you get a closer look at them? Maybe go in? They don't know you, right?"

"Unfortunately," Connors said, "we have a situation here. Someone is setting buildings on fire with people inside and blaming my agent and d'Hout. The death toll is getting pretty high. Americans aren't real popular right now in Cuenca. I'd just as soon stay in my car as long as I can."

About that time, something caught Connors's attention in his rearview mirror. A large group of men appeared from a side street and were only a few yards from his car. They splashed through the rain with flashlights, torches, and some very large clubs. They chanted in Spanish, "Americans go home! Cuenca for *Cuencanos!*"

Through the phone, Van said, "What's that?"

"Like I said," Connors told him, "I've got a situation here. Let me call you back in—" Williams listened, but the line was dead.

Sunday, 12 January
12:04 a.m.

George was close to panic. No doubt the priest was in shock by now. Albert had disappeared. The ICE agent had promised to check out one quick passage of the tunnel, but there had been no word from him in six hours. George knew that only because his watch hands glowed in the dark.

The watch was the only thing he could see, and it reminded him of how much he missed Carol. She had given him the watch for his birthday. It was a Citizen Eco-Drive, the nicest watch he'd ever owned.

"You know I'm terrible about breaking watches," he'd told her when she gave it to him.

"That's why I gave you a really nice one," she said. "You have to learn to be more careful with it. Besides, there's something written on the back." Over candlelight and wine at Mark's American Restaurant in Houston, he turned the watch over and read the words "Always make time for us."

George and Carol weren't much on public displays of affection, but she reached across the table and kissed him. It was one of the most romantic moments of their married lives. Sitting in the black tunnel, George said aloud, "I'm trying, babe. I'm trying."

George's mind played another trick on him. He thought he heard Carol saying something, far in the distance. She called to him. Then she called again. "I'm here!" George yelled. "Right here."

George thought he saw a momentary bit of light coming from the passage below. A voice called out again. "Hello? George?" It was Albert.

"Right here!" George cried out. "Where have you been? Right here; I'm here! Keep coming!"

Shafts of light bounced off one wall and then another, then they were gone. Albert called out again, "Keep talking, George. Let me know if I'm getting close."

The voice still sounded far away and echoed badly off the walls. "Right here," George yelled. "Keep coming!"

George looked back at his Citizen watch and counted down the minutes. He and Albert kept yelling back and forth to one another. In three minutes, George could hear Albert's footsteps and smell an earthy odor. The beam of a flashlight suddenly shot up from below George, startling him.

"You found the city?" George almost yelped for joy. "You brought help!"

Albert's head popped up from below as he made his way up the rungs of the ladder. "It gets weird," he said. "It gets very weird."

"What are you talking about?"

"First, apparently we weren't headed back to the city," Albert said. "Where I came out was anything but a city. It was a jungle of twisted trees so thick I could barely find my way through them. It turns out I was in a polylepis forest, according to some German campers I came across. Fortunately they spoke enough

Spanish and English that we could communicate. The whole place looked like some enchanted land from a fairy tale."

"The Paper Tree Forest!" George said. "That was the spot where Miguel said he would meet us. You found it? How? It's in the complete opposite direction we thought we were traveling in."

Albert said, "The only thing I can imagine is that the tunnels wind so gradually, we simply didn't notice how they changed direction. I know the side tunnel I took cut in a different direction, but it didn't go far enough to take me all the way under the mountain and into the Cajas National Park. That simply wasn't possible. The only explanation is that the entire tme, we were moving in a giant arc."

As Albert spoke, he set two large pieces of wood down on the floor of the tunnel. He also pulled out several strips of cloth. "We can use these to bind the priest's leg. It was really tough explaining to the campers why I needed to borrow supplies, how I ended up in the middle of the mountains with no coat, no nothing, and yet didn't want them to accompany me."

"Why didn't you get them to come along?" George asked. "We sure could have used their help."

In the glow of the borrowed flashlight, Albert frowned. "We made a promise to the priest we would keep this tunnel system a secret," he said. "We have to keep our word."

George felt ashamed. "Of course, you're right. All I'm thinking about is saving our hides."

"Speaking of which," Albert said, "we have to get back to Padre Domingo. I also have the campers' first aid kit. I told them my wounded comrade was so far away that I had to travel fast and light. But they need me to get this flashlight and kit back to them. They are up there for two weeks."

With the beam of the flashlight illuminating their way back through the tunnel system, the two men raced toward Padre Domingo. As they ran, Albert pulled out a couple of granola bars. "Compliments of Gustaf, Grit, and Max, our new friends from Frankfurt. *Bon appétit.*"

George wasn't sure food had ever tasted so good. "Got anything to wash this down with?" he asked. Albert pulled a bottle of water out of another pocket.

"I feel like I'm traveling with Felix the Cat and his magic bag of tricks," George said. He suddenly felt giddy. Not only were they going to be able to save the priest, but they also had a way out that didn't put them back on a collision course with Ordóñez. As they ran, Albert said the Germans also had a satellite phone.

"I'll hold off on calling until we can get back. Then we will call in the cavalry and get some help."

It felt freeing for George to be able to stretch his legs and run down the long tunnel passage. However, in the beam of the flashlight, it was now clear that the tunnel did, in fact, wind ever so slightly as it progressed.

Albert called out in Spanish, "Padre, can you hear me? Padre? We're coming. Hang tough, Father. We're on our way." After stopping momentarily to catch his breath, George took the lead, both in jogging and in yelling toward the priest.

They heard no response, only their own voices echoing off the tunnel walls.

"You think he's okay?" George asked.

"In my line of work, you can't afford to speculate," Albert said. "So what do I do? Speculate all day long. Speculate and pray. And keep reminding myself to stop doing the first and concentrate on the second."

The flashlight illuminated some sort of designs on the walls, but George and Albert had no time for art appreciation. Padre Domingo's life hung in the balance.

Finally, they heard a groan ahead of them. Their pace quickened, with George taking the flashlight and zooming ahead. "We're here!" he called. "We're here!"

When they reached the priest, they found that he had removed his outer cassock and used it to catch the blood and elevate the wounded leg. The dark garment was now covered with blood. The priest was lying on his back and moaning. His *collarino* shirt was covered in perspiration, and his eyes were rolled back in his head.

"It's okay, Father," Albert told him in Spanish. "We're here. We're going to get your leg bound and get you out of here."

"Doubtful," George found himself thinking. "We still have to carry him all that way, then through all the dips and turns to get to the exit Albert found. Then what? We'll still be in the middle of nowhere. This is really bad."

Albert interrupted George's growing pessimism. "I need you to hold this," he said. The ICE agent set two of the thick branches from a polylepis tree on each side of the cleric's broken leg. He next reached into his pocket and pulled out two cords of thick twine he'd borrowed from the German hikers, splinting the leg in place.

"I'm gonna need to buy those folks a really nice meal," Albert said as he continued working on the leg. "Here, George, hold this in place for me."

"Any chance they followed you back to the tunnel?" George asked. "We could use their help getting the priest out of here."

"I know what you mean," Albert said, tightening the cords, which caused the priest to let out a sudden gasp of pain. "But we gave our word, and the padre is right. We don't know what these tunnels hold. They're not ours, and we don't have any right to announce them to the world." The priest again shuddered in pain, moisture suddenly appearing on his face like rain.

"What's the plan for getting him out of here?" George asked.

"The fireman's carry," Albert said. "I lift the father up and carry him on my shoulders. You'll hold the light and go ahead, making sure I don't trip on anything or fall down some hole. We'll have to take turns, though. Let's move as quickly as possible."

"What will that jarring do to the broken leg?" George asked.

"Not as much as leaving him here. I just can't think of another plan," Albert said. "You good?"

George nodded and helped Albert hoist the priest onto the agent's shoulders. Again the priest's body was racked with pain, and he let out a sickening moan. While Albert worked to shift the priest's body on his shoulders, George picked up two extra pieces of polylepis wood Albert had brought, along with the priest's bloody cassock.

Leading the way, George shone the light on the floor and occasionally against the walls. He noticed odd hieroglyphics every now and again. "This is a scientific and historical treasure trove," he said. Albert was too focused on carrying his burden to reply, so they moved on in silence.

After a few minutes, Albert said, "George, I feel something running down my leg. Did I spill some water?"

George looked. "Blood. Not yours." They picked up the pace, hoping their efforts to save the priest weren't in vain.

CHAPTER 31

Sunday, 12 January
2:17 a.m.

Carol sat up in bed and said aloud, "George is alive. I'm sure he is. But he's in danger. He needs prayer."

She had no idea where the thought came from but didn't pause to doubt it or wonder if it was just her exhausted imagination. Her faith taught her that God still spoke to people today as he had in the Bible. She believed this as much as she believed anything, and it completely shaped her approach to life. Bounding out of bed, she put on a robe and went to their home office. She logged on to a couple of social media sites, where she and friends often communicated. There were hundreds of promises for prayer and wishes for the best regarding her missing husband.

Carol worked furiously on the keyboard. "Anyone awake at this hour?" she typed. Then she typed again. "If you are, I believe

George needs prayer. It's not for him, though. Someone with him is in danger. It's just a feeling. I haven't had any communication with him. He's still missing. Please join me."

In spite of the hour, responses began pouring in. "Couldn't sleep. Now I know why. You got it." "Thanks for letting me know. You can count on me." "Will do."

Carol jumped when the cell phone she'd laid on the desk began to ring. "Carol?" the voice said. "It's Brenda. I was awake and saw your messages."

"Anything else from the people claiming to be George?" Carol asked.

"The last time Hugh communicated with them, they were becoming increasingly ugly, wanting to know exactly where the treasure was," Brenda said. "Hugh told them everything he knows, but they can't seem to figure out where the beloved grove is. I don't know how they expect him to figure it out, since he's here and they're there. Besides, we got the indication from Van Williams, the FBI agent, that the embassy was sending someone to help. Surely he or she can get this figured out."

Sunday, 12 January
2:20 a.m.

Dean Connors's pulse raced almost as quickly as his car as he headed out of Cuenca. So far he'd been fortunate to avoid police and army patrols. However, he had just run over at least two people while escaping the mob that surrounded his car. Cold air streamed in the shattered driver's side window where a tire iron had smashed the supposedly shatterproof glass.

Connors had been talking to Van Williams. He had known a group of angry men was approaching his car from one direction. What he didn't see was a second group coming from the other way. He first realized it when the tire iron smashed the window.

A large arm reached in to grab Connors but came up with only his cell phone. Connors instinctively reached to counter the arm but was distracted when a club began pounding on the passenger window. Two more clubs slammed into the glass of the windshield. Connors realized he was hopelessly outnumbered. His only option was to put the car into gear and hit the gas.

A sick *thud-thud* sound came as he watched two of the men disappear under the car when he pulled away. The thought of those two men being run over increased the adrenaline rush inside Connors's head. If he was arrested, his diplomatic immunity might secure his eventual release, but he would surely be thrown out of the country. And that process would leave no one to help ICE agent Albert Pujols escape his captors.

Now, having no map of the area and without a cell phone, Connors lacked any idea where he could go to hide and regroup. He knew Cuenca sat in a valley at roughly eighty-two hundred feet, surrounded by the towering Andes Mountains. When he had driven through those mountains from Guayaquil, he had passed through a dense cloud forest that was part of Cajas National Park. As the car gained elevation near the top of the mountains and followed a pass into the Cuenca Valley, Connors could see enough in the headlights to be reminded of Scottish highlands.

If he could make it back to that remote area known as the Cajas, he thought, he stood a good chance of hiding out until he could secure a map or come up with a plan. There was only one thing in his way. Where the highway wound through the national park, there were guard stations manned by armed patrols.

What were the chances that members of the mob surrounding his car had already informed the police of another crazy *norte americano* "attacking" innocent *Cuencanos*? Connors knew he had no choice but to plow through the mob as they surrounded his car, which had diplomatic plates on it for everyone to see. They began pounding on it and hurling anti-American curses.

Connors imagined heavy doses of alcohol and anger had mixed in the heads of the Cuenca residents to create a lethal combination that threatened his safety. He simply wasn't going to let that happen. Now, as he headed toward the only haven he knew about, the Cajas National Park, he couldn't afford to get pulled over by armed guards.

Connors passed a few houses on the side of the road and a makeshift sign that read CULEBRILLAS. Connors was fluent in

Spanish and knew the name meant "shingles." He wondered if that was a reference to a geographical feature, some industry, or an outbreak of chicken pox.

Slowly cruising along, he saw a smattering of ramshackle houses lodged between the road and an alternating array of steep-sided mountains and precipitous cliffs. Many of the houses looked as if the slightest tremor might send them right over the edge. Connors wondered how houses perched right against the mountain avoided being leveled by landslides.

Past a house with a roof made of corrugated metal sat a simple roadside food stand and a couple of makeshift barns. Three rusty trucks sat just off the roadway. One of the trucks seemed to be nosed right up against the edge of a steep drop.

Connors surveyed the scene. There were no lights in any of the houses and no headlights from cars coming up or down the mountain pass. Down the road, he knew, was the government checkpoint where he would surely be detained simply because he was an American trying to leave Cuenca with smashed car windows late at night in the midst of a manhunt for gringos.

Slowing down his embassy car, Connors killed the headlights. Waiting until his eyes adjusted to the dark, he backed the car up to the truck nearest the cliff. Again looking around, he saw no signs of life. People in this roadside burg were surely so used to cars passing by that they paid them no mind.

He put the car in park. The sounds of a river rushing somewhere in the distance, along with the wind howling over the pass, created a curtain of white noise. Connors hoped the sounds would cover his actions long enough he could create a diversion that permitted him to escape into the Cajas.

He switched the car's dome light to the off position. Then he slipped out and again looked around for any signs of life. He crept over to the pickup. Someone had wedged large rocks in front of the tires to keep the vehicle from rolling over the side.

Connors removed the rocks, tossing them over the edge. Then he opened the truck's driver side door, which creaked mightily. The pickup was easily a quarter of a century old.

Connors disengaged the hand brake, pressed the clutch with his left hand, and turned the steering wheel to get the truck moving. Leaning into the doorframe and shifting his weight backwards and forwards, it was only a moment or two before he could feel the truck begin to rock.

Now he pressed with all his might toward the front of the truck and felt it roll toward the edge. Giving it another shove, he reached over at the last moment and pulled on the headlight switch as the truck clanked and thunked over the edge of the cliff, hurtling into the abyss.

Connors didn't waste a moment. He ran to his car, the engine still running, rolled it several feet farther, stopped again and began honking his horn and yelling at the top of his lungs. "Help! Help! A vehicle went over! Help!" he yelled in Spanish. "For the love of heaven, someone come help! Emergency!"

A light came on in one of the nearby houses, then another, and a third. Sleepy, leery natives poked their heads out to see what was going on. Connors continued his screaming but, noticing his embassy tags, reached into the car and switched off his headlights, hoping they wouldn't draw attention from the startled inhabitants.

"Someone went over!" he yelled in Spanish. "I saw it! Help! We need lots of help!"

In a matter of minutes, the streets were filled with a couple of dozen people peering into the darkness toward the headlights dangling on the side of the mountain three hundred feet below. "Where's my truck?" a man wanted to know.

Connors, speaking only Spanish, said he thought the vehicle that went over might have taken the truck with it. "People need help," he insisted. "Is there a police station or emergency personnel nearby?"

"There is a checkpoint just down the mountain," a young boy said. "They are the nearest officials."

"Who'll go and get them?" Connors asked. "We need the men to stay here and see what we can do. Someone else must get help. Are there telephones where you can call?"

"At this hour, it is faster to go and get them," a woman said. "Telephone service is spotty." It was just the answer Connors was hoping for.

"Go then," Connors said. "God go with you. Lives are at stake. Hurry!"

A half-dozen women bundled themselves against the nighttime cold and set off at a quick walk down the mountain. "Let me move my car," Connors said, "and then we will decide what to do." He wanted the car well out of sight when the police appeared and wanted to know what had happened and who had witnessed it.

Pulling to a spot where the car was aimed downhill and well away from the lights of the houses, Connors picked up a rag and nonchalantly laid it over his front license plate. With everyone looking down the side of the mountain, no one noticed what he had done.

Wandering back into the mix of people, Connors heard some of the men suggest tying ropes to a nearby arrayan tree. That way, two or three of the stronger men could descend to attempt a rescue. Connors encouraged an active discussion of the pros and cons of the idea since it was important they not discover that the only vehicle that went over was the old truck. That would lead to questions Connors didn't want to answer.

Twenty minutes later, two police car sirens could be heard as the vehicles wound up the mountain. Hearing the cars approaching, Connors turned to the people who gazed over the side into the darkness. He renewed the descent-by-ropes idea as if it were the finest thing he'd ever heard.

The dozen sleepy men were so busy looking over the edge and discussing how and when other cars had gone over in the past, they didn't seem to notice Connors was a gringo. His mastery of the Spanish language allowed him to pronounce words in such a way that he might appear to be a light-skinned Castellan from Ecuador's elite class.

Encouraging one man to go for ropes and another to make sure everyone had good gloves for the descent; Connors began to make his way toward the fringes of the small group. By the time the police cars came roaring up, Connors had slipped into the darkness near his vehicle.

Several officers climbed out, clearly irritated at being summoned at this hour. They began questioning the people about who had seen what. Connors eased the door of his car open and glided inside. He kept the lights off, slid the car into gear, and prayed the white noise from the wind and river would allow him to complete his plan. With everyone looking down the side of the mountain, Connors put the car into low gear and pulled away.

Rounding the next curve down the steep mountain road without headlights, however, was more of an adventure than Connors had bargained for. He decided the only way to make sure his car didn't actually careen off the side was to risk turning his headlights on. As he did, he saw he was less than twenty-five feet from the edge and going straight over at the point where the mountain road curved.

He involuntarily held his breath, swung the wheel hard to the right, and applied as much brake as he dared without locking them up. He felt the front tires slide a bit in the gravel. The back tires held, and he was able to keep the car on the road. Since Ecuadorian roads lacked rails at the sides of steep mountains, there was little margin for error. Connors had used every centimeter of his.

Checking his rearview mirror, he saw no vehicles behind him. Nor were there any on the road ahead. After three more switchbacks, however, he saw a sign that said in Spanish, SLOW DOWN. GOVERNMENT INSPECTION STATION AHEAD. ENTERING A NATIONAL PARK. ALL VEHICLES MUST STOP.

Connors hoped the officers had left the gate unattended. No such luck. Nearing the gate, Connors saw a lone uniformed man, hardly more than a teenager, inside the small booth next to the road. His legs were propped up on a desk as he snoozed in front of a large window running almost the entire height of the building. Glad he had kept the license plate covered with the rag, Connors suddenly gunned his vehicle and began honking his horn.

He next jumped out of the car and ran up, making sure he affected a Castellan air of authority in his deportment and voice. "Your comrades insisted you come at once!" he yelled in Spanish. "They said, 'Do not tarry.' They need you, now!"

Being the supervisor of United States embassy security, Connors didn't have to wonder how such commands sounded. He carried them off in a manner that indicated questioning orders was not an option. The previously sleeping guard was confused. "I was told to stay here and guard the road," he said.

Connors knew the Latin American psyche and how shame was often used to control people. "And were you guarding it, or were you sleeping?" he said, noticing the man wore the single stripe of a private.

"I w-was…It's not my fault…You see…Uh…"

"Your commander sounded very displeased and said he needed you at once. He said to remind you who was in charge and said that this isn't the first time you have been told to do something and were slow."

His last comment was a calculated risk. "If you do not come immediately, I am to drive back and inform him. What are you going to do? I'm not going to risk the commander's anger, so if you aren't going, tell me at once so I can fulfill my obligation and inform him."

"I'm going, I'm going," the private said. "Are you driving me?"

"I was told to stay here and stop traffic until you returned," Connors lied. "You go."

"In your car?"

"No, not in *my* car," Connors barked. This fellow really was slow. "Do you not have a vehicle of your own?"

"Only my motorcycle," the guard said. "I paid for the gas myself."

"And you can't invest it in following orders to save the lives of people who have driven off the side of a cliff?"

The private couldn't stand the humiliation any longer. He went to the side of the building, fired up his small bike, and sped off into the darkness of the winding mountain road. Connors imagined the face of the sergeant when he saw this dense private puttering up on his little motorcycle in a few minutes.

Scanning the guard hut, which stood wide open, Connors saw no one else. He stepped inside and quickly eyed the telephone. Picking it up, he heard the dial tone. Connors called the twenty-four-hour emergency line for the United States embassy in Quito. Sgt. Victor Menchaca answered.

Quickly apprising Menchaca of the situation, he asked that the ambassador be informed immediately. "That's a problem, sir," the sergeant said. "The ambassador had a family emergency in Virginia and flew out today."

That wasn't good. On the international front, escalating tension between Venezuela and the United States often played out in Ecuador, which owed much to both countries. As Ecuador increased its intimacy with Venezuela and Iran, there was an equal amount of increasing tension with the United States.

Hence, the embassy staff had been greatly reduced, both out of protest for Ecuador's political affiliations and as insurance in case the embassy was ever attacked. The current staffing levels meant Connors was largely on his own, because the ambassador would be taking a number of Marines with her as protection.

"You want me to upgrade this, sir?" the sergeant asked.

Upgrade was embassy shorthand for elevating the current situation and notifying Washington. If that happened, there was a very good chance this could become an international situation. With mobs attacking Americans, maybe that was best.

But were there really mobs? Or had he only been the victim of an isolated episode? Surely there ought to be a travel advisory regarding the situation, but upgrading it to the level of an international incident? The blowback from that on the embassy and on Connors could be quite serious.

Once this situation was resolved, the Ecuadorian and United States governments would look for scapegoats on whom to blame the situation. Connors knew he and ICE Agent Pujols were low level enough they would make excellent targets.

"Let's hold off," Connors said. "But I do need you to do one other thing. I need you to find the number for FBI Agent Van Williams. He's in Midland, Texas, and he's monitoring the situation, along with some computer techs there. Let him know what's happening. Ask him to keep it on a need-to-know basis. Maybe we can come out of this in one piece. The fewer people who know about it, the better."

Connors hung up. Raising the gate with an automatic lever, he climbed back in his car and gassed it down the mountain and into the remoteness of Cajas National Park and the Paper Tree Forest. Shivering from the wind and cold pouring in through the smashed window, he tried not to think about how desperate his situation was. He also wondered about d'Hout and Agent Pujols. What if the same mob that attacked him found them? Not a productive thought, so he cast it off. He pressed the gas harder and sped off into the darkness.

CHAPTER 32

Sunday, 12 January
3:46 a.m.

The weight of the priest, whom George was now carrying, and the lack of sleep, conspired to make the American feel dizzy and almost unavoidably sleepy. Until forty-five minutes ago, Albert had been carrying the priest as they took turns. Both men were so exhausted that they could barely think.

"I'm sorry," George said, "but I gotta rest for a few minutes. Guess I'm the weak sister of our group."

"Hardly," Albert said. "I was just too tired to say anything. Why don't we close our eyes for a few minutes and then hit it again?"

As they laid the unconscious priest down, Albert said, "I was brought into the world as a Catholic, but for the last few years, I haven't been much of anything except absent. I was telling God a minute ago that I gotta do a better job to pay back what this priest did for me."

George was unsure what to say. After a moment of silence, he heard Albert ask, "You're a Protestant, right? Protestants and Catholics don't get along, right?"

"I don't know about that. It probably depends on where you are."

"What are the differences between Protestants and Catholics? I mean the real differences and not the nitpicky stuff."

"You're asking the wrong guy," George said, yawning. "All I know is the Bible talks about serving God by doing for others. This priest risked his life to save us. Now we're doing what we can to save him."

"Religion is doing good works," Albert said. "I guess that's what I thought, too."

George considered for a minute and said. "Good works? No, I don't think so. You do certain things because you're an ICE agent, things ICE agents are expected to do. But lots of people could do those same things. That wouldn't make them an ICE agent. In fact, it might make them imposters, if they claimed they were one of your fellow officers. You do those things because you're an agent, but doing those things doesn't make you an agent. I think it's the same thing with Christianity. We do certain things because we're Christians, but doing those things doesn't make us a Christian. Listen, I gotta get some sleep."

"Me, too," Albert said. He closed his eyes, and they both drifted off, each resting a supportive hand on the priest, hoping he could hold on just a little while longer.

Sunday, 12 January
3:48 a.m.

Connors pulled off the road at a large wooden sign that read CAJAS NATIONAL PARK. It was quite a work of art, with carved and painted markings showing the national park, its main highway, and various trails leading off to Tres Cruces, the Inca Trail, Paper Tree Forest, and an assortment of waterfalls.

Connors checked his rearview mirror for any other traffic, then looked far off into the darkness ahead of him. Nothing. He slid the gearshift into park but kept the engine running and the headlights aimed at the sign. As he stepped from the car, a biting wind hit him. The temperature in the Cajas was always chilly, but at night it could be dangerously frigid.

He scanned the large map of the seventy-one-thousand-acre park. In many ways Cajas reminded him of Great Basin National Park back in the United States. The almost unending moonscapes, broken by deep forests, dizzying peaks, and pristine lakes and rivers, evoked both awe and an almost primordial fear. All it needed was a large cave system to make the picture complete.

Connors felt exhaustion wash over him and he wondered for a minute where he was. He shook his head hard and rubbed his eyes. This wasn't Great Basin. There were no caves. He was smack dab in the middle of South America. He rubbed his eyes and slapped himself on the cheeks to shake off the siren call of sleep. He knew he must remain focused on saving himself, Agent Pujols, and the missing George d'Hout.

Connors studied the map, seeking a place both accessible by car and remote enough he could escape detection for a few hours. He eliminated the idea of driving on toward Guayaquil. Once the guards he tricked became aware of the deception, their second outpost nearer the port city would be on high alert.

Knowing heavy fog and rains made deep mud a danger, he also sought a location where his car wouldn't get stuck but wasn't visible from the road. With his finger, he traced a gravel trail through one section of the Paper Tree Forest. If the map was to be trusted, the trail seemed to rest on the side of a nearby mountain aimed toward Cuenca.

Taking a piece of paper and a pen out of his pocket, he jotted down the kilometer markers to reach the forest. No doubt there were countless smaller roads along the way, which the map didn't indicate. He didn't want to accidentally take the wrong one and end up lost or stuck in a bog. Stories of hikers and vacationers getting lost in the Cajas and dying were commonplace enough, even Connors, who was experienced in taking care of himself, knew to respect this wilderness.

As he climbed back in the car, an idea struck him. How long would it take the guards to realize they'd been tricked into letting someone pass? Once they did, would they be motivated enough to come after him? It was possible that the private and the people of Culebrillas thought he was a person of elite Spanish status rather than a gringo from America. That might make them reluctant to try to apprehend him. On the other hand, if they decided he was a gringo, that might give them extra motivation to capture him.

Taking out a piece of paper, Connors wrote in Spanish, "Rendezvous with others at Tres Cruces. 8 a.m." He then crumpled up the piece of paper and set it on the ground, testing to see if the wind would carry it off. As it began to blow, he snatched it and found a rock to set on one corner. Thus secured, he hoped it would look like the paper had lodged under the stone.

If the sentries did come looking for him and found the paper, it might buy him a few hours, since Tres Cruces was in the other direction. Then, to draw attention to the place, Connors made sure to gun his engine and leave deep tire marks in the gravel. Seeing the tracks as they passed should get the men to stop and investigate the location.

Sunday, 12 January
4:05 a.m.

"Sorry to disturb you," the voice on the other end of the phone said. "This is Sergeant Menchaca, US embassy, Quito, Ecuador. Is this Special Agent Van Williams?"

Williams suppressed a yawn, looked at his bedside clock radio, and said, "It is. You have news for me?"

Repeating the message from Connors, the sergeant also apprised Williams on the lack of embassy personnel to go to the aid of Connors and ICE Agent Pujols, as well as the risk of an escalation to international incident status. "I understand," Williams said. "Are there any CIA assets who could help?"

"That's above my pay grade," the sergeant said. "However, Special Agent Connors didn't indicate I should contact anyone. Do you have any suggestions?"

"Fresh out," Williams said. "When I got in touch with Connors, I was sending in the cavalry. What do you do when the cavalry needs cavalry?"

Sunday, January 12
5:22 a.m.

Albert woke with a start. He'd been dreaming about playing catch with his seven-year-old son, Matthew. The boy was standing close by and rared back to throw the ball, which flew right at Albert's head. He'd dodged to avoid the incoming missile when he felt his head bump into something just as unyielding. It was the side of the tunnel where he lay sleeping.

"George," Albert said in a whisper through the blackness of the cave, "you awake?"

At the same time, Albert felt for the flashlight and clicked it on. "I think it's time we get going." He touched the priest, getting a moan. "Padre, how're you feeling?"

To George and Albert's great relief, the priest spoke. Weakly, barely above a whisper, he said, "Are we to the old city?"

"It seems this tunnel actually winds around," Albert said. "We are close to Cajas National Park."

"It curves?" Padre Domingo thought about that. "Like the back of the puma or a snake. Not surprising." Then he drifted off into a fog of pain, sleep, and unconsciousness.

George stood up, stretching and yawning. "You lead with the flashlight, and I'll take the priest. Any idea how much farther?"

"I have to confess that these tunnels are totally disorienting," Albert said. "We could be very close to the side tunnel leading to the Paper Tree Forest or miles away. I have no idea."

Albert lifted the priest onto the back of d'Hout, bringing forth another moan of pain from the cleric. Refreshed by their nap, the men moved quickly, barely taking time to notice the additional decorations on the wall as they passed. "Pretty spooky place," Albert said. "I'm glad we found a way out. This is not the place to spend the rest of our lives."

"Hey, what's that ahead of you?" George asked. "Looks like the drop down to the side tunnel."

"I think so," Albert said. "You know, we really should have been using something to mark our trail so we don't end up backtracking."

"Don't think I have anything," George said. "Not even a belt."

"We can use one of these extra sticks from the Paper Tree Forest. I'll set it beside the hole, pointing in the direction we came from. That way if we have to use this passageway again, we know which direction takes us back toward the church and which way leads to...well, to wherever it leads."

Sunday, 12 January
6:30 a.m.

The first hints of daylight were peeking over the Andes. Connors's car sat off the main path into the Paper Tree Forest, concealed from the highway by a grove of polylepis trees and a thick band of cedars and wild quinoa. Stepping from the car, Connors bent to return his Sig P228 to its ankle holster. Noticing some quinoa nearby, he grabbed the tops of several plants and rubbed them between his hands. Dozens of red kernels appeared as the chaff was carried away by the frigid wind.

Connors popped the heads into his mouth, thinking they tasted like slightly bitter wheat. He knew eating raw quinoa was discouraged since it could cause stomach cramps. But he decided only a handful wouldn't hurt and might keep his hunger at bay for a few more hours.

He looked around for signs of life, then craned his neck back toward the highway. In a couple of hours, traffic from both tourists and those traveling on business between Guayaquil and Cuenca would make the road congested.

Hidden at the edge of the forest, Connors noted how remote the area seemed, with only the cloud forest, lonesome wind, endless sky, and peaks of the Andes as company.

Then, at the edge of a nearby polylepis grove, Connors saw what appeared to be a tent. A blond-headed man emerged and, like Connors, surveyed his surroundings. The embassy man ducked behind the quinoa plants. He then calculated the distance between his position and the tent, along with how to get there undetected.

The paper trees ran up the side of the mountain, their twisted branches stretching as high as forty and fifty feet, much taller than their Australian relatives, which looked more like scrubs. Because of the weak branches and gnarled shape, the area they covered seemed dense and impenetrable. That would work in Connors's favor as he attempted to navigate through them without being noticed. The wind would cover any noise he might make while climbing over, ducking under, and sliding around the maze of branches.

Past the trees, Connors noticed large stone outcroppings cut out of the boxlike canyons by ancient glaciers, giving the park its name. Those stones would also provide cover, behind which Connors could hide. He wanted to know who the campers were and see if there was a way he could use their presence to his advantage.

Before setting out, Connors pulled out a pocketknife and used it to unscrew the license plates from the embassy car. He then opened the driver's door and slid them under the seat so no one could identify the car too easily. Next, he checked his revolver and slid extra cartridges into his pocket. He then locked the car and set out.

Connors noticed the unusual branches on the polylepis trees, as rough as the scales of a crocodile, as thin as dried skin peeling off the back of a sunburned man. The reddish-brown bark contrasted vividly with an assortment of mosses and leafy plants, ranging across the color spectrum from shamrock to olive to mint. A large blue-green hummingbird whizzed overhead and disappeared amid the lush vegetation.

Then something in the distance caught Connors's eye. It was a large stone structure. Refocusing his eyes past the dense tangle of trees, he observed that the moss-covered stones of the building almost caused it to fade into the landscape surrounding it. Possibly two hundred yards across and thirty or forty feet tall, the building had stone steps on the left that led somewhere inside. The stone wall had turrets every twenty or so yards. A fortress of some kind?

There were no signs of life around the building. Staring at it, Connors thought it might even be a prison or a monastery. A monastery, yes, that was it. But one that appeared abandoned. A noise from the campsite drew his attention back that direction. A fair-complected man was putting on a backpack, while another fellow threw water on their cooking fire.

The men were discussing something and motioning toward the castle-like structure. Connors worked to get closer to them, careful not to make noise that would give away his presence. Watching the men, Connors hoped they were Americans. If he could rely on their patriotism, it was possible they could be of assistance in his getting back into Cuenca to help Pujols.

A distant shout grabbed Connors's attention. The campers also looked up, startled. Their gaze turned toward the monastery, as did Connors's. Two men emerged down the long staircase to the left of the wall. One, a slender man with gray hair and a beard, ran toward the campers, almost as if being chased. The second darker-skinned man appeared to be carrying some heavy burden.

A second later, Connors realized what he was seeing. It was Agent Pujols and a man who fit the description of the missing George d'Hout! Connors couldn't believe his eyes. For a moment he was going to step out into a clearing and shout to his agent. Then he decided to pull back and assess the situation.

Though he couldn't understand what was being said, clearly d'Hout was yelling for assistance. The hikers ran toward him and then past him to assist Pujols with his large bundle. As it was lowered to the ground, Connors realized it wasn't a bundle at all, but a man.

As the unconscious or dead man was laid out on the ground, Connors had the chance to see his clothes—clearly the second layers of garments worn by a Catholic priest. Was this the priest who had allegedly died in the church? If so, his survival was the best news Connors could have hoped for. It clearly meant his agent and d'Hout were the priest's rescuers, not his attackers.

The two campers soon called back to the tent, and a woman emerged. She carried a red box with a large, square white cross on it. Working in the small clearing, Pujols, d'Hout, and the three campers began to inspect the patient.

One of the campers then rose and walked back to the tent, emerging in a minute with what Connors thought was a satellite phone. From his hiding place, Connors watched the man, who seemed to be checking a GPS device and then giving information to someone on the phone.

Meanwhile, Pujols, d'Hout, and the other two campers continued to work on the priest. After a few minutes of trussing up a leg, the group gently lifted the injured man and carried him back to the camp. He slumped against them in whatever direction his body weight shifted. As they reached the campsite, the man on the satellite phone hung up and gave what appeared to be very good news.

Connors watched as Pujols and d'Hout bumped their fists, celebrating some sort of victory. Relieved that Pujols had successfully rescued d'Hout and gotten him out of Cuenca, Connors wanted to run out and greet the pair. However, something—a small voice in the back of his head—kept telling him to just watch for now.

CHAPTER 33

Sunday, 12 January
7:21 a.m.

Professor Knight pored over one last map and then rolled it up, storing it in the side of a leather field bag that sat on the square kitchen table. "Miguel, more coffee," he ordered. "You can see from the kitchen when my cup is almost empty. Why do I have to ask you for a refill each time? Is this your way of passive resistance? You know what that kind of behavior got your ancestors."

Miguel carried the coffeepot into the dining room area and poured more coffee, his face a mask of indifference. He knew exactly what resistance had earned his people. Since the fifteenth century, human rights for Cañari Indians had been nonexistent. Only in the last fifty years had the indigenous people experienced anything remotely similar to rudimentary social justice. And, as his situation clearly indicated, exploitation of Cañari was still far more common than most people realized.

The Cañari had been a matriarchal society, ruled by a queen who would even lead them into battle. When the Incas appeared on the scene in 1460, they found that the Cañari fiercely resisted their attempts at conquest. However, they employed a mixture of kidnapping and rape, political cajoling, and threats of complete genocide to convince Cañari queens and tribal leaders to "marry" the Inca lords.

Once the Cañari queens were subdued, the Cañari men would obey their commands. However, to teach the Cañari a lesson about the consequences of disobedience, thousands of their males were wiped out in some of the most brutal mass killings in all history. Others were deported far to the south to work in Inca silver and gold mines or to harvest Inca crops.

Miguel wondered when liberation would come for his own family. Years earlier, he disobeyed advice from his elders and moved to Cuenca from his native town of Deleg. They warned him never to trust anyone outside the tribe, a piece of advice he deeply wished he had heeded. It seemed that everyone he met was interested only in exploiting him and his people.

However, when he first came to Cuenca, it was because of an opportunity to operate a series of stalls at an open-air market with a large tourist trade, as well as a loyal following by locals who did their shopping there. Within a year, Miguel had saved enough money to put a down payment on the house Roberto Ordóñez and the professor currently occupied. He also made enough to pay for private school for his girls at a modest Catholic institution near their home.

Miguel's plans before the arrival of Roberto Ordóñez centered on slowly bringing more and more of his family to Cuenca to work. The standard of living was higher than in Deleg, and Cañari children might even one day be able to afford a university education. Such an accomplishment by his family would make them heroes of Cañari lore, people who had finally overcome victimization by the Incas, Spaniards, and the ruling elite of Ecuador.

But clearly there was one more battle to be fought. It was a battle to overthrow Ordóñez and his henchmen. Patient to a fault, Miguel simply had to wait for the right time to begin his rebellion.

As Miguel thought about that, he watched the professor sipping his coffee. Both Miguel and Knight turned toward the staircase when they heard Ordóñez coming down. "Are you ready for your big day at the museum, exploring ancient maps and locating our treasure?" Ordóñez asked. Without looking at Miguel, he gestured he was ready to be served his coffee.

"I have what I need right here," the professor said. "You're sure everything is cleared for me to have complete access to the map room at the Banco Central Museum?"

"Complete access," Ordóñez said. "And in return, you will find where that treasure is hidden by this evening. It is not a suggestion or a wish. It is an order."

"I see," the professor said. "A deadline? Because...?"

"Because I have just gotten off the phone with a customer, a German businessman with whom I have done quite of bit of dealing in the past. He is absolutely fascinated by all things South American. He bought a number of pieces from our little Bolivian adventure. Now he wants more. I have a few pieces from Bolivia I had been holding back, but I need more."

"Is he coming to South America?" Professor Knight asked.

"He's already here," Ordóñez said. "The trip was scheduled some time ago. Did I fail to mention it? Perhaps because I had faith we would have already found what we were looking for with Mr. d'Hout. This German and two associates have been hiking and camping along the Inca Trail. Now they think they simply must have some nice trinkets to take back to Germany with them on their private plane."

"Did you tell them The Toucan here in Cuenca sells a wide assortment of souvenirs?" Knight asked

Ordóñez wasn't amused. "They are good customers, and we are going to have something nice to sell them," he said. "There is simply no question about it. It will help us get some of the merchandise out of the country quickly. Furthermore, this fellow loves to brag to his friends in the international community. That will open the door to more sales down the road."

"I see. So there's no problem as long as I find the treasure in the next twenty-four hours."

"You went to great lengths to tell me how valuable you are. Now is simply your opportunity to prove it."

After watching the professor gather up his things, Ordóñez added, "There is something else."

"Another deadline or perhaps one more veiled threat, Roberto?"

"You will want to know about this. As I mentioned, our German client will be buying some things. But we need to have some other nice pieces for him. It seems he's also interested in doing a bit of bartering."

"Oh?"

"Yes. The most interesting thing happened. It seems they were camping near some ruins in the Cajas when who do you think appeared in the middle of the night, seeking help for an injured priest?"

"I have no idea," the professor said, picking up his satchel and putting the strap over his shoulder.

"It is a man named Albert Pujols. He's in the company of a slender fellow with gray hair and a beard, and a priest who just escaped from a fire here in Cuenca but suffered a broken leg in the process."

Knight dropped his bag and stared at Ordóñez. "They're alive? In the Cajas? How?"

"I have no idea," Ordóñez said. "But it's true, nonetheless. They have been promised a helicopter to get the priest to the hospital in Cuenca. And of course, it will be necessary for d'Hout and the ICE agent Pujols to accompany him."

"A helicopter?" the professor asked. "The hospital here doesn't have a helicopter."

"No, but I do," Ordóñez said. "It is already being dispatched from Quito, where it was being used on a different project. Estimated time of arrival in the Cajas is two hours. My German customer already has instructions, as does the helicopter pilot, that Mr. d'Hout and Agent Pujols are to be on that bird, no matter what."

"Your plans from there?"

"Well, since the priest already died in that horrible fire, it wouldn't be proper for him to suddenly reappear like some modern-day Lazarus. There is a great wilderness area with few trails located in a cloud forest near Cerro Candelaria. I have it on good authority that once the helicopter is over that site, the priest will lean over for a better view and simply fall out of the helicopter."

Professor Knight smiled. "Will it be necessary for Mr. d'Hout and this law-enforcement person to go after him to make sure he has a nice trip down?"

"The agent, yes," Ordóñez said. "We still have need of George d'Hout. Remember, you haven't found our treasure yet. Mr. d'Hout is necessary to make sure we get full cooperation from his brother in case your efforts today are less than satisfactory."

"What about a helicopter landing in the Cajas? Will it be seen? What if there are questions?"

"There won't be. My German friend and his associates will be accompanying the group to make sure there is no more trouble with the agent and d'Hout."

"Your German customer is graduating from buying stolen artifacts to participating in a triple homicide," Professor Knight said. "That's quite a leap. Are you sure he and his friends won't get cold feet? That could jeopardize the entire operation."

"Call it adventure tourism," Ordóñez said. "I trust the German at least as much as I trust you. Now, don't you have an appointment? Tick tock."

PART THREE

Sunday, 12 January
8:06 a.m.

Hugh d'Hout dialed Van Williams. "I have narrowed down where the treasure is," he said as soon as he heard the FBI agent's voice.

"Right," Williams said. "You said it's near a beloved grove of trees."

"No, I mean I know exactly where it is," Hugh said. "I've been poring over hundreds of scholarly websites as well as some done by plain old crackpots. I believe there is a maze of tunnels that runs under the city of Cuenca. There's no consensus of opinion as to how they got there. However, here's the deal: the common thread linking the tunnels is that they run from the ancient Cañari and Inca site near the city center out to all the Catholic churches."

"And?" Williams asked.

"And if I'm right, one of those tunnels runs right under an arbor dating back hundreds of years and dedicated to the Virgin Mother. In other words, the pirates didn't bury the treasure. They simply hid it in one of the tunnel's secret passages."

Hugh continued. "I also found some information indicating that the tunnels could actually run as far toward the coast as Guayaquil. In other words, maybe the reason no one could find the pirates and the treasure all those years ago is that they were traveling underground."

"How did you find this when no one else has managed to do so?" Williams asked. His voice wasn't accusatory, but skeptical.

"One of the things I've learned over the years is that academics utterly disdain crackpots and pseudoscholars," Hugh said. "The pseudoscholars—guys who write books about aliens seeding our planet with humans thousands and thousands of years ago—are just as disdainful of academics. The thing is, the scholars aren't always right, and the goofballs aren't always wrong. I've simply done an academic overlay; I've looked at everything I could find on Cuenca from both the academics and the crackpots. It makes perfect sense."

Williams wasn't sure what to make of Hugh's supposition. On the other hand, if he was wrong, they wouldn't be any worse off than before. "What are you going to do with this information?" Williams asked.

"I wanted to give you time to alert your people on the ground. After they have time to get into position, I'm going to inform the people holding George, hoping whether or not the treasure is there, they will converge on the spot and be arrested. When can you let your contact in Cuenca know?"

Williams weighed what he should tell Hugh d'Hout regarding the situation. However, his silence spoke volumes. "What's wrong?" Hugh asked.

"Two people looking for George have both disappeared," Williams said. "It's almost as if the earth opened up and swallowed them."

"That tends to verify my tunnel theory. So this information doesn't really do us any good, does it?"

"Stay close to your computer and phone," the FBI agent said. "If I hear from the people down there looking for George, I'll contact you, and we can put the plan into action."

Hugh hung up, slumped back in the large black swivel chair in his office, and stared at the ceiling. He let out a weary breath and mumbled, "Lord, I know we're all going to die sometime of something, but I pray it's not George's time to die down there."

Meanwhile, Williams picked up the phone and called the desk at the Quito embassy. "Any word yet, sergeant?"

"None," the voice said.

"If you hear from Connors, I need to speak to him at once. It's of vital importance and may help end this thing."

"I'll let him know, sir," the sergeant said. Then he paused and added, "If we hear from him."

Sunday, 12 January
8:30 a.m.

Professor Knight knew South Americans moved to their own drumbeat. *Tranquilo* and *mas tarde* were phrases roughly equivalent to the American expression "chill out." Knight sat outside the curator's darkened, locked office in the basement of the Banco Central Museum, anxious to get into the research files. He was close to the treasure; he just knew it. The fact that it was a Sunday and the museum didn't normally open until noon meant nothing. He wanted in, and he wanted in now.

Further, with d'Hout and Pujols on the loose, it was imperative to get the treasure and get out of Cuenca. Knight knew the people of Cuenca were in a lather to catch and kill the two men, but what if the men got help before the crowds got them? Besides, angry *Cuencanos* had very nearly attacked the professor when he was on his way into the museum. Fortunately, Ordóñez sent two of the security guards along and they ushered him into the museum unharmed.

Another twenty minutes passed, but finally the museum curator walked up. Her business suit and perfectly styled hair made it easy to see she was among the country's elite. Like Ordóñez, she had probably studied in the United States and returned to her country to take her place as a person of prominence.

Knight couldn't help but wonder what a beautiful, undoubtedly smart woman like her might add to their team. The only issue would involve making sure she wasn't encumbered by morals or ethics. That was the kind of baggage with which their team couldn't afford to be saddled.

Then Knight caught himself. "What team?" he thought. "They would turn on me in a moment. I know it. I need to worry about myself. In fact, what are the odds that I could find this treasure and then dissolve our little partnership? Surely a fine woman like this would make a much better partner than any of the idiots with whom I'm currently working."

The woman walked up to him. "You are Professor William Knight?" she asked in Spanish.

"I am. You will permit me access to all of your files and maps on the ancient city outside your walls here. It's been arranged, yes?"

"Mr. Ordóñez has promised us a very generous donation in return for my full cooperation…as well as my being willing to come in before the museum actually opens and when our research facilities aren't normally available…it is Sunday."

The professor eyed her like a prize specimen. He could tell she was uncomfortable with his appraising looks. "Señor Ordóñez has made sure you will cooperate in every way, yes? How fortunate for me."

She ignored the obvious pass. "I haven't introduced myself. My name is Karina Mora, and I will provide whatever you need." Or did she?

"You may regret saying that," Professor Knight thought. "The last woman who made that kind of offer still hasn't been located." Then he stopped himself. He was beginning to sound like that Inca cur, Juan. One night of unbridled sadism didn't make him like *Muchacho* Juan. He was a better person than that, and he must never forget it.

Aloud he said, *"Usted es muy amable."* You are very kind. Then he asked to be led to the room housing the ancient maps of Cuenca and the Azuay Province. It was time to find that treasure.

CHAPTER 34

Sunday, 12 January
8:35 a.m.

"Miguel, where is Juan?" Ordóñez snapped at the Cañari, who was cleaning up the breakfast dishes.

"In the tunnel," Miguel said. "I believe he is checking and cleaning his guns."

"Tell him to come here at once," Ordóñez said. To himself he mumbled, "If Professor Knight is correct and the German loses his nerve, it could jeopardize everything. Besides, the ICE agent is no doubt very cunning. I can't take chances."

"What, Señor Ordóñez?" Miguel asked as he was about to enter the bedroom with the secret passage to the tunnel.

"Get Juan and stop eavesdropping, you virtual midget!" Ordóñez yelled in Spanish. He followed it with a chain of expletives that trailed Miguel into the closet and then down the ladder, fading as he entered the dim light of the tunnel.

Juan had two pistols before him on a small table and was oiling them, massaging them with tender affection. He was humming a traditional tune his mother had taught him called *"El Candor Pasa."* The look of love quickly faded to contempt when Miguel appeared. However, Juan said nothing. He just stared at the Cañari, one hand on the pistol, a second one holding the oil rag. Juan slid that hand to his right until it rested next to two ammunition clips. "Do you wonder if I will kill you right this very second?" Juan asked.

Miguel ignored him. "Señor Ordóñez wants you upstairs."

Juan returned to rubbing the gun with the rag. "You built this tunnel, yes? Or did you find it already here and take credit for it? Isn't that what Cañari dogs do? Take credit for the greatness of others?"

"What difference does it make to you?" Miguel said, not blinking or backing down.

"Because I need to spit," Juan said. "I was trying to decide whether to spit on the floor or on you."

"I invite you to try either one at any moment," Miguel said flatly. "But for now, Señor Ordóñez wants you upstairs."

A yell from above indicated that Ordóñez's tiny amount of patience had expired. Juan tucked one of the pistols into his waistband and bolted up the ladder. "Coming at once! Miguel didn't tell me you wanted me." Juan scrambled up the steps and through the hatch in the closet.

Miguel stared at the second pistol and the clips lying on the table. He could pick them up and end this now. He could insist that Ordóñez set his family free from wherever they were being kept and then kill both men. The bodies could be dumped into the tunnel, the passage sealed, and this nightmare would be over.

But what about Professor Knight? He would have to kill the professor as well. That shouldn't be too difficult. The man was a weasel, not a pit bull. Disposing of him wouldn't be much of a challenge. But then he would go through the rest of his life knowing he'd killed three people in cold blood. Knowing how evil they were—would that soothe his conscience? Or would he be racked with guilt the rest of his days? There was no clear way to know.

Miguel stepped toward the table, glancing back at the ladder and the light from the bedroom above. He took another step. From overhead, "Hey, *muchacho*, you better just be admiring that gun and not touching. You touch my pistol, and your brains are going to be splattered all over this nice cave you claim to have dug."

"I have no use for guns," Miguel said, not looking up. "They are not the way of our people."

"That's right," Juan said, slithering back down the ladder. "Your people are still living in the Stone Age. Now, Ordóñez wants you upstairs, too. We have work to do."

Miguel took two steps back from the table, turned, and followed Juan up the ladder. "Patience," he thought. "That has always been our virtue. Great patience."

Once they were upstairs, Ordóñez called the two men to the table but didn't invite them to sit. "I have been thinking about what the professor said this morning. George d'Hout and the snitch undercover agent have both been located and are in Cajas National Park."

"Impossible!" Juan protested. "They're dead."

Ordóñez scowled. "Do not interrupt me," he said. "They have been found, along with the priest. The priest has a broken leg, but they are all three very much alive. I have dispatched one of my helicopters to collect them. But here is the thing: Fortunately for us, the person who found them is one of my customers. He has offered to kill them, but I think we need to make completely sure the job is done to specifications."

A large smile replaced Juan's shock. "I have never let you down, Señor Ordóñez," he said.

"That is an ironic thing to say, considering it was you who let them waltz right out of Cuenca and into the Cajas. If it weren't for our customer stumbling onto them, our entire operation would be in jeopardy."

"I will accompany the helicopter and make things right," Juan assured him.

"No," Ordóñez said without emotion. "You most certainly will not. My confidence in you must be reestablished, but not on this. It is too important. I will attend to this myself. However, I do have a job for you."

Ordóñez thought for a moment. "Besides, you like to kill too much. What if you lose control and kill our German customer?

That wouldn't be good for business. No, I have something else you must do."

Ordóñez laid out Juan's assignment, leaving nothing to chance or judgment. First, he was to go to the Internet café and e-mail d'Hout's family, attempting to make sure George d'Hout himself hadn't contacted them.

"You are to be subtle," Ordóñez said. "Continue to communicate with them as if you are George d'Hout. See what they say in response. Then let me know. But you must hurry, as the helicopter will be here shortly. If George d'Hout has communicated with the outside world, try to find out exactly what he told them. We must know which bridges are safe to cross and which ones must be burned. Then advise Professor Knight. He is at the museum near the Cañari ruins."

"You mean the Inca ruins," Juan said.

Ordóñez ignored the trifling dig at Miguel, who was standing nearby. The ruins had been occupied by both Cañari and Inca civilizations before the arrival of the Spanish. Instead, he said, "Miguel, drive me to the peak of Turi, where I'll meet the helicopter. Then come back to the house and comb it carefully for any traces of things left behind by either the ICE agent or George d'Hout. Anything you find—anything at all—will be put in a bag and at nighttime dropped into the river. We have to cover our tracks on the slim chance that these two escape."

"And if they do," Miguel said, "you will escape in your helicopter. What about the rest of us? And how will I find my family? I have done everything you asked. I want my family released."

Juan sneered, but Ordóñez shot him a warning glance. The sneer faded into a chameleon look of concern for the Cañari man. Ordóñez seemed to be pondering his response to Miguel's request but then ignored it. "Those are my instructions," he said. "When I have other instructions, you will be notified."

Turning for the front door, Juan asked, "You have your cell phone, Señor Ordóñez? Should I call you from the Internet café to let you know what I learn?"

"No, I won't be able to hear anything in the helicopter, and I don't believe there is the capability to text from those places. Let the professor know anything pertinent. And then return to the Internet café, and I will call you for an update when we have completed our task."

Ordóñez waved a hand of dismissal to the two native South Americans but then pulled it back down. "And Juan, one thing more," he said. "Regarding the level of heat you have turned up against gringos, I believe you now need to be as adept at turning it down. We need our little American *touristas* coming here. There are plenty of rich ones in the herd, and they make very good customers for my various businesses, including this one. The first little old couple that gets beaten up or killed—it will be all over the Internet. That would be very bad for business, both ours and that of Ecuador. If that happens, some of those in positions of authority who currently help us might turn their backs, or worse. I am holding you responsible. Do you understand?"

Juan's face flushed. His contempt for those of European descent, including Americans, was deep, almost to the DNA level. His people were the rightful rulers of Peru, Ecuador, and

Colombia. He was, he felt certain, a direct descendent of the great Inca kings, Manco Capac, Capac Yupanqui, and Huayna Capac, the last of whom had been born right here in what would become Cuenca.

Didn't Inca legend insist that one day the great people would rise again? Didn't it make perfect sense that the rebellion would start right here where the ancient city of Tomabamba could rise from the ashes? A new Inca king would lead them. Inca kings ruled with a mighty fist, never afraid to spill blood. Wasn't that him, too? He had already chosen his new kingly name: Yupanqui Juan Pacheco. And now Ordóñez wanted him to do whatever it took to diffuse the situation and prevent blood from spilling. Infuriating.

"I'll take care of it," Juan said. Those who crossed Ordóñez had a very short life expectancy. What good was it to be an Inca king if he never lived to claim his throne?

Juan peeled back the large curtains across the picture window at the front of the house. White clouds adorned the sky, forming a crown for the Andes Mountains on all sides. The cottonwoods along the river waved gently in the breeze. A security vehicle waited down the block, just as instructed the night before. Juan walked out, told the two men inside to follow him at a safe distance, and began a leisurely morning stroll through the crisp air to the Internet café.

Sunday, 12 January
8:42 a.m.

Connors ducked lower behind the heavy foliage of his hiding place when the sounds of sirens suddenly split the cold morning air of Cajas National Park. High clouds hung over the mountain peaks like steel curtains. Connors estimated cloud cover at about twelve thousand feet. But below the clouds, he made out hundreds of waterfalls cascading off the sides of distant mountains. If he could see far enough to spot faraway waterfalls, there was the possibility the authorities could see far enough to spot him.

He looked up toward the winding main highway, where he watched the police vehicle round a bend, slow down as the occupants checked side roads for tire tracks, and then roll farther along the steep grade to the next crossroad.

If the authorities found and then fell for the note he'd left by the highway sign, he would know soon enough. His vantage point gave him a clear view, even though the spot was several miles away up the side of the mountain. The lights of the police car bounced off the mountains and a couple of large ponds near the road. Connors hadn't seen the ponds in the darkness. The effect of the lights' reflection on them was nearly hypnotic.

As he stared at them, a buzzer went off in his head. "Those guys want to arrest you, Pujols, and d'Hout. International incident. You haven't had but a moment's sleep. That's a fact. Time to get busy."

Connors refocused and assessed the situation. At the hikers' campground, Pujols and d'Hout appeared to be eating some breakfast while the blond hiker talked to them. The hiker kept gesturing toward the nearby ruins of the monastery or fortress. Connors was much too far away to hear what they were saying. However, he could tell Pujols and d'Hout were being evasive based on the way they kept glancing at each other as they spoke. Their body language, something Connors always focused on, was closed off, indicating there was something important they weren't telling the hiker.

Meanwhile, the other male hiker and his female companion were looking after the priest at the mouth of the tent. Every few minutes they would give a report of some kind. Then either d'Hout or Pujols would go over and look in before returning to the campfire and refreshing what appeared to be large cups of coffee. Steam curled out of the cups from which they drank. The scent of coffee drifted across the meadow to where Connors had hidden both his car and himself.

"Why not just go over there, borrow their satellite phone and call for help?" Connors kept asking himself. But something was holding him back. It wasn't a cognitive thought but rather a gut instinct he couldn't shake. Looking back toward the main road, Connors saw a second police car pull up alongside the first. Four officers were surveying the Cajas, cupping their eyes with their hands to look across the vast expanse of cloud forests, bogs, ponds, mountains, and waterfalls.

Crouched in his hiding spot behind a eucalyptus tree, Connors saw one of the men take out a pair of binoculars and survey the scene again. First he aimed them toward Tres Cruces, the highest peak in the area at over fifteen thousand feet. The peak sat well above the tree line and was currently covered by clouds. Resting atop South America's continental divide, the area had both spiritual and geographic significance for locals and tourists alike.

The barren land looked like an island sitting at the top of the world, a sea of clouds protecting it from the rest of humanity. As Connors thought about the spot, he realized that because Tres Cruces was so barren, it wouldn't take the police but a moment to realize he wasn't there. In fact, if the cloud cover cleared, they could probably tell from several miles away. So much for his brilliant plan.

Looking back toward the police cars, Connors realized the officer with the binoculars was looking right toward him. He instinctively ducked. Had something on his body caught a reflection from the sun? When he looked around, he realized it wasn't him the officer was staring at. It was his car. Though it was hidden in deep trees, the sun had broken through the clouds just enough to glare off something. Windshield? A piece of metal? It didn't matter. He couldn't hide any longer. It was go time.

Sunday, 12 January
8:45 a.m.

"Van, I've got something," Hugh said into the telephone. "I was just contacted again by e-mail. They are still trying to come across as George, but I think there are two different guys writing. This one is a lot more...sycophantic...I don't know. It permeates everything he says."

"Maybe you should apply for a job as one of our profilers. What did this person say?"

"Let me read part of it to you. 'I have to now know the secret. I need everything, dear brother. Don't hold anything back, as time is getting short. You are a great compadre in times of need. Let me commend your knowledge. I will buy you a round of drinks for helping me.'"

Hugh snorted. "This idiot doesn't know that George rarely if ever drinks. That's just not something he would say. This can't be George."

Van Williams said, "I'm more concerned with the wording. Telling you not to hold anything back and that time is growing short. Hugh, I can't raise my contact down there. Because of that, I'm flying blind. But I think you need to tell them everything you know. At least that way, if I do get my contact down there, I'll have a place to send him."

Hugh agreed, saying he would write back to whoever it was and reveal his theory that the treasure was actually in a tunnel running beneath the arbor dedicated to the Virgin Mary. He would also share his belief that the nearest access point to the tunnel was the Fourth Level entrance in the Inca tombs nearby.

After hanging up from the FBI agent, Hugh called Brenda into the room. "Get Carol on the phone," he said. "We're reaching a critical point in things. You both need to be praying for some divine intervention."

CHAPTER 35

Sunday, 12 January
9:01 a.m.

Roberto Ordóñez put his cell phone back into his pants pocket and summoned Miguel from his usual place in the kitchen. "That was my helicopter we heard passing overhead a few moments ago. The pilot reports it is a beautiful day for flying. I believe it will be a beautiful day for some skydiving as well. At least for the priest and the undercover agent."

"Would you like me to come along?"

"Don't they teach you Cañari to count? There are eight seats in the helicopter. The pilot and I are two, along with our three customers, d'Hout, the agent, and the priest. Besides, how would you help?"

"Juan has told me you prefer to not get your hands soiled with these matters. I hoped I could finally earn your trust, as well as the freedom of my family, if I performed this task for you."

Ordóñez stared at Miguel but could read nothing in the man's eyes. "I will consider your offer. Here's my phone. Call a security car to take us up to Turi to meet the chopper."

Miguel stepped outside into the perfect morning to call a security vehicle to the house. As he hung up, the phone vibrated in his hand. He looked at the number. It was one he recognized from the Internet café. That meant Juan was calling. Miguel reached down and hit the "ignore call" button.

Twice more Juan called, and twice more Miguel hit "ignore." Then he thumbed through the settings switch to eliminate the calls from the call log. The next time Juan and Ordóñez were together, Juan would insist he'd phoned, and Ordóñez would point to the fact that there were no missed calls. Anything that created dissension, Miguel was eager to employ.

Sunday, 12 January
9:06 a.m.

Connors stayed low but moved as quickly as his tired legs would carry him. He knew his brain was weary from lack of sleep, so he was extra careful with each step through the heavy undergrowth of the cloud forest. The campsite of the three hikers could be reached in about five minutes by staying just under the cover of the thick forest at the side of the nearby mountain.

His plan was to sneak up on them, listen to their conversations, and get possession of the satellite phone. Then he would call the embassy in Quito for help. He knew he would have to explain his stealth to Agent Pujols and wasn't sure he could. However, every time he thought of just walking into the camp, alarm bells sounded in his head. The question was, if there was danger, why didn't Pujols sense it, too? Maybe he didn't have any choice but to go straight in, since he had the injured priest to think about.

But no one seemed in much of a hurry to help the fellow. There had been one call on the satellite phone but no action since then. Was that what the police on the mountain road were for? Were they looking for the campsite? No, that wasn't possible, since the campsite was in a clearing and easily visible from the road. The police had all but ignored it.

Then facts began to click. Pujols and d'Hout were wanted men, accused of multiple murders across the mountain in Cuenca.

Surely the police had seen them through their field glasses. Why hadn't they swarmed in to arrest them? Was it actually possible that someone in Cuenca was keeping the lid on this situation so it didn't boil over to other communities? That spoke of someone with incredible influence and very deep pockets.

Also, if the hiker on the satellite phone wasn't calling for police, who was he summoning? Was it possible that the same person with deep pockets was the person on the other end of the line? Connors stopped his combination of running, ducking, and slogging through the wet undergrowth to crouch down and reassess.

"*Guten Morgen*," a soft, surprised voice suddenly said, not more than ten feet from him. The female hiker was adjusting her clothes and fastening her belt. "*Ich wurde auf die toilette zu gehen*," she said.

What language was that? Certainly not Spanish. Dutch? No, that wasn't quite it. German? Yes, German. "*Lo siento*," Connors said, assuming his normal pose as an Ecuadorian elite until forced to admit to anything else. "*No hablo alemán*." He was apologizing for not speaking German.

"Do...you...English...speak?" she asked in a halting voice, "My English...is...only fair."

Connors considered, as if having to translate in his head. "I do speak English," he answered but made sure to say it with a Spanish dialect. "I didn't mean to surprise you."

"We have"—she tried to think of the word—"*gäste*...guests in our camp. I needed"—she thought of the word—"the toilet to use. And here is another *gäste*."

Connors said, "I was hiking and saw your camp. You have a man hurt, so I didn't want to intrude."

The woman looked toward the tents, translating in her head. "He is...a priest who was...brought to us. Those two men found him...they said. I am...not sure...I believe them."

She considered how to translate what she wanted to say. "From those ruins, they came. What was a priest doing in there? They said they found him wandering around, lost and hurt. One of the men came to us last night, wanting a flashlight. We...how you say? ...offered to go as well...but he declined. Then he and the other man this morning appeared. It seems...odd."

"Have you summoned help?" Connors asked.

"Gustaf has a satellite phone," the woman said in halting English. "He is very...*reich*...he has lots of richness. So do his friends. He called one of them who is sending a...how you say? ...helicopter."

"*Claro*," Connors said in Spanish. Then, still feigning trouble with his own use of English, Connors said, "You are Gustaf's friend? You are rich, too?"

The woman blushed. "No," she said. "When you are...how you say? ...not ugly to look at, it is sometimes a...substitute for money."

"My name is Rafael," Connors lied. "Your name?"

"Grit," she said. The name didn't suit her, Connors thought. She should have been named Fawn or Bridgett, something reminiscent of a girl from an old Rod Stewart song.

"Come back...to our...camp. You are soaked. We have fire. You can warm up. You went hiking in those clothes?"

"Really just for a walk," Connors said. He shot a look up toward the mountain road to see where the national police were. "What is going on up there?" he asked. "Are they part of the group with your rich friend?"

"No," Grit said. "Gustaf says he doesn't like police at all. He is also wondering what they want. He is supposed to meet a man who will sell us some wonderful artifacts that will make our…"—she searched for the word—"adventure complete. Gustaf said the police are very corrupt here and will steal the artifacts from us. He said they should be…how you say? …avoided."

It was becoming clear to Connors what was going on. Gustaf had hiked in, using the Inca Trail to avoid detection. He was planning on buying treasures from Ordóñez or someone of his ilk and then escaping back across the Inca Trail into Peru. Connors's suspicions had been spot on. "Yes. I would love some coffee. Lead the way."

Sunday, 12 January
9:15 a.m.

Led into the map room, an expansive collection of original works dating back to the earliest days of the Spanish conquest, Professor Knight couldn't believe his eyes. To a serious collector, the maps in this room might have been worth at least a fourth as much as the treasure they were seeking. Even as he studied them, Knight was figuring out how to extricate one or more from the possession of the Central Bank Museum without alerting officials.

Hearing something stirring and a loud voice in an outer room, Knight felt like giving a big library shush to the offender. This place was, for a lover of history, almost sacred ground. There was a 1562 Diego Gutierrez map—he'd thought the only surviving one was in the Library of Congress in Washington, DC—as well as a 1764 Bellin and a 1719 Chetalain, both exquisitely detailed. Three of the maps were by one of the most prolific cartographers of the Spanish conquest, Paulus Minguet, including detailed maps of Guayaquil and Cuenca. These were not copies but the actual maps. Why would the museum, or the bank that owned it, let him actually put his hands on them? Yes, they made him wear gloves, but these items were priceless or nearly so. Didn't they understand what they had here? "And that," the professor thought, "is why people like the lovely curator and her bosses don't deserve to keep such treasures. They fail to properly value them."

The professor scanned the maps with adoring eyes, searching for clues as to where in Cuenca the treasure might be. On one, he traced a line with a gloved hand, and...

There was that noise again. Who was being so loud?

Professor Knight looked up and saw Karina coming into the map room with a start, as if goosed. Her eyes were focused on the professor. She was trying to convey something, but what?

Then the professor realized someone was pressed close behind her. Juan? What was he doing here? The curator received another nudge. Her eyes had a wild look in them, as if warning the professor to run before it was too late. Where could he run? This room had only one doorway, and the Inca was blocking it.

"*¿Como estas, muchacho?*" Juan asked, sounding as if he were the most carefree man alive. Then he gave Karina another push, directing her to a chair near the large table where the professor was examining maps. "I didn't know there were such pretty girls hanging out in the basement of museums. No wonder you like history so much. There is a great deal here worth extensive study." His eyes surveyed the curator the way the professor had surveyed the maps.

As Karina sat down, Professor Knight noticed Juan's right hand, which held a pistol. "You know this man? What is going on here? This isn't right! What's happening?" Karina was having trouble processing.

Before Knight could answer, Juan said, "We are *somos socios*. Business partners." He looked from Karina to the professor. "And, business partner, I have some very good news. You may put away all your maps. I know where the treasure is. All we need now is for this *bonita muchacha* to tell us how to get to it." Juan rubbed the area just under Karina's right ear with the barrel of his pistol, causing her to cringe away from him and let out a frightened whimper.

Professor Knight glared at Juan. "Are you completely insane? This museum is owned by the most powerful bank in Ecuador. They have a small army of people upstairs with enough firepower to start a war. And now you're going to bring them down on us. What the devil are you thinking?"

Karina's eyes were so wide, they threatened to pop out of her head. What was going on here? "What's the matter, *muchacha*?" Juan said. "You didn't think a bookworm like the professor would have an amigo like me? You know, this place is full of surprises. You didn't think the professor could have such a handsome associate? I didn't know such a dry place could have something so fresh as you. You and me are going to be very good friends before the day is over."

The professor glared at Juan. "Leave her alone!" he bellowed. "What were you thinking, coming in here like this? The place is owned by a bank. Didn't you think about all the cameras and security equipment? We paid a great deal of money to have access so no one would be the wiser until it was too late. And now you're going to bring down the whole thing when I am so close to finding the treasure?"

Juan interrupted the professor's onrush of angst. "You're too late. It was not you, but me who discovered first where the treasure is."

"You're out of your mind."

Juan's smile became a snarl. "Later, you will regret that remark, *muchacho*. But for now, you should know there was another e-mail, and it had everything—where the treasure is and how it has eluded everyone."

"Let's leave this woman here and step into the outer room to discuss it," the professor said.

"She's heard so much; she is almost our newest partner," Juan said. He flashed the pistol, not quite pointing it at the professor but not working to keep it aimed away from him either. "Let's talk right here. Besides, we need this fine lady's help with one or two details."

Juan slid into a chair beside Karina, motioning to the professor that he should also be seated. The Inca rested an elbow on one of the maps as he glanced toward the door to make sure they were not being watched.

"That map is priceless," the professor said. "Get your arm off of it."

Juan's eyes narrowed. "I come telling you I have found where the treasure is, and all you can say is my elbows are on the table? That's not very friendly, *muchacho*."

A maniacal smile crossed the Inca's face. The professor knew Ordóñez found this sociopath completely useful, but Knight decided it was about time for *Muchacho* Juan to go the way of the buffalo.

Juan turned to the curator. "What's your name, *muchacha*?"

"Her name is Karina," Professor Knight said. "Quit pointing the gun at her."

"Wow," Juan said. "You two just met? I've heard of love at first sight, but this is crazy."

"I'm a married woman," Karina said. "I've done nothing except show this man to the map room." She saw Juan was moving a hand close to her shoulder. She jerked away from it with all the disgust of a homecoming queen shirking the advances of the class loser.

"And now you are going to show us how to get into the Fourth Level," Juan said, not missing a beat.

"The level of the dead in the Inca ruins?" she asked. "You cannot go there. I cannot go there. It's strictly forbidden. Besides, many people would see us. The entrance is right in the middle of the archaeological park. You'd be stopped immediately."

"We're not going that way," Juan said coolly. "You are going to show us the other way to get there—the secret way."

"What are you talking about?" the professor asked. "What secret way?"

Juan related everything Hugh d'Hout shared in his e-mail, including the fact that there should be an access point into the tunnels about where the basement of the museum was located. The professor waved a dismissive hand, saying, "That's ridiculous. This d'Hout has bought into a bunch of crazy speculation and nonsense. It doesn't exist."

"Let's find out," Juan said, again brushing the barrel of the pistol against the side of Karina's face. "Here is the situation. You, pretty lady, are going to the Fourth Level, the place of the dead. You can either go there on your own power by showing us how to get in from down here, or your spirit can wander there after I put a bullet in your brain. Your choice."

Professor Knight looked the woman straight in her terrified eyes. "I know this man very well," he said. "He's not bluffing. If you know, you should tell him. He'll kill you without the least thought or remorse. Your only hope is to do what he says."

"If you fire a gun down here, it will echo, and people upstairs will hear it," Karina said, her voice shaking. "It will be your destruction, too."

"A good point," Juan said. "Very considerate of you to think of us in this way." He stood up, reaching his left hand into his pants pocket. A large knife came out, which he opened, revealing a silver blade at least five inches long and with a serrated edge that gleamed. "You want me to caress your pretty face and neck with this instead of the gun? I can do that. No problem. It's very quiet. But I'm told it hurts a great deal. That's why I will cover your mouth, to muffle your screams, as I demonstrate the way my ancestors would disembowel the beautiful virgins they sacrificed to Inti. You believe in Inti, the sun god?"

Karina gave no response. Juan pressed on, "You believe in Pachacamac? I imagine Pachacamac's spirit is strong in a place like this, with so much art and culture. Pachacamac is a god who's very hungry for some blood. He hasn't been fed in a very long time. You want me to feed Pachacamac with a big helping of you?"

Tears gushed down the curator's face, and the veins in her neck bulged. "Now," Juan said. "Inti and Pachacamac are whispering in my ear. They say I should kill you. Then the professor and I will find the secret tunnel on our own. What do you say?"

The professor considered intervening, but the look on Juan's face told him that wouldn't be a smart move. Karina shook her head slightly. "I don't know for sure. You're talking about an area of great secrecy. I've been told that if I even go near this place, it will mean not only my job but also criminal prosecution. It's an area said to go below the bank that has never been excavated, at least not that I know of. Not while I've been here. It's an area protected by national law."

"It is an Inca area, yes?" Juan asked, still smiling.

Karina nodded. "And I'm an Inca," Juan said. "I'm the descendant of Huayna Capac, the Inca lord who was born near this very spot. I am simply exercising my ancestral rights. Take us there now, or..." He held the blade near his mouth, his tongue flicking it. "Or my friend and I taste your blood."

Sunday, 12 January
9:16 a.m.

Carol picked up the phone to find Brenda on the other end. "Hugh says he's made contact again with these people, whoever they are."

"Any word on George?" Carol asked. Her voice was calm and even.

"Nothing," Brenda said. "How are you holding up?"

"I'm going to be okay," she said. "I've been reading from the Book of Psalms, and I'm going to be okay. I believe George is going to be okay, too. 'He who dwells in the secret place of the Lord shall be protected by His shadow. The Lord is our refuge and fortress. He protects us from the hunter and keeps us safe from snares.'"

Brenda said. "If this were Hugh, I'd be a puddle."

"I've been a puddle," Carol said. "What else do you know about what's going on?"

Brenda explained what Van Williams said and how he was trying to get in touch with the agents in South America. She also promised to call as soon as they learned anything. "We're praying with you," Brenda said, hoping Carol's confidence wasn't just a trick her mind was playing on her to keep her from going insane. "I guess we'll know soon enough," she thought, hanging up the phone.

CHAPTER 36

Sunday, 12 January
9:18 a.m.

Connors followed Grit toward the tents, staying a couple of steps behind her left shoulder and trying to steer their path away from the clearing so they wouldn't be visible from the mountain road or the camp. The two made small talk, Connors giving the impression that he not only lived in Quito now but had grown up there.

"You are very light skinned," Grit said.

"Castilian," he said. "Lots of Spanish blood. What part of Germany are you from?"

Continuing toward the camp, Connors saw d'Hout and Pujols sitting near the breakfast fire. Pujols noticed Grit as she returned to camp Then he made eye contact with the man who accompanied her. Suddenly he stood straight up in a move of recognition and surprise. Being slightly behind Grit, Connors was able to immediately shake his head in a warning to play it cool.

Pujols took a half step back, but his sudden move alerted George and Grit. The German woman looked around in puzzlement at Connors. "Our visitor looks like he knows you," she said.

"Hmmm," Connors responded. "Maybe he's seen me somewhere. Who did you say he was?"

As they walked into camp, Gustaf and the other German emerged from the tent where the priest lay. "He seems to be resting comfortably. My friend Max has some first-aid experience. He thinks all will be fine once the helicopter arrives," Gustaf said. "And who is this? Another visitor?"

Connors stepped forward, extending his hand. "Rafael Ramirez," he lied. In Spanish he said, "Grit offered me a cup of coffee. I got a little wet hiking and sank into some mudholes."

The group walked toward the fire and the waiting pot of coffee. Both the German named Gustaf and Connors attempted to subtly position themselves so no one was behind them or out of their lines of sight, like two Old West gunfighters positioning themselves in case someone started shooting.

"I was told you have a satellite phone," Connors said in broken English. "I need to use it, as I am also having some car trouble. I'll be happy to pay you for it, as I know it's expensive."

"That'll be fine," Gustaf said. "However, I am waiting for an important call. Therefore, it will be a few minutes. I must keep the line open. We have an injured priest in the tent, and a helicopter is on the way to get him to a hospital."

"An injured priest? Out here?" Connors asked. "How did that happen?"

Gustaf looked toward Pujols and d'Hout. "My friend and I were hiking and found him," Pujols said, still trying to figure out what was going on with Connors.

Gustaf held a cup of coffee in his left hand. He said to Albert, "Now explain to me again, because we saw you come out of the ruins. Is that where you found him?"

"Not exactly," Albert said. "This area is very confusing to me, but it was past the ruins a ways."

"It's lucky you found him," Connors said in broken English. "Where are you both from?"

"I'm from Houston, Texas," George said, "and my friend here is—"

"I'm from Texas, too," Pujols said, not looking at d'Hout. "Big state, though. We only met down here."

"In Cuenca?" Gustaf asked. "I have some friends in Cuenca." It seemed to Connors that he saw Gustaf move a hand toward a jacket pocket.

"What was that sound? Was that the priest?" Connors asked. Everyone looked toward the tent. In that instant, Connors, who was squatting, pulled up his pants leg. He slid away the retention strap and grabbed his pistol. Pujols saw what Connors was doing. A millisecond later he used his body like a bowling ball, rolling into Max's legs and knocking them out from under him.

Gustaf threw the coffee cup at Connors, causing it to glance off the man's right temple and the coffee to hit him in the eyes. As Connors looked down to wipe the hot coffee away with his free hand, Gustaf's pistol came out of his jacket pocket. He pointed the gun and fired. Connors heard the bullet zing past his ear and then heard a cry of surprise.

He glanced behind him to see Grit falling backward. The bullet missed Connors but hit the woman square in the kneecap. She collapsed in an explosion of pain, bone and blood exiting the back of her pants with the bullet.

"No!" Gustaf yelled. "I didn't mean to—"

In less than a second Connors rolled again and came up firing. Three shots hit their target, and Gustaf flew backward. The four reports from the two guns echoed up the mountains of the Cajas like thunder from an afternoon storm. Pujols rolled Max, pinning him to the ground and delivering a ferocious blow to the man's face. He hit him again and then two more times to make sure he was out of commission. On the other side of the campfire, Grit howled in pain as blood spurted from the bullet hole in her pants.

George, completely surprised by the lightning quickness of what had just happened, watched Connors with the gun, not sure whose side he was on or understanding what had just happened.

"Don't shoot us!" he yelled toward Connors. "We mean you no harm."

"He's with us," Pujols said, "which means the Germans aren't."

Connors stood over the body of Gustaf. In all his years with the Diplomatic Security Service he'd never so much as shot at another human, much less killed one. In spite of his years of training, he felt frozen. Looking at the dead man, a wave of conflicting emotions threatened to smother him. However, the anxiety disappeared when a sudden, loud buzz came from Gustaf's jacket pocket. The satellite phone.

"Get her quiet," he instructed d'Hout. "Not one sound."

George attempted to put a hand over her mouth, but Grit suddenly began fighting like a wounded bear, attempting to bite him and clawing wildly. Pujols came over and, in one motion, knocked her unconscious. George looked shocked.

Albert gave George a it-had-to-be-done shrug and said to Connors, "All clear, Chief. Good to see you."

Connors grabbed the phone, thankful it had not been hit in the exchange of gunfire. "*Ja*," he said.

"Gustaf, listen...very good news," said the voice on the other end. "I have two men who are at one of my archaeological sites. They have literally just started into a new chamber. It promises to hold exquisite artifacts, and you will be the first one, besides myself, to see them. Are your three guests secured and ready to be transported?"

Connors held the phone away from his mouth, trying to remember what Gustaf sounded like. Nothing came to him, so he simply repeated the small amount of German he knew, "*Ja. Ja. Was sonst?*" What else?

"I can barely hear you," Ordóñez said. "The helicopter is very loud. Do you have a cold, my friend? All that time on the Inca Trail, yes? We will meet at Tres Cruces in forty-five minutes. Have the priest there and make sure the other two are restrained."

Forty-five minutes? There was no way Connors, d'Hout, and Pujols could get to Tres Cruces in that amount of time, escpecially with police up on the main road. But if they didn't, Ordóñez might smell a trap and bolt away. They needed to capture this increasingly dangerous criminal. However, they also needed to get away from this campsite, which would be swarming with national police in about ten minutes. Connors scanned the area toward the ruins. Past them was another clearing on the other side.

Connors covered the speaker of the satellite phone with his hand and asked Pujols, "Did Gustaf speak Spanish or English?"

"Some of both," the ICE agent answered.

Connors went back to the phone and, doing his best to slaughter both English and Spanish, said, "Police on the road to Tres Cruces. I need you to come to the clearing by the monastery ruins. It's near where we're camping. There's a small lake. We'll be there. Get here quickly if you want these three."

Ordóñez said, "Police nearby? What's going on?"

Connors yelled in Spanish, "Get here quick and you won't have to worry about any of that. Quick!"

"Be there!" Ordóñez yelled into the phone. "We cannot wait. We will land, board you, and take off. If you're slow or there's a problem, our deal is off."

"We'll be there and ready for you," Connors said and severed the connection.

Sunday, 12 January
10:10 a.m.

Connors looked up toward the mountain road and noticed the police were taking their sweet time moving toward the campsite. Pujols said, "They must have called in reinforcements. Not in any hurry to get shot when they don't even know for sure what's going on. What's the plan?"

"First, introduce me to your friend," Connors said. "I'm guessing you're George d'Hout."

Albert said, "George, this is Dean Connors, head of embassy security in Quito."

George said, "I take it there was no choice but to kill that man. I mean...I'm just not used to..."

Suddenly, the intensity of the entire ordeal swept in on d'Hout like a hurricane, knocking him off his emotional moorings. He looked at the dead German and his two unconscious confederates. There was a lump in George's throat, and he found it hard to talk.

Pujols put a hand on his shoulder and looked at Connors. "He's been through a lot," the ICE agent said. "Several people have been murdered by Ordóñez's bunch. We barely escaped. The priest with the broken leg in that tent over there saved our bacon."

Connors said, "We need to get rolling. We've got Ecuadorian national police closing in. Ordóñez is going to be here in his helicopter in a few minutes, and we need to be ready."

Pujols let out a low whistle. "The Germans were calling Ordóñez? I'm going to change your name to Cavalry Connors. You got here just in the nick of time. We escaped Ordóñez once. I have a feeling he isn't prepared to let that happen again. How'd you find us?"

"Weird luck," Connors said, "I was looking for you in Cuenca and literally got driven out of town by an angry mob. I ended up here and was shocked to find you here, too."

"I know we need to go," d'Hout said, "but I have got to talk to my wife. Please!" He wiped his eyes. "Please, just for a minute. I can use that guy's satellite phone."

Connors looked at the dead man. "He won't need it," he said. "But you've got to make it quick. Like two minutes or less."

Grabbing the phone, George quickly figured out how to make an international call. The phone rang twice, and a tentative voice answered, "Yes?"

"Carol, it's me," George said. "I'm okay. I love you, honey. Talk to me. I need to hear your voice."

"So it worked!" Carol said, sounding overjoyed. "Hugh's plan worked! I'm so excited. What an answer to prayer! I love you, too, honey. Are you okay? When are you going to be able to come home?"

George's face registered confusion. "Worked? You mean prayer? I was sure you were praying for me."

"Of course, yes. But I mean Hugh's plan. It worked."

"Tell me what you mean. What does Hugh have to do with this?" George looked at the dead man and the two unconscious Germans.

Carol quickly related the events of the past several days, including Hugh's ongoing conversation via e-mail with the criminals. Then she told him about the morning's exchange. She said she was sure the kidnappers had let George go because they now knew the location of the pirate's treasure under the "beloved grove" near the Inca ruins.

"So you think they're on their way there now?" George asked. "And where is it, again?"

After Carol explained, George related the conversation to Connors and Pujols. George told Carol he loved her and would call back soon. Connors took the phone and dialed Van Williams. The FBI man agreed it was likely at least some of the gang was currently on their way to the treasure's alleged location.

Hanging up, Connors asked, "How many people in Ordóñez's outfit?"

Pujols said he knew of four, plus a couple of dozen armed guards from a regional security agency Ordóñez either owned or was paying to provide muscle.

Looking at his watch, Connors said, "We've got about twenty minutes to make this work. Let's get busy." Pujols pulled guns from both of the German men and tucked them into his belt.

"We need to switch clothes with these German guys," Connors said. "Make it quick. George, has Ordóñez seen you in that outfit?"

"For several days," d'Hout said. "By the last day, he was probably smelling me in it, too."

"Perfect," Connors said. "When the helicopter lands, you and I are going to walk out so they can see us. You're going to stay right in front of me, so Ordóñez can't see my face. Albert, you stay in the trees with your back to the copter. Find some kind of a hat or cap from these guys to put on. We need some clothes from the priest, maybe his pants. We can lay them back under the trees so it looks like you're guarding him. Get the shoes, too."

"What about these people?" George asked, motioning to the three Germans and Father Domingo. Then George looked at the priest again. The man's eyes were open but glazed. George tried to think of something to say in his limited Spanish. Nothing came to him. Instead, he kneeled down and took the priest's hand.

"You saved my life...our lives," George said. "Thank you." Then he remembered the words for which he was searching. "*Gracias, mi hermano.*" Thank you, my brother.

"These people are staying here," Connors interrupted. "The police will find them. They'll get the priest some real help. Plus, this will occupy the local cops so we have a chance to nail Ordóñez."

Pujols asked, "If it doesn't work, if Ordóñez smells a rat, do we take the chopper down? A couple of bullets to the fuel tank?"

Connors thought about the political fallout from such a move. "I'm hoping it doesn't come to that. You and I can get out of the country as *personae non gratae* through diplomatic channels. But it might make it tough for d'Hout. Let's work our play with the idea that this comes off like a charm."

CHAPTER 37

Sunday, 12 January
10:11 a.m.

"Yes, this is Karina Mora down in the museum archives. We've had a little electrical outage, and we need two good flashlights," the curator said into the telephone in Spanish. She listened. "No, we don't need an electrician right now. Actually I have some rare pieces out, and I don't want anyone coming down here and bringing a lot of dust and dirt into the room. Just set them outside my office, and I'll retrieve them."

She listened again. "Yes, Señor Tavarez, I know you take very good care of me. Yes, you're my favorite maintenance man. But now just isn't a good time to fix them. Just the flashlights, please. And leave them outside my office door."

Karina hung up the phone. "*Buena muchacha,*" Juan fairly purred. Then he looked at the professor. "You watch for the flashlights, and then we can start after the treasure. Don't screw up, *muchacho*, or there will be one less person to divide up the treasure between."

"Now you're giving me orders?" Professor Knight asked. "I don't think so."

"You're going to talk to me like that, *muchacho*? Embarrass me in front of this pretty lady? You know baseball?" Juan asked the professor.

"Some, but what does that have to do with—?"

"You got one strike for being stupid and for me having to find the treasure. You got two strikes because you embarrassed me in front of this *chiquita bonita*. Third strike, and you are way out. Fourth Level out." He pointed the pistol at Professor Knight and said, "Boom. Just like that. Boom. Get me, *muchacho*?"

"I get you. Completely." The professor slipped out of the map room after Juan turned off the lights. That left Juan alone with Karina, who swallowed a whimper as Knight left. The professor padded across the basement, looking for security cameras. He saw none. How could a museum owned by the most powerful bank in Ecuador not have security cameras everywhere? If there were, he might wait until he was out of Juan's line of sight, then wave like a madman to summon help.

When guards came, the hot-blooded Juan would be quick to shoot, which meant he would be killed before he could rat out the professor. But then, what to do about Karina and everything she'd heard? Surely Juan would kill her first. He always had a shoot-first, ask-questions-later mentality. But such considerations were for naught, since he saw no cameras. "Ridiculous," he thought. "Don't they know there are bad people in the world?"

He walked past a room dedicated to the history of Ecuadorian currency and a couple of empty offices. Then he came to the office of Karina Mora. He went to turn the handle and found she had obviously locked it as she was leaving. He stopped and listened. Was that the sound of someone coming down the stairs? Was he going to be caught out in the open with questions about where Karina was and no answers?

He backtracked to the currency exhibition and turned his back to the maintenance man, who was heading for the curator's office door, two flashlights in hand. The man tried the door and also found it locked. Professor Knight focused his attention on the exhibition, not looking at the maintenance man.

Setting the flashlights down by the door, the man reached into his pocket and pulled out a large ring of keys. Sorting through them, he found the one for which he was searching. He inserted it into the door and turned it. "Señora Mora?" the man called in the dark.

He then tried the lights in her office and found that they worked fine. He left the office door open and the flashlights resting on a table. Stepping back into the lobby, he looked around at all of the lights. Then he began walking toward the professor. He was pulling something else from his pocket as he came. Were there security cameras Professor Knight had somehow missed? Was this man an undercover detective of some kind? The two men made eye contact as the maintenance man's hand snaked deeper into his pocket.

Just as the maintenance man was about to speak, the door to a series of research rooms opened. Karina emerged. "Where are my flashlights?"

"They are by your office," Tavarez answered, a definite Quechua Indian accent in his voice. "Which lights aren't working? I can fix them."

"They are in the guarded rooms," Karina said. "You know you cannot go in there."

The man ducked his head in a sign of submission to authority. "I'm sorry," he said. "I like to help."

Karina kept her face a mask of stone. "I'm sure there are ways for you to help upstairs. Thank you for bringing the flashlights. Now I have work to do. Good day."

As the man walked off, Professor Knight let out a long, slow breath. He looked at Karina, then past her. Through a crack in the door to the archives room, he saw the point of Juan's pistol. Behind that was one leering eye. Both were trained on the back of Karina's head.

The door opened a bit farther, and Juan peered out, looking around the basement for any other signs of life. There were none. "Hey, *muchacho*," he said to the professor, "it was very good in the dark with your girlfriend. She has all the right equipment for my expedition. I may check it out again later."

Professor Knight looked back to Karina, who was trembling. He saw her looking at the stairwell that led to the main floor and the building's exits. "Don't do it," the professor said. "You won't make one step. He's a very good shot."

"You're right," Juan said, coming up behind Karina and tucking the gun in his pants. "Now you and I are going to get those flashlights. And then we're going to go find that treasure."

"We can't," she said.

"We've been all over that," the professor answered. "We can and we will."

"No, you don't understand," she said. "Even I don't have keys to get into the sacred areas. There are multiple locks, and I don't have the keys to any of them."

Juan smiled. "Fortunately," he said, caressing the gun through his pants, "I brought a locksmith kit that can help me penetrate even the most difficult places."

"She gets your point," the professor said. "Let's focus on one treasure at a time."

Juan walked her over to retrieve the flashlights. "Now where, muchacha?"

"Past the display on currency," she said. "There's a closet against the far wall. We start there."

Juan asked the professor, "How much you figure this treasure weighs?"

"Maybe three hundred, four hundred pounds," he said. "Hard to say for sure. In a few minutes, we won't have to speculate, if you're correct in your assumptions."

"They're not my assumptions," Juan said. "They came from that gringo George's brother. If you're saying it's stupid to trust a gringo, you're probably right, *muchacho*."

Juan turned to Karina. "You have some kind of a rolling cart down here? Something you move books or equipment with?"

She nodded and directed him to one in a nearby supply closet. "With this," he said, "we can roll the treasure out."

"Back through the bank?" the professor asked. "Not likely."

"The gringo's brother thinks the tunnels go all over Cuenca," Juan said. "We can find another exit. No need to come back through here again. But before we leave this area, how old are those maps you were looking at?"

"I get the idea," Professor Knight said. He walked back into the map room and began rolling them up. Crisp edges broke off several, no matter how carefully he tried to handle them.

"You are about to destroy priceless maps," Karina said. "They cannot tolerate the light and the weather of the outside. They'll fall apart."

"This is your fault, not mine," the professor said, continuing to work.

"What? My fault?" she shot back.

"You were foolish enough to let me in here. Your fault. A lack of good judgment."

Sunday, 12 January
10:50 a.m.

George, Connors, and Pujols sprinted along the edge of the forest, out of the line of sight of the national police. The officers had found Connors's car. While two of them examined it, the others carefully walked toward the camp. They knew there had been gunfire. Just as suddenly, however, all signs of life at the camp disappeared. They were in no hurry to walk into an ambush. They preceded, guns drawn, at a snail's pace.

In the distance the thrumming sounds of rotors echoing off the mountains of the Cajas could be faintly heard. It raised goose bumps on George's back and arms. He looked at Pujols. "I don't think I've really been afraid the whole time," he said, "but I'm afraid now."

"Pretty natural," Pujols assured him. "Before, you didn't know what to expect. Now you do. Soldiers going back into combat for the second and third time are always more afraid than newbies."

"I'll have my gun drawn," Connors said, "Agent Pujols has the German's guns. If you see something, anything, that tells you danger, you drop down to the ground, and I'll open fire."

"And if we get all the way to the helicopter?" d'Hout asked.

"When you get to that last step, reach up like you're going to grab a handhold," Connors said. "Then you duck. Get on the ground, under the copter if possible. I will give Ordóñez the chance to surrender. After that, what happens is up to them. You don't come up until I give you the sign. And watch the landing skids. Don't let them pick you up if they try to take off. Your best bet is to be right under the center of it."

George looked at Albert, who gave him a thumbs-up. "You can do this," Albert said. "No problem."

"Doubtful." Looking at his hands, George saw they were shaking. Where was his inner fortitude, the never-say-die attitude that allowed him to compete as a runner for as long as he could remember? Was it still being held hostage by Ordóñez, the professor, and *Muchacho* Juan?

Pujols turned to Connors, who was checking his pistol. Speaking quietly, the ICE agent said, "Dean, I'll do whatever you say, but I want you to consider rethinking this. Why not put me out front? Let George hang back in the trees, dressed as one of the Germans."

"I thought of that," Connors said. "What happens, though, if they open fire on us and take us both down? Then d'Hout is right back where he started, and neither one of us can help him. These guys are really dangerous; I don't have to tell you that, right? We need an army, not two guys. I'm trying to give us our best chance at getting the drop on Ordóñez."

"I understand," Pujols said. "George really is a good guy. He's held up really well through this."

Connors said, "I just killed someone, Albert. I understand what you mean about being under stress. We also stand on the verge of an international incident. The Ecuadorians are being courted by the Iranians, the Venezuelans, the Cubans, and every other country that's crossways with the United States. On top of everything else, if this doesn't come down just right, it will turn into another example of the imperialist United States beating up on a bunch of poor Ecuadorians. And who'll bear the brunt of that embarrassment? You're looking at him. So I get 'incredible stress.' But let's focus on getting these guys. We can fall apart later."

The chopping sound of the blades' vortex grew louder, its *thrum thrum thrum* echoing off the mountains. All three men looked up through the trees for signs of the copter. Across the wide expanse, George noticed that the policemen approaching the camp were also looking around. They were frozen in place, perhaps wondering if they were about to be attacked.

In certain remote areas of Ecuador, ambushes by drug cartels and smugglers were all too common. Many good policemen and army personnel had died over the years in such skirmishes. However, around Cuenca and the Cajas, the violence had been virtually nonexistent. Everyone, even drug cartels, understood the impact of destroying the tourist trade. However, people had once thought the same thing about Mexico, and look at what was going on there. These officers were not going to take any chances, so they retreated for cover until they knew what was going on.

Connors tried to decide whether the officers' retreat was good or bad. On the one hand, it would reduce the chances he'd get shot by one of the Ecuadorian police. On the other hand, it would also make it harder for them to rescue George if Ordóñez somehow took him and Pujols out. Glancing up again, Connors saw the chopper, probably some country's army surplus, coming into sight.

Pulling on one of the caps he had picked up in the tent, along with sunglasses, Connors stepped out from under the trees and waved. The noise from the helicopter's approach was almost deafening now. The bird swung into view but didn't come straight down. It circled as if someone on board were assessing the situation. "Come on, you son of a—," Connors thought, but a sharp sound cut him off.

Looking around, he saw a policeman across the field; the man had a rifle and was aiming it right at him. He heard the *zing* of a bullet coming close by. Frantically, he waved at the helicopter to come on down. Then he retreated under the trees. In a moment he emerged, pushing d'Hout out in front of him, George's hands behind his head.

Connors leaned close to George's ear and said, "I gotta make this look right." Then he roughly swung d'Hout toward the police, as if warning them they were about to shoot a hostage. George was glad Connors was pushing him along. Otherwise he wasn't sure he'd have the courage to keep walking. The noise from the helicopter was now so loud that it sounded as if it were inside George's head. He glanced up and saw it coming down right in front of them.

As the chopper reached the tops of the trees, George made eye contact with Roberto Ordóñez. Ordóñez smiled broadly and nodded approvingly, as if seeing an old friend. George looked, as best he could, into the helicopter to see where Juan and the professor were. He saw only Ordóñez and the pilot. Turning his head slightly, George yelled, "I don't see two of the others. They must be going after the treasure."

"Keep walking," Connors shouted into d'Hout's ear. "Remember what we talked about. You're in front of me, so I don't have the best view, but we need to make sure the people on the chopper can't see my face. Is that Ordóñez?" George nodded.

Connors leaned in close to his ear again. "See any guns?" George shook his head. Connors and d'Hout were no more than ten yards from where the helicopter was about to touch down. Connors loosened his grip a bit on the Sig. He remembered attending a seminar in which a Drug Enforcement Agency representative had been lecturing. The man had said it was increasingly difficult to fight terrorists and drug cartels because these people considered life cheap and weren't afraid to die.

"We hold life as precious," the lecturer said. "That is our greatest strength and our greatest weakness. But remember, as long as we let them be the predator, that makes us the prey."

"Not today," Connors thought. "Today, these guys are the prey."

The helicopter was inches from touching down. Connors thought he saw some movement in the back of the bird. Had he? Maybe not. Ordóñez was looking right at them, so he didn't dare peek too far out from behind George's head. If Ordóñez caught on to what was happening, he had a clear shot to kill both he and George.

George watched Ordóñez in the front passenger seat of the chopper. Ordóñez bowed his head slightly, as if welcoming two visitors to his home. George froze, causing Connors to almost run into him. "C'mon," Connors yelled. "Keep moving."

CHAPTER 38

Sunday, 12 January
10:55 a.m.

Karina stood before a door with a double deadbolt lock and a sign in Spanish: Absolutely No Admittance under Most Severe Penalty of Law. "Uh-oh," Juan said. "We don't want to break the law, do we, pretty lady?" He had a gun shoved into her back as they snaked through the dark corridors beneath the bank, most of which Karina insisted she had never visited and didn't know existed. Even for the curator of the museum, these areas were seriously off-limits.

Juan reached his other hand to touch her back. "You ever do anything that was really bending the rules?" he asked, like a snake hissing in her ear. "You ever a bad girl?"

"Can we focus on the job at hand?" Professor Knight asked.

"I will focus on what is at hand later," Juan said, touching Karina again, "after we get the treasure."

Professor Knight looked at the curator. Terrified. He had to admit he liked that in a woman. "You have a key, or does Juan use his gun?"

"I swear I have never been down this far," she said. "If there are keys to this, I have no idea where they are."

"You are the curator of this whole museum, and there are places in it you have never been?" Juan asked. "That's absurd. I should kill you right now for lying."

"I'm not lying. I was told to leave these areas alone. They're sacred. I was trusted, and I have honored my promise to not disturb these areas. I don't expect you to understand that…"

Juan stepped forward, shoved Karina to the left, and shattered both locks with two quick pulls of the trigger. Shrapnel from the bullets and locks sprayed, hitting all three of them.

For a moment Karina thought she had actually been shot. She looked and saw bloody spots on her hands. Suddenly an intense burning registered all up and down her arms, on the side of her face, and just below her right knee.

"You idiot!" Professor Knight screamed. "Why didn't you tell us to get back?"

Juan, nursing his own small wounds, smiled as if he were a mischievous child firing off a bottle rocket too near a thatch roof. "Pain makes you know you're alive," he said. "And look, the door isn't locked anymore. Shall we go get my treasure?"

Professor Knight looked into the eyes of Juan Pacheco as he pushed open the heavy door and roughly shoved Karina inside.

"His treasure?" Knight thought. In spite of the pain and blood, he was sure he'd just heard Juan say they were getting his treasure. The look in his eyes was wild, even crazy.

The professor leaned in close to Karina and whispered, "You see it, don't you? This Inca's mental canoe really is about to go over the psychological waterfall. I'm your only chance of salvation."

"Shut up and keep moving," Juan said. Karina had fallen a few steps behind. He reached back and pulled her up to him. "Tell your girlfriend there's no time for whispering secrets, *muchacho*."

Juan insisted the professor and Karina go ahead, then grabbed the rolling cart and pushed it through after them, shoving it into the back of Karina's legs. "Women's work," he said. "Push the cart."

She took it as Juan and Professor Knight looked for a light source. Finding none, they switched on the flashlights the maintenance man provided. "We are very close," Juan said. "This isn't part of the bank. This is my people's work. Look at the walls."

The ceiling of the area they were now in was not squared off at ninety-degree angles. The entire structure was rounded, as if they were inside a giant, hollowed-out snake. There was also a bit of an echo that hadn't existed before. "The spirits of my people are here," Juan said. "The kings are calling me."

Professor Knight looked at Karina, who stepped closer to him. Or was she just stepping farther away from Juan? Juan looked sharply at both of them. He motioned with his pistol to keep moving forward. Professor Knight said, "I suspect the two of us can get the treasure back to the safe house. And if we keep the curator with us, it will be handy. Trying to watch her and hold on to the treasure will be tough, though. But together I think we can do it."

Juan said nothing. He was like a hunting dog closing in on a rabbit. Knight thought he saw the Inca actually sniff at the air, trying to pick up the scent of something ahead of them. They walked on in the darkness, the two flashlights picking up nothing but desolation in the ancient tunnel.

Juan said, "The gringo d'Hout's brother says these tunnels are everywhere in Ecuador and Peru. He thinks that's how the pirates got here from Guayaquil without getting caught. Why didn't you tell Señor Ordóñez about these tunnels, Mr. History Man?"

"Stories of the tunnels were investigated by the Ecuadorian government back in the 1980's," Knight said. "The government said they checked out the stories, and there was nothing to them."

"You trusted the government, made up of the descendants of the conquistadors?" Juan asked, incredulous.

They came to a Y in the tunnel. "We go right. I can feel it, like a magnetic pull. My ancestors are telling me to go right. How does it feel walking the same paths the dead walk, *muchacho*? Does it make you feel close to death? He pulled the gun out of his pants and waved it a little. "Think how many sacrifices my people could have made if they'd had some of these. But the knife is slower, more religious. Hard to cut out a heart with a bullet."

He looked at the professor, who was sweating profusely in spite of the mild temperatures in the tunnel. "What you thinking about, *muchacho*? You look scared."

"I was...was just remembering when Roberto and I met in college. We could tell from the start we were going to be lifelong brothers."

"You are reflecting back on your life. Why do you think that is?"

"Just remembering how tight Ordóñez and I have been over the years, that's all. We are about to reach the treasure, right? I always reflect on what makes us a good team at times like this."

"You sound like a woman," Juan said, eyes on the tunnel in front of them.

"And you sound like you have no need of anyone," the professor said. "The great Inca king Huayna Capac had trusted lieutenants. You sound like you need no one."

Juan stopped and turned to the professor. "You know how many advisers the great king had?"

Professor Knight smiled. "Four was an important number to your ancestors. The king had four intimate advisers. Those would have each had four, and so on. Even the god-king Huayna Capac had to seek advice from time to time."

Professor Knight kept walking, not making eye contact with Juan. He could hear the rolling wheels of the cart Karina was pushing. "And you know what happened to those advisers when they gave bad advice?" Juan asked. "They got disemboweled in front of the new ones. That made it clear there was no margin for error in the advice given to the king."

All three suddenly stopped. Beams from the two flashlights picked up a line of clay pots in front of a small passage. There were roots growing through the top of the tunnel and a clear smell of earth, plants, and age. The roots looked like tentacles blocking the path. Some even stretched to the floor and resumed their downward path.

The pots had been shattered, giving the appearance that someone had picked them up, checked their contents, and dropped them. "These were put here to indicate a spiritual wall," Karina said. "They were filled with certain ingredients to attract one type of spirit and to keep another type away. Whoever dropped them had no respect for Inca religion. They were looting the place."

"Look at that," Professor Knight said. He pointed to a place where a foot had stepped on a piece of pottery, shattering it and leaving an indention in the dirt, ashes, and crushed pieces. "Notice how the shoe print is pointed. And here's another one. There's no left or right shoe print. They're both the same. That doesn't prove it was the pirates d'Hout and Edward Davies, but it certainly fits the type of shoes they would have worn."

"There were doors leading to this place," Juan scoffed. "Anybody could have made these footprints, even the curator lady."

Karina turned sharply and said, "Maybe you know nothing of respect for antiquities, but others do. I'd never do such a thing. These areas are sacred! When it was discovered that they were here, they were preserved—closed off to stop looting, not to encourage it."

Juan responded by slamming the pistol into the side of her face. She crumpled to the floor of the tunnel like the shattered pottery, her knees and hands cut by sharp clay shards. She winced in pain, rolling up into a ball of tears, bruises, blood, and misery. Juan pulled back a leg to kick her in the head.

"We need her alive," the professor said. "Besides, you don't want all that beauty spoiled when it comes time to celebrate your victory."

Juan's scowl melted into a toothy, childlike grin. "Now that's what I like in an adviser. You are thinking good. Help her up and get that cart past all the rubble. We need it for my treasure."

Knight searched around the broken pottery with his flashlight, settling on a mound of what appeared to be dirt about two inches high and six inches wide. There was no other dirt like it on the floor. "See that? It tells us the pirates came this way. They used llamas to carry the treasure. And no one has been here since. If they had, they would have disturbed these mounds. We're on the right track."

"How do you know that, *muchacho*, from little mounds of dirt?"

"These are llama turds. They've disintegrated into their more base properties, but it's what we need as proof we're on the right track. If we wanted to walk all the way back to Guayaquil, should those tunnels still exist, we would simply follow the trails of llama droppings."

"I'm not surprised you'd know so much about crap, *muchacho*. Let's go get my treasure."

With mock sympathy, Juan turned to Karina. "You don't look so good. What happened to the pretty lady I met earlier? You ever been with an Inca king before? I didn't think so. You're going to be with one now, right after we get my treasure."

CHAPTER 39

Sunday, 12 January
10:56 a.m.

George kept his eyes toward the rear of the passenger compartment of the chopper. He was sure he'd just seen movement there. What was it? The helicopter's noise was deafening, and with the police across the wide field, taking aim at them, it was more than George's senses could absorb. The real question was whether Connors had noticed the movement.

Close to the helicopter now, George felt a pulsing in his ears. Was it his blood pressure or perhaps the sound of the chopper blades banging the air? Then he realized it was Connors, acting as Gustaf, who was bumping the side of his head with the magazine end of the pistol handle. Leaning into the side of George's head, Connors was working to keep his face hidden from Ordóñez.

He was also saying something, but it sounded like, "Don...le... mov...side...ful."

As George started to turn his head to see what Connors was telling him, he saw Ordóñez raise a hand and glance over his shoulder to the rear of the craft. The barrel of a shotgun was sticking out the open door of the chopper. George followed the barrel to see Miguel's face. The Cañari made eye contact with George, his eyes sending a strong, unmistakable message. *Get down!*

George saw Miguel cock both barrels of the shotgun. Again the Cañari indicated George should duck now. What was Miguel about to do? A flood of information washed over d'Hout so fast, he struggled to take it all in.

Suddenly, it was clear. Miguel was attempting to free him and liberate his family in one motion. Somehow he'd gotten Ordóñez to trust him with a weapon, or he'd taken it by force. Now the Cañari was about to shoot the man he thought was George's captor. Being hidden in the back of the helicopter, he was then in a position to hold the shotgun on the back of Ordóñez and the pilot and demand that his family be set free. Connors and Albert, posing as the Germans, were in grave danger.

"No!" George screamed, but the sound disappeared into the rotors of the helicopter like a teardrop in a river. George jumped back, trying to use his body to force Conners out of the way. He and the security chief were locked in an awkward dance of scrambled limbs and confused motions.

A sudden sound pierced the helicopter's drone, the explosion made by the right barrel of Miguel's shotgun. Seeing George shove himself into the German, at the last possible second Miguel had moved the barrel just a hair to the left. Paramo grasses and scrubby vegetation exploded to the right of Connors.

For a moment, George felt dizzy. He knew the helicopter was in front of him and that Connors was beside and slightly behind him, but he had the sensation of moving forward and staying in the same place all at once. A sudden attack of vertigo? Refocusing, he realized the effect was created by the fact Connors was not in place but was actually stepping back in what appeared to be slow motion. The pistol Connors had been holding also appeared to be moving in slow motion, flying out of his right hand and arcing toward the ground. Something else was wrong. Connors's arm was no longer a suntanned brown, but a volcano of reddish-black lava flowing from a thousand vents.

Was that blood? Connors had been shot. The security chief stumbled backward, rolling as he crashed to the wet ground. Where was Albert? He had to warn him. George turned and saw Pujols pulling out the pistol he had taken from the Germans and firing at Ordóñez. He sprinted out from under the cover of the trees. The shot went wide. Pujols squeezed the trigger again, but the gun's firing mechanism malfunctioned. Nothing.

George saw Pujols behind him running toward the helicopter. He turned his head back to the bird and saw Miguel, who was pointing the shotgun at him and indicating he must get in. "What is he doing?" Ordóñez screamed into his headset to the pilot. "I specifically told the idiot not to open fire unless I gave him the signal."

A sullen, determined voice interrupted whatever the pilot was about to say. "I am through taking orders," Miguel said. "You are going to free us. You are going to free my family. Or I will kill you right now. Once this man is aboard, you will take off and take me to my family. Now!"

"I trusted you!" Ordóñez screamed back. "You begged for a chance to prove yourself. It's why I came back to get you and allow you to come with us. You are a Judas! A Judas, you ridiculous little Cañari freak! I'll kill you. You're a dead man, you Judas."

George couldn't hear the exchange in the headsets, but he could tell Miguel and Ordóñez were furious. When Miguel pointed the gun toward Ordóñez, George began to back away. He saw Miguel's lips form the word "no" as the Cañari shook his head. Was George now a pawn in Miguel's schemes, as he had been in Ordóñez's?

At once, Miguel looked past d'Hout and pointed the shotgun toward who he thought was a second German running toward the helicopter. George reached up and grabbed the end of the shotgun, using it to pull himself into the chopper. "If you shoot him, you won't have anything left against Ordóñez!" George screamed so loudly his voice cracked.

He wasn't sure how much Miguel heard past the headset he was wearing, but when he pointed toward the front of the helicopter, the Cañari got the message.

Sunday, 12 January
11:01 a.m.

Looking to the back of the helicopter, which wasn't easy because of the safety harnesses he was wearing, Ordóñez saw George was blocking Miguel's view. He used the moment to reach for his own pistol and click off the safety. Before he could reach over his shoulder and fire, not too concerned about which person he hit, Ordóñez felt the pilot urgently tapping his left shoulder.

"The other one," the pilot was repeating over and over. "The other one. He's shooting." A bullet hit the front window of the helicopter. Shatterproof glass kept the windshield intact, but the shot had only missed hitting Ordóñez through the open cockpit door by inches. Without waiting for permission, the pilot lifted the bird off the ground in a violent motion. Ordóñez aimed at the gunman running toward the helicopter and squeezed the trigger, but his shot sailed wide.

The helicopter lurched forward and up. Ordóñez looked back again and saw George fall backward toward the helicopter's still open door. Miguel held the shotgun in one hand and grabbed George with the other, preventing him from falling out. The chopper was now above the tree tops and gaining altitude quickly.

As the helicopter turned, Ordóñez saw the national police below him rushing to the Germans' tent. The man who pushed George toward the chopper was writhing in pain on the ground.

Another man, possibly one of the other Germans, had turned and was sprinting toward the ruins of the monastery.

Now the chopper was moving forward instead of up, and Ordóñez couldn't see anything else. The entire episode had taken only a few seconds, but it felt like an eternity. Roberto glanced backward to see the shotgun still pointed at him.

"Tell him to fly to where my family is," Miguel said into the headset he was wearing.

"If you shoot," Ordóñez said, "you will almost certainly hit the pilot. That means the helicopter will crash and you will die. You didn't think of that, did you?"

"And you will die, too," Miguel said, never missing a beat. "I've been dead inside since you took my family from me. I will not live again until you give them back. So I am already dead. You cannot kill me. You, on the other hand, want to live. So you are the one who stands to lose the most if I pull this second trigger."

"I believe we can settle all of this once we've gotten out of this area. We cannot wait on the treasure. It is now imperative we make our escape. Of course, you may go with us."

Miguel continued, "You have insulted me. You have insulted my people. You are the evil that has afflicted my people. You are the *sagra supay*, the greatest of all devils. To kill the devil is not only a possibility. It is an obligation."

"The devil?" Ordóñez asked into the headset. "Juan possibly, yes. Me? No. I have taken good care of your wife and family. I've taken good care of your home, which you were very kind to let us borrow. In fact, I am going to pay you generously for allowing us to rent it. How much do you want?"

"I want my family," Miguel said again. "I will tell you no more. Fly me to where they are. Now! Radio to the people holding them and tell them to bring my family to where we land. Then you may fly away, and I will rejoin my family."

Miguel watched Ordóñez reach up and make an adjustment on the headset control. Suddenly he couldn't hear anything being said, though he could see Ordóñez talking to the pilot.

George pulled the Cañari's headset to the side and yelled, "He switched to a different channel. He and the pilot are talking but don't want you to hear." Miguel couldn't make out what George was saying but read his expression and frantic hand signals.

The Cañari stood, as best he could in the cramped helicopter, leaned over the middle row of seats, and jammed the shotgun into the area where Ordóñez's neck met his shoulders. Ordóñez twisted around in disgust. Again the Indian released his right hand from the trigger to signal toward his headset that he couldn't hear. As he did, Ordóñez raised his right hand over his left shoulder and squeezed the trigger of a pistol he had been concealing. One second Miguel was leaning forward. The next, he was slumped over the middle row of seats.

Ordóñez pointed the pistol at George. No emotion. No anger. Just a businessman taking care of business. He signaled for George to remove the headset from Miguel and put it on. With the pistol pointed at him, he was in no position to argue. Once he had it on, he sat down on the back row of seats. Ordóñez's voice crackled in his ears. "I want you to know I have done what Miguel asked. You might say I fulfilled his last wish."

George said nothing. Just stared. "You see, all this little idiot wanted was to be reunited with his family. I was merely fulfilling his wish. They have been dead for several days now. I am hardly in a position to run a hotel. Keeping guests for an extended period of time is not my line of work. Too expensive. He wanted to see them, so I was putting him in the best position to do just that."

The helicopter zoomed over the Andes and back toward Cuenca. Low, dark clouds rolled over the mountains like a beast, threatening to consume all it encountered. The morning sun, that object of Inca worship, was the first to be devoured. As it was swallowed, the day grew dark.

Sunday, 12 January
11:08 a.m.

"Miguel," George thought numbly. "I thought he was my guardian angel. Can angels die?" This was a good man, a good man in a horrific position who was simply trying to get his family back. He'd tried to help. In so doing, he mistakenly shot another good man, Dean Connors.

George didn't fear for his life. He didn't dread being murdered, which would surely happen somewhere in the not-too-distant future of this never-ending nightmare. He only missed Carol. He felt alone. He felt hollow, like a cantaloupe from which the meat and seeds had all been cleaned out and only the slightest bit of flesh and rind remained.

His glazed eyes stared ahead, his back rigid against the rear seat of the chopper. In the front, Ordóñez was smiling, his head turned over his left shoulder toward d'Hout. George didn't want to hear any more. He couldn't. He took off the headset and absently threw it past the slumped corpse that had once been Miguel and onto the middle row of seats. Tears filled his eyes.

Focusing just a bit on the motion in front of him, George realized Ordóñez was still trying to communicate with him. He worked harder to focus his eyes, but they rebelled. They had seen too much. The waving became a bit more insistent, stopped for a moment, and then was replaced by something else. Ordóñez was pointing the pistol straight at him.

A surge of adrenaline replaced the numbness. The survival instinct was taking over. George's head turned slightly so Ordóñez was centered in his line of sight. Ordóñez pointed to his own headset and then to the one lying helter-skelter near Miguel. George looked at Miguel. A lifeless body and blood. Following the trail of blood as it ran down Miguel's torso and to his legs, George saw it was slowly making its way toward one of his athletic shoes. He moved the foot back a bit.

He looked back up. Ordóñez's smile was harder, his head tilting a little to say, "Put on the headset, or I will kill you where you sit."

Why? What could Ordóñez say to him? What would he want to say to Ordóñez? Nothing came to mind. Numbness seeped back in. George saw Ordóñez's thumb flip off the pistol's safety. George edged forward, grabbed the middle seats, and pulled himself up. To get the headset, he would have to reach past Miguel's body.

As he did, blood got on his hands. He wiped it on the seat and kept working his way to pull Miguel close enough to get the headset. As he did, he noticed the shotgun. It was propped askew, half on and half off the middle row of seats. He looked up at Ordóñez.

Roberto Ordóñez was smiling even bigger now. He shook his head in a don't-be-a-naughty-boy manner. As he did, the pistol extended a bit farther toward George. As George pulled up to get past Miguel, the body shifted backwards and fell onto the floor at George's feet. Blood was everywhere. George thought he was going to throw up.

He focused on the headset, slipping it on. "Do you know I considered including you in my organization?" he heard Ordóñez say. "You know computers; you are bright. You surely have connections in the United States and possibly elsewhere. I am very disappointed in you, Mr. d'Hout. And now you have infected Miguel here with whatever this poison is. So today I have lost not one but two men with the potential to do great things for me and for themselves."

George wished he had left the headset where it was. "But do not fear, Mr. d'Hout," Ordóñez continued, "because at least one member of your family has been very cooperative. What is your brother's name? Hugh—is that right? He has done what you would not. He has told Juan and Professor Knight exactly where the treasure is. They are on their way there now."

Sunday, January 12
11:10 a.m.

Carol d'Hout felt a quick stabbing pain that instantly reminded her of going into labor. It was as if something kicked her right in the ribs. At the same instant, a feeling of dread came over her. "George," she muttered. "Dear God, please keep George safe."

As an evangelical, she believed it was not only possible but expected that a child of the King would appeal to that King in times of trial. For her, praying was as much a part of life as breathing. It was more than just a laundry list of wants and needs. It was also listening, meditating, reading scripture, and knowing the scriptures were written as much with her in mind as the original recipients.

She listened now. There was no audible voice. Nothing anyone else might pick up on. But there was a clear impression that the danger in which George previously found himself had again reared its head. There was nothing psychic about her feelings, and she approached them cautiously. "Lord, I don't know what's going on, but I'm claiming protection for George."

She thought about something she'd heard her brother-in-law, Hugh, say before. "We are all going to die someday of something. Lord, I pray it's not George's time today. Bring him home safe."

CHAPTER 40

Sunday, 12 January
11:11 a.m.

Riding in the helicopter, George was struck by how close the Cajas National Park was to Cuenca. Just over the next mountain, really. The mountains were beautiful. He looked at them as if they were the last things he would ever see. Quite possibly they were.

As he did, he remembered the words: "I will lift my eyes unto the mountains. From where shall my help come?"

Ordóñez's voice crackled in George's ear. "What did you say, Mr. d'Hout?"

Realizing he said the words aloud, he said, "Nothing. Just thinking of an old song."

"I would prefer you focused on helping us recover that treasure, Mr. d'Hout," Ordóñez said. "It is the only thing that might save your life."

The helicopter was near Turi, the highest point in Cuenca. It circled to land. Again, George found himself focused on the words. Were they from the Bible? He couldn't remember. More words came to him, but he kept them inside this time—something he once read, something he heard in church. "The Lord is my light and my salvation. In whom shall I fear? When evil men advance against me, they will stumble and fall. In the day of trouble, the Lord will keep me safe."

George took a deep breath and felt his body relax a bit. He couldn't explain why. The danger was just as real, and closer than ever. They would soon be reunited with Ordóñez's henchman, Juan. George had seen repeated examples of the things of which Juan was capable. Nonetheless, he almost felt calm.

"I must be in shock," he thought. "No other logical explanation." He stared out the window of the helicopter. There was a sensation at his feet. Miguel was there, of course, or rather Miguel's body. A few seconds passed and there it was again, a sort of tapping on one of George's ankles. He looked down. One of Miguel's hands was slowly, painfully making its way from where it lay at his side and then up George's leg past his knee.

The body was so bloody, George didn't want to look. But the hand was moving. George looked up to see if Ordóñez's head was turned toward the back of the bird. Both the pilot and Ordóñez were watching the ground grow ever closer. In a few seconds, they would be landing.

At George's feet, Miguel's hand now attempted to pull at something. Glancing up to make sure Ordóñez wasn't looking back, George leaned down and put his hand next to Miguel's. Before George could grab it, the hand fell, landing on the Cañari's stomach and pushing back his shirt just a bit. The movement revealed a pistol tucked in the waistband of Miguel's pants.

As George pulled the gun free, Miguel's hand moved again, his index finger touching George's wrist. There was blood on it, deep crimson and sticky. With the finger, Miguel traced the shape of a cross on George's wrist. George watched the finger work, then followed it up the arm, the shoulder, and the neck to Miguel's face. Miguel moved his lips. The Cañari was saying something. What was it? There was too much noise to make it out. George tried to lip-read, but were the words in English or Spanish?

Then George knew what it was. "*Mi familia*," Miguel mouthed. My family. Miguel's eyes were looking at George, then past him. Then at nothing at all.

"Miguel," George thought. "Michael. Just like the archangel. Thank you."

There was a bump, and George looked up. The copter had landed.

"Señor Ordóñez," George said into the headset, "I have a confession to make."

"A confession?" Ordóñez said. "You were with a priest. Perhaps he is who you should have spoken to."

"It concerns you," George said, "so I need to tell you."

"Go on."

"My brother and I, we have known about the treasure for a long time," George said. He was on unfamiliar ground and not sure he could pull it off. "We also knew others might try to find it. We had a code and backup plans. I don't want to die, and I see that I'm not going to get away. If my brother told you the contingency location—the dummy location—instead of where the treasure really is, well..." George let his words trail off.

"Why don't you tell me where the treasure is, and we won't have to worry about false locations," Ordóñez said.

George said, "I feel really addled right now. Please tell me where Hugh instructed your people to go. If it's wrong, I can tell them how to get out of it. I'm trying to help, but I think in all of this I have a concussion or something. I feel terrible. If I pass out..."

"You will have no opportunity to stop them, so even if you are lying, I don't suppose it matters. They are headed to the beloved grove near the old Inca settlement in the heart of city central. Your brother said the treasure is actually buried under the grove in a series of tunnels. Access points are underground."

George let his head dip a bit, and he tried to make his eyes swim in their sockets. Refocusing, he looked straight down at his lap. The pistol was loaded, the safety was on, but George fixed that.

Ordóñez said, "Now, why don't you set the record straight on where the treasure is and spare your life?" George looked up and saw Ordóñez pointing the pistol at his face.

"I don't feel very good," George said, leaning left. As he did, he brought the pistol up over the seat with one motion and pulled the trigger again and again and again and again and again and again. He waited for the answering shots and the bullets that would rip into his flesh.

None came. George stayed ducked down listening as the helicopter rotors slowly spun to a stop. Then he could hear the wind outside. Then came a gigantic boom. George involuntarily ducked down farther. After a few seconds of quiet, he looked up to see dark clouds of a fast-approaching storm rolling in over the mountains. The skies had been clear a few minutes earlier, but now Cuenca was immersed in a thunderstorm.

In the front of the helicopter, the bodies of Ordóñez and the pilot lay slumped. Each had gaping bullet wounds to the head. George looked outside, but no one was around. Everyone had run for cover from the sudden downpour. Was it also possible that the sounds of gunfire had been mistaken for early peals of thunder?

George pulled off the headset, discarding it on the back seat. He picked his way past the middle row, grabbed the shotgun, and then moved to examine Ordóñez. The smuggler's eyes were raised to heaven, but he was currently about as close to that location as he would ever get, George thought. Staring at the bodies of the pilot and Ordóñez, George waited for the same sick sensation that hit him when he saw Miguel shot, and before that, Connors. Nothing. Not this time.

Climbing out of the helicopter and into the rain, George moved up beside Ordóñez and unbuckled the harness, holding the body in place so it wouldn't fall out. Then he frisked the clothes until he found the cell phone in a pocket. The task was difficult, but George dislodged the phone. Standing beside the helicopter, the storm drenched George, but it also washed off Miguel's blood from his arms and clothes, mixing it with the brownish-red mud and disappearing in rivulets.

Dialing the phone, George entered the country code for the United States. "Hello, Carol?" he said. "It's George. I'm okay. I can't explain everything that's happened, but I'm free."

Sunday, 12 January
11:30 a.m.

"Her purse!" the professor suddenly said, stopping dead in his tracks and holding up a hand.

Karina's arms and legs ached from stooping over the cart and pushing it through the long tunnel. She stopped but kept focused on the floor. Her hair was matted, her clothes, arms, and legs bloody. Juan, leading the group, his flashlight surveying the path ahead of them like a jaguar in search of its next meal, pivoted.

"What now, *muchacho*?" he said, his voice dripping with annoyance.

"We didn't get her purse," Professor Knight repeated.

"So? Who cares? Maybe I should just feed you a bullet. Maybe you aren't a trustworthy adviser at all."

"When no one can find her, but her purse is still there, that will be a sign something untoward happened. If, however, her purse is also gone, that means she slipped out, and no one saw her leave."

Juan looked at Karina and appeared to be considering the professor's words. "You mean you didn't grab it? What were you thinking?"

The professor said, "You need to hurry back and get it. In her condition, if we take her all the way back, she will just slow us down. I will stay here with her and wait for you."

A huge smile crossed Juan's face. "I don't think so, *muchacho*. I have a better idea. You go back and get the purse, and I will stay here with the pretty lady."

His eyes rolled over Karina with such lechery that she recoiled against a far wall and crouched in a fetal position. Hysterical sobs and shrieks emanated out of her, echoing off the walls and ceiling of the tunnel. Juan sprang forward and raised a foot, preparing to stomp her.

The professor said, "That's why I must stay here and you must go. She is a hostage, not a plaything. After we are done and safely out of here, you can do whatever you please with her. Do not compromise our mission, especially when we are so close."

Juan's eyes raged. Karina looked up to see his left hand plunge into his pants pocket and pull out the pistol. The professor was watching Juan, his hands in front of him, palms down in a sign he meant no harm. "Think about it, Juan. The maintenance man saw her, and he saw me. When she comes up missing, he will tell someone he saw me. And he might have seen you, too. We don't know. When they look for her, there has to be no evidence of foul play. They have to look for her somewhere besides the museum, especially since she requested flashlights. Someone is bound to catch on, perhaps quickly."

Karina watched Juan's demeanor change again. He tucked the pistol back into his pants. "You're a good assistant. But only an assistant. I see why Señor Ordóñez keeps you around."

Sunday, 12 January
11:59 a.m.

It was all Professor Knight could do not to roll his eyes. This buffoon would be comical if he weren't so deadly. The professor wished for a smartphone so he could covertly record the idiot's words and then play them back for Ordóñez. Such boastings and claims to authority were clearly treasonous. If Ordóñez heard them out of Juan's own mouth, they would be dealt with in short order. But such recording devices were also considered treasonous. Authorities, especially from Europe and the United States, could use such technology for spying, tracking, and listening in. One way Ordóñez managed to evade capture for such a long time was by keeping his operation as low-tech as possible.

"How do I know you will not do anything foolish while I'm gone?" Juan asked.

At this, Professor Knight reached into a place he normally reserved for meetings with potential patsies like George d'Hout and Karina Mora. He looked Juan straight in the face and lied for all he was worth. "I am not oblivious to which way the wind is blowing and how things are changing regarding leadership roles," he said. "Nor am I stupid enough to think my life would be worth a mite if I cross you. When you return, you will find both of us here. I will do my best to get the lovely Karina Mora up, on her feet, and cleaned up, ready for what promises to be a splendid rest of the day. What else would you like me to do while you're gone?"

Juan straightened up a bit as the words soaked in. "Even a gringo can see I'm destined to be an Incan king. Is that right, *muchacho*?"

Seeing that his flattery was having its intended effect, the professor continued. "It's Sunday, so many of the bank guards are off today. There will be guards working the museum, though. It's important no one sees you. No one. The job is to get the purse and any other personal belonging she put in the office. Then lock the office as if our curator was heading back home. We'll wait for you here."

"Tell me again why we shouldn't bring her with us and all three go."

"Look at her. If anyone catches sight of this…this mess that used to be the lovely Karina Mora, they'll send in the Marines. You're a master at hiding, not being seen. That's not something I have ever had to do. I don't want to get us caught."

"Like a caiman, an anaconda, or a jaguar. Even you see it, *muchacho*, is that right? And they are deadly, yes? I am deadly. If you cross me in even the slightest way, I will kill you both and sacrifice your blood as the first offering of a new Inca reign."

Still curled up into a fetal position, Karina whimpered. Juan leaned in close to the professor, his acrid breath burning the professor's nostrils. "She is my snack, and I will save her for later. Don't touch my snack, *muchacho*. It is mine." Then he added, "You be right here, *muchacho*. No going on farther. Period. Right here. *¿Comprende?*"

The professor thought of a thousand things he could say, starting with "Care for a mint or some gum?" He swallowed the thought and reapplied his earnestness like a fresh coat of paint. "Your *muchacho* will watch over the pretty curator and make sure she doesn't get any ideas. Then you will lead the way, and we will find this treasure. Or, better said, you will find it, and I will help."

Juan's eyes twinkled. He was gone in a moment. Incas were renowned for their speed and stealth. The light in the tunnel was now reduced by half, and it was focused on the floor. There was movement, and Knight turned to where the curator was crouched. "I know your little friend Juan seems like a person who would just as soon kill you as kiss you," the professor said. "He plans on doing both, but not in that order. I, on the other hand, am doing everything I can to spare your life. I want to help you.

"In fact," he almost whispered, "I have a plan to save your life, but you must trust me completely and do everything I say, down to the smallest detail. I am your only hope. Do you understand me?"

Karina gave a slight nod but stayed ducked. "You must recompose yourself and be the professional woman I met earlier. Juan is a predator. The old, the weak, and the wounded are eaten first. You don't want to be eaten, do you? And, by the way, I'm not so sure we are only speaking metaphorically."

Karina Mora tried to stand and gather her dignity, but this latest revelation or threat or whatever it was pushed her back toward the floor. Seeing her curl up into a fetal position and hearing a moan escape her, Professor Knight knew he had gone too far in his little game of manipulation. "I was exaggerating,

Karina. You must regain yourself. You are a beautiful, desirable, strong woman. That will intimidate him and keep him at arm's length. What you are doing now will only make him want to have his way with you the second he returns."

Professor Knight aimed the flashlight at Karina but stepped toward the far wall, giving her space. "I cannot trust you with the flashlight," he said, "but I will leave it trained on you while I look away. You get your clothes in order and fix your face."

Of course, Professor Knight was lying when he said he wouldn't look. Any peek at all at the beautiful Karina was too good a thing to pass up. So he enjoyed it very much when he saw her adjusting her blouse and attempting to move her hair back into place. He was not as pleased when he saw her stooping, apparently trying to fix her shoe.

She picked up a sharp piece of broken pottery and tried to palm it. When the professor spoke, he made her jump like ice water down her back. "Is there something I said that perhaps gave you the misconception that I am weak or won't kill you myself?"

Karina dropped the pottery shard, which made a dull clanking sound as it bounced and broke and came to a stop. She felt her life doing the same thing. "I...I...I," she stuttered, but no other words would come.

The professor's first inclination was to come after the woman and beat her. That would never do, if for no other reason than it was exactly how Juan would have behaved. Juan was a buzz saw, an animal, a brute. Professor William Knight was different, the way a scalpel is different from a chain saw.

"I am disappointed," he said in a crisp, clear manner. He was in command, and she would obey him. "Can you tell me which of the instructions I previously gave that were unclear?" There was no response other than a slight tremor of the lips and hands. "A good sign," the professor thought.

"Your silence tells me you did understand what I said but chose to disobey," he continued, a teacher talking to a naughty child. He spoke slowly. "This time I will demonstrate great tolerance and forgiveness. You will see me as the person who controls the third member of our little group. You will also see me as the person who holds your life in my hands. Juan is a cobra, but I am the snake charmer. He may seem more deadly, but it is I who calls the tune. Is that clear? He is poison, but I direct where that poison goes. You saw it earlier. I am here with you because I sent him away. The question is, do you want to be here, so to speak, or gone?"

Professor Knight watched her. More trembling. "Look at me full in the face, Karina," he said. This was where he would most precisely apply the scalpel. "You were bad. If you are bad again, we will kill you. In the same way I have determined how to keep the authorities from looking here for you, I will make sure no one ever—and I mean ever—finds a single trace of you. Are you married?" He already knew the answer by her ring and earlier comments.

She nodded.

"Children?"

She nodded again.

"How many?"

She stuttered, "Three," and began crying.

"It's a shame, the professor thought, "because they'll never see their mother again. But the world is full of tragedy. What's one more?" Aloud, he said, "Of course there's no reason we can't bring this to a successful conclusion, and then you will be reunited with your loving husband and little ones. If, that is, you do everything I say. Everything."

Karina looked at the professor and wiped her eyes with the back of one hand. "What does your husband do?" Professor Knight asked.

"He is an executive at the Banco Central," she said. "It's how I got this job."

Professor Knight wondered what the word for "nepotism" was in Spanish. Obviously, if there was such a word, it didn't carry the gravitas here that it did in the United States. "An executive? Tell me more."

Karina saw a chance for her survival. "He's the number-three man. We make a very nice living. I know he would pay to make sure I come out of this unharmed."

She looked in the direction Juan had run, back toward the museum. She lowered her voice and said, "I would make sure he paid you. Just you. But you must make sure nothing happens to me. Nothing at all at the hands of that pig."

Professor Knight smiled. What he felt like saying was, "Never play a player, sister." What he did say was, "I'm sure we can work out something very satisfactory for all concerned. But my previous conditions are unchanged. If you fail to do one single thing

I say, your very well-off husband will go back to wherever he found you and get a younger, prettier replacement. And you? You will be gone. Disappeared. Your children will live their entire lives wondering where you went and why you abandoned them. Do we understand each other?"

Karina stood. "How much farther do you think it is to the treasure?"

"The pots to ward off evil spirits mean we are getting very close to the tombs. The grove under which the treasure is supposed to be concealed is about two hundred yards past the entrance to the tomb outside, so maybe about that same distance underground. What's your estimation?"

"I thought you were robbing the tombs," she said. "What grove? What are you talking about?"

The professor realized he had said too much. On the other hand, how could they use her as a hostage and keep her ignorant of the treasure? She would find out sooner or later.

"In 1687, two pirates made off with the Orellana treasure, which was hidden in Guayaquil. We believe they came this way and hid the treasure. However, they were unable to retrieve it. We are about to collect it on their behalf. And you will be right there to see it. The only question is, will this be the last thing you ever see?"

CHAPTER 41

Sunday, 12 January
12:33 p.m.

National police continued to search the monastery ruins in Cajas National Park but could find no trace of the man they had seen running that direction. The other man, writhing in agony, had been stabilized, and an ambulance was on its way from Cuenca. A sergeant asked the commanding officer on the scene what he thought.

"Drugs, probably. Helicopter coming in and taking off all of a sudden. A deal gone sour, it looks like to me. Too bad, too. I thought we'd kept the big-league guys out of our sector. We're going to have to crack down harder on this slime; do a better job of watching the Inca Trail. That's my guess on where the people in the tent came in. Had to be. No paperwork on them indicating they came in through one of the checkpoints."

A voice from inside one of the tents summoned. "Lieutenant, I need to see you." Entering the tent, the senior officer made eye contact with the man dressed in black, his leg splinted.

"Father Domingo?" he said. "I got a bulletin saying you were dead—died in a fire. You're alive!"

The lieutenant dropped to his knees. He wasn't normally an emotional man, but tears of joy flooded his eyes. "You're alive," he repeated and reached over to give the priest a hug. The other policemen looked away, not wanting the commander to later be embarrassed his men had seen him cry. Such things were not proper.

"Father Domingo baptized every one of my children," the lieutenant said to everyone and no one. "How did you come to be in this place, among these people? What did they do to you?"

The priest smiled weakly. "*Mijo*," he said, "it is as good to see you as it is to be seen. Where are the others? The two men who brought me here? They are good men who are being framed. You must help them."

The lieutenant was confused. Which two? There was a dead man, a female with a gunshot wound to the knee, and the man who was shot in the arm. And of course the final suspect, who disappeared in the ruins. But he would be found in short order.

Another voice summoned the lieutenant. "This one is singing like a bird," a policeman said. "Something about not knowing about the smuggling but willing to testify. It doesn't make sense."

Turning back to the priest, *his* priest, the lieutenant said, "We're going to need your help to sort this all out. Ambulances are on the way. You will be on the first one."

"No," Padre Domingo insisted, taking the lieutenant's arm in his weak hands. "Who is the most injured?"

"There's a guy out there who took a full blast from a shotgun in his arm," the policeman said. "Probably going to lose it. Keeps trying to talk to us in Spanish, but he's in so much pain, he keeps going back and forth into English. Not sure what's going on there."

"He should go on the first ambulance," the priest insisted.

"There's room for two. You can both go, but I will make sure there's an officer to keep an eye on this guy. We don't know what his story is. Besides, Padre, your leg isn't looking real good. We're going to have to get it attended to. How does it feel?"

"Actually, I can't feel it at all right now, so that's a relief," Padre Domingo said. The lieutenant looked away and blinked back tears. That was not a relief. He crossed himself and asked St. Michael, the patron saint of police officers, and St. Jude to intercede for this man so he might keep his leg.

"Are you praying?" the priest asked.

"Yes, Father."

"Then also pray to St. Gerard for two Americans," the priest said. "Their names are Albert Pujols and George d'Hout. They saved my life, and I have tried to help them as well. Then, *mijo*, you must give feet and hands to your prayers by helping to find them. They may still be in danger." The lieutenant understood. St. Gerard was the patron saint of those falsely accused.

Sunday, 12 January
1:00 p.m.

George d'Hout held the cell phone he had taken from the body of Roberto Ordóñez. He had never talked to Van Williams previously. He thought he remembered his brother, Hugh, mentioning the federal agent and their friendship a time or two but wasn't really sure. However, when Agent Williams heard George's voice, he responded as if the computer consultant were an old friend.

"My wife said you urgently needed to talk to me," George said.

"I'm so thankful you're okay, George," Williams told him. "Can you give me a status update on a man named Dean Connors and a man named Albert Pujols?"

"It's Connors I'm worried about," George said. "He took the brunt of a shotgun blast in his right arm." George explained what had happened in the Cajas, feeling, however, that the explanation was taking up precious time.

Twice he interrupted himself to say, "Agent Williams, I appreciate the need to be thorough, but the fact is, two very dangerous and deadly men are probably about to get away with a very large treasure. If they do, they'll also escape prosecution for a double handful of murders. What do I do to stop them?"

"I appreciate your willingness to help," Williams said, "but you're a civilian, and you said yourself that these are dangerous men. What you can do is not put yourself back in harm's way."

Then Williams asked, "To the best of your knowledge, was Agent Pujols captured?"

George resisted the urge to tell the FBI man about the tunnels and instead said, "The last I saw him, Albert was heading toward some ruins. It was the route we took to get from Cuenca to the Cajas."

"Your brother seems to think there are a series of tunnels in that area dating back to pre-Colombian times. What do you know about that?"

"The fact is, I can't say," George said.

"Look," Agent Williams said, "I don't care about tunnels or treasure or any of that. I care about catching two murderers and bringing them to justice."

There were sudden sounds of many sirens ascending the road from south Cuenca to Turi, where the helicopter had landed.

George ducked into a small restaurant about fifty yards from the helicopter. Because of the heavy rain, no one was out walking around, and no one had discovered the bodies inside the chopper. A woman and her teenage son were wiping down tables in the restaurant. The handwritten sign out front advertised plate lunch specials for two fifty. George, rain dripping off his clothes and hair, asked both of them questions in English. They simply shrugged. Satisfied they didn't understand, he continued his conversation with Van Williams.

"Agent Williams," George said into the phone, "there's an army of sirens coming this way. I'm not very far from the helicopter, and someone may have seen me leaving it. The rain is coming down in buckets, and I need to use it as cover to get away. I'll call back when I can."

"Just don't do anything..." It was the last thing George heard before clicking off the phone. He ordered *"un plato especial"* when he came in, not knowing if that was the correct way to say one special plate or not. It got him his food, however. He was too hungry, famished really, to run out on the beans, tortillas, gigantic kernels of roasted Inca corn, and some kind of stewed meat.

The sirens were now piercing through the rain and fog like a bulldozer through chocolate ice cream. It wasn't ambulances, as George had guessed, thinking someone had seen the two men hunched and lifeless in the helicopter. It was police cars. They appeared to be the same police cars George had seen in the Cajas, but who could know for sure?

George chomped a tortilla and looked out the front window of the small restaurant. Guns drawn, the police formed a circle around the chopper. Once the officers saw the two bodies inside weren't moving, they closed in, pulling them out and letting them fall hard to the muddy, rain-drenched ground.

George watched, but also looked around the restaurant as casually as possible for a way to slip out the back. He quickly realized, however, that the establishment backed right up against the side of the mountain. There was only one way in and out. A feeling of panic came over him. Had he let himself get captured again?

Looking out the window, George could see one of the men reach into his vehicle and pull out a bullhorn. Turning the volume to full throttle and testing the microphone system, the lieutenant could be heard for hundreds of yards through the driving rain. The lights and sirens had attracted many people out of the places from which they'd sought refuge from the storm.

"I am Lieutenant Ramon Ascasubi," came the voice in Spanish. "We are looking for a *norte americano* named George d'Hout. He was probably in this helicopter. We need to take possession of this man as quickly as possible. Please help us to find him."

George didn't understand what had been said but recognized what sounded like his name, only pronounced Hor-hey De-hoot. Laying some pocket change on the table, George kept his face low and made for the door.

The teenager working in the restaurant suddenly bolted out of the kitchen, yelling something in Spanish. Taking that as his cue, George exited and began running down the hill through the sheets of driving rain. The food made him feel both revitalized and slowed down. His feet were made of concrete as he ran down the muddy hill, looking for any opportunity to escape.

Behind him, a police car now whizzed in his direction. It flew past him, giving George a moment's relief. But as it came to the next curve, the brakes were applied much too quickly for the road conditions. The car skidded to a stop inches before the edge of the cliff, did a very tidy donut, and now blocked George's route of escape.

The lieutenant stepped out of the car and looked at George. No guns were drawn. "Señor d'Hout," Lt. Ascasubi said, his voice totally calm, *"Soy amigo de Padre Domingo. Estás a salvo, señor. Estás a salvo. Te lo prometo."*

George felt like a deer surrounded by hunters. *"¡No entiendo!"* he yelled. I don't understand.

Lt. Ascasubi said, "I am English not so good. But the friend with Father Domingo. You no danger. You safe. *¿Comprende?*"

George wanted to run, but the way down the hill was blocked by Ascasubi's car. An officer near Ascasubi was about to draw his pistol. Ascasubi motioned for him to stand down. Up the hill, two more cars moved to block all routes of escape. With the mountain behind him and a cliff in front, his options were to give up or jump. Dead, he couldn't help anyone, so he raised his hands in surrender.

Lt. Ascasubi was already reaching for the radio in the patrol car and calling for a translator. The rain continued coming down in buckets. Everyone—Ascasubi, George d'Hout, and the officers—was soaked to the bone. Hanging up the patrol car radio, the lieutenant told two officers to escort George back to the restaurant at the top of the hill.

At a table, George and the lieutenant tried to talk, but it was a jumble of *"no comprende"* and "What? I'm sorry, but I don't understand."

It was 2:20 before a translator arrived, an American retiree named Patsy Webb who worked for an English-language bookstore and taught at one of the Catholic high schools a couple of hours a day. When she came to the table, Lt. Ascasubi introduced her to d'Hout.

"You're George d'Hout?" she asked.

"Yes. Do I know you?"

"No, but a priest was just talking about you on the radio a minute ago," she said. "I was listening to it as I pulled up. They were talking about the way you and another guy were framed for crimes you didn't commit. It's a live news conference from the hospital. They said the priest refused to go into surgery and get his broken leg worked on until he could set the record straight for everyone in Cuenca. You're a celebrity."

"Doubtful."

Patsy repeated the story to the lieutenant and his officers in Spanish. Several of the men immediately wanted to question d'Hout about who framed him. Ascasubi cut them off. "How do the men in the helicopter fit into this?" he asked George.

"The man in the passenger seat is the leader of the smugglers," he explained. "He killed the man in the back of the helicopter and was about to shoot me. I fired back, killing both him and his pilot." George said via the translator, "This may seem a strange question, but please tell me your perceptions of American law enforcement working down here."

Ascasubi weighed the question and then put his answer on the same scale. Finally, through the translator, he said, "I hope you won't be offended, but most of the time when American officials come down here, they want to tell us how it's going to be. There is no asking, no collaboration. We are dumb Latinos, and they are the great white gods from the north. With a few it's different. You have to take them one at a time."

George was satisfied with the answer. He explained how he had come to be in Ecuador and how Pujols and Connors had been trying to save him. He also explained that Ordóñez operated with such impunity that it seemed hard to believe there wasn't a certain level of official involvement, or at least a willingness to look the other way.

"Therefore," George said, "they didn't know who they could trust. Hopefully, Padre Domingo is right, and we can trust you."

"Tell me where the rest of this gang is, if you know, and I will provide the actions that back up my words," Ascasubi said. "These men are cancers. They must be extracted."

Sunday, 12 January
3:51 p.m.

Juan was rarely struck with a sense of reverence or solemnity. Now, however, he felt both. "I was led here," he kept saying. "My ancestors want me to have it. It is mine."

In front of them, tucked in a side tunnel winding under the archaeological park, was a treasure that made the haul in Bolivia look like something from a child's piggy bank: emeralds, *reales*, pieces of eight, gold *escudos*, gold and silver ingots, silver bars, and an assortment of baubles no doubt pilfered from the women of Guayaquil during the 1687 raid. It all lay before them.

"How could you have let this go all this time?" the professor asked Karina. "It could have been yours if you had only dared to go and seek it out."

"First, I knew nothing about it. Second, as I have said, this is a sacred area. It was off-limits."

"Fortunately, we are not as squeamish about such things. Now your loss is our gain," Knight said. "Breathtaking."

Karina Mora's breath was taken away as well, but for a different reason. As the trio wound their way through the Inca's Fourth Level, they found Inca mummies, skeletons of dead llamas, and several dozen Indians up and down the tunnel in front of and behind where the treasure lay. Some had obviously been trying to run and were speared or shot in the back.

"Why?" she kept saying over and over. "Why did these people have to die?"

"They were used by the pirates to haul the treasure," the professor explained as if demonstrating how two and two equals four. "They were no longer needed."

"They could have been set free," Karina said. "What if they had families back in Guayaquil?"

Juan ignored her sentimental tripe. He was trying to get a grasp on just how much all this might be worth. The professor, however, was more than happy to educate this obviously naïve woman on the ways of the world. "I'm surprised a curator would be so simple minded," he said. "How could the pirates turn them loose? They might talk. They knew where the treasure was hidden. They knew about the tunnels. That would never do."

"I know about the treasure," Karina said somberly. "I know about the tunnels."

Juan and the professor glanced at each other. Professor Knight hoped Juan remembered they might need a hostage if things went wrong later. Further, he had had no opportunity to speak to Juan about it, but there was every possibility that they might clear another fifty to hundred thousand dollars by holding Karina for ransom.

Whatever camaraderie was rekindled between Juan and the professor by the discovery of the treasure melted with Karina's next statement. "Now that the treasure is found, Professor, don't forget that when we were alone earlier, you promised you would speak to your lackey and make him promise to free me." The word *lackey* in Spanish was *lacayo*; the word hit Juan's ears like a slap across the face.

He sprung up from the place where he'd been kneeling in front of the treasure stacking reales. "What? *Lacayo?* Who are you calling a *lacayo?*"

Karina remained a picture of composure. "I didn't say it. Your friend there did. He told me you worked for him and were nothing more than a stupid snake, poisonous but with a small brain. He, on the other hand, was the snake charmer and could make you do anything he said."

The professor's face flushed. He also sprang up, his eyes filled with indignation as he started for the curator. It was no longer a question of when Juan would kill this woman. He would take care of the matter himself.

Racing past Juan, the professor suddenly lost his balance and tumbled face-first into a llama skeleton and decaying bits of bayeta bags. Looking back to see what had tripped him, he saw Juan's leg sticking out. The professor's eyes traced the body all the way up to the maniacal face. "And after you tell me not to touch the merchandise because we need to be focused on the mission," Juan bellowed, "then I find out you want me to go for the purse so you can play touchy feely. That won't do, *muchacho*. Now you pay."

One of Juan's hands held the pistol. The other produced the large knife with a serrated edge like shark's teeth.

"Juan, use your head. She's turning us against each other. You're playing right into her hands."

"So again you're calling me stupid?" Juan said. "I don't have to trust what she says. It's coming right from your own lips; lips I

535

am going to cut off and paste on that llama head. This is a place of death, *muchacho*, so you are going to be right at home."

Remembering how Karina had reached for the pottery shards earlier, Professor Knight glanced down and saw some nearby. He reached down for one. As he did, the lightning motion of Juan's blade bore every resemblance to the cobra from Knight's metaphor. As the blade sliced into the fatty part of the professor's hand between the pinky and wrist, Juan pulled back. He was eager to make this as slow and painful as possible.

The professor cried out. "Juan, stop this! You're not using your head!"

"Stop calling me stupid," Juan said. This time his hand thrust up and sliced a gash along the professor's left jawline. "That could have been your throat or your tongue, *muchacho*. How many times do you think I can cut you before you bleed out? What do you think is the world's record for that? I think I'm going to make a new world record."

The professor's heart raced, making the blood pour from the neat slices along the jaw and hand. Professor Knight pressed the jaw into his shoulder to soak up some of the blood. He was a logical, even conniving man, but everything was happening too fast. He had to slow things down so he could think. He must find a way to open Juan's eyes, so blinded by fury.

"Juan, if you kill me, who's going to help you get the treasure out of here?" Professor Knight pleaded. The words sounded pitiful. What must they sound like to a psychopath like Juan Pacheco? "I am your servant. But I cannot serve if you kill me."

For the next twenty minutes, the deadly dance continued. Each time the professor tried to stop Juan, Juan sliced him just deep enough to draw blood, but not deep enough to hit any major organs or blood vessels. Each time he was sliced, the professor would cry out and beg. Then he tried to reason with Juan, and the process repeated itself.

"Thirty-four cuts so far," Juan said, proud of himself, "but I got to give it to you, Professor. You're still standing. You keep extra blood for just such occasions?"

Juan laughed at his own remark. The professor leaned against a wall. Below him was a puddle of blood; it was starting to get sticky and coagulate around the edges. Knight wanted to fall, to let his heavy legs have a moment of rest, but he knew he dared not. He would be finished for sure. So he leaned and bled and cried. His brains and cunning were an Aladdin's lamp, but he couldn't find the right words to unleash the magic inside.

Meanwhile, Juan practiced his stroke, working on one motion and then another—a jab-and-twist, a lunge, a slice, a backhand uppercut. Which ones produced the most pain, the most blood, or a combination of the two? He appreciated the professor's resilience, since most people would have curled up into a little ball by now, making it hard to do really good work.

CHAPTER 42

Sunday, 12 January
4:30 p.m.

Lt. Ascasubi was in charge of the operation, but two captains and even a couple of members of the police oversight commission stood with him at a bridge where Avenida Doce Abril intersected with Las Herrerias Bridge. George stood back, unable to make out anything but a word or two of what was going on. The translator was standing beside him. She said, "I'm not sure how much I'm supposed to be telling you."

"I was abducted by the men they're after and was framed for murder by them," George said. "I've also seen firsthand how they work. I need to know everything so I can help the police."

"That's fine," the translator said. She thought she should say something encouraging. "You seem no worse for the wear."

"Doubtful," he said. Men walked by in bulletproof vests with assault rifles. Moving toward Ascasubi, George asked the translator to help him. "Lieutenant, can you tell me what's going on?"

"This is the place where your brother said we're most likely to find an access point to the place where the thieves were heading. We're getting ready to go in, but we don't have a special weapons and tactical force like you do in the United States. The men you see here getting ready to go in are volunteering for the duty, risking their lives to capture these criminals."

Ascasubi continued. "They didn't have much trouble finding the tunnel once they knew what they were looking for. It's amazing that these things could have been here all this time, and nobody knew."

"We need to talk about that," d'Hout said. "It's very important to Father Domingo that these tunnels stay a secret. I imagine that makes it important to you as well."

Ascasubi watched some men go by. "You know how the Incas kept secrets?" he asked George. "They killed everyone who knew. Fewer mouths to keep watch over."

"Now you're sounding like the guys who kidnapped me," George said, not entirely comfortable with the words.

"I'm one of the good guys," Ascasubi assured him through the translator. "We are sending the officers in any second. First, we have to catch them. Then we will address the issue of securing the tunnels. It is a priority."

Four policemen in assault gear entered the tunnel. Police had cordoned off the area so far back in every direction that civilians couldn't see what was going on or where the police were headed. Ascasubi said, "It's roughly two blocks to the area under the grove. You can see it over to your left, about eleven o'clock in your line of sight. The assault team will cover that distance in a couple of minutes. Then we'll see what happens."

George said, "It's possible the thieves aren't there yet. It's also possible they already came and left."

Through the translator, Ascasubi said, "Your optimism is encouraging. Nonetheless, we'll do our best to catch them."

Once police figured out where the tunnel entrance was and how to open it—which was done indelicately with a battering ram—the men switched on lights attached to their rifles, along with secondary lights attached to their headgear. The headgear lights made them look like military-grade cyclopses. They were also targets for anyone lurking in the dark.

A few hundred yards inside the tunnel, their radios could no longer communicate with Lt. Ascasubi. They were effectively cut off from the outside world. However, Ascasubi explained to George, the criminals might attempt to backtrack and escape from the museum entrance. Therefore, six officers joined the regular guards near the front door of the museum and were told to check anyone coming out with anything even remotely resembling a package containing guns or stolen goods. Further, all gringos were to be searched, since a gringo was believed to be one of the leaders of the group.

So far, the police had rousted six Americans—four college students spending a semester abroad and a couple of retirees from Oklahoma, who didn't understand what *abrir su bolsas* meant.

The couple looked at each other. "Maybe they're having one of those fund-raisers for Jerry's Kids," the wife said.

"They're police, not fire fighters. Besides, we're not in Altus. They may not even have Jerry's Kids here."

"Well, I'm going to contribute anyway." She pulled out a five-dollar bill and tucked it into the hand of one of the policemen attempting to search her bags. The police were too stunned to speak when she said, "For the children...*para los ninos*." The couple walked off with an extremely self-satisfied look.

Back in the tunnel, the four officers switched off their headset radios, just in case they were being picked up outside. Once they were sure the radios were powered down, the point man said, "We face a dilemma. Señor Ordóñez and Juan promised us this would never happen."

The man at his right shoulder said, "It didn't appear the American recognized us. I was watching. Before, he saw the security guard uniforms. Now he sees the police uniforms. Nothing else."

The point man said, "He's not our problem, at least not right now. Our problem is what we do when we come across Juan. You know that's who it's going to be. We must be in agreement before we encounter him."

Sunday, 12 January
4:46 p.m.

Much deeper in the tunnel, Juan continued his sadistic brand of surgery on his former partner. Still leaning against a wall but too weak even to raise his hands to block the regular visitations of the knife, Professor Knight said, "I'm cold. Where are we? Is this Mount Chim...Chimbor...I'm cold."

"Death is getting close now," Juan said. "Your spirit wants to fly away, but it will be trapped here forever."

"Why is the snow red?"

"Snow?" Juan started to laugh. "I've seen a lot of people die before, but you take the cake. Best death ever. Don't let anybody tell you different. *Muchacho*, you're a trip."

"The snow is red," Professor Knight repeated. "I'm cold. Can you help me? I'm so cold."

"I can help you," Juan said. "You want me to help you not be cold?"

"Very much," the professor said. "Thank you, kind sir."

Juan furrowed his brow. "*Muchacho*," he said sourly, "you made me forget my count. How many was it?"

"How high?" the professor asked. "Mount Chimborazo is twenty thousand five hundred sixty-four feet at the summit." His tongue was thick, his head was woozy. "The Battle of Chimborazo was fought in 1534. Sebastián de Belalcázar and his army of conquistadors defeated the Inca army led by Rumiñahui. It was..." Knight dropped to his knees. "It was a rout."

"Really?" Juan asked. "Well, in the Second Battle of Chimborazo, it looks like the Incas are winning. How tall is the mountain?"

"Twenty thousand five hundred sixty-four feet," the professor said. "Very cold."

"Well, this is twenty thousand five hundred and sixty-five." With that, Juan made a flourish with his knife, took it quickly and deeply across the professor's throat, and then stepped back to examine his work.

The heartbeat was so weak, blood flowed rather than spurted out of the open arteries, a waterfall of crimson down the front of what used to be Professor William Knight. He fell forward, his head peeling back upon impact with the floor like the pop-top on a can of cherry pie filling.

It was then that Juan turned. He didn't like to brag—actually, he loved to brag—but nonetheless, he said to Karina, "What do you think of your snake charmer now? You too impressed to speak, pretty lady?" Juan kept staring at the professor's body, impressed with his work. "I said..." Juan turned to look at Karina.

His fury renewed, Juan turned and spat on the body of the professor. "Look what you did!" he screamed. "You can't even die right." Looking up and down the tunnel, Juan tried to determine which way the woman ran. He decided she must have gone back in the direction of the museum. It would be pitch black, and she would be too afraid to go forward with no idea what might lie ahead. Then he heard something to his right, in the distance, away from the museum.

"Are you afraid your boyfriend won't protect you?" Juan called into the dark tunnel. "Come to me, baby. I'll be your new boyfriend."

No answer. But there was a strange sound, like many feet shuffling. Then someone trying to be quiet, then more shuffling.

A shiver ran up Juan's spine. He wasn't superstitious, but on the other hand, no one could deny the powers of the dark forces. And in this tunnel system, leading right through the Fourth Level, those powers would be especially strong.

"Where you at, pretty lady?" he called, somewhat more meekly, into the darkness. "You want to share this treasure with me? Be my baby?"

No answer. More shuffling, then everything stopped. Another shiver crossed Juan's body. He moved back over to the treasure, pulling the cart near him; he began loading the treasure on it. First ingots, then pieces of eight and *reales*. The cart was getting heavy, and he didn't have a quarter of it loaded yet.

Juan knelt, busy about his work. Then he felt something wet soaking through his pants leg. He shined the flashlight down on the professor's blood, like a gory glacier moving toward him. Repositioning himself and continuing his work, he heard another noise. This time it came from his left, back toward the museum.

He taunted, "I'm gonna get you, you—" Then there was a gasp and a muffled scream. It was a woman's voice…or was it? Juan stood up. How could he load the treasure and go after this infernal woman at the same time? The treasure would have to wait. He couldn't take a chance on her getting back to the museum and summoning help.

Another muffled scream and then silence. It was definitely a woman. What had she seen to make her scream? Seen? These tunnels were darker than any pit of hell. She couldn't see anything. That must have been why she'd screamed. She must have run into something or maybe tripped over one of the skeletons.

There was another possibility, Juan thought. What if the spirits were roused to stop this woman so Juan could bring back the Inca Empire? What if the spirit of Huayna Capac had grabbed her? After all, it had been in this Fourth Level that he had seen William Knight for what he really was, a sniveling usurper and traitor. Maybe the spirits were holding the curator for him. It was every macabre, sadistic fantasy he'd ever had rolled into one: Inca skeletons holding the curator while he tried to find an even slower, more terrible way to kill her than he had the professor.

There was another noise back to the right, like someone kicking something. Then a beam of light, at least it appeared to be a beam, shot through the tunnel like lightning. And like lightning, it disappeared as quickly as it had come. In spite of his bravado, it was the third time in less than five minutes Juan Pacheco was covered in goose bumps. He didn't like it. Looking longingly at the treasure, he switched off the flashlight and listened.

There was definitely the sound of several feet coming his way. He switched the flashlight back on, but held it close to the floor. He made his way past the blood puddle where the professor lay, past numerous skeletons of llamas and Indians, then to the graves of the Inca royalty. Juan stayed low and moved quickly, a shadow concealed by darkness. When he got to the row of smashed pottery that blocked the way back to the museum, he was dismayed he hadn't found the curator yet.

His angry profanities echoed off the tunnel walls as he continued on. Then Juan stopped and smiled. He aimed the flashlight toward his watch. It was after four o'clock, the time the museum closed on Sunday. The maintenance man or perhaps a security guard would go into the basement, look for Karina, and see she was gone. They would assume she left unnoticed and proceed with lockup. She'd work backward, first through the doors where Juan blew off the locks, then to the six or seven for which she had keys. "Keys! She doesn't have her keys. They're in her purse and that's back with the treasure. She's just as trapped as before."

Juan heard another sound behind him. A suppressed cough? Ghosts and spirits don't cough. What was going on back there? Maybe Ordóñez was through disposing of the priest and ICE agent, and was coming to check on his progress. Maybe he had found another way in. Then horror struck. What would Ordóñez think when he found the professor dead and Juan nowhere in sight? Would there be mistaken allegations of treason and a double cross?

Juan was angry and in need of the security guards Ordóñez kept around. They could help him nab the girl and explain things to the boss...for whatever amount of time Ordóñez remained the boss. Juan hadn't forgotten the crystalline revelation that had come his way regarding his role in restoring the Inca Empire to greatness.

Wanting to grab the curator, continue loading the treasure, and see what was making the shuffling noises all at the same time, Juan paused and did nothing. Then he spoke aloud. "I am an Inca king. Kings are gods. What I do is right. I am the giver and the taker of life. Blood flows where I walk. I am feared and worshipped. What I do is right because it is what I do."

It was a dangerous thing to say, especially if Ordóñez was waiting in the darkness. However, the time had come to lay his cards on the table. What better place than the Fourth Level to declare himself an heir to the Inca throne? In a state of elation, Juan turned in the direction of the museum. He envisioned ancient Incan *chasqui* runners, famed for their ability to travel hundreds of miles without stopping. He attempted to channel their spirits; then took off, almost flying through the dark corridors of the tunnel. As he ran, he fantasized about catching Karina Mora and providing himself a double portion of human gumbo. The professor had been the appetizer. Karina would be the main course.

CHAPTER 43

Sunday, 12 January
5:19 p.m.

An explosion of thunder and lightning cascaded around the group that stood by the police cars, but no one jumped except George. He was talking to the lieutenant near the entrance to the tunnel. Again the sky opened and dumped buckets of rain on them. Lt. Ascasubi, born and raised in Cuenca, thought no more of it than a parrot would think of feathers. George, however, shivered as the rain soaked his clothes again. The translator was also shivering.

"Let me open up the police car, and you can—"

"Albert!" George cried. "Albert escaped into the tunnels. That's why nobody has found him yet. He could be lost down there. And if Juan and the professor are in there, he could run right into them. I've got to help him!"

Lt. Ascasubi barely understood a word. He did, however, see d'Hout breaking for the tunnel. Springing to stop him, the lieutenant shouted in Spanish to the translator, "Tell him there could be a shootout in there. It's very dangerous. He cannot be permitted in there."

As the translator reached the third sentence, Ascasubi relaxed his hold on George's shoulders. George used that moment to make a beeline for the entrance. His runner's agility helped him avoid Ascasubi's attempt to re-grab him. Ignoring the yells of Ascasubi and the translator, he disappeared into the tunnel.

Concern for Albert, along with previous experience in the blackness of the tunnels, turned George into a prairie dog zipping through its burrow. He kept one hand on the wall as a point of orientation. He knew there might be downward tunnels like the one that injured Padre Domingo, but as he sprinted though the black gloom, he knew it was a chance he'd have to take.

Sunday, 12 January
5:47 p.m.

Juan knew he was approaching the first door back into the museum. No footsteps. No breathing. All was darkness save for Juan's flashlight. However, the batteries had lost a bit of power, and the light was slightly fading.

Almost to the door, Juan started to raise his flashlight to it. Then he heard something beyond it in the tunnel. "Karina? Where are you? You've been a naughty girl. Come to me, your new boyfriend, to beg for forgiveness."

He raised the flashlight. There she was, standing in the middle of the corridor, bloody, disheveled, and shaking. "Professor Knight was shaking, too," Juan said. "You cold? Come here and I will warm you up."

The flashlight went into the other hand. Juan grabbed his knife from his pocket. It was still sticky from its earlier work, but there would be time to clean it later. Karina backed up.

"Where you think you're gonna go, muchacha?" Juan asked. "Besides, you just passed the way back into the museum, you dumb broad. It's right over there." Juan swung the flashlight around, making a quarter turn and then...He turned back again. What was that? Another person?

"Hello, *muchacho*," Albert Pujols said. "Miss me?"

Juan swung the flashlight to shine the light in the ICE agent's eyes, but Albert said, "I've got a pistol and I'd love to use it. Put the flashlight down."

"With pleasure, *muchacho*," Juan said, clicking the light off and dropping it in one motion. Darkness enveloped the threesome. Juan and Albert lunged toward one another in a death match. Juan knew Albert would be reluctant to fire his gun, afraid of hitting the woman. He, on the other hand, had no such concern. He would reach out, try to get a piece of the ICE agent with his knife, then fire his pistol in that direction. All he needed to do was use his free hand to get it out of his pocket.

Sunday, 12 January
5:51 p.m.

In the darkness of the tunnel, George watched the four assault team members standing transfixed by what they had found. The treasure was hypnotizing. They barely paid attention to the goo that had once been William Knight. George couldn't exactly see the treasure, but the four gun lights and the four headlamps all focused on the same indention in the tunnel made it easy to know where it was.

George listened to a series of low whistles and exclamations by the officers. The spell the treasure cast was broken by two quick gunshots and a cacophony of echoes rattling through the tunnels. All four snapped to attention, bringing their weapons to the ready.

"This way, now!" the team leader yelled and bolted toward the sound. The three other members jumped in behind him. One slipped in the coagulating blood. Catching himself, he stopped and looked back down the tunnel as if he'd seen or heard something. He shined his lights in that direction, but they picked up nothing, so he took off to catch up with his fellow officers.

George rose from his prone position on the floor and slowly stood. He had been listening to the talk among the four policemen/security guards. True, he couldn't understand more than a few scattered words. However, their tone and conspiratorial manner told him what their words failed to deliver. He believed these men were seriously considering trying to steal the treasure for themselves.

Then George remembered Juan saying some of the members of his security detail were local police. For all he knew, these men were more loyal to Ordóñez and Juan than they were to Lt. Ascasubi. And then there were the gunshots and the way they had run. Was Albert in the tunnels? If so, was he the shooter or the one being shot?

George ran for all he was worth, watching the eight lights of the rifles and headlamps bobbing ahead of him in double time. George continued following the lights. He jumped when three more shots rang out, first two and then a pause, followed by a third. There was also a scream, perhaps from a woman.

Sounds of a skirmish, cursing, and clawing were partially drowned out by the banging of boots on the tunnel floor in a quick one-two-one-two order. George was only about twenty yards behind the assault team now and closing on them when they stopped and leveled their weapons on a rolling, struggling pair.

Juan and Albert were locked together—kicking, gouging, biting. Behind them stood a woman, herself bloody and bruised. The lights from the assault team startled all three, and they froze.

"Everyone on the ground!" the assault team leader screamed in Spanish. "Now! Or we open fire."

The four policemen swarmed in and knocked the two pistols away, then scooped both men up and slammed each one against opposite walls of the tunnel. "Watch yourself, *muchacho*," Juan warned in Spanish. "You better not forget who pays your salary.

That's you, right, Esteven? Hey, Pablo, Chico, Pauly! You boys are just in time."

Karina was moving toward the police to thank them for saving her life. But hearing Juan's words, she immediately retreated to her position against a wall several feet away. "Watch that one," Juan said. "She's on a real high horse, but I'm about to get out my riding crop and give her a lesson she never forgets."

One of the assault team members looked at Albert Pujols, who remained silent, an assortment of cuts, bruises, gashes, and contusions all over his body.

Across the tunnel, Juan caught a look at Albert in the headlamps. He bent to pick up his knife, which had been knocked to the floor in Albert's initial lunge. Juan said, "This one's like a freaking ghost. He keeps coming back from the dead. Where'd you come from, muchacho? How'd you get down here to crash our little party?" He wiped blood from the knife onto his pants leg. There was also some on his hands. He licked it off.

Albert remained silent, staring. "You met my personal security detail?" Juan asked. "Their day job is cops, but ain't they something when the lights go down. Men with families got to make a living. Mr. Ordóñez pays them real good, don't he, *muchachos*?"

The assault team leader looked at his comrades. Then he looked at Juan. "Señor Ordóñez is dead," he said.

"That isn't funny," Juan said. "Señor Ordóñez doesn't like it when people make jokes at his expense."

"He won't mind this time," the team leader said. "He was killed by the American you kidnapped, that guy named George d'Hout."

"Seriously?" Juan asked. "Seriously? That's perfect! I can't believe it. The gods are conspiring to bring about my rise to power even quicker than I could've imagined. The professor's dead. Ordóñez is dead. That means I'm your boss now. And we get to split up all that treasure. Did you see that treasure back there? You had to have passed it. Unbelieveable! And what about the little Cañari Miguel?"

"Also dead," one of the assault team members said. "Not sure what happened there, but when we got to the helicopter, we found Ordóñez and the pilot dead in the front and Miguel dead in the back. Ugly business."

"And how did you find me to assist with this pig, this United States federal agent trespassing on our land?" Juan asked. He spit the words *United States* like they were poison.

"You have a problem," the assault leader said. "There are about thirty cops at the outlet of the tunnel. They're waiting for you with guns cocked and ready."

Juan was unfazed. "Fortunately, we have a second avenue of escape through the museum."

"Six guards at the front door," the assault leader said.

Again, Juan was ready. "Perfect. You march me out through the bank. You call for cars. Then you get us out of there before the ones at the tunnel entrance know what's going on. Did you see the size of that treasure? Because Ordóñez is dead, there is only one person who will decide how it's divided. Me. And like I said, I choose to split it with you, equal shares."

"Ahem," George said, clearing his throat. He came walking out of the darkness and stepped into the eerie lantern glow of the assault team's lights. "Albert, would you tell them what I'm saying? Officers, I think Juan here is offering to split the treasure with you. My Spanish is terrible, but that's what I'm pretty sure I'm hearing. To do that will mean killing me and my friend here. You'll also have to murder this woman, because it doesn't look like she's with Juan, at least not of her own free will."

He turned his attention to Juan. "And guess what? The priest who was inside that church you burned down, the guy you very nearly killed, he was on the radio earlier today telling everyone what really happened. Everyone in Cuenca knows. I suspect by now everyone in Ecuador knows. You have nowhere to run, *muchacho*. You are done."

George stepped in front of the policemen and intentionally made eye contact with each one. "Keep translating, Albert. So you guys are faced with a choice. You're either going to be heroes for bringing in a hated criminal or loathed by everyone for being part of a lawless gang that has killed indiscriminately, including some of their fellow law enforcement personnel."

Albert was being guarded by one of the officers. Taking George's cue, he stepped toward the man leading the assault team. "The other thing is, if you decide to keep the treasure, you're not done. George is right. You'll have to kill the three of us. Then you'd be on the run for the rest of your lives. Your families will be hated and your children rejected by schoolmates, the offspring of traitors. Heavy load to bear."

From behind where George stood, another voice interjected in Spanish. "This is all very interesting in theory, but that's all it is, a theory."

It was Lt. Ascasubi. "And I will tell you why it's theory. It's theory because it's based on the idea that these four officers have a choice to make. The choice between following this gentleman and being rich"—he motioned toward Juan—"or continuing to financially struggle, taking two and three jobs to make ends meet."

The four policemen looked at each other, but none spoke. It was quiet in the tunnel. Ascasubi continued. "And you're wrong, Mr. d'Hout and Mr. Pujols. They wouldn't have to kill three people. They would have to kill four, because they would also have to kill me."

No one stirred for several seconds. "Which way do you want us to take the prisoner out, sir?" the assault leader asked Ascasubi in Spanish.

An officer aimed his rifle at Juan Pacheco. Another took the Inca by the shoulder and prepared to move him to the center of the tunnel. The officer standing near Pujols took a step away from the ICE agent, indicating he was no longer being held as a suspect.

Karina Mora let out a deep breath and walked to Lt. Ascasubi. She introduced herself and asked if someone could please get her family on the line and let them know she was all right. As the group began to move back toward the treasure, Juan suddenly launched a karate kick into the crotch of the policeman nearest him. The Inca turned to run into the tunnel's darkness back toward the center of town.

"*¡Bajar! ¡Bajar!*" yelled Ascasubi. Get down! Karina and George hit the ground. Albert leaned back against the wall, knowing what was coming. Three assault rifles and Ascasubi's handgun all were raised and fired within a millisecond of one another.

For a moment it looked like Juan was flying. Bullets grabbed his body and thrust it forward before slamming it into the floor of the tunnel. The ghoulish dance was caught by the lights on the rifles. Hitting the ground, Juan's body made an *ooooph* sound like air escaping from a punctured tire.

George watched Juan go down. As the Inca sank, George leaned back against a wall and slowly slid down until he was seated on the ground. The smell of gunpowder filled the air. Smoke could be seen curling into the rifles' lights as it exited the muzzles. Karina broke down crying, finally believing her nightmare was over. Ascasubi offered her a handkerchief, which she gratefully accepted. Albert walked over next to where George sat, grabbed a piece of wall, and slid down beside him.

They sat in silence. Their ordeal was over. They were alive.

"That was pretty brave," Albert said to George as they watched the policemen inspect the body of Juan Pacheco. "I wasn't sure which way things were going to go. You did good."

"Turned out the police lieutenant was right behind me, so it wasn't so brave after all," George said.

"But you didn't know that, did you? You still get my vote for doing a first-class job. You might even make a pretty good cop."

"Doubtful," George said. "Very doubtful. So how did you get here? This is a long way from the ruins in the Cajas."

Albert said, "There are ancient stories about how *chasqui* runners would cover unbelievable distances racing along the Inca

Trail. People always said it was because they were chewing coca leaves. That may be true. But I've discovered another reason."

"Oh yeah? What?"

"They were on a mission," Albert said. "I was trying to get back to help you. Turns out I completely overshot where I was trying to reach. Maybe I took a wrong tunnel. Next thing I knew, when I stopped to take a break for a minute, I heard somebody running toward me. It was that lady."

"She a hostage?"

"Apparently," Albert said. "She got away when Juan and Professor Knight started fighting, though I doubt it was much of a fight. Anyway, I grabbed her and got her calmed down. Then here came Juan, and you know the rest."

"I don't want to get all mushy, but I'm really relieved you're okay," George said. "I didn't get much of a look, but it seems the professor came to a pretty horrible end."

"Juan tried to do the same thing to me," Albert said. "You and the assault team came along in the nick of time. We were going at it pretty even, but he was strong, almost possessed. It was like fighting a wild animal; he was a fierce warrior."

"He was a lunatic," George said. "A complete and total nut case."

CHAPTER 44

Sunday, 12 January
9:00 p.m.

"I have spoken with the proprietors of the Posada Del Angel Hotel and they would like you both to stay there free of charge in honor of all you have done," Lt. Ascasubi said in Spanish to Agent Pujols.

They stood in a hall of Mount Sinai Hospital, sirens sounding somewhere in the distance. An attendant rolled a wobbly gurney past them.

"That's very kind," Albert said. "Let me see how the patients are doing and talk to George."

He stepped into a room where Padre Domingo was in one bed and Dean Connors was in the other. A curtain dividing the room had been pulled back. Connors stared at the ceiling. The priest dozed off, his leg elevated with hoists. Officials from the diocese had been in and out for the last several hours. For now they were gone, promising to return tomorrow. A team from the embassy was on their way to Cuenca, and the ICE agent had been asked to wait in the city to speak with them.

"How you doing?" Pujols asked Connors.

The security chief stared at the ceiling. "They say the arm can't be saved." He tried to smile, but pain rolled over his face. He fought back against it and said, "The upside is maybe I'll get some reprieve from all the paperwork this little misadventure is sure to generate."

George, sitting in a chair in the corner, bowed his head. He had no more tears. However, guilt and self-recrimination racked him to the point where he very nearly doubled up. "What should I have done?" he asked, his voice barely audible. "You told me what to do, but I completely blew it. I keep playing it over and over in my mind. What should I have done?"

Pujols walked over to George and put a hand on his shoulder. He wasn't sure what to say, so he just stood there. It was Connors who spoke. "George, can you come here?"

"I'm so sorry," George said. "You told me what to do, how to play it. But it still happened. You still got shot." George was too ashamed to make eye contact, so he stared at the floor.

"Agent Pujols will tell you this again," Connors said, "because you're going to need to hear it many times. You did nothing wrong. We were in a hopeless situation. If anyone did something wrong, it was me. I put a civilian in harm's way. At the time, I couldn't think of another way to go. We do the best we can.

Tragedies happen. Bad people are out there, and they do bad things. You didn't pull that trigger..."

George looked up. He wanted to defend Miguel, who had also been placed in a hopeless situation and had simply done what he thought was best.

"I know," Connors said. "Miguel was a good person. I believe that. George, the world can be a pretty ugly place. Anybody who doesn't believe there's evil out there hasn't spent much time looking around. But you never gave up. Agent Pujols didn't give up. I'd like to think I didn't give up. None of that stops tragedies."

Connors grimaced again. The pain medication was wearing off. "You want to help?" he said. "Find the nurse who's packing the good drugs and get her in here pronto."

George stepped out into the hall, which was gleaming white, accented with aqua-blue tiles and greenery. He hurried to the nurses station and then realized he didn't know the words with which to request more pain killer for Connors. Little groups of black chairs lined the halls every few feet. George collapsed in one and stared at the ceiling.

He had been on a seemingly endless emotional roller-coaster ride—excitement about the job, irritation at being stood up, pure fear because of what he'd encountered, and now crushing guilt. There had also been moments of diamond-sharp spiritual clarity. Where had those gone?

He remembered a plaque hanging in Carol's bathroom. It read, "Do not be like children, tossed to and fro by every wind. Instead, believe in the truth and cling to it."

"I've read that a thousand times," George said to himself, feeling old and tired. "It's not quite as easy to heed as it is to read."

A nurse walked by, as did Albert, who pulled up and sat down next to George. Had the ICE agent walked by before? He must have, to get the nurse when George didn't. "I have some good news," Albert said. "We have a couple of very nice rooms in a cozy little hotel for as long as we need them. Then the embassy will see about getting you back to Texas."

George said nothing. Albert asked, "When's the last time you talked to your wife?"

"A couple of hours ago. She's gonna want details about what happened. What do I say?"

"On the phone? Not too much. But when you get home, you need to tell her everything. Get it out, so it doesn't eat on you. You've been to war, George. You've seen things most people never have to see. It's okay to be shaken up. I'd worry about you if you weren't."

"In some really significant ways, though, I've failed myself," George said. "I didn't always respond with the intelligence, the composure, the…the maturity and spiritual insight I claim is a part of my life. That's the thing…I feel like a lot of the things I believed about myself took as big a blast as Dean Connors's arm. But I can't amputate my self-image."

"George, you're feeling what a lot of people experience in your situation, including soldiers and law enforcement people. They're trained to deal with these kinds of things, but they still struggle. When we were in the tunnel, the only way we were going to get out was to keep moving. You're in a sort of tunnel right now. Don't pitch a tent there. Keep moving…back to your wife, your life, and the things you believe in."

George looked up, his hands folded in his lap. "You think Connors will forgive me?"

"There's nothing to forgive, but if you need to be forgiven, then yes, I know he will."

"Can I borrow a phone to call Carol again? I want to give her an update."

"Of course." Albert smiled. "Tell her the people here are hailing you as a hero. It's the truth. It must be, because that's what they're saying on the radio. And they never get it wrong."

CHAPTER 45

Thursday, 23 February
7:30 p.m.

The phone rang twice before George answered it. He didn't recognize the number. "Hey, George, it's Albert. Albert Pujols," said the voice on the other end of the call. "I wanted to give you an update."

"Update? Sure."

"I just got off the phone with Dean Connors. He asked me to call you. He's in rehab at a hospital in Maryland and doing really well. Next week he's scheduled for the first fitting of his new artificial limb. He says he's already been out to the shooting range twice to start the process of qualifying with his pistol left-handed."

"That's great. Really fantastic."

"Tell me how you're doing."

"Well, I'm seeing one of the ministers at our church every week," George said. "He's a licensed professional counselor, so he's supposed to know what he's talking about."

"And?"

"And I'm also seeing a psychiatrist my doctor recommended. My wife thought it was a good idea, too. There are some pretty bad dreams. He also gave me something to help me sleep."

"Is it working?"

"It is; the medicines and being able to talk about it with the psychiatrist and counselor. It's helping. And Carol has been incredible. She just listens and lets me talk. Not once has she blasted me for being an idiot and ignoring her premonition to not go down there."

"Are her premonitions ever wrong?" Albert asked.

"She bats about four hundred. But that's still good enough to get you in the Hall of Fame."

"In baseball, but not in life," Albert countered. "Maybe that's why she's not beating you up. She thought something might go wrong, but there are probably plenty of times she had the same feeling and everything turned out fine."

"So how are we supposed to know?" George asked.

"We aren't. That's part of the adventure, part of the journey."

George didn't know what else to say. There was an awkward silence. Then he said, "You still working out of Quito?"

"Actually, I can't say," Albert responded. "Security, need-to-know basis, things like that. But I did get some pretty incredible news today. You want to hear it?"

Wednesday, 25 April
8:23 a.m.

"I can't believe you want to do this," George said. "I told Albert there was absolutely no way you would go for it. And I'm fine if we don't. We really, really don't have to."

Carol zipped up the final suitcase and motioned for George to carry it to the car. "You sound like a broken record," she said. "We're going, and that's all."

Carol climbed into the passenger seat. George put the last suitcase in the Honda Pilot and backed it out of the garage. Carol watched the garage door go down as they pulled out of the driveway. "We're meeting Hugh and Brenda at the airport," she said. "They texted. Their flight from Midland arrived twenty-five minutes ago. You were taking the dog to the kennel."

"Everyone's making too big a deal over this," George insisted.

"Oh sure, you go to Ecuador and have some big adventure, but when I want to go, when Hugh and Brenda want to go, you don't want to go. Killjoy." She smiled to make sure George knew she was teasing.

At the airport, Hugh and Brenda were standing with a tall man in a golf shirt and slacks. His hair was sandy colored and close-cropped. His glasses were steel rimmed, his eyes steel blue. After hugs were exchanged between Carol and Brenda, Hugh said, "George, Carol, this is a very special person, and he wanted to come along for the festivities. Meet FBI Special Agent Van

Williams, who coordinated the efforts here to locate and rescue you."

Williams gave an embarrassed smile and shook hands with George and Carol. "I'm really glad to finally meet you," he said. "I'm also looking forward to meeting Dean Connors and Albert Pujols."

"Connors is going to be there?" George asked. "That's fantastic." Then he got quiet. After an awkward silence, he said, "But I confess I'm also very nervous to see him again. He, uh, lost his arm. It was my fault, or at least partially my fault. At least I'm putting it into words. Getting it out. That's what I've been told I'm supposed to do."

"I talked to Connors on the phone a couple of times," Williams said. "He told me it was an issue for you. Maybe on the plane your wife and I can trade seats, and we can talk a bit. A few years ago I was on assignment in New Jersey. My partner got killed. I know one hundred percent what you're going through."

George looked at Carol. She said, "Brenda and Hugh already told me Agent Williams wanted to come, so you guys can talk on the plane. It's fine."

An announcement indicated the flight was boarding for Panama and then on to Guayaquil. "We are retracing this whole thing?" George said. "Is that really necessary?"

Hugh said, "For you, maybe. For the rest of us, absolutely. Besides, the other George d'Hout really is our ancestor. I want to know where he went and what he did. I may write a book about it. Or at least a blog on the Internet."

"No tunnels, though," George said in a quiet tone. "The officials there have really gone out of their way to get that whole thing hushed up. Who knows what kind of problems might occur if people start getting into them."

"Not a worry," Hugh said. "But we want to see everything else."

"You are such a little kid," Brenda teased her husband as they got into line to board.

After a couple of hours on the plane, Carol excused herself to go to the ladies' room. When she returned, she asked Van Williams if he would like to trade seats. When Van came to George's row, George unbuckled his seat belt, slid over into the middle seat, and gave Williams the aisle position.

After some small talk, Williams invited George to share what had happened. Over the next hour and a half, they each discussed their personal struggles in coming to terms with tragedies.

After a period of silence, Williams said, "I noticed in all your discussion—and I realize we haven't talked all that long—you've expressed a lot of regret. However, one thing I haven't heard you say is that you regret killing Ordóñez and the guy piloting the helicopter."

"Should I?" George asked. Williams had switched to listen-only mode, so he didn't answer. George continued. "The pilot... maybe I should feel bad about him, but honestly, in my mind he'd been just like Juan Pacheco, a bloodthirsty henchman and psychopath. I don't know that. Nobody's talked much about him. But Ordóñez, no, I don't feel bad about it. He was going to kill me. There's no doubt. I watched him murder Miguel. If anything,

I wish I could have killed him before that happened. Are those feelings wrong?"

"I don't think so," Williams said. "You were in imminent danger. You did what you had to do. And that's my point about all of this. I'm not preaching, except to the choir, because as I said earlier, I've struggled with these same issues. But you did what you had to do when you had to do it. Connors did what he had to do, and so did Pujols. You feel bad, but when you really dissect what happened, are those feelings well founded? You stopped one evil man and, according to Pujols, intervened to keep Juan from getting away."

They continued talking, and by the time the plane landed in Panama, they felt like old friends. After changing planes, they had another hour and a half to talk before landing in Guayaquil. "Whatever you do," George said to the group, "hang on to your luggage claim checks. It was right here the trouble started."

For the next two days, George played tour guide, showing them Parque Seminario, with its giant iguanas; Cerro Santa Anna, which overlooked the entire city and river; the banana and cocoa plantations; and the open-air markets.

CHAPTER 46

Sunday, 29 April
8:30 a.m.

The five Americans packed their bags and prepared to take a private van over the mountains to Cuenca. Standing outside the hotel, the same one where his misery had begun, George said to Hugh, "I can't tell you how much I was dreading this. I kept feeling like it was all going to start again. Having Carol here, along with you and Brenda, has been really therapeutic."

"Don't forget the G-man," Hugh said. "Of course you feel safe. We brought our own strong arm. You thought about Tuesday? What are you going to say?"

"I don't have a clue," George confided. "Not one clue."

"I bet you'll completely wow them," Hugh predicted.

"Doubtful," George said.

Tuesday, 1 May
3:00 p.m.

Crowds had begun filling Aguilar Stadium, home of the professional soccer club Deportivo Cuenca, two hours earlier. Vendors were doing a brisk business, selling everything from hot dogs to roasted guinea pig and buckets of beer. In the home team's locker room, officials from the US embassy in Quito, along with representatives of the Ecuadorian government, reviewed with everyone where he or she would sit, what the schedule of events would be, and how he or she was to react.

The locker room was so full of people and activity that when Dean Connors arrived, George had difficulty getting to him. As George waded through the mass of humanity, Carol in tow, his heart beat violently. Facing the embassy security chief, he wanted to speak but suddenly wasn't sure what to say.

They stared at each other for a few seconds. George was filled with trepidation. Connors looked…well, what was the word?

Carol stepped forward. "I'm Carol d'Hout, George's wife," she said. "I want you to know how much I appreciate everything you did to save my husband's life. I also want you to know you are in our prayers every day."

Connors smiled. Out of habit, he extended his right arm, which had a temporary prosthesis on it. He pulled it back, reached out with his left hand to shake, then pulled her in for a hug. "I'll tell you the truth," Connors said, "the more Albert

Pujols has told me about your husband, the more I'm wondering how to find a little more time to get to know him. Albert thinks very highly of him."

Van Williams, who was chatting with embassy personnel, saw the three talking and made his way over. "We visited on the phone," he said by way of introduction. "I'm Van."

The natural bond between two law enforcement officials kicked in, and George and Carol were able to let them carry the conversation. Then a man in a black suit with an earpiece called for everyone's attention. The room fell silent. He said everything twice, once in Spanish and again in English.

"*El presidente* will be entering the room shortly," he said. "We request your courtesy in remembering this is not a time to discuss politics or policy, nor will those topics be broached during the public presentation. This is a time to honor the unceasing commitment of good people here in Ecuador and in the United States, along with all other countries of the world, to stand together against crime."

With that the president of Ecuador entered the room. No one spoke except when spoken to. When the president got to Dean Connors, he said, "I have spoken to officials here in Cuenca, including the lieutenant who brought this situation to a resolution. His name is Ascasubi. He said it was regretable there had not been more of a foundation of trust between our two countries, because that might have expedited a successful conclusion."

Connors was unsure what to say that didn't involve policy or politics. He chose to say, "The lieutenant did a very good job."

When the president turned to George, he said, "You were lured here under false pretenses, and I understand that in spite of that, you helped bring down evil men and destroy their organization."

George blushed and said, "I'm just glad to be invited back under better circumstances. It's not hard to see why so many Americans are relocating here. You have a beautiful country."

Once the preliminaries were over, George and Albert were escorted to front row seats, where Lt. Ascasubi was waiting for them. The rest were ushered to a VIP section. When the Ecuadorian president was introduced, wild cheers broke out along with spontaneous singing. It was a soccer stadium, and the event carried the energy of a championship sporting match.

All the law enforcement personnel involved in the case were presented with medals of valor. George was presented with a special award for civilian bravery. The mayor of Cuenca was also brought on stage. He and the president presented George with a key to the city. "Señor d'Hout," the president said, "as I searched for exactly what I wanted to tell you today, in front of all these people, I came across a quote from a great man from your country. His name is Martin Luther King Jr."

The president paused, and then continued. "This man said, 'He who passively accepts evil is as much involved in it as he who helps to perpetuate it. He who accepts evil without protesting against it is really cooperating with it.' Another great man, Albert Einstein said, 'The world is a dangerous place to live; not because of the people who are evil, but because of the people who don't do anything about it.'"

The president paused again for effect, and then said, "You did not choose to have this happen to you, but when it did, you responded, in spite of the fear you must have felt, with bravery and resolution. The people of Cuenca, the people of Ecuador, salute you. You have helped to preserve our national treasures and rid the world of a group of very bad men."

After the ceremony, which lasted too long for George's taste, Lt. Ascasubi and Albert walked up to him. "The lieutenant wants me to tell you he has a surprise," Pujols said.

"Oh," George responded, afraid it was another invitation to a ceremony he didn't want to attend but couldn't graciously turn down.

Ascasubi ushered a short, thick woman with a flat face and large nose up to him. She wore a white hat with a black band. She had three little girls in tow. They were dressed identical to the woman, including the white hat. Ascasubi spoke, and Albert translated. "This is Señora Santos. She wanted to meet you."

George looked at her politely but vacantly. Then he said one of the few bits of Spanish he was confident in, "*Mucho gusto*." Nice to meet you.

In spite of her dark skin, George could tell she was blushing. Her peasant dress indicated she was a simple woman who was not used to such highbrow events. She spoke barely above a whisper to Lt. Ascasubi.

"She says her gratitude is great, but she lacks the words with which to express them," Albert translated.

George looked to Albert for help. What was this all about? However, Albert was happy just to let d'Hout dangle in the wind.

Finally, Albert said again, "This is Señora Santos. She says you made her husband's last days bearable because she knows you showed him decency. You also were—and I'm quoting here—'an avenging angel sent from God.'"

George smiled at Señora Santos and then turned to Albert. "I'm as lost as last year's Easter egg."

"You most certainly are," Albert said. "They don't hunt Easter eggs in Ecuador. Strictly a religious holiday here."

"And back on task," George said, "why is this lady staring at me? Who is she, and what's she talking about?"

Lt. Ascasubi decided to try out a little English. "This...is... Señora Santos...the...how you say? ...*viuda*...the widow...of Miguel Santos."

"This is Miguel's wife?" George blurted out. "That's impossible. She's dead! Are these her kids? They're dead, too."

Albert was glad Señora Santos didn't speak English. He said, "We thought so, too. But apparently not. The guys who were holding her, when they got word Ordóñez was dead, simply let her and the girls go and beat it for parts unknown."

"So Ordóñez was lying about them being dead?" George asked. "Why?"

"Maybe he didn't know it was a lie," Albert said. "We can't say for sure. It's possible the guys grew fond of the woman and her kids and simply didn't have the heart to off them; sort of a modern-day Snow White and the huntsman. The other possibility is maybe Ordóñez's order never got conveyed. Like I said, nobody knows for sure."

The Ecuadorian Deception

Señora Santos spoke again. "Tell him I want him and his family to come to our house. He knows where it is, near the Yanuncay River. We will serve them a fine meal of native specialties. Today I bought some very fine *cuy* to prepare."

After Albert translated, George asked him, "*Cuy*? You're kidding, right?"

"She's counting on you coming." Albert beamed.

Ascasubi said more to Albert, who translated. "He wants me to tell you the president intervened on the family's behalf, when we realized they were alive. A portion of the proceeds from the legal sale of the treasure, probably to the Banco Central Museum, will be used to make sure the children get a good education and Señora Santos is taken care of."

"Santos?" George asked. "Doesn't that mean 'saint'?"

"Yes," Albert said. "Miguel's name in English could be translated 'Saint Michael,' like the archangel. A guardian, a protector."

George said, "Ask Señora Santos what time dinner is." He was thinking about roasted guinea pig and trying to force a smile without much luck.

"Cheer up," Albert told him. "You might just love the taste of guinea pig."

"Doubtful," he started to say, but then he caught himself. "Who knows? I just might. After all, what's life without a little adventure?"

Made in the USA
San Bernardino, CA
13 October 2014